PRAETORIAN

***

The Cleansing Fire

By S.J.A. Turney

For Leni & Gavin

Awesome people

Also by S. J. A. Turney:

The Marius' Mules Series

Marius' Mules I: The Invasion of Gaul (2009)
Marius' Mules II: The Belgae (2010)
Marius' Mules III: Gallia Invicta (2011)
Marius' Mules IV: Conspiracy of Eagles (2012)
Marius' Mules V: Hades Gate (2013)
Marius' Mules VI: Caesar's Vow (2014)
Marius' Mules VII: The Great Revolt (2014)
Marius' Mules VIII: Sons of Taranis (2015)
Marius' Mules IX: Pax Gallica (2016)
Marius' Mules X: Fields of Mars (2017)
Marius' Mules XI: Tides of War (2018)
Marius' Mules XII: Sands of Egypt (2019)

The Praetorian Series

Praetorian – The Great Game (2015)
Praetorian – The Price of Treason (2015)
Praetorian – Eagles of Dacia (2017)
Praetorian – Lions of Rome (2018)

The Damned Emperors (as Simon Turney)

Caligula (2018)
Commodus (2019)

Tales of the Empire

Interregnum (2009)
Ironroot (2010)
Dark Empress (2011)
Insurgency (2016)
Emperor's Bane (2016)
Invasion (2017)
Jade Empire (2017)

The Ottoman Cycle

The Thief's Tale (2013)
The Priest's Tale (2013)
The Assassin's Tale (2014)
The Pasha's Tale (2015)

The Templar Series

Daughter of War (2018)
The Last Emir (2018)
City of God (2019)
The Winter Knight (2019)

Roman Adventures (Children's Roman fiction with Dave Slaney)

Crocodile Legion (2016)
Pirate Legion (2017)

Short story compilations & contributions:

Tales of Ancient Rome vol. 1 (2011)
Tortured Hearts Vol 2 (2012)
Tortured Hearts Vol 3 (2012)
Temporal Tales (2013)
Historical Tales (2013)
A Year of Ravens (2015)
A Song of War (2016)
Rubicon (2019)

For more information visit www.simonturney.com
or follow Simon on:
Facebook Simon Turney Author aka SJATurney (@sjaturney)
Twitter @SJATurney
Instagram simonturney_aka_sjaturney

Italia & Africa in 190 AD

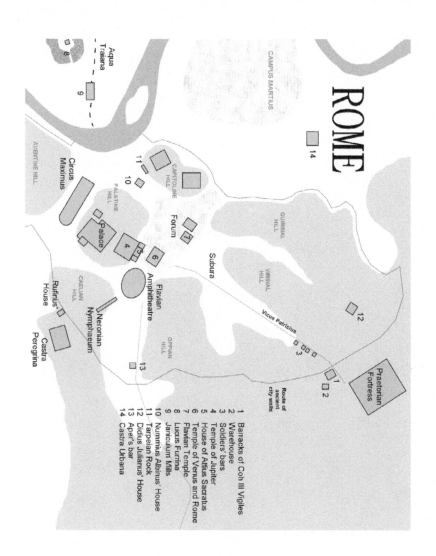

ROME

1 Barracks of Coh III Vigiles
2 Warehouse
3 Soldiers' bars
4 Temple of Jupiter
5 House of Attius Sacratus
6 Temple of Venus and Rome
7 Flavian Temple
8 Lucus Furrina
9 Janiculum Mills
10 Nummius Albinus' House
11 Tarpeian Rock
12 Didius Julianus' House
13 Aper's bar
14 Castra Urbana

Also available online at:
https://simonturney.com/downloads/praetorian-maps/

Part One

Purification

Year of the Consulship of Aurelius and Sura

190 AD

Casus ubique valet, semper tibi pendeat hamus; Quo minime credas gurgite, piscis erit.

(Wherever you cast your hook, it is in the least expected pool you will find fish)

- Ovid: Ars Amatoria

I – THE PLAYGROUND OF EMPERORS

BAIAE, CAMPANIA. LATE SUMMER

The sister of the divine emperor Commodus, Annia Aurelia Fadilla, had proved to be a somewhat difficult proposition for Rufinus. In unpleasant ways, she reminded him of Lucilla, the oldest of the siblings, who had almost put him to death all those years ago in that sprawling villa on the road to Tibur.

Not that she was wicked and scheming. In fact, Fadilla was clearly staunchly loyal to her emperor brother, even at a time when Rome was seething with uncertainty, and Commodus' erratic behaviour was becoming a worrying matter for everyone. And she was not the cruel mistress that Lucilla had been, for her slaves were more content than most. But it was also more than the fact that she physically resembled her older sister. There was a sharpness to her tongue and a flintiness to her gaze that promised trouble, even if it never delivered.

It meant that Rufinus was constantly on edge in her presence when he probably didn't need to be and the others, who had not spent time languishing under the rule of the emperor's harpy sibling, had no comparison to worry them, so it was only Rufinus that suffered so.

It made it all the harder for him to keep his eye on the target.

Optio Equitum Appius Numerius.

It had taken months of peeling away the rotten layers of the onion to find the stinking heart of the thing, and he'd begun to despair of actually getting anywhere with it, but finally he felt that he was closing in on the centre of the malevolence.

He had taken on a commission among the *frumentarii*, the 'grain men', who formed the secret eyes, ears and occasionally knives of the emperor, hidden among the legions and the rest of the army, seeking out treason and crime. Vibius Cestius, one of the subtlest and most dangerous men he had ever met, yet also one of the most honest and true, had spent a single market cycle initiating Rufinus into their ways, for he would not need to know much. His assignment was going to be straight back to where he knew best: the Praetorian Guard.

Cleander had fallen from grace, and badly, his head carried back to Rome on the tip of a spear, angry citizens fighting over the rest of him for some souvenir. The corrupt monster who had ruled Rome in the name of the emperor was gone, grain was plentiful once more, and even the plague had abated. All should have been good. But the simple fact was that Cleander had been in unopposed power for years, and his network of informants, clients and villains had spread into almost every sector of society, especially the imperial administration and the military.

It was said that the emperor and his chamberlain and new consilium were busy rooting out the web of villainy in the palace and the administration, but the rot had gone deep in the Praetorian Guard which had been Cleander's mailed fist, and that had become a prime concern of the emperor and his cadre of loyal agents. What use, after all, was a bodyguard who had spent years reneging on their vow and serving another who *undermined* the emperor?

Rufinus hadn't really known how to start, but as always Cestius had ideas. During Cleander's reign of terror the Praetorian Guard had been torn apart with conflicting loyalties. The frumentarii had as always remained loyal to their master. But the way an insidious master controls a force is to select a single thread and seize it, pulling until the whole garment is tugged in the same direction.

Cleander's thread had apparently been that shadowy remnant of a bygone age: the speculatores. Originally a separate unit within the Guard, the speculatores had served as scouts, spies and assassins for the emperors before Hadrian's creation of the frumentarii. After their official disbanding by Trajan they had continued to be of less *official* use, the arm of the Guard that carried out the less wholesome orders of their master, shuffled back among the Praetorian cohorts and hidden from records.

Cleander had drawn the speculatores to his cause, and they had in turn brought in other critical officers and men of the Guard. The problem was that the speculatores were by their very nature secretive and hard to uncover. Their details were controlled by an *exactus*, a record keeper, who was one of their number. They had, in fact, been so subtle that Rufinus had served alongside them for years without knowing of their existence. Now that he knew of them, the occasional unexplained absences of certain men from his cohort who had been pulled out for special duties began to make sense.

Rufinus had brought to justice more than a score of Cleander's worst lackeys over the last month, but only now had he finally set his sights upon a member of that elusive speculatore unit. Optio Equitum

Appius Numerius. A junior cavalry officer, Appius had been one of those riders who had butchered citizens and children outside the gates of Rome on Cleander's orders. Rufinus had been instrumental in trying to bring down the wicked chamberlain's enemies. And because of his ties within the speculatores, the moment Cleander had been branded an enemy of Rome and fallen to the mob, Appius and all his dubious cronies had slipped back into the Praetorian Guard seamlessly as though they had never done anything wrong, the records of their crimes expunged by the men who kept them, as corrupt as the villains they protected.

Appius Numerius.

A cavalry officer, commanding a turma of thirty Praetorian riders of the Second Cohort, Appius had been more careful than those Rufinus had hunted down previously. And while he'd had plenty of evidence for the others that he'd been able to take to the authorities and have them condemned, Appius had maintained a clean appearance, with no dirt clinging to him. All Rufinus had was the word of a man who had then thrown himself from the rocks before Rufinus could bring him in.

He'd spoken to Cestius about it. How did he bring down a villain that he knew *was* a villain, but for which there was no evidence? Cestius had simply reminded Rufinus that he was one of the frumentarii now – the emperor's knives, who had the authority of the emperor himself to act in matters of imperial security. Appius had to die for his crimes, and no one needed to know about it. If it did come out into the open, Rufinus could always show his identification as one of that shadowy unit and walk away a free man, though that would effectively end his usefulness in hunting down rogue Praetorians, so that would have to be the last-ditch option.

Rufinus had spent many days trying to find a way to get to Appius in the Castra Praetoria, but the place was too busy and Appius too careful, and the opportunity simply never materialised. Then he had learned that the man and his turma of riders were being attached to the retinue of the lady Fadilla, who was to journey to Aenaria and take the waters there in an attempt to shift a lingering minor ailment.

It had taken Rufinus three solid days of coaxing and several surprisingly expensive bribes to the exactus of the Second Cohort to secure his transfer to that unit. Though the Second was as under-strength as all the others and short of two centurions, his own tribune had not wanted to lose him. In the end, though, he'd secured his place in that cohort as the third centurion. A further two hefty bribes and more persuasion had seen his century one of the two infantry units assigned to the lady Fadilla alongside Appius' cavalry.

This hunting criminals was an expensive business, and Rufinus was grateful that all his considerable pay-outs would be recovered from the vaults of the frumentarii in due course, even if it required a lot of paperwork.

Eleven days ago, Fadilla had left the city in a rich carriage with a considerable train of slaves and servants, along with three giggling ladies from the higher circles of Rome – a vapid bunch with more fingers than brain cells. They had travelled down the Via Appia with Appius' cavalry riding ahead, the century of Bubulca split to each side of the procession and Rufinus' own century bringing up the rear with the pack animals, the big, black menacing shape of Acheron padding alongside, causing the soldiers to bow out of the way, avoiding the fierce looking dog as best they could while retaining formation.

At no point on the journey had Appius made himself vulnerable, remaining in the close company of his riders at all times, and Rufinus had begun to feel the building frustration as the entire party took ship from Puteoli and sailed for the island of Aenaria with its renowned healing baths of warm mineral springs. An entire market week on the damned island had ensued with Rufinus impotent to do anything. Once they had settled in and the lady had confirmed that she would be spending eight days in treatment, Appius had taken his leave, boarded a ship and returned to Puteoli with a couple of his men to make the most of the bars and brothels and great entertainment venues of the city. It would have been Rufinus' perfect opportunity, but in a stroke of idiotic ill fortune, centurion Bubulca had slipped from his horse that same damned afternoon and taken a head wound that left him dazed and in need of days of recovery.

Rufinus had been left as the only intact officer of three units and could hardly abandon his post. So, he had commanded two infantry units and left the cavalry to themselves as they oversaw the protection of the emperor's sister during her stay. Rufinus had spent his spare moments walking Acheron to where he could stand on a wide balcony that looked out towards the mainland where Appius was almost certainly carousing and making himself a perfectly viable target at the one time the young frumentarius could do nothing about it.

Optio Appius had only returned to Aenaria the night before they were due to leave.

Chance had thrown Rufinus his one shot at the last moment, though, and he was determined to make use of it. Their return sailing to Puteoli went horribly wrong. The ship's steering rudder broke not far past the Misenum cape and forced them to their left, towards land on the wrong side of the bay. Instead of heading back to Puteoli that morning, and then a straight journey north to Rome, they landed at Baiae. There, while Appius had made arrangements with the ship's trierarch to move on the next day once the ship was repaired, the gaggle of empty-headed ladies with the princess gushed over the legendary beauty and reputation of Baiae and suggested that they make use of all the facilities while they were marooned here for an unexpected day.

Baiae was, and always had been, the playground of the rich. Cicero had had a villa here, as had Julius Caesar and the emperor Nero. Hadrian had been here when he died. The town itself was a small affair, if well-appointed, centring around a huge and sprawling thermal bathing complex and a mysterious temple to the underworld, surrounded for several miles by the country estates of the rich and famous. The lady Fadilla and her entourage settled easily into one of the villas on the town's upper terraces, long owned by the imperial family, and then headed down to make use of the facilities.

Leaving Bubulca's century guarding the villa, Rufinus and Appius took their Praetorians, numbering seventy-odd in all, down to the baths to protect the empress. The entire complex was a massive affair built upon three levels of terracing, and sprawling along the slope, all consisting of four separate bathing establishments.

This was no simple rich visitor, though, but the emperor's sister. As she and her cronies entered the Baths of Venus, the Praetorians moved ahead and had the baths cleared. Mercifully, there were few visitors at this time of the day, and it had not taken so long to clear them out. All male staff had been temporarily dismissed, and the baths were now attended purely by gentle female slaves. Appius and Rufinus assigned their men around the baths' periphery at every door and window, every furnace and access point. No one was to interrupt the lady at her leisure with her friends and her slaves. No one unauthorised was getting into the baths of Diana.

It was then, as the lady lounged in the warm waters of Baia and the accompanying guards sealed the place tighter than a clamshell, that Rufinus' one opportunity arose. Appius Numerius had been sneezing violently that morning and decided that he would never have a better chance than now to take advantage of their location.

The steam rooms and sulphur baths here were almost as renowned as those on Aenaria. Appius would use the baths.

Rufinus fretted for a moment. Centurion Bubulca was back up at the villa with his men. With Appius strolling off to the Baths of Mercury a few hundred paces away, Rufinus was effectively in charge of the empress' security. Still, there were more than seventy men guarding the baths. Unless something went spectacularly wrong, they all knew precisely what they were doing, and Rufinus did not plan to be long. He spent a few moments more doing a circuit of the complex, making sure the place was sealed and his men were all in position and, happy that the empress was secure and that the Praetorians would all assume Rufinus was simply patrolling somewhere, he slipped away.

The Baths of Mercury was a smaller complex than those of Venus, but apparently at least as popular. As Rufinus stepped into the apodyterium, he could see that nine of the niches for clothes were already full. Two of them, at the end of the room, contained Appius' gear. Rufinus chewed his lip and crossed the room, disrobing and folding his own kit, slipping it into the next two niches and offering the slave an extra donative for watching them. Moments later he was in a towel and wooden clogs, clip-clopping into the baths.

No one had seen him slip his pugio dagger from his sheath as he changed and hide it beneath the folds of his towel. Breathing steadily, he moved inside, navigating by heat. He knew that Appius was here for his cold and would therefore be in the warm bath or the steam room. Given that, he headed towards the glow of warmth, and then found the signs on the walls, pointing to the various rooms, many of which were clearly chambers hollowed out of the mountainside rather than constructed buildings. Baiae was known for the vents of sulphurous steam and the natural hot waters that bubbled up from the ground, after all.

Aware that Appius would recognise him instantly, Rufinus pulled part of his voluminous towel up and over his head in the manner of a priest and moved to the hot bath. The room, with its intricate mosaic floor and walls painted with scenes of cavorting sea nymphs, was occupied and he immediately shrank into himself as he entered, but swiftly realised that neither man was Appius Numerius. A fat man with an almost entirely bald head sat in the water at the far end of the hot bath, and an old man with white curls sat nearby with his back to Rufinus.

With an apologetic smile, Rufinus bowed back out of the room. He didn't bother with the warm room or the cold one. He was certain

Appius wasn't there, and he wouldn't be in the attached leisure facilities with their libraries, bar, food store or gymnasium. That realistically meant he had to be in the *laconium* – the steam room – the natural place for a man trying to rid himself of a troublesome cold.

Passing through the small hallway he approached the place, seeing the wisps of steam already puffing out along the corridors. A slave stood near the doorway to the laconium. He would have to be absent. There had to be no ready way to trace this back. As he stepped confidently towards the slave, he affected a Dacian accent, something he remembered quite clearly from his long sojourn in that hard-but-beautiful frontier land.

'I am hungry,' he said to the slave in a thick accent and with a deep growling tone. 'Fetch me bread and cheese. And wine. *Good* wine.'

The slave, unaccustomed to being sent for such things when he was clearly here to help with oils and strigils and to hand out towels, frowned in confusion.

'Now,' barked Rufinus, and the slave jumped and scurried away.

Good. Not only one potential witness disposed of, but also a man who would remember only an arrogant easterner with a deep voice. Tucking the towel around his face to hide his visage as much as possible, Rufinus slipped through the door and into the steam room.

The place was not well lit, with just a narrow chimney rising from the top of the domed chamber roof, traversing through the rock to the air above, as well as two oil lamps that merely added to the temperature. The heat here, supplied by the natural vapours of the earth itself, was intense, hotter than any laconium Rufinus had ever encountered. Though the source of that heat flowed beneath the floor and through the walls themselves in carefully added tiled flues, the room remained steam-filled anyway, for a great labrum of cold water stood in the centre, constantly giving off clouds of vapour that filled the room.

Even as Rufinus slipped in, he saw a broad-shouldered man with an immense neckbeard emerge from the steam cloud and scoop up a cup full of cold water, tipping it across his arms and then his torso to refresh himself before disappearing back into the cloud and his seat somewhere at the edge of the circular chamber.

Rufinus frowned. He listened carefully. Above the general hiss of steam, and the very distant chatter of life outside in other areas of the bath, he could hear the distinctive sounds of breathing and movement from only two sources in the room. Just Appius and the neckbeard then. Remaining perfectly still, Rufinus listened. A sneeze followed by a rasped cough located the cavalry optio readily enough. He was at the far side of the chamber, and Rufinus, now confident he knew whether the occupants were in the steam, slipped from his wooden shoes, leaving them next to the door.

The floor here was far too hot to attempt bare-footed, but this required silence, and he simply climbed up onto the raised bench that ran around the entire room, crouching and padding almost silently along it in bare feet.

The figure of the optio coalesced in the eddying mist for a moment, and Rufinus acted in an instant. Appius was clever and dangerous, so in order to do this right, Rufinus had to be even more so. Before Appius could even call out, Rufinus had dropped to the bench next to him and the dagger that had been concealed in his towel was now at the villainous optio's neck, the point drawing a single bead of blood from the man's throat apple.

'Appius Numerius, I know you're clever,' he said in little more than a whisper that he hoped would not carry across the room in the boiling steam. 'So, I know you are well aware that I have you at my mercy. You have your back to the wall, quite literally, and I have a very sharp knife at your throat. You might be quick, but you have to be damn sure you're quicker than me if you feel like moving. And I can assure you that you're not. Do you understand?'

Appius, unable to nod without cutting his own windpipe, hissed an affirmative.

'You were one of Cleander's lackeys. There is no use in denying it, for I have it on very good authority from another villain who now resides in an urn.'

A tense silence now. No denial.

'I represent certain authorities who are unwilling to see the emperor's guard tarnished by such men as yourself. In fact, you might say I have made it my task to see each of you pass the final river for what you've done, and you especially, as a murderer of children, deserve it more than most.'

Appius' lip wrinkled unpleasantly, but he remained silent.

'I would love to see you dead, Appius Numerius, for the sake of all those you butchered in Cleander's name. But the sad fact is that I am hunting bigger fish than you. I know you are of the speculatores, and I know that your lot have their own records clerk who himself is off the records. He is the man I need right now. And I need him enough that I'm willing to make a deal with you to get him. You tell me who he is, and I will withdraw this knife and leave. Then you

10

run. Run as fast and as far as your legs can carry you. I will never stop hunting you, but in exchange for that name I will move you to the bottom of the list and give you plenty of head start.'

Silence.

'It has taken me some time to identify you, but do not think you are unique. If you *won't* give me the name, I will still take immense satisfaction in removing you from the world of men, and I will simply find another of your ilk from whom to draw the name. Don't waste this opportunity.'

'You're one of the grain men, aren't you?' hissed Appius.

'Yes, though first and foremost I am Praetorian. A *true* Praetorian who holds to my oath. The name. Your speculatore exactus. His name in return for your chance at survival. And I am not the most patient man in the world these days. When the steam clears and old neckbeard over there sees us, I will have no option but to cut your throat and run. So, come on. The name.'

There was a silence again, but this was a different silence. Rufinus knew his silences well. This was not one of defiance, nor of indecision. This was one of fear. Fear was easy to manipulate. He prodded gently with the knife and a small trickle of blood ran down Appius' neck. The man swallowed as lightly as he dare.

'Gaius Calidius. Fifth Cohort.,' the man whispered finally.

Rufinus nodded, committing the name to memory. There was, of course, the possibility that Appius was lying, but the acrid ammonia smell of urine rising from the man's nethers and the repeated bobbing of that throat apple spoke of true fear, so Rufinus didn't think so.

Gaius Calidius. Fifth Cohort.

'When you run, do it straight away. Don't stop to speak to your men. If you're still around when I leave this building, then your head start counts for nothing.'

Carefully, he withdrew the knife and slipped to his feet, backing away from Appius along the bench and disappearing into the steam. Unarmed and still fear-driven, the man had not moved. Rufinus reached the end of the bench and dropped, slipping his feet back into the wooden shoes. Standing straight, he left the steam room, dagger once more secured beneath his towel.

In the room outside the slave had returned with a small tray, upon which sat a platter of bread and cheese, a souvenir glass etched with a stylised picture of the bath complex and two small jugs for wine and water. He looked worried. Rufinus smiled at him and took a step forwards.

11

Appius had to be desperate now, as Rufinus realised, alerted by the pounding of wooden shoes on the floor behind as the optio ran towards him. Of course, the man might well be on the run, precisely as Rufinus had advised. But for some odd reason, Rufinus didn't think so. He could almost feel the malevolence pounding out ahead of the man like a wave. Kicking off his wooden clogs, he took two steps to his right, nodding a warning at the slave, who stepped back, confused.

Appius Numerius emerged at a run from the cloud of steam, face twisted into a feral snarl. In his hand he held a strigil, a curved bronze scraper used for removing oil and impurities from the skin as part of the bathing process. From the fact that he brandished it raised, like a cavalry sword, it seemed unlikely he was about to gently scrape the oil from anyone's flesh.

Rufinus acted instantly. It would be hard to kill efficiently with a strigil, but far from impossible, and if anyone could do it then a cold-hearted killer like Appius could. But Rufinus was ready. He'd been half expecting something like this anyway. As Appius' hand swept down with the improvised weapon into the space where Rufinus had been and now only his wooden clogs stood, the frumentarius spun mid-leap, his hand grasping Appius's wrist and jerking it down.

Something in Appius' arm broke, for the sound of snapping bone echoed around the chamber before being lost beneath the optio's scream. His ruined arm kept moving now, still guided by Rufinus' strong hand, and came down in an arc, digging the bronze edge of the scraper into the cavalryman's neck. The flesh resisted, for the weapon was not sharp, but Rufinus was strong and his opponent now panicked and uncontrolled. In the blink of an eye the strigil had torn a jagged line across Appius' throat.

The optio dropped to floor, gurgling and shuddering, and Rufinus stepped back. The slave was shaking almost as much as the dying man, and Rufinus swiftly rescued the wine and water from the tray before they fell, then grasped the souvenir glass as it toppled. Calmly, as though nothing untoward had happened, he poured a glass of well-watered wine – a small one, for with his history he dared no more – and then placed the jugs back on the tray.

'Sorry about the mess,' he said casually to the slave, in that same Dacian drawl. He had been attacked and defended himself, in front of witnesses, but still it was better to stay unidentified in all of this. Swigging down the wine in front of the spasming body and the shocked slave, he smiled and went to replace the glass, but thought again. It was a souvenir, after all.

12

With a last smile, he stepped over the now still body of Appius Numerius, killer of children, and left the room. Mere moments later he was back at the apodyterium, having paused to wash off the spatter of blood in one of many cold water labrums, where he retrieved his gear, dressed swiftly and, whistling a jaunty tune, left the Baths of Mercury.

He was just outside the main door when the screaming began deep in the complex behind him.

Moments later he was back with his men, strolling around the periphery of the other baths where the emperor's sister relaxed. He quickly made sure he was on the far side to the baths where he'd pursued Appius. The last thing he wanted now was some curious administrator dragging around a slave who could identify Rufinus and looking for a Praetorian officer to complain to.

As he sank to a marble bench in the shade, he mused.

Gaius Calidius. The records man for the speculatores. He would have the full list that would detail all his friends within the Guard and give Rufinus ample to work with. From there he would be able to dig out the *really* big fish. With luck, by Saturnalia he would be able to say the rot was arrested and the Guard cleared of this infection.

It would take time for the administrators here to unpick what had happened in the baths, and if it ever somehow came out that a second Praetorian had tucked his uniform into a niche in the changing room, they would be long gone by then. Rufinus was not going to log the disappearance of the optio, for sure, and the lady Fadilla was aware that the man had spent an entire week of her convalescence carousing in Puteoli, so she would likely assume he had ended his time drunk in an alley or some such. By the time it was all unravelled, the imperial party would be on the way home, and the only word that would reach Rome would be that Appius Numerius had attacked some Dacian bather in Baiae and died in the process.

Neat.

Now to move on to the records clerk.

13

II – A WIFE'S PLACE

ROME. LATE SUMMER

R ufinus rolled his shoulders as he approached the house on the Caelian Hill, suspiciously close to the camp of the frumentarii, and unpleasantly close to an aqueduct he had once had to run along in the middle of the night with angry men in pursuit.

He had taken out a loan with Severus, who seemed to have almost bottomless pits of money these days, and purchased for Senova and himself a rather nice moderately sized town house, with a glassware shop occupying one flank and a basket seller on the other. Both quiet and non-pungent establishments with tame opening hours. It was, to Rufinus, the good life.

Publius, his brother, who had spent so many months in self-imposed exile in Cemenelum to avoid the machinations of Cleander, had come back to Rome in the aftermath of the chamberlain's fall and had immediately taken on their father's rather poor town house, fighting litigation for ownership, though once Severus had been persuaded to put his consular weight behind the case, it had resolved very quickly. So, Publius had a house in Rome and was now in some mid-level post in the city's water supply administration, and Rufinus and Senova had their own home, the repayments to Severus a pittance given his healthy wage as a Praetorian centurion. All was good.

One thing still baffled him regularly, though: the status of he and Senova. Under their pseudonyms the previous year they had been a married couple, and it had felt natural. Now they were themselves again, yet nothing seemed to have changed. Everyone had continued to treat them as a married pair, despite the fact that in the word of law, they were not. Moreover, he might lose status as a patrician married to a freedwoman, which would be troublesome given his position. And there was, of course, the fact that the Guard, just like the rest of Rome's military, forbade marriage among their members, with the exception of senior officers. So Rufinus and Senova were not married, were not allowed to be married, and probably *should* not be married. Yet against all expectations it appeared that they still were.

Turning the corner, the house came into sight, the frontage freshly painted and both flanking shops open for business. He stumbled to a halt and took a deep breath at the sight awaiting him. Twelve lictors stood outside the house looking bored, togate and with their fasces bundles of tied rods held tight, some perusing the baskets and glassware on show. Rufinus knew the horse that was tied to the stone ring in the gutter too, as well as the soldier in only tunic and cloak holding the feed bag. He knew who they had escorted.

Lucius Septimius Severus, Consul of Rome and one of the most powerful men in the empire. These days Rufinus' patron, too. On his more sleepless nights he tried to tot up just how indebted to the man he was now, and when forced to give up because he ran out of numbers and superlatives, sleep was even further off. Still, Severus had only ever been supportive and helpful and though he had often demanded things of Rufinus, they were always asked with good reason, and the Praetorian had always been in agreement in the end.

For years Rufinus and Senova had lived under assumed names, wearing other personas like masks, hiding their real identities. In truth, Rufinus was still adjusting to being able to be himself again in public, not having to hide his name for fear that the chamberlain's spies would seek him out, but it still made him twitch to have such blatant attention drawn as the entourage of a consul outside his house. Needless to say, folk all up and down the street were gathering in small knots watching, hoping to elicit a greeting from one of the two most influential men in the empire.

Taking another deep breath, Rufinus adjusted the hang of his tunic and strode towards the house, wishing he'd bothered with the old-fashioned bulky toga which he knew Severus would be wearing. Some days, especially warm ones, it was natural to forego the archaic dress for something more practical. He wore his Praetorian tunic, white with the red borders, denoting his centurion status as clearly as the vine staff jammed under his arm.

The eyes of the public narrowed as he passed. The Praetorians were still a subject of worry among the people of Rome. No matter how much the new prefect, Laetus, and his men tried to rebuild the reputation and to make clear to the people that it was Cleander and a few corrupt officers that had butchered civilians in the emperor's name, the violence of that day a few short months ago remained fresh in everyone's mind. It would be a long time before the man in the street trusted a Praetorian.

And that was as it should be, Rufinus mused irritably. His months of hunting out corruption had only highlighted just how deep the infection had gone. Some days he wondered if the whole Guard might be at fault. Perhaps Severus was right that the Guard needed to be disbanded entire and then rebuilt from fresh stock. Still, none of those in power would sanction such a thing, so it remained a dream of a notion.

Approaching the door, he nodded to the soldier with the horse, a bay mare called Phaethon. The soldier bowed his head respectfully in reply. The lictors regarded him with interest. Rufinus felt a sly smile slide across his face. The traditional guards of a consul should really be with him. That they might be loitering in the street like boys skipping their lessons told Rufinus all he needed to know. He could imagine what had happened. The men would have prepared to follow their master inside until Senova had forbade them, probably because of the state of their shoes, looking at them. How the world turned that a woman he had met as a British slave girl with heavily accented bad Latin now told the second most powerful man in the empire he couldn't bring his guards into her pristine home. That made him laugh. What made him laugh all the more was that Severus had clearly acceded to the demand without argument.

He knocked at the door and Naravas pulled it open suspiciously, eyes gleaming and iron-banded club in hand in case one of the lictors might get ideas. Upon seeing the house's owner, the big Numidian slave, a gift from Severus and one of several, pulled the door wide and bowed. Rufinus made his way inside and as soon as he was across the threshold, the big dark-skinned man waved his club in warning at the gathered lictors and then slammed the door in their faces.

Rufinus swept off his cloak and threw it at a peg on the wall not far from the shrine of the household gods, which it missed entirely, landing in a crumpled heap. Sighing, he moved on. No matter how much the years passed by and what lofty position he reached in Rome, the gods continually reminded him that in his heart he was still a clumsy young man.

He could hear murmured conversation and occasional deep rumbles of laughter from the consul and followed the sound through the atrium and into the corridor that led into the peristyle. He shivered as he passed the wall decorations. One of the best fresco painters in Rome had been commissioned and had finished a month ago. To the left was a traditional tromp l'oeil view of countryside from a balustraded walkway. It would have fitted in any Roman

16

villa, but for the imagined view upon which it looked out. Rufinus had never been to Britannia, but he now felt as though he had, for this view had been designed by Senova based on her homeland. Cliffs and forests, jagged moorland and rivers could have been anywhere, so had she really needed to add the detail of the small settlements of round huts apparently made of wood and animal poo? Was that strictly necessary? Still, it was better than the other wall, from which a goddess glared, looking suspiciously like Minerva. But he knew it was Brigantia, the goddess of Senova's tribe, and the painter had contrived to give her a bitter and accusing face that seemed to look down on Rufinus as he walked past. He wondered how soon he could get away with having some sort of accident in the corridor that would require redecoration.

Moving past the accusing goddess of the Brigantes, he took another calming breath in the air of the peristyle garden with its twin half-moon fountains and neatly trimmed box hedges. Hemda, the gardener, was so busy sculpting a shrub into a perfect orb that he failed to notice his master pass by. To some extent that was to be expected. Rufinus naturally spent three nights in four sleeping in his quarters in the fortress, and only joined Senova at the house on his time off. It seemed to be the way of things among the centurions and other officers, all of whom had unofficial wives in the city.

Hemda was another African, from somewhere in the mountains east of Carthage. On days when suspicion was Rufinus' watchword, he wondered at the fact that his house seemed to be full of Africans and considered the faint possibility that Severus, being an African himself, had filled the place with his spies. On other days he brushed the notion aside, but it still came back to haunt him from time to time.

The voices issued from Senova's tablinum. Some houses, he mused, had such an office for their owner and the wife *didn't* need one. That Senova had an office of her own and refused to give over space for one to her husband said more about their relationship than Rufinus liked. When he had argued about the unfairness of such a thing, she had asked him if he had an office space in his centurion's rooms at the Castra Praetoria. He'd had to admit that he had, and that seemed to end the conversation. Some things were not worth arguing about, especially since Senova always won anyway.

He approached the doorway of the office. The door stood wide open, allowing the air to circulate, and as his feet crunched on the gravel on approach, suddenly a great black hairy shape bounded from the room and slammed into Rufinus' legs so hard he almost went over the nearest box hedge. Recovering himself he made a fuss of Acheron, rubbing behind the dog's ears. The great animal smelled of lavender and Rufinus felt disapproval rise. If Senova insisted on bathing Acheron she could at least give him a masculine scent and not some flowery aroma. It didn't suit him. But then he remembered what Acheron sometimes smelled like and had to acknowledge that lavender was at least an improvement. Acheron was no young pup these days. At a rough estimate, Rufinus put him at thirteen years, and he knew from his youth at the villa that old dogs acquired a natural aroma that was hard to shift. He also worried that Acheron's sight was slowly failing. He ran into Rufinus' legs surprisingly often these days. Still, he was active and happy, and that was what mattered.

With the black beast trotting alongside him, he entered the office. His heart drummed out a worried beat as he took in the room. The walls were covered in hand-written lists, notes, maps, charts, receipts and documents, each of which might be considered dubious to have on display, especially with the door wide open and a consul present. He would have to remind Senova to be a bit more circumspect. Carefully, too, unless he wanted to be sleeping back in the camp again tonight.

'Gnaeus, well met,' smiled the consul, his tanned face creasing between his curly hair and his elaborately twirled forked beard. He rose and crossed to shake hands with the Praetorian.

'Consul.'

'I think we have known one another long enough for you to call me Lucius,' the consul said, an eyebrow cocked. He turned and swept an arm out to encompass the room. 'Your wife is a marvel, Gnaeus.'

There it was again. Wife. At some point he was going to have to work out what to do about that.

'A marvel, consul?'

'Lucius. And yes. I have been married twice. My first was a distant relative of Trajan and as high-born and well-placed a woman as you could know, and Julia is the daughter of a priest-king, as educated a woman as you could hope to find and a student of literature and philosophy, and yet neither of them might have assisted me in such a mighty task as this.'

Rufinus nodded unhappily. In truth, while he would always be grateful for help in his task of rooting out the corruption in the Guard, he felt that the frumentarii and the emperor would probably disapprove of his wife taking an active part in it. That being said, it worked well. She had a quick mind and was inordinately logical. Her insight into connections, movements and finance among the conspirators had led him along routes he would have been unlikely to find on his own. Moreover, he could hardly have kept such details as all this in his rooms at the fortress. But then if he'd been allowed an office in his own house...

'How did Baiae go, Gnaeus?' Senova asked bluntly. Rufinus winced. He wished she wouldn't be so damned careless and outspoken.

'It... went,' he answered weakly.

Severus chuckled. 'Come now, Gnaeus. The only Praetorian within a mile of this place is you, and all your staff have been vetted. You can speak freely in your own home. These are no longer the days of Cleander.'

Vetted. He bet they were. All Africans who owed Severus. Spies...

'I dealt with Appius. In the end he somewhat condemned himself and I would have been blameless, but I left unidentified anyway. The fortress will soon receive a report that he came to blows with a Dacian bather and died as a result.'

'You become more subtle with each passing month,' Severus smiled. 'Association with Cestius is doing you good.'

'I got a name.'

Senova nodded and reached for a piece of vellum and a pen. 'Go on.' Rufinus looked worriedly at Severus, but he nodded.

'Gaius Calidius of the Fifth Cohort.'

'Fifth Cohort,' Senova repeated as she wrote. 'Good. Gens Calidia makes him a plebeian, yes?'

Rufinus nodded. Sometimes he forgot that Senova was not born Roman and every day was still a learning experience for her. 'There have been praetors in the family, but yes. Very much a plebeian gens.'

'So, we don't expect him to be connected in high circles?'

'I suppose not. It'll all be through patronage. See what you can find out about him. Anything I can use for leverage will be helpful. I need his record books. They will give me the names of most of the men I'm looking for, but I could do without having to beat it out of him.'

Senova nodded. 'I'll spend some time in the tabularium tomorrow, and there are a few people I can speak to as well.'

Again, Severus looked impressed. 'This one is worth a thousand dowries, Gnaeus.'

'To what do we owe the honour of this visit, consul?' Rufinus said, changing the subject as Senova pinned the new name up on her wall of information, and then used two strands of thread to link it to other items in her web.

'Lucius,' Severus said again. 'In actual fact, I came to bring some documents your wife asked for in her ongoing research, and it is happy coincidence that you arrived. I think perhaps I ought to update you with the latest news from court, since you have been away near half a month now.'

Rufinus nodded sagely. 'Thank you.'

'There are worrying currents,' Severus said quietly. 'In almost every sector of society. This is not information to be bandied about openly, Gnaeus, but you and I have been at the heart of matters in recent years, and your current position in some ways requires you to be conversant with all rumour and news. What do you know of the emperor recently?'

Rufinus shrugged. 'He is back in control of Rome and the empire. The people eat well, disease has abated, riots have ended and Cleander is gone. I have only heard the people speak in awe of the emperor. All seems to be back in order.'

'*Seems* is the relevant word there, Gnaeus. The emperor revels once more, but he pays attention to the games and the races, to giving banquets and doling out largesse. He has more or less handed over the reins of state to Eclectus and Laetus.'

Rufinus frowned. 'They're both good men.'

'But the emperor should not be placing his authority in the hands of others. Look how well it ended with Perennis, or with Cleander. He needs to guide the chariot of state himself. Instead he seems more interested in training with his gladiator friends, driving chariots and hunting beasts.'

Rufinus bridled. 'There is nothing wrong with that. I swore an oath...'

'Yes, I know,' snapped Severus. 'And it does you credit that you think so highly of the emperor. You are loyal. We're *all* loyal, Gnaeus. But we also have to be aware. You know whereof I speak.'

Rufinus nodded slowly. 'The succession.'

'The emperor has reigned for a decade now, Gnaeus, and still there is no successor in line. His wife has gone, sent to exile and death, and his mistress seems to be barren. There are no close relatives whom he might realistically consider for adoption. Some think he might go down the route of his forebears and select an heir for adoption outside the dynasty. But whatever the case it is

20

happening too slowly. I am watching cracks appear. The senate is extremely disapproving of the emperor's attitude and activity, and not just the ones who had connections to Cleander. The wall is starting to crumble, Gnaeus, and I watch hungry men manoeuvring. Clodius Albinus is in Britannia, and that place has three legions and is closely tied to Germania. It is a power base of great proportions, and you already know he covets the throne. And Pescennius Niger is at his country estate, but his factors continue to work, and it appears he seeks the governorship of Syria. You know how important that could be?'

Rufinus nodded. It had been a governor of Syria who had revolted against Marcus Aurelius a few decades ago. It made his skin prickle to think of men actively positioning themselves and waiting for the emperor to fall. Did none of these men have any honour?

'We knew of those two. They were always going to be ones to watch.'

Severus nodded. 'But now they gather power like the pleats of a money pouch pulling closed. And they are not alone. Sulpicianus and Didius Julianus both look to the future, if perhaps less blatantly than our old friends.'

Rufinus' lip curled. He didn't like this treasonous-sounding talk. Before he could stop himself, he found himself saying 'And what of yourself, consul? The second most powerful man in Rome and with the governorship of Pannonia to look to? The most powerful military position in the empire?'

He flinched at what he'd said, yet Severus did not appear to be offended. Indeed, the consul nodded gently. 'It is in the interest of Rome that we do what we can to ensure stability. Should the emperor die without the succession secured, which is a concern when his private life is spent hunting lions, driving chariots and fighting gladiators, then we need to be prepared. With Albinus in the north and Niger in the east and the unknown Claudius Lucillianus in Aegyptus, if I secure Pannonia, then I have a strong force able to move in any direction at short notice in support of the status quo and to put down would-be emperors.'

'In favour of whom?' Rufinus found himself saying. 'If the emperor should die without an heir, why not this Lucillianus? Or Sulpicianus? Who would you support in opposition to them?'

Severus straightened. 'I have been working in close concert with Pertinax…'

'Ah, Pertinax.' Rufinus struggled for a moment. The old general, the victor of Dacia and a careful, sensible man who Rufinus had met on more than one occasion, and the strange thing was that he could see Pertinax in the purple. He shook his head to rip the image from it. What was he doing? Commodus was the emperor of Rome and until he no longer sat upon the throne, he deserved Rufinus' utmost loyalty. He turned an angry look on Severus.

'It should be beneath us discussing a successor to the emperor. He is hale and hearty. He is only thirty years old. He could yet take another wife. There might well be a successor.'

'And he might be eaten by a lion. Or take a sica in the belly in a training session. Or his chariot overturn and smear him across the sands. Or there might yet be men who seek his fall in the senate. Since the days of Nerva the emperors have had the foresight to have the succession lined up throughout their reign. It is the only way to ensure a stable transition. That the emperor does not see that worries me.'

He sighed. 'Gnaeus, I tell you again that I am loyal to the throne. As loyal as you. But I am far from blind, and I will take whatever steps I must to ensure that should the worst happen the throne will fall straight into the hands of someone strong and worthy.'

Rufinus sagged. Why did it sound so sensible when Severus said it thus? 'So, you would have Pertinax?'

Severus frowned. 'No. I told you I was working *with* Pertinax. He is too divisive. There are men who would refuse to accept him.'

'Then who? You?'

Severus burst out laughing. 'It would be a sad day for Rome if I took that throne, Gnaeus. I am a soldier, not an administrator. And the worst thing of all? I can all too easily see myself on that throne, which is why it certainly should not be me. Pertinax is the same. Any man who would want the throne is probably a bad choice.'

'Then who?' Rufinus said, befuddled.

'Pompeianus.'

Rufinus blinked. 'What?'

'Tiberius Claudius Pompeianus. The clear choice.'

'I...'

'You know Pompeianus. You know him well. Tell me he is not the right choice?'

Rufinus simply frowned. The old general. He was; of *course* he was. He was the *perfect* choice. He was already part of the imperial family, having been Marcus Aurelius' son-in-law, and consequently Commodus' brother-in-law, even if through that witch Lucilla. He was subtle, clever, brave, had been a great general under the previous emperor, and had managed to survive even his wife's plot against the throne. A man who played the game so well that most people didn't even realise he was playing it. And a man who had never, to Rufinus' knowledge, had any aspiration to rule.

'He would be... yes, the clear choice.'

And Commodus liked him. When he had thrown out all his father's advisors, he had felt compelled to keep Pompeianus. When the general's family were executed for their part in the conspiracy a decade ago, he had survived with a clear record. It was just possible even that the emperor might be persuaded to adopt his brother-in-law. It was a stroke of genius. Moreover, he was once more impressed with his African patron. He had for a moment seen Severus as a power seeker himself, but the discovery that he worked to put in the succession the one man who might be able to hold it all together impressed Rufinus.

Severus sat back in his seat. 'If things decline or anything untoward happens, Pertinax commands the Urban Cohort, who we know to be free of corrupt influence. He will be well placed in the city to secure Pompeianus. And I will have the lion's share of the veteran legions on the Danubius, ready to leap to his defence should any other claimant start to move from the periphery of empire. If you have cleared the threads of Cleander from the Guard, then they too could be relied upon.'

'Neat,' Rufinus said finally.

'You approve.'

'In principle. But only as a safeguard. I will support no move against the emperor. Commodus is the ruler of Rome by divine right, be dynastic descent, and by popular choice.'

Severus nodded. 'Quite. But I fear we have focused on one strand of news to the exclusion of all others. I had many tidings to impart.'

Rufinus nodded, walked over to kiss Senova, then sank into another chair and ruffled Acheron's head as he curled up at his master's feet. Over the following half hour, the consul caught him up on all affairs in the palace and the administration of Rome. Finally, having exhausted his news, Severus rose and stretched. 'Time I departed,' he said. 'I hope to enjoy a brief sojourn at the baths before I settle in to being badgered by plaintiffs for a few hours. Good to see you back and to hear that your task continues well. Cestius made a good choice in you, as did I. My wife is having a small party. Just a few score of the most noisy and irritating high-born ladies of the city. I would deem it a great favour if the two of you would join us two nights hence? I could do with the support of a sensible male, and

Senova, you might prove the only woman who can match my wife's wit among that throng of pigeons.'

Rufinus snorted, but Senova was there straight away. 'We would be honoured, Consul. Thank you.'

As the consul shook hands with Rufinus, kissed Senova on the hand and then left to be shown out by Naravas, Rufinus sighed. 'Great. An evening of being subjected to the vapid mob of Roman matrons.'

'You heard the man, Gnaeus. He needs us. We shall be an island of sense in a sea of the senseless.'

'Have you been reading Ovid again? I don't like it when you get all poetic.'

Senova gave him a withering look, and he sighed. 'We have to do something about our marital status.'

'We are married.'

'But we're not, Senova. Some fictitious centurion and his woman are married. We're us again now.'

'Alright, but we cannot be wed again, Gnaeus. Not with you in the Guard.'

'I know. It's frustrating. But what will the rich and noble women at Severus' dinner think of us? Of you?'

'If they think at all, it sounds as though it will be miraculous. Do not fret so over such things, Gnaeus. All will be well.'

'I hope it will. In the meantime, I need to think about the next step. I will have to move on Calidius as soon as possible. If he hears that his fellow speculatore in the cavalry has died in a fight he might become suspicious and more careful. Ideally I could do with facing him before news of Appius reaches the fortress.'

Senova nodded. 'I will have everything there is to know for you by nightfall tomorrow.'

Rufinus chuckled. 'Severus is right, you know? You *are* a marvel.'

Yet still, as he went across the house to get changed, he managed to 'accidentally' leave a scrape across Brigantia's accusing eyes.

III – UNPICKING THE THREADS

The Castra Praetoria never really slept. With cohorts and centuries of soldiers on duty in the city and the palace, accompanying various notables of the imperial court and family, or overseeing imperial projects and the like, there were always men coming and going at all times of the day and night. And, of course, of the ten cohorts based here, unless the Guard was required by the emperor on a campaign, there were always at the minimum four or five cohorts in the fortress on various ordinary camp duties, ready to be called up for emergencies.

As such, despite the lateness of the hour, Rufinus moved through roadways where men chatted, lights burned, and conversation hummed. He strode with purpose, for that was always the best way to go unnoticed in camp. Anyone who looked authoritative and busy was clearly not worth attention, after all. And wearing his centurion's crest and with the vine stick jammed under his arm, no guard was about to stop him. He had left Acheron at home, though. Sometimes subtlety was required, and Acheron was many things, but subtle was not one of them.

He turned over in his mind everything Senova had told him as he walked.

Gaius Calidius may be the records keeper for the speculatores, but he was also the exactus of the Fifth Cohort. Naturally. He would need to occupy the same rank and role in the open guard registers if the speculatores were to keep their identities unknown. He was plebeian, but from a wealthy branch of his family, most of whom seemed to have disowned him. He certainly owned no property and was a client of no one important. Yet, clearly, he was still receiving a sizeable purse of coin from them on a regular basis. As yet Senova had been unable to identify why his family might be paying him off despite having cast him out, but it might well have something to do with his gambling.

The man was apparently notorious for it. Not only wagering on the games, the races and other great events, but also down to the grimy business of dice in back street drinking pits, and even of illicit fights held in warehouses and cisterns, against the law and out of sight of the Urban Cohorts and the vigiles.

Rufinus might not know why Calidius received money from his family in addition to the healthy pay grade of a Praetorian exactus, but he sure as shit knew where the money went. Senova had been scathing of the man's behaviour, though Rufinus had been moved to defend him. It was a self-destructive habit, of course, but Rufinus had been put through the grinder of addiction in his time, and he knew damn well how easily it took a grip on a man; how simply it could turn a good man sour. Calidius was an addict. That was not necessarily his fault.

Moreover, Senova surely had every affidavit and record from the trials, the proscriptions and the general shower of faeces that had made up the days after Cleander's fall, and yet despite some digging through the day, she had been able to unearth not a single word against Calidius. It was, of course, possible that the man was horribly guilty of something they hadn't got a reference to, since evidence of crimes from that regime would be emerging for years yet, but it was equally possible that the man was entirely innocent.

The speculatores might have been in the pay of Cleander, but some folk would see the entire Praetorian force as that, and just as Rufinus knew there were men in the Guard entirely innocent of corruption, so there would also be the same among the speculatores. He would not condemn a man without evidence. All too often over the past few months he had chased down and cornered villainous Praetorians and been forced to deliver the ultimate justice to them. On occasion it had been Acheron who'd done so, mind, which tended to get messy. But this was different. He had to get the information from Calidius, for the man was the password that would open the door of knowledge. With his muster lists, Rufinus would have the names of every speculatore in the Guard. But without any evidence of crimes on the clerk's part, he would not consider beating it out of him. Even the *threat* of violence seemed to be a step too far when the man might be entirely innocent.

That was what had led to this late evening stroll.

As he turned a corner into the next street it became clear that he was now in the barrack region of the Fifth Cohort. The dirt-stained whitewashed plaster of the barrack blocks was painted with their cohort's insignia, a deep blue background making the white stars and moons and the golden scorpions and lightning bolts almost leap out from the wall. Almost as pretentious as the First Cohort, he grunted to himself.

The narrow street between the blocks was empty apart from one soldier who was sitting outside his room's door being noisily sick into the gutter. At least he wouldn't be much of a witness if this went wrong. In theory a centurion had every right to enter the room of an inferior, and if it was brought before the prefect nothing would come of it, but there were certain proprieties, and the tribune and centurions of the Fifth would be incensed that Rufinus had the audacity to enter the room of one of their men without prior consultation. Moreover, if the other speculatores learned of it, they would have warning of what was to come. Thus, the fewer witnesses the better.

The drunken guardsman didn't look up, aware only of a passing figure and not even his rank, let alone identity. Rufinus strode on to the end of the block. The exactus' office/sleeping chamber was at the end of the block opposite that of the standard bearer, as it was with every cohort in this fortress. Rufinus tried the door. Locked.

Time for his little trick. From his belt pouch he produced the ring with the six keys. The exactus' office door was sealed with a warded lock like all the others in the fortress. The problem was that originally the entire fortress had been outfitted by the same people in a short space of time, and due to the difficulty of producing more than a thousand doors with more than a thousand locks, they had been mass-produced. That meant that in the early days of the fortress there had been only four types of lock used. In the nearly two centuries since then there had only been two major overhauls requiring new lockable doors, and each of those had used only one run of locks. The result was that a man with six keys could open every standard door in the Castra Praetoria. Oh, not *every* door, for the officers' houses were different, as were those of the granaries, principia, armoury and so on. But if you wanted to get into a man's room you needed only one of six keys.

The exactus' door opened with the third, and Rufinus slipped inside. As he closed the door behind him and looked about, he immediately formed an opinion of Calidius as a fastidious, neat and organised man. His office and living space was the tidiest room Rufinus had ever seen. It was late summer, and the day's heat could still be intense, while the nights were beginning to bring a little chill, and while the man was out in the city, he had the place warming with a well-stocked brazier. Even there the man's tidy and careful nature showed, for his office was carefully organised such that the brazier was covered with a mesh to prevent coals leaping out, and was positioned carefully in the corner away from the main furnishings so that should it somehow fall there was precious little chance of it doing more than charring the flagstones.

A quick scouring of the room turned up nothing of interest to Rufinus, which surprised him not. In short order he narrowed down the location of anything important. A chest stood in the corner. Quite a large chest, heavy and strong. It had a good lock, judging by what he could see, and the manufacturer had hinged the lid with interior hinges to prevent simple access. There were men in Rome, especially in the frumentarii, who could open locks like this with special knowledge and skills. Rufinus was not one of them. He did not have the fingers for such dextrous, subtle work, his hands being those of a boxer.

But he'd learned much in the time he had known Vibius Cestius, the most cunning man in the world. One thing he'd learned was that people had a tendency to focus on the detail without turning the whole thing and looking at it from another angle. Such was the case with lock-fitters. It would take an expert thief to open that lock, but if you simply looked at it properly, there was another, more obvious, solution.

The entire lock plate was attached to the box with four bronze rivets. Tongue poking from the corner of his mouth, Rufinus pulled out his special bag from his belt. Placing it on the floor beside the chest, he drew it open and located the chisel-tipped knife. In mere moments he'd got it under the flange of the first rivet and was levering it out. It came away with a click and fell into his hand. He examined it. It had survived well. Quickly, he repeated the process with the other three, and peered at them all. Two had bent on removal. Ah well.

With a sense of satisfaction, he simply lifted the plate from the box, lock and all. Pulling open the chest, he went methodically through the contents with increasing frustration. The cohort's records were kept in immaculate order. But only the *Fifth* Cohort. There was nothing in there that might be something to do with the speculatores. For a moment he considered that the two groups of records might be combined somehow, that the speculatore lists might be hidden in plain sight among the others, but he quickly dismissed that notion. If anyone senior going through the records of the Fifth found them, it would cause trouble. No. They were hidden somewhere else.

For another quarter of an hour Rufinus searched, to no avail. Wherever they were, they were too well secured. Frustrated, he replaced the chest lid, returned the plate to its place, lock back in situ, and produced a hammer from his bag, as well as a small square of fleece. Using the latter to deaden the sound, he hammered the rivets back into place, then found two matching ones from the wide selection in the bag and finished repairing the chest. Moments later, he was slipping out of the door and locking it again. He might have found nothing, but at least there was no sign that he'd been there. He was just leaving as a guardsman rounded the nearest corner with a bag of charcoal. He saluted Rufinus, who nodded in return. As he left, Rufinus noted the man unlocking Calidius' door, going in to bank the brazier so that it kept burning in its owner's absence. Gods, but Rufinus had been lucky not to be inside when the man had arrived.

Time to move on to plan B.

Calidius was on one of his nights off, which he contrived to somehow have every other day. He would be somewhere gambling. The races for the day had ended, as had all the amphitheatre's events. If he remained true to form, the exactus would either be at an illicit fight or in one of the Praetorian-frequented taverns playing dice.

There was an illegal fight going on tonight. Senova had given him the details earlier, and he'd known better than to ask her how she'd discovered this. Sometimes it was better to live in blissful ignorance.

Stealth had not succeeded. Next came bribery. Threats would be the last resort, so he would now meet the man on familiar terms. Giving the watchword at the western gate, he slipped quickly through and out into the city. He was dressed in his tunic and cloak, with his military belt, vine staff and sword. He was not going past the pomerium, the sacred city boundary beyond which weapons of war were forbidden, so he could easily remain openly armed.

It took a quarter of an hour to find the warehouse and Rufinus boggled at the audacity of it. The building was directly across the street from the barracks of the Third Cohort of the Vigiles, the firemen who doubled as night-watchmen, supplementing the Urban Cohorts. An illegal fight held across the road from the men who should be stopping it. Such fights flaunted laws, for they were always held using cheap slaves, usually stolen ones, and were to the death, thinning out a pool of manpower already scarce through plague and war. Such laws had been instituted at the insistence of the lanistas who were being undercut for private events by these seedy gatherings.

At the door, Rufinus nodded to the man inside and handed over a small fee, which saw the place opened up to him. Inside, he saw the uniform tunics of several of the vigiles, which explained a lot. At the centre of the warehouse a makeshift arena had been formed from wooden hoardings, and inside it two slaves, and not the best stock from the look of them, hacked one another to pieces, wearing a mishmash of second-hand, battered gladiator armour. The crowd all around bayed for blood, and money was changing hands constantly.

Rufinus squinted, concentrating as he moved around. He was sure he could identify Calidius. He'd spent a short while watching the man's office from the end of the street in the afternoon, had quickly identified him and had lodged the image in his mind. The man had a curled beard and short hair, which had been an odd thing only a decade ago but seemed to be a growing fashion. He had, however, clearly been afflicted with some pox in his youth, and there were small bald patches in hair and beard which made him fairly recognisable.

That was why half an hour later Rufinus emerged into the street once more in increasing irritation. While it was faintly possible, he'd missed the man in the packed warehouse, he didn't think so. Calidius had not been there.

Plan B2.

Moving two blocks west, he reached the northern end of the Vicus Patricius and began to saunter down the well-lit, busy and effluence-filled street. He called in at the *Hades' Falx* and treated himself to a well-watered wine as he peered around at the occupants. No sign of Calidius. There was not a hint at the *Black Grape*, nor at the *Spit and Polish*. The fourth bar produced gold, though. Calidius sat at a table in the corner with two other men, both in Praetorian white, a stone board covered in pieces between them. Even as Rufinus bought a drink and watched, Calidius wiped his opponent from the board. The other two men at the table huffed in anger and snapped faintly threatening insults at Calidius, who grinned, sliding their piles of money over to join his.

As they left, Rufinus made his move. Approaching the other side of the table, he gestured to the seat. 'Do you play dice too?'

Calidius frowned at him. 'Why?'

'Because I'm feeling lucky and you have a huge pile of cash.'

The exactus shrugged. 'I play dice games, but tonight I'm playing stones.'

'I don't play stones, but I intend to leave tonight with that pile of cash.'

Calidius' brow rose again. 'Do you indeed? How lucky are you?'

'Very.'

The exactus, a calculating look on his face, slid the board aside. From a bag beneath him, he produced a dice-rolling tower and a small pouch, which he tipped out to produce a collection of exquisite looking dice. Rufinus gave them a once over. 'Very nice. Which one rolls the sixes and which the ones?'

The clerk narrowed his eyes. 'You think I cheat?'

'I think anyone who sits at a table in a bar with that large a pile of cash is not relying on chance.'

The man glared at him for a moment. 'My dice are perfectly fair. You prefer others?'

Rufinus fished in another of his belt pouches and lifted a closed fist. Opening it, he let two dice drop to the tabletop. 'The fairest dice you will find in Rome,' he announced.

The exactus frowned at them, then gathered the pair up and rolled them. Sucking his teeth, he repeated the process again and again, each time with apparently random results. Satisfied, he nodded. 'Very well, we use your dice.'

Rufinus settled in, produced a stack of coins and put them on the table. He bet on the numbers, slid coins across, and Calidius did the same. Rufinus scooped up the pair of dice, gripped them and then cast them into the dice tower. A five and a three. Just as he'd predicted. Calidius frowned at him 'Let me see those again.'

Rufinus scooped them up from where they had rolled out of the tower and dropped them into the man's hands, who rolled them a few times. Random results. Still frowning, he huffed and pushed coins over to Rufinus.

'Beginner's luck,' the centurion grinned.

The second cast was Calidius', and neither of his numbers came up. The pot grew, and Rufinus achieved no success on the third throw. The pot grew again. The fourth throw went to Calidius, who smiled in satisfaction and pocketed the entire pile. 'Perhaps the night is not your friend after all, centurion?'

Rufinus shrugged. 'I've coin left yet, and I feel luck all around me.'

A short while later Rufinus netted a pile of coins twice the size of that Calidius had won, earning him more hard and suspicious looks. The next hour went on much the same, with Rufinus winning now more often than losing, and when he did, generally winning the larger sums. Periodically, overcome with suspicion, the exactus would demand to examine the dice, and Rufinus would oblige. Once or twice the man would insist they play with his dice, but quickly Rufinus proved them to be weighted, and so they went back to Rufinus' ones, which clearly were not, despite the centurion's suspicious level of success.

31

As the evening progressed, Rufinus became wealthier and wealthier, and Calidius' pile of winnings diminished constantly. With the desperation of the addicted gambler, the exactus knew he should stop and walk away early in the game, but simply could not bring himself to do so. Thus, he fought to the bitter end, and despite everything, Rufinus found that he felt an odd sympathy for the man he was depriving of coins at a disgusting rate.

They had been at the table for just over an hour and a half when the last of Calidius' coins changed hands. Rufinus knocked back the last of his cup of watered wine. He'd had four, which was more than he liked to, but he didn't want to draw too much attention, and in taverns people drank.

'Buy you a drink?' he said to his dejected opponent.

Calidius flashed him a look that was in equal parts anger and remorse. 'I think you've done quite enough, thank you.' He gathered up his dice tower and board and stones, slipping them into his bag with shaking hands. Rufinus swept up the dice in his big fist and used his other hand to open the pouch at his belt. Carefully, he let all eight dice drop from the fist he had kept closed all night, its size easily capable of hiding six small seemingly identical dice, wedged in the lines in his palm and between fingers. The dice that each rolled a specific number, and the pair that were truly fair, all distinguishable to their owner by the very faint differences in finish. He really ought to be ashamed of himself. He had not been brought up to cheat. Look what prolonged exposure to Vibius Cestius was doing to him.

As Calidius stormed out of the tavern angrily, barking at men to move out of his way, Rufinus pinned his cloak about his shoulders and rose, tightening the strings on his bulging purses, and slipped out in the man's wake.

He followed the exactus back up the Vicus Patricius, watching and listening as the man continually kicked things in anger and misery, swearing when he hurt his foot, and muttering about fortune and gods and 'bastard centurions' as he went. Rufinus allowed him to slip away from the busy road into one of the smaller cut-throughs that led towards the west gate of the Castra Praetoria, and then closed behind him.

'Calidius!'

The figure, now a darker shadow within the gloomy empty narrow road, stopped and turned.

'You.'

Rufinus closed on him, and the man took several steps back. 'I'm not armed.'

'And I'm not drawing my sword,' Rufinus replied.

'I know who you are,' the exactus snapped. 'The one they talk about. Should have realised it when you first sat down. The one who was Perennis' pet. The one Commodus himself rewarded and who Cleander condemned. The one covered in torture marks. The one with the bastard hound who tells senators what to do.'

Rufinus blinked. In a way it described him, but he wasn't sure he liked the picture that painted. 'I'm not your enemy, Calidius.'

'Evidence suggests otherwise.' The man backed up against the brick wall at the side of the narrow street. Rufinus held his hands out to his sides. 'Do you want your money back, and more besides? I can make that happen.'

'Not by singing a happy tune, I'll wager.'

Rufinus tried to keep his demeanour friendly and comfortable. 'You know what I do?'

'Some say you hunt Cleander's spies.'

'Some are very astute. I am in the business of bringing to justice men who sold out their oath in favour of a would-be despot. Men who deserve everything coming to them, and many of them fellows of yours among the speculatores.'

Calidius flinched. 'I did nothing wrong. Never took a sestertius from the chamberlain. Never killed a citizen of Rome. Never even drew a blade against them.'

'I believe you. And in all the evidence we have against your friends, your name appears not once. I am not after you. I don't *want* you. But I *do* want some of your friends. I have names and descriptions from witnesses, and some I think I know, but I cannot confirm identities without the records of the speculatores. Records you control. I want your muster, pay, assignment and transfer records.'

'Piss off.'

'I only want them for one day, and then you can have them back.'

'I can't.'

Rufinus took a single step forwards, arms still outstretched, and Calidius flinched again. 'Listen,' the centurion said encouragingly, 'I don't want you. No one does. Not only will I give you back your winnings and pay you helpfully for your aid, but when this all comes to a head, I can make sure that no shit sticks to you. That you stay clean, with a clear military record. You could be one of very few speculatores that comes out of this better than they started, with imperial favour. I can offer you that, but only for your help. I need those records.'

'You have no idea what you're asking,' Calidius said, a hint of panic creeping into his voice.

'Oh, I do. But I give you my word that as I bring my investigations to a close, I will keep your name out of it. And you will still have your records should anyone ask. I'll just have a copy to work from. Imagine if you could live the rest of your career out not looking over your shoulder and waiting for the headsman?'

The exactus shivered. 'It's not a small thing. I would want huge assurances. *Written* assurances. And I couldn't stay here. I would need a new name. A new assignment somewhere else. Somewhere cushy, too. It would not be cheap for you, what you ask.'

Rufinus nodded. 'I will pay your price. Just give me the records.'

'Come to my office.'

With the man leading the way, they moved through a few back streets and then out onto the main road leading to the Castra Praetoria's west gate. There they both gave the password and were admitted without argument. Rufinus immediately became watchful, gaze tracking each figure who passed, aware that being seen in Calidius' company might trigger something for the right person. Swiftly they moved out of the main roads, taking the narrow alleys between blocks until they emerged at the end of the Fifth's barracks.

They crossed the street and Calidius produced a key, opening his door with worried looks in both directions that made Rufinus smile, given that he'd already broken in here with ridiculous ease so recently. Inside, the exactus hung up his cloak on a peg on the far wall not far from the brazier and beside his sword baldric that hung on a similar peg. Putting his belt pouches into a box on the desk, he motioned for Rufinus to lock the door behind them. The centurion did so, leaving the key in the door.

'The records. Just the ones for the speculatores, but I want all of them. I have plenty of detail about murderers, extortionists and other criminals in Cleander's pay, but without adequate details, I cannot necessarily marry them up with men from your unit.'

'Where will you send me?'

Rufinus shrugged. 'You only need to be away until the Guard is cleansed of rot. You can hide under an assumed name until them. Believe me, I know. I spent a year in Dacia and the east. I have friends in places both high and low. How would you like to be assigned as a private guard for an imperial villa in Baiae? The best posting in the empire, I reckon. The best weather, lovely place, sea

34

and sand, plenty of bars and night life. And since the imperial villas are generally unused over winter no one to boss you around. You could more or less have your own little palace for the winter. And I could maybe arrange a pay increase too? Sweeten the pot for you?'

Calidius still looked worried and unsure, chewing his lip.

'It's still so risky. Believe me, I fear you. You and your dog. But there are men in the world I fear more.'

'Not for long,' Rufinus rumbled in a menacing tone. 'Soon those men will be glaring out from the top of spear shafts over the city's old gates. And you'll be living the good life. I will see to that. You have my word on it. And all for just a little help tonight. I'll have the records back for you by nightfall tomorrow.'

Twitching, Calidius stepped over to that wide space around the brazier that had been left clear in case the thing toppled, and he dropped to the floor. With a little industry, he lifted out a loose tile across which Rufinus had walked half a dozen times earlier. The sneaky little bastard. From inside, he pulled a collection of documents, each in a leather wallet, all unmarked.

'You have no idea how important these are,' the exactus said, his voice wavering as he swallowed nervously and rose to his feet once more.

'Oh, I do, Calidius. They are, in fact, critical. With them, Cleander's rot can be cleared out for good.'

The exactus nodded, still visibly worried, and lifted the wallets, tilting them and loosening the tied thongs so that the vellum and parchment pages slid from the wallets.

'One day and I'll get them back to you.'

'I don't think so,' Calidius said suddenly, his voice acquiring a certainty that had been absent thus far. As Rufinus felt a surge of panic, the man stepped back and lifted the grille over the brazier.

'No!' Rufinus leapt forwards from where he'd been standing by the door, but Calidius was quick. In a heartbeat he dropped the records into the glowing orange coals and let go of the grille, which fell atop them. Yelping and blowing on his fingers, which had been singed in lifting the hot ironwork, he stepped away.

'No,' shouted Rufinus again, diving over towards the brazier, but in a moment of unexpected bravado, the exactus ripped his gladius from the scabbard hanging on the wall behind him and dived between Rufinus and the brazier, brandishing it. He might only be a clerk, but even a clerk in the Guard was as well trained with a blade as any legionary. Rufinus was under no illusion as to the danger, but he had to get those documents.

The vellum and parchment had quickly caught fire and were already burning, and Rufinus could see his chances of cleansing the Guard vanishing before his very eyes in a puff of carbon. Damn the weak-willed man! Or possibly strong-willed, depending how you looked at it.

'Stay back,' Calidius warned, gesturing with the sword. Rufinus felt panic setting in. He needed those documents, and they were now burning thoroughly. All his skill at tactics and planning a fight were of no use now.

'Sorry, friend,' Calidius muttered, 'but you have no idea who you're dealing with. I'd rather die here on a sword point than them find out I sold them out to you. Self-preservation.'

Rufinus acted before he'd really thought it through. He was still wearing his cloak and, gripping it with his left hand, he lifted it and leapt. His left fist, protected only by a handful of wool, closed on the exactus' blade and he gripped tight. He felt the sharp blade through the wool as the man tried to pull it out of Rufinus' tight grasp, and he gasped as the sword's edge cut through both wool and palm flesh in one move, but still he did not let go. His other hand came around in a powerful right hook, sending Calidius sprawling backwards, yelping, sword falling from hand as his broken jaw came loose at one side. He stumbled into the brazier, which overbalanced and tipped out onto the stone floor.

Through blind luck the exactus managed to avoid the burning coals as he hit the ground and thrashed in pain and panic, but Rufinus ignored him now. His attention was on the brazier and its contents. His hopes were dashed in moments. The documents had been alight too long. There was no saving them. Calidius had been efficient as always, utterly destroying the records even as Rufinus demanded them face to face. Damn the man. Rufinus had felt him teetering on the edge of accepting the offer. A moment longer and he might have done so.

Heart pounding and misery roaring through him. Rufinus kicked at the charcoal, seeing if there was anything left. One single page remained partially untouched, though already the flame was racing along it, eating up the knowledge it contained. Desperately, Rufinus tried to stamp out the fire, but his hobnailed boots would not do the job. He watched in dismay as the flame engulfed all that was left.

The day had been an almost complete failure.

Almost.

As the blue-gold edge of flame swept across that last fragment of parchment, annihilating it, he had seen one name in the moments before it became a charred and blackened nothing.

Attius Sacratus.

He turned to the thrashing figure of Calidius. 'You've just cost me months of work, and all for a little cowardice. The end result for these traitors will be the same, I'll make sure of that, but when this is all over there will be no protection for you. You've cast your lot in with the villains now. Good luck with them.'

Turning his back on the cringing, whimpering clerk, he strode from the room, unlocking the door and emerging out into the night air. He felt the anger and the humiliation burning in him. He'd had the best chance tonight that he'd hoped for in months, and it had gone up in smoke, quite literally.

All he had was another name now. It was slim pickings, but it was all there was. He would have to find this Attius Sacratus and hope the man had information of his own.

Back to work, then, he sighed.

IV – JUST ONE LEAD

Cestius had an odd look on his face as he traipsed across the atrium, through the painted corridor and out into the peristyle with various slaves following him. Rufinus stood outside Senova's office with his arms folded, enjoying the morning sunshine, but less so the gentle aroma of multi-species dung carried from the surrounding streets on the gentle breeze.

'Vibius? Any news?'

The visitor waved the slaves away irritably and gestured for Rufinus to head into the office, face still looking... what? Embarrassed? Surely not, as he never seemed that. Contrite? Perhaps. Irritated most definitely. An odd combination.

Rufinus entered the office, where Senova sat rubbing the bridge of her nose with finger and thumb, tired of working through documents. She turned slowly, smiling a weary greeting to their friend as Vibius Cestius gave a suspicious look around the garden and then closed the door. Rufinus had never seen the man looking so disturbed. It was a weird thing to witness.

'What is it?'

Cestius leaned his back against the door and rubbed his hands together. 'Tell me what you found out about Attius Sacratus.'

Rufinus shrugged and turned to Senova, who closed her eyes once more, recalling what she had done over the past few days. 'I've been through four years of records from the Castra Praetoria that Gnaeus brought me, and I still have two more years here to get through, but every year we go back makes it less likely we'll find anything in my opinion. If he was active under Cleander, his records should be available now. He's not on any lists for postings, pay, muster, requisitions or *anything*. It's almost as if for the Praetorians he doesn't exist.'

She waved a hand wearily towards the wall. 'I've searched every page of public record we should be able to find. There are three Attius Sacratus' in Rome, which doesn't help, but one is a wine merchant, one is a slave trader and the other is apparently a socialite. A ton of money and busy climbing the patronage ladder with an eye on the senate. None of them show any hint of being involved in the Guard. I have a clerk digging out their property records for me so that I can see if there's anything to find there, but that won't be until tomorrow. This man is a ghost, Vibius.'

The frumentarius nodded. 'He is. And there's a good reason for that.'

Rufinus' eyes narrowed. He took a single step forwards. 'You don't mean…?'

Cestius nodded. 'He was seconded from the Praetorians into the frumentarii over a year ago.'

'What?'

'Quite. It shouldn't have happened, really. We've never knowingly had one of the speculatores move into the frumentarii. I think it's more a professional rivalry thing than a rule. They were the emperor's eyes when we were the emperor's knives. But the problem is, with them being distributed among the Praetorian cohorts with little record, it's hard to know who they are. So now, we are forced to consider the possibility that Sacratus was not the only one of his unit who is currently among our number.'

'Can you say, "conflict of interest"?' Rufinus grumbled.

'Quite. A unit that seem to have thrown in their lot wholly with Cleander serving among another unit whose loyalty was kept unwavering for the emperor. I would love to have a little chat with this Attius Sacratus. This is a little embarrassing and suggests that we might need to attempt a purge of our own people even as you do so with the Guard. I truly wish you'd been able to secure those records.'

'Me too,' sighed Rufinus. 'Believe me, I tried. At least we got a name. An important one, by the looks of it. So, what can you tell me of Sacratus? He's still with your number?'

Cestius shook his head. 'The man's too clever and cautious, clearly. As soon as he left the Praetorians, the speculatores wiped his records so that as far as the administration is concerned, he never existed there. That's why you can find nothing. Then, somewhat conveniently, the moment Cleander fell, Sacratus came down with the plague. He was invalided out, then miraculously got well and, as you can probably guess, his records were wiped. The man truly is a ghost. He has no service history in either unit. In fact, the only records you'll find show that he was from Beneventum and from a relatively unimportant family there. He has no surviving relatives.'

He drummed his fingers on his forearms. 'Sacratus is the man you see climbing the social ladder in Rome now, though. He seems to have inherited property and businesses that have made him a man of means. Personally, I see them as ill-gotten gains from his time under Cleander, though of course there will be no record to be found of any of it. It makes me twitch that we had a grain man who was probably passing on important information about our activities to Cleander. It makes it something of a surprise that you stayed hidden during the period of your "death". Anyway, Sacratus now has property in Rome and is looking to gain influence and power.'

Rufinus cracked his knuckles. 'Sacratus might be all-but invisible, but I would be willing to bet that a man in his position, who was among the most secret of soldiers and the most well informed, will know more about the speculatores than many of his peers. He could be the source of information we need. A human record book.'

Cestius nodded. 'But a hard one to open.'

Rufinus gave him a dark look. 'I'll open the bastard, don't you worry.'

A tutting noise came from the corner. 'Try not to kill him before you get anything out of him, dear.'

Rufinus rolled his eyes at Senova. 'Of course. You have his address?'

Senova rifled through the documents on her desk. 'House at the end of the forum, below the Palatine and facing the amphitheatre and the Temple of Venus and Roma. Jammed between two small temples. Hard to miss.'

Rufinus nodded. 'I know the one. Pass it quite often when coming and going from the palace. A good position to keep an eye on the activity of the city's most important people. This will have to be done carefully. Can't just drop into his house and demand information. Not if he's that good. We need to know everything about him and his place first. Cestius, can you dig out anything at all about him from the frumentarii? I know you said his records were wiped clean, but there must be threads, else you wouldn't know about him at all. Anything you can find out might help.'

He turned to Senova. 'Look into his history in Beneventum and his past year in Rome. The two occasions he's broken cover. I want to know anyone he owes, anyone he cares about, and anyone he is either in close company with or at odds with. Anything I can use for leverage when I have him over a barrel.'

'And you?' Senova said.

'I am going to have a good look at his place. If I need to get in there undetected and surprise him, I need to know what I'm up against. That house is in an extremely busy and visible location, so this will have to be planned meticulously.'

There was a sudden bang from behind Cestius and the wooden door shook in the frame, knocking the frumentarius forwards. He sprang away from the door, hand going to the knife at his belt, but Rufinus just chuckled and opened the door. The great, black hairy shape of Acheron padded in, looking accusingly at Cestius.

'He doesn't like locked doors.'

Senova smiled. 'Are you taking him with you?'

Rufinus shook his head. 'Not this time. This is just reconnaissance, and Acheron tends to stand out. In fact, I'm going to dress as boringly and nondescriptly as possible.'

'Then you'll need to walk him before you go. Look at him.'

Rufinus sighed. 'This is important. Can't one of the slaves…' but his gaze had met that of Acheron, whose head was tilted to one side. 'Alright. A quick walk down by the aqueduct, and then I'll get going.'

It was almost an hour later when Rufinus emerged from his house in a plain grey tunic draped down to the knees, below the traditional military height. He had a small utility/eating knife sheathed at his belt, a small scuffed purse, and a plain undyed cloak of light wool. His boots were the ones he used for walking the dog, civilian affairs without the studs, but scruffy and old. He was so average he would vanish among the crowds of Rome.

The morning was wearing on now, and he planned to spend perhaps an hour or a little more checking out the place and then return for lunch, unless something specifically piqued his interest. He emerged into the street to find the tide of humanity already strong, and slipped in among the crowds gently, joining the flow down the hill towards the heart of the city.

As was the norm these days, his watchful gaze slipped all about as he moved, looking alternately bored or interested depending upon where it fell, but in truth all the time watching for anyone paying attention to him. There should be no real need to do so, in fact, but after his time in this city wearing the guises of different men, and a sojourn in Dacia, he had learned the value of being thoroughly aware of his surroundings. To his relief, there did not seem to be anyone watching or following him, and his gaze inevitably slid to the monuments of his own past as he moved.

The Castra Peregrina of the frumentarii where he had spent odd times throughout the past decade and where he was theoretically now based. Conveniently close for Vibius Cestius to just drop in from one place to the other unexpected and unnoticed.

The aqueduct where he had run for the palace in those desperate dark days when he'd been trying to save Perennis. He'd almost toppled to his death from that great bridge, and Cestius *had* fallen, breaking an arm.

The settling basin where in his first year in the Guard he had been forced to leave Scopius. A defining moment in his life, really. He'd only wanted to threaten the man, to stop the bullying bastard from making Rufinus' life hell, but in the end Scopius had forced him into a grisly fight that left the man drowning and changed everything. It had been the first time Rufinus ever killed a Roman, let alone a soldier. It certainly hadn't been the last.

The memories of the great amphitheatre that loomed ahead came thick and fast. The place he had saved the emperor's life. The place he had won his silver spear that he had later lost. The place where he had finally confronted Lucilla's private killers.

He forced his attention from reverie now, as he turned towards the forum. Beyond the grand conical fountain, he could see the Via Sacra marching up the slope between the Palatine and the great temple. The arch of Titus stood proud across the street at the high point. And there, on the left, he could see a featureless wall with a high quality door. Nothing more. That was all there was to see of the house from the road. It had its own private balneum – a small bathhouse – as Rufinus could clearly tell from the wisps of steam rising in groups above the place, leaving the building through vents in the roof.

A small temple to the genius of the Caesars stood on the corner before it, butting up against the house's eastern edge. Access from there would be difficult to say the least – likely impossible. Just on the off chance, he slipped through the crowds and made for the temple. Three citizens were inside, making devotions, and a low-ranking priest's assistant was busy talking earnestly to one of them. Rufinus took his opportunity to look around the temple as he made his own offering of coins. It was a small and fairly basic temple, well decorated and with a somewhat generous statue of the emperor at the rear, towering over the altars in his painted glory. There were no apparent rear doors or other chambers. The only way to access the house from this temple would be slipping across the roof and down into the garden, and the location made that unlikely. The streets around here would never be empty, even in the middle of the night. Satisfied that he had ruled this out, he moved on, back into the daylight and, slipping into the tide of humanity once more, headed up the Via Sacra towards the forum.

He could see the tips of trees within the house's private garden, tucked away behind that wall. It was a rich place, clearly. The door was the only clear entrance, and the wall featureless to either side. He would have liked, in a perfect world, to have spent time studying the wall and door, but one of the critical factors of Rufinus' visit was to be unnoticed. Sacratus was clearly a subtle, clever and careful man, and Rufinus needed to blend in with the crowd. As such, he paid as much attention as he could in passing, but without staring. There was a small glazed aperture close to the door, just the size of Rufinus' palm – probably into the doorman's alcove, so that he could observe visitors before opening the door. A knocker on the door was shaped like a dolphin.

Then he was past and moving on. Just as the temple of the Caesars butted up against the house's eastern end, the temple of the Lares, the public spirits of Rome, did the same at the western end. Hoping that his investigations under the cover of worship were not some sort of dreadful impiety, he slipped from the tide of people into this place. Another devotion and donation of coin, muttering rote prayers while surreptitiously sliding his gaze around the room. Once more, the temple was of a standard plan. No hope of accessing the house from the west unless it was from the temple's roof, under the gaze of half the city centre's eyes.

No. That was three sides of the house out of the question. Sacratus had chosen his abode well. It was a veritable fortress. There was only one hope, then. Passing beneath the decorative triumphal arch across the street, he turned to his left and climbed the slopes of the Palatine. Here and there he could see men who were clearly Praetorians and tried to avoid them. They were probably perfectly innocent, but it would hardly make him less conspicuous if a Praetorian recognised him and hailed him in the street.

At the north-eastern corner of the Palatine stood one of the city's larger temples: that of Jupiter Victor. On a grand platform a century old, the temple itself stood at the centre of a square of ornate gardens, all of which was surrounded by a portico. The corners of the roofed surround hosted enclosed rooms that served as ancillary buildings for the main temple, and the southern and western sides of the temple were solidly walled with ornate fake columns and arches built into the structure beneath the portico. The north and east, though, were of open colonnades, looking out as they did over the edge of the temple platform, some sixty feet or more down to the city below.

Entering the temple complex by the ornate triple arch in its western face, he milled about among the various citizens who were here to show their devotions, and the slaves serving the temple's priests. As he did so, his eyes continually fell upon the populace of Rome, watching for anyone paying too much attention. Satisfied once more, he slipped through the gardens to the north. Dipping beneath the portico, he approached the arcade with the low balustrade, looking out over the city.

As though simply enjoying the calm of the day, he wandered over and leaned on the balustrade with both elbows. Apparently enjoying the view, his eyes were in truth turned down, looking over the north side of the platform to the house of Attius Sacratus. He could see the temples to either side and confirmed that his chances of crossing either of their roofs unnoticed were tiny.

The house filled the middle third of the space between the two temples, a mass of tiled roofs from the outer blank wall to the terrace foundations, two square gaps in the roof showing the location of atria. The western end was filled with the bath suite and a small yard where logs were stacked, and the furnace slave's quarters lay. The eastern end was a very pleasant private garden.

Rufinus felt his heart jump to see a small group of figures in the garden. One was togate, and he was instantly sure it was Sacratus. He was with visitors and a slave, sharing drinks. Rufinus chewed his lip. It was quite by chance that his gaze slipped left and right as he leaned out over the balustrade and the vertical drop beyond the house. It was this pure luck therefore that he spotted the other figure leaning over the balcony a hundred paces along.

He forced himself to stay still, rolling his eyes right, though apparently still watching the city below. That was how he saw the man glance surreptitiously his way for just a heartbeat. That was all the confirmation Rufinus needed that the man was watching him. He had to be good to have gone undetected this long, unless perhaps the man was set to watching Sacratus' house and had simply picked up Rufinus here. Either way, he was now being observed by someone.

Was the man watching Sacratus and therefore interested in Rufinus on the side, or was he here simply because he had been following Rufinus? The answer might well make all the difference. If he was following Rufinus, then he was almost certainly an enemy. If he was watching Sacratus, then perhaps he was a friend.

Only one way to tell.

Straightening, he turned and strolled away from the portico, back across the gardens. He desperately wanted to turn and look back, but that would be too obvious if he *was* being followed. As he passed between a well-tended flower bed and a maze-like box hedge arrangement, he approached a slave who was brushing leaves and dirt from the path. Hailing the man, he paused beside him.

'Can you tell me, is the temple open during the night?' He was fairly sure the answer was yes, having served on the Palatine for much of the last decade, walking back and forth past the place. Certainly, at night there were people there and torches lit.

'The temple remains open at all times for the glory of Jove,' muttered the slave as if reading the words from a speech, 'though the devotee will find a reduced staff in the hours of darkness.'

Rufinus nodded. It was good to know, but the best thing was that in speaking to the slave he'd had the brief opportunity to glance back carefully. The man from the balustrade, wearing a nondescript brown tunic and with short curly hair and beard, was halfway across the gardens, casually sauntering and looking this way and that at the gardens. Rufinus was no longer under any illusion. The man was following him.

Trying not to look suspicious, he slipped through the arches and back out of the temple complex. He was beginning to form a plan. The balcony with its view down over Sacratus' house was the only realistic approach, and at night there would be fewer people around in the temple, if any. The shadows under the portico would hide his activity well, too. It was dangerous, but it was a start. In the meantime, he would have to concentrate on his new friend.

As he turned right and headed back down towards the forum, he tried to decide what to do about his pursuer. Did he want to confront or evade the man? Who could he be? He ran his thoughts over what he'd seen. Nondescript dress. Average and currently fashionable hair and beard. He was either very ordinary or very good at pretending to be ordinary. What of his shape? He'd been of average height. Rufinus cursed himself for not having noticed more.

Back on the Via Sacra, he spotted a stall at the street side where a man was selling copperware. Smiling to himself, Rufinus wandered over and started to peruse the wares. Swiftly he found a tray of beaten copper hanging from a line amid several jelly moulds and pinched the corner of it between thumb and forefinger. Apparently examining it, he turned it this way and that.

'Bay-est kwaleetee,' the stall owner said in some thick southern accent. 'Corp-err pew-err and no-ting else.'

Rufinus nodded just as he got the angle right and had a lovely reflected view of his secretive companion across the street. In a heartbeat, he took in everything he could and then turned it again.

'Eight dee-narii. You wan?'

Rufinus sniffed deeply. Horribly inflated price, of course, but he couldn't be bothered to argue. 'Actually, yes. Thank you.' Taking the tray, he handed over the coins much to the stall holder's delight, thoughts still focused on the figure behind him.

The man was not a Praetorian. He had a thin and reedy build. Far too slight for the army. That meant he was neither Praetorian nor speculatore. Moreover, he was probably not a frumentarius either. That meant he was a private hireling. And a good one, at that. As such, he would know as little as possible about his employer. Better to evade him and then be more watchful than to confront him, Rufinus suspected.

He turned into the next alley, and at the far end paused before turning towards the Flavian temple. The man turned into the alley a moment later. Rufinus ducked around the side of the building and ran. Up the Vicus Statua Verris he pounded, drawing attention from the folk in the street. Turning left behind a small knot of men arguing with a street side philosopher, he pounded halfway along and then slipped into an archway. Ahead, the bakery was in full operation, slaves turning the great stones to grind the grain, men hurrying this way and that with bags and the like. Rufinus slipped to the side and disappeared into a shadowed niche.

He could not see out from his little hideaway, but he heard pounding footsteps turn into the alley, then grow louder and louder. The steps paused at the archway he'd taken, and he felt his pulse racing at the proximity. Once more, he considered actually confronting the man. He heard the feet pace a few steps into the bakery entrance and stop. The man was no more than six feet away from Rufinus. He held his breath.

As he heard the man turn, he risked leaning a tiny bit to his left and was treated with a momentary glimpse of the man from the rear. In that brief moment, Rufinus decided he had been right to hide and not confront the man. As the figure stepped away again, out into the street, Rufinus peered at the gleaming blade in the man's hand.

It was not a soldier's weapon, and not a private utility knife. It was a curved and razor-sharp sica. The weapon of a gladiator more often than not, which suggested who this man might be, though he lacked the blubber so often found on an arena fighter. But it was also a traditional weapon in Dacia, which added a second worrying possibility. Either someone had hired a gladiator to follow and possibly kill Rufinus, or his old friend Optio Daizus from the Thirteenth in Dacia had finally caught up with him. Neither was an encouraging notion. The man could well be a gladiator, and a good one if he relied on speed to avoid injury rather than bulk. Certainly not the sort of man Rufinus wanted to tackle without knowing more of the man's abilities, and certainly not while armed with only a fruit knife and a copper tray.

The man turned left at the end and hurried on along the street, heading the way he must presume Rufinus had gone. This was all something of a worrying development. Rufinus should be able to find out if anyone connected with Daizus and the Thirteenth had come to the city from Dacia. Between them Senova and Cestius could determine that. But although that was a possibility, Rufinus was more inclined to favour the idea of a gladiator in the pay of someone as yet unknown in the speculatores.

Certainly, Rufinus was now making enough waves in his investigations to have drawn their attention. Until recently his targets had been lesser folk and their fates easily explained away as accidents, but the death of Optio Appius Numerius in Baiae had now become common knowledge in the camp and, though no one could connect it to Rufinus, it would have any other conspirators connected with him looking over their shoulder. And though the clerk Calidius had lived through Rufinus' confrontation, he was now languishing in the Praetorian hospital with a broken jaw, watched over by Mercator and Icarion, the only two men of the whole Guard in whom Rufinus felt he could place absolute trust. The man's disappearance from duty, and his injury, would be adding to the suspicion of the other speculatores.

They had clearly decided that Rufinus' prying had gone far enough.

He stepped out into that alley once more, looking this way and that. He'd left it long enough now and strode off back the way he'd come. Out in the street he re-joined the flow of humanity and made his way back down to the amphitheatre and then around the Ludus Gallicus and along the Neronian nymphaeum, heading home. It suddenly occurred to him that if he was being targeted by his enemies, then Senova was now in danger. He would have to do something about that. He couldn't imagine she would agree to leaving town again as she had during the Cleander operation, but he would certainly have to improve her security somehow.

His mind was elsewhere, busily considering Senova's safety, when the attack came suddenly and from out of nowhere. The man suddenly emerged from his right, from among the many life-sized statues in the great nymphaeum. Soaked from hiding among the waters, the attacker was on Rufinus in a heartbeat, that keen-edged sica swiping in for the kill.

The man was definitely a gladiator. The blow was perfectly aimed for Rufinus' neck and had come unseen from the side. Had Rufinus not been holding an overpriced copper tray, he would have been on the ground in a moment, pumping out his life. Instead, out of pure instinct the tray had come up and deflected the blow at the last moment, the curved edge scraping out a spine-tingling noise as it screeched along the copper surface, carving a deep rent in it.

Rufinus remembered one of his fellow soldiers back in his early days in Marcomannia during the war describing what happened next. Mummius had said that people were just animals, and like all animals, their instinct when they sensed danger defined their response. They would instantly become a wolf, or a fox. The wolf would turn and face the threat, determined to bring it down and nullify it. The fox would run, outpacing the danger.

Rufinus, it seemed, was currently a fox. By the time the assassin had recovered from his failed slash Rufinus was already off. Without looking back, he flung the ruined tray and was rewarded with a clang and an angry shout, but he didn't wait around. He was running.

On another day, when he was armed for a fight, he might have been a wolf, but he was under no illusions here. He was currently outclassed and had been very lucky to survive that. And there was another factor, of course. A few hundred paces up the street, Senova waited in their house. What if this man was not alone and other killers with razor-edged sicas were busy there?

His feet took on an extra turn of speed at that, and he was off. Only when he passed the aqueduct did he pause and look back. There was no sign of the sodden gladiator in the road. He stopped and took a deep breath, then turned and ran on.

His relief when his frenzied hammering at the door resulted in its being opened by Naravas with a frown was almost total. Clearly nothing untoward had happened here.

Yet.

Pushing the surprised doorman inside, he turned and slammed the door shut behind him.

'Have we had any visitors?'

The big Numidian shook his head. 'Not since you left, Domine.'

'Thank the gods.' He turned wild eyes on the doorman. 'Lock and bar that door. You only open it for Vibius Cestius or the consul Severus. No one else, without coming to see me first. Got that?'

Naravas nodded. 'Trouble, Domine?'

'I strongly suspect so. Do you have any training with weapons, Naravas? Other than your club, I mean.'

The Numidian gave him an odd look and broke into a grin, white teeth shining out of his dark face. In answer he held out his arm and pulled up the sleeve of his plain tan tunic. Rufinus blinked at the tattoo on the upper bicep that he'd never seen before. A lion above a simple 'III'.

'You were a legionary in the Third.'

'Yes, Domine.'

'How in Hades did you end up being a slave?'

Naravas snorted. 'Who ever said I was a slave, Domine?'

Rufinus blinked. 'But you're a doorman. A household slave that Severus...'

He tailed off. Severus had given them Naravas. They had assumed he was a slave, but in truth that had never actually been said. 'But we don't pay you...'

Naravas laughed. 'I'm in the service of the consul, Domine. Don't you worry. I'm paid quite well.'

Rufinus shook his head in wonder. 'I've probably treated you like shit, man.'

Again, a laugh. 'Actually, you've been pretty polite. If I *was* a slave, I'd be laughing my arse off about my soft owner.'

Rufinus couldn't stop the slight blush that rose to his cheeks. A suspicion settled on him. 'Half my staff are from Africa. Are you all men of the Third sent here by Severus?'

'Of course not, Domine.'

'Good.'

'Half of them are from the Pannonian legions sent here by Cestius.'

'For Jove's sake, does no one tell me anything?'

Naravas shrugged. 'It wouldn't change anything. We're here to look after the lovely lady while you do what you have to. It would be better if you didn't really draw attention to this and just kept treating us the way you have so far.'

Rufinus sagged. 'Thank you, Naravas. I feel I might owe you all, and I'll probably owe you a lot more, soon. I was attacked not far from here by what I think was a hired gladiator with a sica. He was very good and very fast. And if my enemies are doing things like that, we need to keep this place sealed up tighter than a fish's rectum.'

Naravas nodded. 'It's all in hand, Domine. Go have a cup of wine and relax. Your dog's been whining for you.'

Rufinus nodded, clapped his hand on the man's shoulder in a fraternal manner, and walked off towards the peristyle and Senova's office. He had much to update her with, and now he had an idea of how he was going to get to Sacratus.

V – THE HUNT

Rufinus crouched in the room's corner, wondering whether to rise and move about a bit again. He'd done so half an hour ago, when the cramps had last threatened to set in. He could sit somewhere comfortable, of course, but everywhere comfortable would be in plain sight, which was clearly out.

The approach had been exciting and timed exquisitely. He'd chosen late evening rather than true night, when the city was still busy. That meant that rather than the house being silent and patrolled by Sacratus' men on careful watch, slaves were still about their tasks and the house hummed with activity. An extra peril in one respect, given the increased chance of being seen, but a peril removed in that the sounds of his activity would be easily masked. He was surer of his ability to hide than to sneak, so the choice seemed clear.

He'd watched from the colonnade of the Temple of Venus and Roma as his prey emerged from the house dressed in immaculate toga and, accompanied by guards and slaves, climbed into his litter and traipsed off up the Via Sacra. A dinner engagement, Rufinus had assumed. But he had also noticed the increased smoke from the bath furnaces and a delivery of three amphorae of good wine, so the man was only out for a temporary visit, and not staying the night. No rich man left his baths heating for the benefit of his slaves. That meant that most of the guards would be out, and several of the slaves, and that Rufinus had the chance to work his way in and be ready for Sacratus' return.

Timing and luck.

His second stroke of good fortune had come as he'd left his eyrie among the temple columns, with a slow, careful scan for any lurking gladiators with sharp blades, and made his way up the slope of the Palatine. It turned out to be busier on Rome's most exclusive hill than he'd anticipated. Some sort of party or public gathering had clusters of people around in the streets. Worse, the Temple of Jupiter with its handy colonnade that overlooked Sacratus' house had been full of devotees on some sort of specific visit. Men and women from Sardinia, judging by the accents.

Then it had all changed. As Rufinus had lurked in a doorway, waiting for them to clear a little and becoming increasingly irked with it all, an unexpected distraction arose. Somewhere down by the Flavian forum a fire had started, and the sudden urgency, with all the shouting, drew people away. Rufinus had waited until the area was almost empty and had then made his way over to the great temple. Just as he'd left the street and disappeared into the almost deserted complex, a unit of Praetorians emerged from the palace gates at the top of the street and had begun to move out at speed.

Rufinus had moved across to his balustrade then and looked down. Perfect.

From here he could also see the fire, which had been more worrying. The flames had already engulfed part of the Suburra and the Flavian forum and were by then threatening the spice warehouses not far from where he stood. It was a larger conflagration than usual, but Rome burned with tedious regularity. Several times a market week the vigiles would be active somewhere in the city, putting out flames. This one might be bigger than many, but it was so perfectly timed that it was almost as though the gods had started it just for him.

As the public had largely oohed and aahed and ogled the dangerous flames, and the Praetorians, the vigiles and the Urban Cohorts all put aside their differences for precious moments to band together and deal with the peril, Rufinus had sauntered casually along the balustrade to his chosen point.

He'd then heaved off his shoulder the bag he'd been carrying and in the shadows of the portico unravelled the thin but sturdy rope that had been coiled within. No grapple, for that risked too much noise. Instead, one of Cestius' men had taught him a type of knot that should hold tight enough to carry an elephant yet come loose with a simple shake of the rope. It had taken some recall to get it right in practice. Tying the rope to one of the posts in the balustrade and praying that the whole structure was as sturdy as it appeared, he'd taken a deep breath and climbed out over the rail.

Again, fortune had been his ally. He'd not anticipated how ridiculously exposed and obvious he was going to be hanging on a rope beside a man-made cliff of red-brick and vaulted arches. Luckily, by that time the spice warehouses across the Via Sacra had been burning and the smoke, the roaring inferno and the odd scent of spice that pervaded the air had every pair of eyes turned to the disaster.

Rufinus had hung in the wide open like the most brazen burglar, and not one person noticed.

He'd made the mistake of slithering down the rope for speed, minimizing the time he was out in the open. That gave him a minor friction burn on each hand, but it was only light, and would not inhibit him. His soft boots had touched the tiles of the house roof moments later, and he'd crouched, finally out of sight of most places, except the Temple of Jove above, the roofs of the two adjacent temples, and the upper steps and colonnade of the Temple of Venus and Roma across the road.

Bracing himself, he'd given a tug on the rope, but nothing happened. A momentary surge of panic had swept through him then. If the rope hung there and the fire was brought under control, sooner or later someone would notice it. He'd tugged again. And again. The fourth time he'd given such a mighty jerk on the rope that when it came free, he'd lost his footing, slid down the roof with a ceramic clatter and ended up hanging from the edge of the atrium roof over the expensive impluvium pool with its Neptune mosaic.

Swallowing nervously, he'd dropped lightly to the floor below, grabbing the rope as it slithered down after him and gathering it into his arms. He'd been horribly aware of the noise he'd made, but clearly his luck was holding, for he'd stepped aside into the shadowed doorway of a dining room just as a curious slave appeared from somewhere and looked up at the roof, wondering where the noise had come from. The man had stood there for moments, then shrugged, presumably blaming avian life, and returned to his tasks inside.

Rufinus had heaved a sigh of relief and then, watching and listening carefully, he'd slipped through into the second atrium. It seemed likely that the sleeping chambers would be that way. He'd waited there in another doorway as a slave pottered about doing chores, and thanked Fortuna once more when she made her way into one of the bed chambers carrying the most expensive looking bed sheets Rufinus had ever seen. She'd been in there a short while, then returned with crumpled old sheets and disappeared into another doorway.

Rufinus, now content he knew which chamber was Sacratus', had slipped across the atrium and into that room. The girl had lit two oil lamps, and the room had a low golden glow. It was well-appointed and was clearly the master's chamber. He'd been grateful to see the bed made for a single occupant. Senova had assured him that Sacratus was a single man, from her research into public records, but

Rufinus had still been prepared to have to deal with an innocent bystander. Now it seemed that was a worry he could put aside.

The bed chamber was the clear place to wait. Apart from Sacratus himself the only people who might come into the room were his slaves, and now that the oil lamps were burning and the bed ready, it seemed unlikely that anyone other than the master would be the next to arrive.

Thus, Rufinus had found a nicely secluded and shadowed corner behind a large wooden cupboard, had coiled the rope as a makeshift seat and had sunk to the floor there to wait. He felt certain the owner would make sufficient noise moving through his house to give Rufinus plenty of warning. For convenience and speed, he had unsheathed his sword and the blade now leaned against the wall close to hand.

So Rufinus had sat, crouched and fidgeted for almost two hours now, waiting for the master to return. Indeed, the oil lamps were beginning to stutter, suggesting that they would not be long before burning out. That meant the possibility of the slave coming back to refill them, which could cause problems, but there was little to be done. From the timing of the slave's preparations, it was clear that Sacratus had overrun and had taken longer than expected. Briefly, and with an unanticipated worry, Rufinus wondered if the man had fallen foul of the fire on his return journey. Rufinus could be hiding in a house while his only lead on the villains in the Guard was burning to death, pinned under a roof joist.

Such imaginings became more and more pervasive as time wore on, and he had to stand once more and shake out numb joints.

That was when he heard it. Commands in a deep, baritone voice that could only be Sacratus. Relief flooding him, Rufinus rose from his rope-seat and picked up his sword, whirling it a couple of times to work out the stiffness in his wrist. One of the lamps chose that moment to gutter to darkness, halving the glow in the room. Luck was clearly still with him.

Listening to the conversation and the footsteps, he heard them pass into the second atrium, just outside the bedrooms. Carefully, light on his feet, Rufinus edged around the cupboard now, so that he lurked by the shadowed wall just around the corner from the door. There he waited, breathless, sword lifted. The man would enter the bedroom, probably followed by at least one slave. Rufinus would step out behind Sacratus and grab him, sword coming around to the throat. Then, in a commanding position, he could have Sacratus order his slaves out and close the door. With a blade at his windpipe,

Rufinus felt sure he could convince the man to spill out his secrets. After all, if not, he might spill out the man's life.

The footsteps closed on the door. Rufinus braced.

Everything went wrong in that very moment.

As the figure stepped into the room and Rufinus moved, he realised all too late that it wasn't Sacratus. Nor was it one of his slaves. It was one of the big-muscled guards that had escorted him on his trip. The man was sooty and smelled of smoke, and Rufinus realised in a heartbeat that in attacking the wrong person he had effectively turned his back on the next person, which was almost certainly Sacratus.

He had no time and reacted on instinct. Slamming down his left foot hard and without even a glance to see what was coming behind him, he pivoted, still gripping the guard, sword coming around to his throat. With the agility that only comes from daily practice and plenty of martial experience, Rufinus spun, his big, strong arms still gripping the man and turning him as though holding a shield.

Within two heartbeats of having leapt onto the wrong man, he'd turned and put the guard between him and the door. It had been a good move. His instincts had been spot on. Sacratus' sword slammed into the guard's gut where it should have been the middle of Rufinus' back. The guard was impaled in an instant, as Rufinus could attest, since he could feel the tip of the blade that had burst out of the man's back digging into his ribs.

Sacratus snarled an oath and yanked out his sword.

The guard in Rufinus' arms screamed and collapsed in a heap that Rufinus instantly let go of before it dragged him down. Rufinus realised now just how sharp Sacratus had been. He'd not sent the guard in first out of some paranoid fear of random trouble. He'd sent the man in because somehow, he'd known Rufinus was there. He was sacrificing the man in order to get the drop on the interloper.

Even now, his own attack having failed as much as Rufinus', the man was thinking swiftly, planning. His eyes narrowed, darted once back and forth as he weighed up his chances against Rufinus, and then he chose. Tonight, Sacratus was a fox, not a wolf.

Rufinus saw in his eye the glitter of a decision made and suddenly Sacratus was off. Leaping the body of the guard, Rufinus gave chase. A second guard who had been across the atrium leapt in the way and Rufinus had to waste precious moments feinting twice to get the man into a dangerously overextended position before dispatching him with a blow to an armpit.

Then he was running again. He could hear Sacratus ahead, bellowing orders to his people. The man was damn good, clever and quick, but Rufinus felt that he was better, at least in a straight fight. The man had instantly decided as much from one look at the interloper and had consequently fled to fight another day. Rufinus gritted his teeth as he ran through into the other atrium. Sacratus was his only lead and he damn well was not going to let the man get away. He needed the information in his quarry's head.

Determination driving him, he met a third guard in the atrium, parrying the man's attack with his own blade and impatiently flooring the fellow with a left hook, leaving him yelping and falling as he ran on. Slaves had been pulled out into the doorways to block them by a harsh master with the urge to flee. Rufinus barged his way through them.

Sacratus was at the house's front door now. Rufinus heard him pull over the shrine to the household gods, creating yet another blockage for Rufinus to hurdle in his pursuit. He heard the man open the door, or possibly his doorman doing it for him and felt the edge of panic. The man was getting away. Rufinus would not get a second chance like this. If the man knew his time was up and his identity known, he would melt away into the shadows again and disappear, emerging in some distant province under another name. It damn well had to end now.

Then Fortuna nodded his way once more.

As he turned into the corridor that led to the front door, he saw Sacratus coming back into the house. Shock hit him as he realised why. The street outside the front door was a wall of boiling golden flame. The fire was far from under control. In fact, it was now spreading south, engulfing the edge of the Palatine and, with it, Sacratus' house. The man couldn't leave into that wall of flame.

Rufinus snarled and pressed on towards the man, who took one look at him and dipped through a side door. His frustration grew when he followed the man and realised that he was simply chasing him round in a loop to the same atrium in which he'd just been stood. Had he stayed there, the man might just have run straight into him. Instead, now the man was back in the atrium where the guard with the bruised face and scattered wits was still on the ground, groaning, while Rufinus was having to push past more discarded blockages to get to him.

There was no way out, and they all knew it. The house had a solid wall on every side, with fire blocking the only door. It was then that Rufinus realised what Sacratus intended. As he rounded the corner to the atrium, he saw feet just disappearing upwards as the man hauled himself up onto his own roof.

Rufinus grunted his irritation and leapt out into the atrium just too late to grab the disappearing feet. Looking this way and that, he settled on the only viable choice: to follow.

Sheathing his sword, he jumped, grasping the antefix below the tiles, its terracotta surface embossed with a gorgon design. The thing held, his fingers hooked over the top, and he pulled up his other arm, swinging it over onto the roof tiles and looking for any grip.

Some preternatural sense made him jerk his hand back just as the sword struck the tiles where his questing fingers had been, cracking and smashing them. For a heartbeat, Rufinus hung there, swinging by one hand from the roof edge. There would not be a repeat of that last blow, though, for he could hear Sacratus scrambling away up the tiles. Better still, as Rufinus swung his arm back up, over the roof, he found a good, solid purchase on a lath beneath the broken roof. In moments, he was hauling himself up. As he scrambled desperately onto the shattered tiles, he saw Sacratus at the apex, slipping down west towards the bathhouse roofs.

He gave chase. His intent was to smoothly rip his sword free as he skittered up the tiles, but he had been forced by time constraints to sheathe his sword without cleaning it and the sticky gore had all-but glued the blade inside, so that even as he crested the roof and slid down the tiles at the far side, he was still swearing and tugging at the hilt. It came free suddenly, and he almost pitched down into the furnace yard. Steadying himself with difficulty, he spotted Sacratus again. The man was on the far side of the baths with their higgledy-piggledy roofs, scrambling up onto the roof of the Temple of the Public Lares.

As Rufinus pursued, his gaze swept around, and he took in the scale of what was happening around them. The helpful little fire that had so aided him in gaining access to his quarry's house was now a blazing inferno that was clearly threatening the whole heart of Rome. The eastern end of the forum was alight, and the blaze spread all the way back into the Suburra. It was now eating the structures on the northern slopes of the Palatine and threatening the great temple from which Rufinus had dangled his rope, and even the very palace itself. Men of every force in the city ran hither and thither in groups with water, extinguishing fireballs only to watch new buildings explode into golden flame next to them. Others, mainly the men of the Guard and the Urban Cohorts, were pulling down whole streets to prevent the spread of the conflagration as best they could.

It was a true disaster in the making.

Yet for Rufinus it could be little more than a distraction. Months of work hinged on getting information out of the man now fleeing his grasp. That had to come before mere fire. If the Guard was ever to be cleared of corruption, Sacratus had to sing a song of traitors.

Gritting his teeth, Rufinus skittered and slid across the bath house tiles and leapt, hauling himself up onto the temple roof with his free hand. Sacratus was at the top of the temple now, standing with a foot on each side of the apex for balance. Rufinus scrambled up into the same stance, and the two men faced one another along the roof. There was nowhere to go. along the street the buildings were a blazing inferno, fiery wreckage filling the Via Sacra below. The road up to the Palatine was scattered with burning beams and was some thirty feet below besides. To the north the temple platform rose, unclimbable without that rope, and Rufinus blocked the way back to the house, much good attempting that would do either of them.

There was an odd silence amid the roar of the fire.

'I should have moved against you when I heard about you last year,' Sacratus said.

'What?'

'When you were a prefect of the fleet. At the time I left you alone. Whatever your goals were they didn't seem to be interfering with mine, so I let you be. That decision has come back to bite me, hasn't it?'

'You didn't simply decide to sell me to your master?'

Sacratus snorted. 'Cleander? Hardly. The man was useful for a time. A patron who thought he controlled me. He got remarkably little out of me. *I* got a great deal more out of *him*. You see, I was frumentarii, whatever else you might think. I was always loyal to the emperor. Had I found myself at any time having to make the decision, be assured my sword would have been in Cleander's neck. But as long as my interests never quite conflicted it was incredibly lucrative to have the confidence and support of both the frumentarii and the Praetorians, while simultaneously taking generous payments from the chancellor.'

'That's low, even for your kind.'

Sacratus shrugged. 'One day, Rufinus, we all get old. Those of us tied to honour and the service might end up with a vineyard or even an estate. Me? I'll end up with property to rival any patrician senator. I'll end up making laws and living an easy life, retired far earlier than the likes of you and with money to enjoy my life. This isn't treachery, Rufinus. Greed, perhaps, but not treachery.'

'Well now your climbing has ended, Sacratus.'

'Oh?' the man said with an interested expression. 'How so?'

'Look about you. Your house is about to burn. Your identity is known. You are the key to my mission and your history of criminal avarice will see you hauled over the coals and probably under the executioner's blade.'

'Oh Rufinus, don't be so dramatic and so blind. I will walk away from this free and rich, fat and happy.'

Rufinus frowned now. 'How do you figure that?'

'I know that Calidius burned all the records. And no one in Cleander's true pay will give you a single name, even under torture. Me? I'm the anomaly. I'm the outsider who worked for the same men as you. I owe the speculatores nothing. In fact, I owe our joint friends more loyalty. And I am the only man with the names you seek who you stand even a chance of dragging them from.'

'With hooks if I have to.'

Sacratus shook his head. 'If it transpires that I have died, all those you seek will go to ground, take flight and change identities. You'll never find them. But if you're sensible and play the game, we can make a lucrative deal. You have the resources of the palace and the Castra Peregrina behind you, while I have what you want.'

'You rat.'

'Don't be daft, Rufinus. You know how the great game is played. It's never black and white. Here's what's going to happen. We're going to sheathe our swords – though you might have to do some serious cleaning first. Then we're going to get down somehow and get out of the way of this fire. You are going to sign a whole load of documents for me, granting me funds, lands and immunity from prosecution. You will assign me a bodyguard and a nice villa in a hidden location where I can wait out the rest of your proscriptions. And when the last of the speculatores is dead, I will come back to Rome and live a good life for the rest of my days. And in return, when I have all those assurances, I am going to give you a list of names and some very damning information that spreads far beyond the corruption in the Guard and will bring down some very important men.'

Rufinus' eyes narrowed.

'I get my good life,' Sacratus said, 'the frumentarii get their traitors, the Guard gets reborn, and you become famous as the man who made it all happen. Everybody wins but the baddies. What do you say, Rufinus?'

Damn it, but it was perfect. It made Rufinus twitch to even consider letting this sleazy bastard off, but when it came down to it, one dodgy arsehole in return for a whole slew of *real* criminals was no choice really. It was a given. And he felt confident that he could agree to this without argument. Cestius would back him to the hilt on it. It would solve all their problems and make the loss of Calidius and his papers palatable.

'Alright, Sacratus. I accept your proposal. The precise details we'll hammer out when were safely away from here. For now, let's get away from the fire.'

The man on the far end of the roof smiled wickedly and slid his blade home into the sheath at his hip.

Rufinus was just contemplating whether it was worth cleaning his yet, since he could hardly clean the inside of the scabbard anyway, when ill fate turned her hand to the game once more. He happened to glance up just as Sacratus' neck sprouted an arrow. He blinked in shock.

Sacratus frowned, oddly, reaching up with his hand to touch the shaft protruding from his neck. He let out a strange gurgling noise and crumpled, slumping to the tiles. The arrow snapped with the impact, and he slid down the slope with a ceramic clatter, pitching out into the Via Sacra and its burning wreckage.

Rufinus stared in horror and disbelief at the trail of blood that ran from the roof's apex down to the edge, beyond which he could no longer see the body of his quarry. The simple importance of what just happened slammed into his brain again and again. Sacratus was dead. Sacratus was his only lead. Sacratus was the only man he would ever likely get that information from. And Sacratus was dead.

A second thought suddenly barged its way in past the repetitive shock. An archer had now had time to nock a second arrow, and Rufinus was standing on the top of a roof, brightly lit by multiple fires. He threw himself down to the tiles just in time, as the second arrow thrummed past and then clattered against the brick substructures of Jove's temple.

Unable to halt his movement now, Rufinus simply slid down the roof's slope and fell into the Via Sacra. In that last moment before he pitched out from the tiles, he thought he saw the shadow of a man between the columns of the Temple of Venus and Roma opposite. That had certainly been the direction from which the arrows had come.

He landed with a thud. He felt something in his leg twist and give way at the impact, though at least he was sure it hadn't broken.

Sacratus had done him one last service by supplying a relatively soft landing. Rufinus hauled himself upright from the mashed corpse beneath, shaking a dizzy head and wincing at the pain in his leg. All around him the street was full of burning wreckage.

A man from the vigiles, busy with his mates hauling a water cart up the street and pushing flaming wreckage out of the way with a long pole, hurried over to help, but Rufinus waved him away with thanks. He could manage.

With difficulty, and slower than he wanted, he limped and stumbled across the Via Sacra, dodging fires and charring wreckage. He reached the steps of the temple opposite which as yet had managed through sheer luck and wind direction to avoid burning. Wincing with every other step, and favouring his right leg, he slowly climbed the podium of the great temple.

It had been many heartbeats by the time he pulled himself up that last step to the columns of the temple. The archer would be long gone. The unseen man had not only almost killed Rufinus, but he had also removed the last hope of naming the corrupt men in the Guard. Rufinus felt utterly dejected. Everything he had done had now come to naught.

But Fortuna wasn't quite done with him yet. As he stood there, filled with misery, his gaze fell to the floor. There were footprints. Fresh footprints amid the ash that had gathered in the shelter of the columns. No one else was in the temple. It was not burning but was perilously close to the flames. No one would come here unless it started to burn. The footprints were new. They *had* to be the archer's. And while they could be any old boots really, they were clearly a soldier's boots from the marks of the hobnails. The trail would vanish once the footsteps emerged into the open, but there, in the lee of the column and fluttering slightly in the hot breeze, lay the answer.

A blue feather.

Not much of a clue, even Rufinus had to admit. But it was something. It was something that gave him a direction at least. Even as he watched, the wind caught the feather and lifted it, carrying it away across the Via Sacra. The feather could only have been there moments without the wind removing it, so it had to belong to the man who'd also left the footsteps.

And there was only one group of men who wore military boots and blue feathers.

He had a lead. Just a small one, but that feather belonged to only one of just twenty men.

VI – A CHANGE OF TACK

'Five hundred men,' corrected Vibius Cestius, leaning back against the wall with his arms folded.

'What?'

'Five hundred, not twenty.'

'How do you figure that?' Rufinus frowned. 'One cohort. Ten centurions and ten optics.'

Cestius rolled his eyes. 'And what do your lot do for parades? Or on festival days? Or whenever you need to look your best?'

Rufinus sagged. 'Parade crests.'

'Quite. Forget narrowing it down to officers. *Anyone* from the First Cohort has a blue feather crest even if they don't wear it all the time.'

'Damn it, you're right.'

He'd been so pleased to have had such a narrow focus after having repeatedly lost important leads that he'd not thought it through properly. The Guard was split into ten cohorts, and though there was by necessity flexibility in assignment, each cohort had its speciality. Rufinus' current unit, the Second Cohort, was the unit generally assigned to the escort and protection of members of the imperial family while out of the palaces. Only one cohort, though, wore the blue feather crests: The First Cohort, with the permanent, rather cushy, assignment to protect the Palatine.

Palace duties.

The favoured ones.

'It's still a win,' Senova reminded him.

'What?'

'You've narrowed down your latest conspirator to one cohort out of ten. Just five hundred men. It can't be hard to narrow it down further.'

Rufinus frowned. 'I'm not sure how.'

'Cohort records, for a start,' she said. 'You can effectively rule out anyone who was on specific duties, as they couldn't have been where you were.'

Rufinus shook his head. 'The fire burned all night and drew attention from every unit in the city. It was chaos. Any man could have taken a few moments out to try and kill us.'

Cestius cleared his throat. 'Any man with access to a bow and the knowledge of how to use it could have, you mean.'

Rufinus blinked. 'Gods, yes.'

'Archery is not a prime skill for legion or Guard, so there cannot be too many men in the cohort who could have had a go at you,' the frumentarius went on.

'But we can't guarantee that such things will be in records. I knew a lad back in my old legion in Pannonia who could skewer a rabbit at a hundred paces with a bow, but there was nothing official about it. He was the son of a huntsman. There might not be a record of such a skill.'

Senova huffed. 'Then you'll just have to examine the cohort from within.'

'What?'

'When you needed to hunt down Appius Numerius in Baiae, you got yourself transferred to the Second Cohort so you could follow him there. Now you need to track a man in the First Cohort. You need to transfer again.'

Rufinus shook his head. 'It's not that easy. Inter-cohort transfers are not common unless it's a promotion or a demotion. It's never done without good reason, and the First Cohort are notoriously hard to get into. They're the top cohort with the best duties, the best quarters, and often direct access to the prefects and even the emperor sometimes. Getting into the First Cohort is like trying to gain access to the House of the Vestals. Near impossible.'

'Surely nothing is impossible for the frumentarii?' She looked back and forth between Rufinus and Cestius.

The tribune sucked on his teeth. 'He's right, Senova. Transfers into the First are like unicorn horns. Known to exist, but no one ever has one. He could fall back on his frumentarii membership, but if he does then that risks his full identity being known openly among the Guard and that puts his whole mission in danger.'

Rufinus sighed. 'Well, however I do it, I need to be in there. She's right. I'm never going to be able to dig deep in the First Cohort without being one of them. I'm going to have to see their exactus and ask him for a favour.'

'Offer him money,' Cestius murmured. 'You know how corrupt these men can be, Positions are bought and sold with worrying regularity. Buy yourself a new commission.'

Rufinus smiled slowly. 'I think I have another idea. But I'll try yours first.'

With the aid of the frumentarius officer, he arranged for the transfer of as sizeable purse, and thereafter saw Cestius out. He spent the noon meal with Senova, or as much of it as possible, given that Acheron kept taking pieces of his food off the table every time he turned his eyes away. Then, finally, with the large black hound at his side, he marched back across town to the Castra Praetoria. Giving the watchword, he made his way back to his barracks and into his room. As arranged, a large purse of gold coins sat on his bunk. He knew better than to enquire how Cestius managed things like this, secretly slipping a large amount of gold into the heart of the Praetorian fortress, but at least it was here.

Cestius was right in that clerks were usually pliable, but this was too important to pin it all on that. He needed that sideways promotion, and he needed it soon. If gold bought him access, then all was fine. But he needed a backup plan, and it couldn't involve the frumentarii unless he wanted his true associations known to all. There was another possibility, though.

Securing the gold, he took a deep breath. This was risky, but it could work.

Strolling out of the barracks, he made his way to the storehouses. At the appropriate one, he opened the door and approached the counter with the lattice-work grille above. Two clerks were deep in discussion over some list of figures, and only looked up as Rufinus cleared his throat meaningfully.

'Yes, Centurion.'

'I need to requisition three pairs of boots.'

Without answering, the clerk slid a tablet and stilus over to him, and then returned to his discussions. Rufinus glared at him, and then bent over the tablet, scratching his request into the wax.

'Don't forget to add the size,' the clerk reminded him without looking up from his list.

Rufinus nodded absently and bent back over his tablet.

CALIGAE SPECULATORIAE – III
MEDIUM LARGE

He slid the tablet back under the grille and the clerk peered at it, then waved his friend to silence. 'You don't look like a scout,' he said, eyes narrowed at Rufinus.

'Second Cohort. We're accompanying General Pompeianus on a hunt. Our infantry boots won't cut it. We need scout wear. Now just sign off the chitty, will you?'

The clerk frowned for a moment more, chewing on his lip, then nodded and retreated inside. Rufinus tried not to heave a sigh of relief. The Caliga Speculatoria would rarely be requisitioned by anyone but the scouts. A lightweight boot without the ubiquitous military hobnails, it was manufactured to be equally effective on horseback and moving quietly through all sorts of terrain. These days it was only worn by scouts, though in earlier times it had been part of the uniform of the speculatores, when they were still openly identifiable.

The clerk returned before long, carrying three pairs of boots. 'These coming off your unit's account, Centurion?'

Rufinus shook his head. 'I'll pay for them myself.'

The clerk nodded contentedly. That would mean considerably less admin work for him, and Rufinus privately wondered how much of his coin would make it into the Guard's vaults. Doubtless this man and his mate would have a good night in town on the proceeds.

Handing over the coinage, he retrieved the boots. All the better if the man pocketed the payment himself. That would leave no trail to follow, after all. Stuffing the boots in his linen bag, he returned to his barracks and slid them under his bed. They were his backup plan. For now, threat could wait while he appealed to greed.

To that end, he left Acheron snoozing on his bed blankets while he went on his visit. The big hound was a very effective guard for his room. A short while later, he was making his way into the headquarters building. All around the courtyard stood offices, and he strode over to the clerk's office for the First Cohort, the door closest to the basilica entrance, a position of prominence. The clerk also had an office in his cohort's barrack region, like all the others, but with the ostentatious bigheadedness of the First Cohort, Rufinus assumed he would favour his office in the headquarters.

The exactus sat behind the desk, scratching his neck and yawning. It was a sign of how self-important his sort could be that he never even bothered standing in the presence of a centurion. Any member of the First Cohort considered even the lowest of their number superior to an officer in another cohort. Rufinus tried not to take it personally, though he felt his lip twitch in annoyance. In a way, he hoped this jumped up little shit wouldn't take a bribe, because he would just love to put the wind up him.

'Yes?'

Rufinus closed the office door behind him. 'I'm here to request a transfer'

The man harrumphed. 'Details?'

'I'm a mid-level centurion in the Second, but I want in to the First.'

'You and every other stick-carrying swagger merchant in this camp. The First has a full complement of centurions. There's no vacancies. Unless my tribune signs you on, or the prefect, or the emperor himself take your case, there's more chance of you sprouting wings and flying away than moving into the First.'

Rufinus nodded sagely, trying to keep the simmering anger down low. He'd anticipated that angle.

'Two of your centuries are currently missing commanders. I know this because I checked the assignment rosters and they've been rotated out. One is, unless I'm much mistaken, on long-term leave in Gaul, and the other is busy coughing up his lungs in the hospital. Plague is my guess. So even if you're expecting your Gallic centurion back, that still leaves one position you could fill, even if on temporary assignment.'

The clerk frowned. 'Neither is free. The centurion on leave is being replaced by his optio. The man is currently in the process of changing role and selecting his own replacement as second. The sick centurion is more senior and, while he's not expected back, there have been miraculous recoveries before. The man is a war hero, and I am not about to replace him until he expires. And when that happens, I already have his optio ready to step in. The man's already been filling in for him.'

'Let me cut to the chase,' Rufinus said quietly. 'I want one of those positions. I will have it. If you're willing to bargain, it could go well for you.'

Placing his vine staff on the desk and fishing into the satchel at his side, he produced the purse. Very slowly and methodically, he removed gold coins in small numbers, stacking them in a line on the desk so that they slowly formed a gleaming wall between the two men.

'Nice tidy sum here. Could buy yourself a little place by the sea down in Surrentum with that.'

A calculating look crossed the man's face as he peered at the coin, the gleam in his eye every bit as shiny as that of the gold.

'And don't try to edge me upwards,' Rufinus advised him. 'That is all there is. It's extremely generous as a donation just to move two officers around. My advice is to take the money, find a way to achieve the transfer and we all live happily thereafter.'

The clerk frowned. 'Either way, to grant your transfer would be to deny a promotion to an optio who has already been confirmed. Can

66

you imagine how irritable your second in command would be if I stopped his promotion and put you him in charge of him? The gold is very generous, but I can't take it. I would make enemies of officers in my cohort, and so would you.'

'Making enemies of an ambitious optio is not the worst possible outcome of all this. I can guarantee you there are less successful options. Take the money. Make the transfer.'

'No. Listen, Centurion, I'm doing you a favour. You don't want to keep an optio back down in the ranks when he's expecting his centurion's crest. That's a dangerous enemy.'

Rufinus snorted, remembering Daizus in Dacia in that very same situation. 'I've been through it before. Trust me. I can handle it. Take the money and make the transfer.'

But the clerk was shaking his head. 'No, and I also do not take kindly to the veiled threat in your tone.'

'You'll regret it when I *unveil* it,' snapped Rufinus, leaning forwards.

'Out of my office,' the clerk barked angrily.

'This isn't over,' Rufinus said through bared teeth as he slid the coins back into the purse.

'Yes, it is. Don't come here again.'

'Oh, I won't.'

Slamming the door behind him as he left, Rufinus stormed across the courtyard angrily. By the time he emerged out into the street, he had begun to force himself to be calm once more. He shouldn't have let himself get angry. He'd half expected that to happen, after all. The First always tried to promote from within, the elite bastards. Still, he'd almost had the man with the gold. He'd seen the clerk teetering on the edge of acceptance. And it had not been that the money wasn't good enough any more than it had been pride in his cohort that had stopped him acquiescing. It had been fear of irritating members of his own unit by accepting a bribe for an outside transfer.

Good, Rufinus thought, nastily. Now I get to frighten the shit out of him instead.

On his way back to his room, he made a detour, calling in on two old friends. Mercator and Icarion, two of his companions from his first days in the Guard, and the only two living Praetorians he would trust with his life, were both in the latter's room, playing knucklebones. They grinned as Rufinus walked in. 'Well hello, stranger,' Merc grinned.

'I've meant to drop in recently, but I've been a little busy.'

Icarion snorted. 'I'll bet. I won't ask, since I'm fairly sure none of us want to know the answer.'

Rufinus laughed. 'Actually, it's about an underhand little job I came. I could do with some help.'

'What is it? Not something that's going to threaten my commission, I hope?' Icarion said. It sounded like a jokey tone, but with a nod to the optio's crest on the helmet hanging on the wall, Rufinus knew there was a little true worry in there. Icarion had served as an optio now for two years, and his centurion was due for retirement in the new year. Unless something went wrong, Rufinus' old friend would be one of the centurionate very soon, which meant he would undoubtedly select Mercator as his optio. Briefly he wondered if it ever irritated his old friends that they had struggled for a decade to secure their first commission while the young Rufinus had joined beneath them and then sailed far past them to officerhood in half the time. No, he didn't think so. Neither of these men would begrudge him anything anymore than he would them.

'I hope not,' was Rufinus' honest reply. 'It could have repercussions, but all being well it won't. I don't want to endanger your pay increase.'

Icarion snorted. 'Me? I need the centurion's pay. This reprobate,' he thumbed towards Mercator. 'Well, you know him and money. He's got more wealth than the temple of Saturn already. And now he's dabbling in property. Owns half a dozen townhouses and villas now.'

'And a latifundium in Veneto,' grinned Mercator. 'And I'm looking at two estates abroad. I'm on the verge of a very nice acquisition.'

Rufinus chuckled. 'All I want is a couple of friends to look threatening at my shoulders while I try and persuade someone to do something for me.'

Icarion winced. 'Pray tell, who are you planning on threatening?'

'The exactus of the First Cohort. I need a transfer.'

'Why would you...'

'Don't ask things when you really don't want to know the answer,' Rufinus advised him. 'Will you help?'

'Of course we will, you daft sod.' Mercator gathered up the knucklebones and slid his money back into his pouch. Rufinus noted with a sly smile that he included the pile of stake money in the centre of the table among his coin. No wonder the man was so wealthy. As Icarion did the same he gave his friend a withering look. 'Alright, Merc. Next off-duty session the drinks are on you.'

Laughing, Rufinus left the room, his two friends at his heel.

They reached Rufinus' barracks a short while later and as Merc scratched idly behind Acheron's ears, the room's owner fished the three sets of footwear from beneath the bed.

'Going hunting, are we?' Icarion murmured.

'Something a little more significant. A little more archaic.'

Mercator stopped scratching and straightened. 'You want us to play Speculatores?'

Rufinus nodded. 'Just long enough to put the shits up the clerk. He won't accept money and I need that transfer.'

'Have you contemplated what will happen if he turns out to be one of them? The next thing you know we'll be found floating face down in a latrine. The very best we could hope for is an exile posting to some shithole like northern Britannia.'

'Don't let Senova hear you say that.'

'Rufinus, this is properly dangerous.'

The younger man shook his head. 'I don't think so. I really don't think this man is one of their number. I'm assuming that the speculatores have only one exactus.'

'Yes, but it might be him.'

'No. The speculatores' exactus is currently nursing a broken jaw in the hospital. You should remember him.'

Mercator's eyes widened. 'Gods, the one we were watching was a speculatore? You never told us that. Have you not heard about him though?'

Rufinus shook his head. 'What?'

'He died a few days ago. Some sort of internal rupture. We assumed it was natural, but if he was one of that lot...'

Rufinus huffed and bit his lip. 'They silenced him in case he talked. They've done it since then too. Put an arrow through a man's neck last night just as he was about to sing me a tune.'

'Rufinus this is dangerous stuff.'

'I know. But I don't have anyone else I can trust. Just you two.'

He gave them a pleading look.

'You got me large, right?' Merc sighed.

'Yes, I remember your giant feet.'

'What's your plan?'

Five hours later, as the horn blared above the headquarters and the watch changed, Rufinus and his friends sat in the dark. The sun had gone down an hour ago, and the shutters on the window only added to the gloominess of the room.

The Cleansing Fire by S.J.A. Turney

'Here we go,' Merc muttered, a hand cupped to his ear. Rufinus heard it too, a moment later. Footsteps approaching on the gravel outside. The three men tensed. Acheron let out a low rumble, and Rufinus gently stroked his head until that noise subsided.

The door opened and a figure stepped inside, dressed just in tunic and boots. Barely had he entered when the door was slammed shut behind him, Icarion sealing the room from where he had stood beside the door jamb.

'What the...?' barked the man in shock, but Merc was already there. He slid the shutter open on the lantern on the shelf, bathing the room in a golden glow.

The clerk blinked, eyes squeezing shut.

'What? Who...?' then his eyes fell upon Rufinus, sitting on the wooden chair by the bed. 'You!'

Rufinus nodded. Beside him, Acheron began to growl again, quietly. The clerk recoiled, but then urgently stepped aside as he remembered that someone was standing behind him, having closed the door. Icarion moved in front of the exit, blocking it further, as Mercator remained seated by the lantern, one leg crossed over the other, his naked blade lying across his lap.

'Who are you all?' the clerk demanded, though his voice now wavered with fear rather than the pompous superiority of earlier.

'I need a transfer,' Rufinus said quietly. 'Normally our own exactus would arrange it and you would only become aware of it when the order landed on your desk. An order you couldn't refuse. But our exactus has had an accident, and we are temporarily forced to look to you.'

'Who *are* you?' the man demanded again, but the answer was already dawning on him. His eyes fell upon the unusual lightweight hunting boots of the man sitting beside the big hound. Glancing at the others' he noted the same footwear on them all and his eyes widened.

'I can't,' he said. 'I'll end up in so much shit.'

'Shit with your mates or shit with me. Time to make up your mind.'

The clerk's face paled. 'What I told you is true. Both centurions might yet come back. In the meantime, their optios are already in the process of promotion. If I put you above either of them, you and I will both be targeted.'

'Leave the optio to me,' Rufinus said. 'The plague-ridden centurion. He'll never come back, and if he does, he'll be too weak for active duty. Give me his century. Tell me his optio's name and I'll square things with him.'

The clerk, frightened but defeated, sagged. 'Two days. It'll take two days to put the request through. Usually takes more, but that's the fastest it will ever happen. And if I do this, you'll never bother me again?'

Rufinus shrugged. 'As long as I never need to.'

The man sighed. 'Two days. You'll be commanding the Third Century, then, alright?'

'Agreed. You made a wise choice.'

Icarion opened the door at a nod from Rufinus and all three, along with the big, black hound, strode from the room. 'Have a good evening,' Merc said with a malicious grin as he left, then shut the door.

'That was oddly fun,' Icarion laughed as they strolled away from the block. 'Is this what it's like to be you, Rufinus?'

'Sort of. There's usually more pain and panic involved, though.'

'What now?' Mercator asked.

'I suggest when you get back to your rooms you dispose of those boots well. I'll do the next bit. Thanks for your help, though, both of you. I don't think he'd have believed it if it was just me.'

The two friends shook hands with him and then headed off back towards their own barracks, and Rufinus sighed. He couldn't go through that angry optio situation again. The time with Daizus had been dreadful. He had to head this one off and that meant appealing to a combination of pride and greed. He'd not got the optio's name, but he was the second in command of the Third Century. Since Rufinus was already in the barrack region of the First Cohort, it was not a difficult job to locate the optio's quarters. On a whim, he checked the centurion's room at the end, first. It was locked up and dark. That was a good sign. If the optio was too power-hungry, he would already have moved in there. Instead, Rufinus found the optio's door ajar and a golden light glowing from within. He knocked politely.

The door opened a moment later, a tall man with a black curly beard and shaved head peering out in surprise. His gaze fell upon the big hound and he took an involuntary step back at the sight. Most people did.

'Yes?'

'Can I come in?'

The man said nothing, merely gesturing inside. Rufinus entered and the door was shut behind him. The optio shuffled into the opposite corner to Acheron. He didn't look afraid, but certainly careful.

'What can I do for you?'

Rufinus sighed. 'You're currently commanding the Third Century with the expectation of receiving your vitis cane in a day or two, I believe?'

'That's right.'

'I have some bad news for you, I'm afraid. The simple fact is that I am about to take command of your century. The transfer is in process.' He caught the look of anger rising in the man's face and held out both hands. 'Wait. I know this is irregular and that you quite rightly expected command. The problem is that this is going to happen whether you like it or not. But I don't want conflict between us.'

'You're going to be disappointed then,' snapped the optio.

'My transfer will likely be only short term. I am not halting your promotion. All I'm doing is delaying it.'

'You have no right...'

'That's where you're wrong. I have every right. Listen. What's your name?'

'Titus Gamburio.'

'Listen, Gamburio, I can see that you're a man of honour. A less worthy man in your position would already be in the centurion's office. That means that you respect him, yourself, the position and the chain of command. As such, I am inclined to both like and trust you, neither of which I say easily or often.'

'That doesn't make jumping my promotion acceptable,' grunted the man.

'It is a temporary measure. And when I move out again, I will make sure that you follow me, for I still want you as my optio.'

The man's eyes narrowed. 'Why would you move on so quickly? Men spend years trying to secure such a role. Where could you possibly hope to advance to from there so soon?'

Rufinus gritted his teeth. He didn't really want to do this, and it was a real risk. But he didn't want this man his enemy, and he needed his help. He would have to trust his judgement of the man's character. He didn't appear underhanded or corrupt, at least.

He reached down into his purse and ignored the coins in there, instead fishing in the compartment to one side. He withdrew his brooch and held it up to the torchlight. 'I would be very grateful for your support while I'm in the role, and my gratitude opens doors.'

The fibula was silver and moulded in the design of a sheaf of grain stalks bundled together suspiciously like a fasces. The IV on it identified Rufinus' unit within that hidden force.

'You're a grain man.'

'Yes. And I have a duty within the First Cohort. When it's done, I'll be gone again, and you'll step into my place. And when you do, you'll have the thanks for the frumentarii for your help.'

The man straightened. 'I am loyal to my oath,' he said, slightly defensively. 'Loyal to the emperor.'

'I thought so. Will you help me?'

The optio nodded. 'What do you need?'

'Well for now I need you to forget what you just saw. You can act a little irritated at my transfer. That would be normal, of course. But when I need your help, I'll call. In the meantime, we just need to be good guardsmen, right?'

Gamburio nodded. 'You have my word.'

Rufinus was smiling to himself at how well he'd handled all this as he returned to his own barracks a short while later. He had secured not only his transfer but the panicked assistance of the clerk and the steadfast support of the man he had unexpectedly supplanted. All was good.

But he was not expecting the message that awaited him in his room.

A small scroll case, just a hand long, sat on his bed. It bore the unmistakable seal of Severus, from his signet ring, and Rufinus frowned as he broke the wax and slid out the vellum within.

FIRST HOUR
JANICULUM
FURRINA STEPS

VII – THE FIRST HOUR

Rufinus' hand went to the knife at his belt, his nerves twanging. Beside him, Acheron clearly felt something too, for a low rumbling growl constantly issued from his throat. Momentarily, Rufinus paused, turned and peered back down the hill. Beyond the darkness of the lawns he could see the buildings of the lower Janiculum hill, mostly dark and sleepy, though the great aqueduct that marched down the slope ran through the massive mill complex that ran day and night to provide flour for the city, five great wheels turning with tortured groans every hour the gods sent. Beyond all that, past the inky ribbon of the Tiber, the city of Rome glittered and twinkled with golden lights.

He may still be inside the city's political boundary, but the heart of Rome felt disturbingly distant from here. He was beginning to have serious misgivings about tonight. Turning uphill once more, he could just see the apex of the roof of the ancient temple of Furrina jutting out from the trees. All ahead was dark.

He shivered. This was not a good place. No one really came here. Even the children who played on the Janiculum during the day kept away from the Lucus Furrina. Yet here he was in pitch darkness making his way into the sacred grove.

Hundreds of years ago the famous Gaius Gracchus had died within this place, fleeing his enemies across the river only to fall in the home of this ancient all-but forgotten Etruscan goddess. Now the place was shunned. Cursed. It had long since lost its college of priests, even in the days before the emperors ruled. No one drank the water from its spring now, the small torrent flowing down to empty into the Tiber untouched. Once a day someone came here and cleaned the temple, tidying its grounds. Cursed it may be, but even a shunned temple to a forgotten god had to be maintained. No one would risk incurring the wrath of Furrina, whoever she was.

Five more steps and he lost sight of the glow of the city behind him. The temple sat at the heart of a small area of greenery and woodland that surrounded a spring. At night it was surprising how utterly rustic this place was, given its proximity to the greatest city in the world. He shivered again. Acheron growled. His fingers fiddled with his knife hilt. Why hadn't he brought a sword? The answer to that was simple, though: he'd walked through the city's ancient sacred centre where weapons of war were forbidden. Praetorians were permitted, of course, given dispensation for official duties, but no one could accuse this of being an official duty, and so he'd left it. He pulled the cloak a little tighter around him with his free hand and once more questioned why he was here.

Severus had sent for him.

Why?

The man was a consul and currently the man was not directly involved in Rufinus' work per se, for all his support and patronage. Why here? Severus had come to his house before now to discuss even delicate and dangerous subjects. What could possibly be so secretive that he would drag Rufinus all the way up here? Certainly, they would be unobserved, but this still felt very wrong. Had the message not borne the signet seal of the consul, Rufinus would have assumed it to be a trick and not come.

Indeed, he was beginning to suspect foul motives here, regardless of the seal. He was starting to consider how easily a seal could be faked if it was well enough known. Probably very easily.

The hairs stood proud on the back of his neck and he pulled his knife, gripping it tight, prepared for trouble. If Severus was here, surely he would have his lictors with him. No, Severus was not coming. This was something else. And there was an extremely high probability that whoever was behind it had violence in mind rather than mere conversation.

Around a corner in the wild grove he turned, the ancient temple appearing in forlorn glory before him. Beside it a basin contained the sacred waters that gurgled up through a hole in a stone cover carved in ancient days. Whoever had designed that spring head might have known the creepy reputation the place would one day carry, for the passage of water and air through the holes in the stone contrived somehow to form a discordant whistle that cut to the bone.

Rufinus shivered again. He almost left then, turning back to the warmth and safety of the city below. But there was one reason not to. It was very unlikely that Severus was here. It was, in fact, highly likely that whoever was bringing him here was one of his unknown enemies, and that meant there was another chance here to find a thread on which to tug. A name or names.

Briefly, and with more than a touch of worry, it occurred to him that a truly devious man might send Rufinus all the way up here merely to get him out of the way while attacking his house and all that he cared for. He quickly pushed that notion away. Severus and

Cestius had filled Rufinus' house with very capable warriors in the guise of slaves. Woe betide anyone who tried to assault that house.

No. This was about him alone.

There was no one on the steps of the temple. But then, it wasn't quite the first hour yet. The chimes and horns announcing the time would ring out at any moment. Tense, teeth gritted, Rufinus strode out across the path before the spring, trying not to hear eerie voices in the whistling, and climbed the steps. The bronze door of the temple was resolutely closed and there was no light from within. The scant moonlight picked out the embossed medusa heads on the doors, and Rufinus found for the first time that the image, considered a good luck sign, actually seemed a little creepy, the ancient monsters watching him as he climbed.

He stomped up the eight heavy steps and turned.

Acheron came to a halt beside him and sat down, still rumbling deep in his throat.

'I know, boy. Me too.'

A distant dull clang announced the first hour and was picked up by other bells and horns across the city. Romans had long since learned to sleep through such things. Life in the city would be unbearable if light and noise kept one awake, after all.

He stood, tense, knife still in hand.

What in the gods' name was he doing? He would wait for a count of fifty and then go home and forget all about this. He found himself listening to the strange whistled melody once more, wondering how the ancient sculptor had managed to achieve it, or whether perhaps it was miraculous accident at work. It was only because he was paying attention to the whistling that he heard the extra sound suddenly beneath it: the thud and thrum of an arrow being released.

Instinct saved his life, as the moment he noticed that extra deadly sound he threw himself to the side. The arrow hurtled through the air where he had been and clanked against the bronze doors of the temple.

'Kill,' was all he said, and Acheron was off.

As Rufinus shuffled over to a pillar of the temple's colonnaded front and staggered upright using it as cover, he watched Acheron race towards the darkened trees and then disappear into the shadows. Damn it but he should have brought a sword. What bloody use was a small eating knife right now?

Ducking out from the pillar once more, he peered at the grove. He could see nothing. Not even movement. Then there came a sudden tableau of sound. Voices. Two voices at least, and maybe more. He could hear the muffled snarling of Acheron and desperate shouts from the shadows.

Risking further attacks, Rufinus emerged from the column and leapt down the steps two at a time, racing for the woods, skidding to a halt as figures emerged. A man in a nondescript cloak appeared from the boughs of the wood, staggering backwards, flailing wildly. He was screaming, and reason why soon became clear. Acheron was attached to his leg by the jaws. The man fell back and for a horrible, gruesome moment, Rufinus saw his face illuminated in the moonlight. The hound had clearly managed to get to the attacker's face, which was ruined and torn and covered in blood. The man was done for, though even as he fell, screaming, Acheron took another bite of his leg.

Rufinus moved again, racing towards them.

Another thrumming noise caught his ear, and his eyes went to the shadowed woods beyond, trying to determine the source before he threw himself left or right. But the arrow wasn't for him. Acheron suddenly stiffened and yelped, letting go of the dying man's leg, then slumped on top of him, howling.

Rufinus felt cold. His heart filled with ice as he saw the great black hound fall.

He was moving forwards again, but as he did a second figure appeared from the treeline, bow raised, and arrow nocked. He pulled back the string hard, and Rufinus felt his world collapsing. He was in the open now with nowhere to hide. If he threw himself to the ground, he would be at the man's mercy, and there may yet be more of them in the woods to back him up too. He could see Acheron shaking on the ground on top of his victim, who had ceased to move, and felt again the terrible wrench. He couldn't help the hound now, and there was nowhere to shelter.

Praying as hard as he'd ever prayed, Rufinus ran.

He raced for the path that led back to the city and a few short heartbeats later there was another thrum of a missile released. He tensed, but never slowed his pace, weaving left and right along the path in order to provide a harder target. The arrow tore through his cloak and scored a line along the ribs at his left side but hurtled on and scraped to a halt along the path.

Voices behind. Still more than one man. He'd made the right decision in running, but what now? Back to barracks? Home? Find somewhere to hide? Yes, that last. His legs were already tired from walking across the city and up the hill to the temple, and his ribs now stung constantly, sending shockwaves of pain through him any time he bent or twisted.

The image of Acheron lying shaking atop the man flooded back into his mind, and with it came a sense of angry purpose that pushed away the fear and the pain. He was being chased. He could hear them. They had no intention of letting him live. But they were also the men he was looking for. They would have information he could use. And most of all, he would make sure they died for what they'd done to Acheron.

Now he was looking ahead as he emerged from the trees once more onto that wide lawn, but not for a place to hide. Instead, it would be a place to hunt. Gods knew he'd had plenty of practice hunting men these past few months, and he'd put that ample experience to use now.

His eyes fell on the Aqua Traiana, the great aqueduct that marched down the hill over to his left, heading into the Transtiberim region of the city. At this point the aqueduct was only eight or nine feet in height, having crested the hill below ground and then gradually changed angle. Ahead, it split its course, one torrent running into the complex of mills and driving its water wheels, the other bypassing it and soon entering an aqueduct bridge that carried it across the Tiber to bring much needed water to the city beyond. The branch that powered the mills was afterwards distributed around the lower Janiculum.

The aqueduct would provide cover for now. He had to get them onto his own ground where he could deal with them up close, where the bow was rendered ineffective.

Acheron...

An arrow hurtled past him, missing him by a mere hand-width, and only then because of his random zigging and zagging as he crossed the grass. Turning left, heart thundering, he raced for the aqueduct. Close by a street ran alongside the waterway. Here the aqueduct was still too low to drive a bridge underneath, but a small low arch, big enough for a man part-hunched, passed through the heavy stonework of the thing, and Rufinus raced for it, desperation driving tired legs. Moments later he was through and emerging at the far side. Ducking around the side of the arch, his gaze swept this way and that. Uphill was too open with wide thoroughfares and no cover. Ahead were streets and a small temple, and down to the right, some way below and before the main bulk of the city, the heavy squat building of the mills stood proud some thirty feet in height, its great wooden wheels hidden within the complex, but their motion creating a low rumble audible even from here.

There. That was the place. But before he could move, he heard the voices of the two men pursuing him. He couldn't hear what they were saying, but he could track where they were. One was moving towards the arch, and the other was heading uphill to where they could cross at the next point. In a moment, Rufinus realised he had the chance to even the odds.

The closer of the two men pursuing him would come through the arch carefully. He would look left and right immediately, and Rufinus would have trouble with just a knife, unless he could somehow surprise the man. A nasty grin crossed his face and he turned, jamming his knife between his teeth, fingers finding the gaps of crumbled century-old mortar between the stones of the aqueduct. After all, he had experience of climbing the damn things, didn't he?

The Aqua Traiana here was only nine feet tall, and in a matter of moments he was pulling himself up, staying low so that he would not be visible at the far side. Raising his head just a touch, he caught sight of the man, who was now very close, moving carefully. He might have had a bow before, but now he'd drawn a gladius and was approaching the arch slowly. Rufinus waited until he disappeared beneath the aqueduct and then swiftly rose to a crouch, turning to the near side of the arch.

He held his breath.

The cloaked figure emerged from the archway carefully, head snapping back and forth, prepared for Rufinus to jump him. It only occurred to the man to look up at the last moment, all too late. Rufinus landed on his back, one hand grasping the voluminous folds of the man's cloak at the back of the neck for purchase and thereby also pulling it tight, choking him. The man gasped, his free hand coming up in an attempt to undo the strangling garment at his throat, but as he did so Rufinus' knife came down hard in an overhand blow.

The knife was only a three-inch blade, but that was more than sufficient. The sharp point slammed with force into the back of the man's hand, sliding between the bones to emerge from his palm, where it continued on into his windpipe.

The man jerked, sword dropping from his fingers at the sudden unexpected death blow. Rufinus ripped his blade free and let go, dropping panting to the ground as the man collapsed before him. Rufinus took just long enough to commit his face to memory as he gathered up the fallen sword. The stricken man had a soldier's physique and a currently fashionable beard and hairstyle. There was little doubt in Rufinus' mind that two Praetorians would not show up for duty in the morning. Three, if he had his way.

Up the hill, the other man emerged from the aqueduct crossing, caught sight of the scene, and barked a furious threat. His hand went to the quiver at his side and began to nock an arrow to the bow. Rufinus turned and ran downhill, jerking this way and that once more. He had to bring the man close enough to deal with him without that damned bow.

His heart was still icy, images of the great black hound slumped over the body near the temple battering him rather unhelpfully as he ran. The mills were close. The sound of pursuit was lost now beneath the roar of the water and the ligneous groaning and creaking of the wheels even muffled as they were within the building. Even as Rufinus closed on the place, a door opened and a man carrying a huge sack emerged, crossing the street to where a pile of such sacks awaited collection and dumping it unceremoniously with them.

The man turned in surprise, shouting 'Oi!' as Rufinus ran past him and in through the door. He almost came to grief immediately, for he'd been expecting some wide hallway of turning machinery and men with grain. What he actually encountered immediately was the Aqua Traiana.

The water sloshed down from the channel's opening at the upper end of the mill complex where it became a mill race, wide and deep and very, very fast, which ran through the building itself, just inside the wall where the wheels turned ponderously, their axles driving other shafts that rose through the building into the second storey. Inside the door, a wooden bridge crossed the water and Rufinus almost pitched from it into the racing torrent before steadying himself.

The angry worker raced in after him but slowed at the sight of the grisly soldier with a shushing finger at his lips, that hand still holding a bloodied knife, the other with a clean gladius by his side. At further gestures from Rufinus, he hurried past and into the mill. Rufinus, plan resolving in an instant, ducked back beside the doorway, throwing away his knife.

Despite the cacophony of mill noises, he heard the sound of the man approaching, military boots clacking on the stone. He braced, perilously close to the edge and the racing water below. The would-be assassin burst through the door a moment later, bow discarded and blade in hand. Rufinus lashed out with his empty hand, combining two moves in one. His palm slammed into the man's chest, overbalancing him, throwing him back towards the racing waters, and at the last moment Rufinus' fingers grasped the man's cloak at the neck.

The pursuer pitched out over the water in shock, with an alarmed bark. He would have plummeted straight in had Rufinus not had a grip on him, but even then, the weight simply pulled Rufinus forwards, threatening to tip them both in. Desperately making an unhappy decision, Rufinus threw away the sword in his other hand and grabbed the door jamb with it.

There they hung for precious moments. The unknown Praetorian was being held out of the water only by Rufinus, who in turn was only held up by a grip on the door frame. He watched as the man marshalled his thoughts and his sword hand tensed, coming round.

'If you use that, we both die,' Rufinus grunted. 'The water is far too fast to fight. By the second heartbeat it'll have carried you beneath that undershot waterwheel. The power in that thing is a thousand times your strength, and the space underneath is about a hand's width. I'll die from the sword wound, but I'll be getting off lightly. You, on the other hand, will get all the delights of drowning while simultaneously being crushed and ground to pieces beneath the water wheel. Would you like to rethink your next move?'

The man's eyes widened, and his sword arm paused. His head turned to take in the immensely powerful waterwheel just behind him and the torrent of extremely fast water that lay in between. Rufinus could see the man imagining exactly what he'd just described, and his face drained of colour. He dropped his sword a moment later, hand searching for the wall and instead grasping Rufinus' arm. As if to highlight his possible future, the sword fell into the water and was immediately carried beneath the first wheel where it clattered and eddied among the timbers, finally bursting free, already bent, to disappear beneath the second wheel. The man swallowed nervously.

'You killed my dog,' Rufinus said in a snarl. 'Every ounce of my soul screams to kill you, but I know you're just a piece in this game, not the player. I want to know the name of the big man among the speculatores. The one who's moving the pieces. You give me that name and I'll let you live. That is my offer and my only one. You won't get another.'

The man coughed in panic. 'You'll only get in worse trouble,' he said. 'You don't want Aper to find out what you've been up to.'

'Aper?'

The man seemed to weigh up his chances for a moment, and then nodded frantically. 'Vectius Aper. Centurion of the Second Century, First Cohort.'

'But he doesn't know about me? He's not the man who sent you? Who sent the blue-plumed bastard at the temple of Venus?'

The panicked man shook his head. 'You wanted a big name. The boss. Vectius Aper's your man.'

Rufinus nodded slowly. Aper was a name he could work with. He was fairly sure that even this Vectius Aper would answer to someone higher, since it seemed unlikely that a centurion was at the top of this particular shit heap, but it was someone to look into, and a man in the First Cohort, at that.

He let go of the man's cloak.

The Praetorian' eyes widening, he flew into a panic, his hands gripping Rufinus' wrist as he hung over the deadly chute. 'We had a deal,' he gabbled. 'You promised.'

'You killed my dog,' Rufinus replied. 'I lied.'

The man's grip on his wrist was tight, holding on for dear life, and Rufinus couldn't shake it. Moreover, he was still relying on his other hand on the door frame to keep him from following the man in. He did the only thing he could. Craning forwards, he sank his teeth into the man's grasping hands.

The assassin screamed and instantly let go. Rufinus saw his white, horrified face for only a moment as he toppled back and disappeared beneath the water. Pulling himself upright safely, Rufinus stood, impassive, and watched. The man appeared above the surface only once between the bridge and the wheel, gasping and coughing, and was then pulled under again by the strong current.

Rufinus couldn't hear the screaming, under the water as he was, but he saw the wheel slow for a few moments, juddering, and then, freed of its impediment, begin to turn once more at its usual pace. Beyond, as it flowed to the next wheel, the water had turned pink.

Rufinus spun to the terrified looking mill worker.

'Sorry about the mess.'

With that he stepped back out of the Janiculum mills and turned, slogging exhaustedly back up the line of the aqueduct. Heart heavy, grief and tiredness fighting for control of his body, he passed beneath that arch once more, along the street and across the lawns. Through the woodland and into the sacred grove of the Lucus Furrina. The moon was out in full now and bathing the world in silvery light. The temple looked more eerie than ever as it shone white amid the dark trees.

Rufinus took only a moment to spot the heap that had been Acheron's victim, and his heart lurched as he realised the dog was not there. Hurrying over, panicked, desperate, wide-eyed and with an

82

oddly out of place hope fighting all the other emotions, he looked at the mangled body. Another Praetorian for certain. A trail of blood left the body, and Rufinus peered at it, following its course. He saw Acheron then, a shapeless black heap on the grass by the sacred spring's pool.

Heart pounding in his ears, Rufinus ran over. Acheron lay by the water on grass slicked with blood.

When he saw the chest suddenly heave up and down in a breath, Rufinus cried out loud. Dropping to his knees beside the hound, he examined him. The broken shaft of an arrow jutted from his haunch, above the left hind leg. Rufinus stared. He'd seen Acheron fall and had assumed the blow to be mortal. Of course, he knew next to nothing about dogs' anatomy, but it seemed more than possible that this might not be fatal. Arrows to *men's* legs did not necessarily kill. He'd seen soldiers recuperate after such wounds during the Marcomannic wars.

Acheron lifted his head, whining, and turned to look at his master.

Rufinus, tears in his eyes, reached down and cradled the head. 'You tough old bastard, you're going nowhere but home.'

'He's here,' Senova said, rushing into the room. Behind her came a flurry of people, several of the house's staff accompanying the pair who had been summoned. Since the plague had once more abated in recent months, the huge number of physicians who had flocked to Rome for the ample work had been somewhat struggling to make ends meet. What it did mean, though, was that some of the best medici to be found in the empire were immediately at hand and open for business.

Alexios was one of those physicians who had maintained a distinctly high reputation throughout, even in a time of plague. Along with his young assistant, the man tottered into the room, rubbing his beard. 'Arrow wound, yes?' he said as he entered the room.

'Yes.' Rufinus stepped aside, leaving the table and its occupant in open view.

'That is a dog,' the physician said, brow creasing.

'I hope he's as talented as he is observant,' Rufinus said, throwing a look at Senova.

'No one would come when I said it was for a dog, so I didn't tell him.'

Rufinus sighed. 'Yes, he's a dog, but he's a very important dog. I want him treated.'

'I am not an animal physician,' the Greek said, his frown still in place.

'Is there any reason removing an arrow from a dog's haunch would be different from doing it for a human?'

'Of course, there is,' Alexios snapped. 'He's got four legs and they bend the other way for a start. He subsided a little, the frown moving from one of consternation to one of concern. 'That being said, the procedure would be much the same, I suppose. I would just have to be very wary of unknown anatomy.'

'He can be saved?' Senova said, voicing the question that Rufinus had refused to do so far.

Alexios shrugged. 'So long as he hasn't lost too much blood then he has the same chances as any leg wound. If the arrow comes out cleanly, then it's relatively simple, and then the only real worry will be infection. So long as he stays clean and well, then he should live, yes. Whether he'll lose the use of the leg remains to be seen, but... well, I cannot say anything for sure. I did mention that I'm not an animal physician, yes?'

Rufinus collected something from the nearby table. An arrow. The one that had missed him and struck the temple door.

'I think we might be lucky,' he said, holding up the arrow.

'This is the sort that the dog was struck with?'

'His name is Acheron, and yes.'

'It is smooth and narrow, without barbs.'

'Quite,' agreed Rufinus. 'Designed to seek holes in chain armour, I think.'

'Then it will be easier to remove. That is a blessing.' The physician looked across at him. 'I am not cheap, even for dogs.'

In answer, Rufinus gathered up something else from the table – the large bag of gold coins Cestius had given him to bribe the clerk. 'Wages for half a year, I'd wager. All yours if Acheron lives.'

Alexios nodded sagely. 'You are most persuasive, sir.' He approached the table and looked over Acheron. 'He is an old dog, is he not?'

'Yes, but that matters not. He needs to live.'

Alexios nodded again, leaning close to the wound. 'Another factor in our favour is the sheer size and build of the dog. Many beasts would have bled out too much be now, and their anatomy would be very spindly and narrow for me to work with. This animal has big powerful muscles and is large enough, in fact, to almost treat as a human. Yes, I think I can work with this. He will live, I'm sure.

How many legs he will walk on I cannot say until he starts to recover.'

Rufinus stepped back. 'Then get to work.'

The physician turned to his young assistant. 'Unroll my tools. Find the spoon of Diocles, my clamps – the largest ones – and the needle. I do not think the arrow has damaged anything critical. Mercifully it has lodged in muscle and flesh only.' He glanced up at Rufinus. 'I will need clean water, both hot and cold, and towels.'

Rufinus was trembling slightly, and Senova laid a soothing hand on his shoulder. 'I'll get them, dear.'

He stood, watching, as the physician went to work. After some time, he became aware that Senova had returned and was standing beside him.

'You said you got a name?'

Rufinus nodded. He'd been thinking about Acheron almost constantly as he'd found a barrow in a nearby shed where the groundskeeper worked and had struggled to lift the dog into it so he could barrow the wounded animal halfway across the city to home. But in those moments where his mind had drifted, it had drifted to that name

Vectius Aper.

Part Two

Investigation

Year of the Consulship of Apronianus and Bradua

191 AD

Non viribus aut velocitate aut celeritate corporum res magnae geruntur, sed consilio auctoritate sententia

(It is not by muscle, speed, or physical dexterity that great things are achieved, but by reflection, force of character, and judgement)

- Cicero: Cato the Elder on Old Age

VIII – NEW CHALLENGES

The two guardsmen snapped to attention as Rufinus passed, and he gave them a casual salute, his attention focused elsewhere. The figure of Vectius Aper, identifiable by the blue edged tunic beneath his toga, padded across the garden with a purposeful gait. Rufinus took a deep breath of winter air, cursing once more the sedate pace to which his investigation had slowed. Almost three months had passed since the attempt on his life at the Janiculum mills and, though he'd made some progress, it had been inordinately slow going.

The night he'd returned with the injured Acheron, who was now well on the path to a full recovery and using all four legs, Cestius had come to see him. How he'd found out about what happened so quickly was just one of those mysteries of the frumentarii about which Rufinus remained in the dark even as one of their number.

'You have a new lead?' he'd said.

'A centurion in the First,' Rufinus had nodded. 'A man by the name of Vectius Aper.'

Cestius had sucked through his teeth like a wheelwright pricing up a cart repair. 'Take this slowly, Rufinus,' he'd advised in a serious tone.

'What?'

'You have a tendency to take whatever lead you have and run at it with your head down before it can duck out of sight. That's not the way to handle Vectius Aper.'

'You know him?' Rufinus had frowned, listening to the sounds of canine surgery in the next room and trying not to picture what was happening.

'I know *of* him. His name is well known among the frumentarii. He has been peripherally linked to a hundred nasty little troubles over the years, but the slippery fellow always oozes out of danger. Nothing sticks to him. His name has been bandied about in connection with several unlawful executions and land seizures under Cleander, but there is no actual evidence connecting him to anything. He's shrewd and careful. If you go about investigating him with your usual cheerful zeal, you'll lose your only lead again.'

'Not my *only* lead,' Rufinus had corrected him. 'The man I just dealt with intimated that Aper is unaware of me, so *he* must have been sent after me by someone else. That means there's at least another higher figure in the First Cohort.'

'You have a colourful history, Rufinus, and thanks to your recent activities you'll have come to the attention of all sorts of villains. If you want to keep doing what you're doing, you need to pull back a little. Slow down. You are frumentarii now. Infiltrate and investigate. Time is not an issue. These men are going nowhere, so take your time and piece it all together. Most important of all, build yourself a story and learn it by heart. If there are men seeking your death, then they have reasons. Find out those reasons and find a way to dismiss them. You can hardly infiltrate while men are trying to kill you periodically.'

Rufinus had sighed. 'I honestly thought I was near the end.'

'This is not a race, Rufinus. You've been lucky so far, but now is the time to start playing seriously.'

And so he had. He had spent months positioning himself and, though it irked him to admit it, Cestius had been absolutely correct. It had worked. Firstly, he'd received his transfer to the First. His optio, Gamburio, had played the part of the ousted officer well, acting resentful and difficult for Rufinus, who had been forced to impose his command on the century. Gamburio, it turned out, was the perfect foil for his subterfuge. The man was so closely tied to his century that Rufinus could almost alter their mood by suggestion through his optio. Over the first month, Gamburio had gradually played the game of acceptance of his lot, through grudging respect to finally warming to his new centurion and becoming a tentative friend. With that came the same from the rest of the century and by the time November crawled into view, Rufinus was finally in a position of acceptance.

It did not escape his awareness that there were men in this cohort seeking his end, and that it could even be men in his own century, and so he began to gradually and subtly disseminate his story, a tale that effectively explained his behaviour, disassociating him from his true allies and suggesting connection to the very men he had been hunting. In a bar one night he feigned drunkenness and *let slip* that he had spent months in Dacia on a special mission for Cleander. That had gained interest from many. Twisting his forced exile into a private special mission to spy on Clodius Albinus and Pescennius Niger he effectively removed any notion of an enmity between himself and the chamberlain whose web of wickedness had bound together so many criminals.

Leaning on a balcony in the palace one day with a centurion he didn't know, he mentioned Baiae and the princess. The centurion had been instantly interested, noting that that trip was when the cavalry optio had died in a fight in the baths. Hadn't Rufinus been the one there with him? Rufinus had nodded and told him how he had seen Appius Numerius falling out with the Dacian but had thought nothing of it. How he had worried and wanted to seek out the man when he'd gone missing, but the princess had been determined to move on. Shifting of suspicion became Rufinus' stock in trade.

Then had come the matter of Attius Sacratus. That was the most important thread of his new story. Someone had watched him with Sacratus and had killed the man, attempted to kill Rufinus, too. That had almost certainly led to the three men hunting him on the Janiculum. Someone had taken offence to him dealing with the former speculatore. Someone who did not report directly to Aper, since it seemed the centurion was unaware of the matter, but it was still important to put out a new version of events to deflect suspicion anyway.

Rufinus had made sure he was in a tavern full of men from the First Cohort when he dealt with that. Someone muttered something about the frumentarii. Rufinus had picked up on that and used it. He'd been waiting for just that cue for weeks. Launching into a 'drunken' tirade about the frumentarii, he set himself staunchly against them in the eyes of the men about him. Leaning forwards conspiratorially, he'd waved his companions closer, but then spoke in tones loud enough to be picked up at the next table by two men who had been paying suspiciously close attention.

'Did you know that one of them hunted me down, the bastard?'

That had raised eyebrows. He'd slurred deliberately as he went on. 'Used to be one of ours, but apparently he'd been working with the grain men all along. Sacratus, the bastard. Said he had evidence that I'd done things for Cleander and that he'd bring me down.'

At that point he'd sat back and waved his hands, palms down towards the table. 'I didn't, mind. Just a bit of intelligence gathering in Dacia, but still. He was busy threatening me – I think he planned to try blackmail – when some helpful passer-by put an arrow in him. I don't condone stuff like that,' he added, trying to look contrite, 'but it was useful, I can tell you. So, don't talk to me about the bloody frumentarii.'

Three little leaks of information over the space of a month, each in a different place and in the company of different people, and yet he could almost feel his new history flowing out among the cohort like ripples from a stone thrown into a pond.

He'd left it at that and as the days passed, he could almost sense his reputation changing. Cestius' advice about pace and subtlety was good. Then had come another hurdle. He had transferred to the First Cohort now, but that hadn't brought him close enough to Vectius Aper. Of the centuries in the cohort, there were only ever two on duty at a time on the Palatine, and the duty roster was so organised that Aper's Second Century was on duty alongside the Sixth, while Rufinus' Third century worked alongside the Fourth. He'd needed to change the rota somehow and couldn't simply have the clerk move it about. It had to be done a lot more subtly than that.

He'd begun a two-pronged attack at the calends of November. On one front, Rufinus began to distance himself from the centurion of the Fourth. He didn't want open hostility, though. Just an uncomfortable working relationship. Over two market weeks of shared duty around the palace, Rufinus made himself unacceptable. His fellow duty officer was born in Rome, but of Syrian blood, his father an Emesene. It had not taken a lot of work to unearth that fact. He had then, in close earshot of the man, told a rather off-colour and slightly insulting joke about Syrians. The man's attitude towards Rufinus had begun to sour that very morning and Rufinus kept nudging it down any time things settled.

Simultaneously, he had acquired through Cestius a set of loaded dice that looked identical to those used by the centurion of the Sixth. He had waited until a day when Aper had been gambling with his fellow centurion and had contrived to swap the dice during a raucous moment. The damage he'd done with that simple act had been instant and impressive. The accusation of cheating had been vehemently denied, but when proved by the fact that the man's dice were definitely loaded, Aper had blown his top, snatched back all his coins and snarled imprecations at the man.

Two days later the duty roster changed. The dicing centurion, seething but unable to defend himself against the accusation, had managed to have his shift changed. The moment it became known that the roster was being altered, Rufinus' Emesene counterpart had requested that Rufinus be transferred. Just like that, in less than a month the Second and Third Centuries had been reassigned to joint duty on the Palatine. Rufinus had his in.

Two months it had taken, but slowly and subtly as it had happened, it had not stirred up any trouble. Indeed, there came no further attempt on his life. Perhaps his story had reached the important ears at last.

His first direct meeting with Vectius Aper had come only two days into their shared duty. As their shift had ended, the centurion had waved Rufinus over and invited him to share wine. Rufinus had done so and had drunk more than he liked to these days, not wishing to appear odd in any way. Aper had quizzed him then.

'You're the one who won the silver spear back when the princess Lucilla tried to kill the emperor.'

'I am,' Rufinus had nodded. 'Though I lost the spear a long time ago.'

'They used to say you were the emperor's favourite.'

A test? A nudge? Rufinus had shrugged. 'Just did my duty. They used to say *Perennis* was the emperor's favourite too, remember, right up to the point the sword went through him. Being an emperor's favourite can be a dangerous bloody game.'

Aper had nodded at that. 'Perennis was a good man.'

'I served him personally.'

'You've got a very cloudy history, my friend,' Aper had said, guardedly.

'Haven't we all?' Rufinus had replied archly, nodding at his companion.

That had made Aper laugh. They had spent the next hour talking of old missions and events, some of which, for Rufinus, were entirely fictitious, and some of which he'd twisted into something else. In the end they had shaken hands and retired.

Rufinus had scrubbed his hand clean that night. Just looking into the man's eyes made him feel corrupt. There was something about the man that simply exuded criminality, and in a perfect world Rufinus would have loved nothing more than to confront him, but the simple fact was that there was no evidence. Just the word of a man now dead that Aper was one of Cleander's criminal speculatores. And in that evening of conversation alone half a dozen dreadful criminal events had cropped up in conversation, yet each and every one had been spoken of carefully, placing Aper elsewhere at the time.

Rufinus would have to manoeuvre the man into damning himself somehow.

December had come around all too quickly. Rufinus had spent less and less time with Senova and Acheron, concentrating on the job at hand. Cestius had kept himself away, against even the possibility that he be linked with Rufinus. Severus had been busy with his consular duties and was preparing to lay down his position in the new year, when he would ride for Pannonia and the governorship there.

And all that time Rufinus did his duty quietly, standing in rain and chill winds, marching around the palace corridors and checking on his men. He had even accompanied the emperor on two occasions, though he'd barely even seen Commodus, who went everywhere with his mistress and a motley collection of gladiator friends now. He had taken to great shows in the arena and seemed to favour a new Herculean image. Rufinus might have wondered about this change in the emperor's attitudes had he not had his eye on a different figure, though he might also have remembered all those years ago in Vindobona when the young Commodus had already identified with Hercules.

In fact, what Rufinus did was watch Aper constantly. In the fortress, in the palace and in the city, whenever he could contrive to be in the same place, he kept an eye on the man. He began to suspect that Aper had a constant slew of criminal activities on the go, all so carefully controlled and hidden from plain sight that Rufinus could only catch the supposed edge of them, like a bad smell floating in the air when the culprit has already left.

Moreover, as December rolled on towards its inevitable conclusion, he had the sense that something was building. There was an increase in the frequency of Aper's activities, and the man began to be more watchful than ever.

Aper would tour the Palatine on duty, and on occasion he would find his way into rooms in which he had no official duty. If he met anyone there, he was very careful. Rarely did he repeat a location, so there was no pattern to anticipate, and when Rufinus had on occasion managed to slip into those rooms just after Aper had departed they had been empty and shown no signs of disturbance. It was extraordinarily frustrating.

There were four men in Aper's century, Rufinus quickly realised, who the centurion relied upon when about his unofficial activities, and Rufinus noted them for further investigation, but the sly bastard never once let his guard drop, and those four men were never alone to be observed, travelling in pairs at all times. Rufinus had managed to sit at a table with them in a bar and had listened carefully to everything they said but had learned not one thing of use.

He had been beginning to despair of ever discovering *anything*, of being able to dig any deeper. He remained certain that there would be someone higher among Cleander's old web than Aper, yet he had seen no sign of it, and even if he'd had anything on Aper he would not have used it, for he felt the need to try and identify this supposed higher power first.

Now, as Saturnalia approached and the cold frosts of winter settled upon the palace, Rufinus emerged from the corridor into the shadows of the colonnade, watching Aper crossing the garden and heading for the imperial apartments. Almost like some sort of dance, Rufinus watched four figures emerge from doorways to either side at the far end of the garden and fall in behind Aper like an entourage. Those same four men as always. Rufinus had known something was up when he'd seen Aper in a hurry to depart the imperial presence, as though late for a meeting. He'd followed slowly, subtly, staying some way back. The addition of all four of his close men confirmed it.

Rufinus waited there, in the shadows, until the five men had disappeared through the door into the complex. He'd noted before the door closed that the figures had turned right. Hurrying now, he made his way around the colonnaded edge of the garden. Across the middle would be faster, but of little use if one of them happened to have stayed behind and then opened the door to see Rufinus running after them across the lawns. No, he skulked at speed in the shadows and soon enough arrived at the door.

Carefully, he peered at the tiny sliver of light at the edge of the door, confirming that no one was standing right behind it. No call for subtlety here. If they were waiting in sight, then sneaking would make it obvious. The simple fact was that Rufinus had as much right to be here as they, and consequently, he strode through the door as though about some task. He kept his gaze straight ahead as he walked forwards into the corridor that led towards the sunken peristyle's balconies, though his eyes rolled uncomfortably to the right in their sockets, taking in what he could of the corridor. In moments he was past and out of sight once more, but he'd seen enough.

Off to the right, near the next set of doors stood a staircase that led down to the less used underground floor of the palace. Down there were whole labyrinths of rooms that were only really known now to the slaves who had to use them. Some dated back even before the construction of this palace, to the great golden house of Nero that had partially occupied the Palatine. Two of Aper's men stood guard beside the stairs. They had shot a look his way as he passed but had written off his presence as he simply passed by at a distance.

His mind raced. Down there was a veritable warren of rooms and even slaves were rare to encounter within. In theory that staircase was the only way down. Most men would believe the tunnels now sealed off by the watchful eyes of two of Aper's men. Rufinus, though, had been guarding this place for a decade now on and off. He had spent time in its bowels in busier days, when Perennis had been imprisoned here. He knew the substructures where the Ninth Cohort went about their grisly work extracting confessions from traitors and then executing the condemned. He knew how to get to those rooms and, apparently unlike Aper, he knew where they joined the labyrinth under the main palace.

Taking a roundabout route so as not to pass within sight of those two men, he made his way out onto the colonnaded upper terrace of the so-called 'stadium' garden. Hurrying along to the far end, he descended the stairs and strode back along the garden, past the few surprised folk whose duties forced them to be out at work in the cold. In moments he dipped back in through a side door, now a storey down.

Inside he entered a long narrow corridor with small rooms leading off, each used by the gardeners and slaves in the maintenance of the great leisure 'stadium'. Past these he moved at speed. At the end of the corridor he paused long enough to remove the extra sash he carried beneath his sword belt, pulling it free, tearing it in two and hastily wrapping the pieces around his boots and tying them. Hurrying on he was satisfied at the dull thuds his feet now made instead of the loud, clear clack of hobnails.

Around half a dozen corridors and rooms, he passed, then slipped through a door that had remained closed so long that it was almost sealed shut with cobwebs. Then out once more into other dark rooms, moving largely by memory and the occasional shaft of light from above. He slowed to a quiet creep as light glowed ahead and reached the hall below the stairs, at the top of which he could hear the two guards talking.

Concentrating, heart pounding, he listened very carefully. The palace hummed with life at all times, a tapestry of sounds, and it took some unpicking of the threads to identify the ones he sought. Two more voices, muffled, distant, ahead and to the right.

Now, he crept. Pausing, he made sure his torn sash covered all the nails in his boots and moved with almost infinite slowness. To be discovered now would ruin everything. As he neared the voices he stopped once more. The conversation was hard to make out, but it seemed to be meaningless chatter of the sort common to men forced to wait in position for some time.

Rufinus couldn't see them and was aware that at this point even with binding around his boots he risked being heard if he moved any closer. Fretting, he wondered what Aper was doing beyond his guards. Fortuna was watching over him, though. Moments later a helpful slave somewhere trundled a handcart with a squeaky wheel through the rooms above, a rhythmic thumping and squeaking issuing through the floor down to these cellar rooms. Taking a breath, Rufinus moved forwards again, keeping his careful footsteps in time with the cart. For just the blink of an eye he caught a glimpse of two more soldiers standing beside a doorway and ducked back into a pitch black recess.

Controlling his breathing and willing his heartbeat to slow, he cocked his head and listened carefully. Thankfully the two guards had stopped their chatter, and he could now make out other voices, only at the very edge of hearing, but one was most definitely Aper's.

Damn it, but he still couldn't make out the words. Whatever it was, though, it was clearly an important meeting. He stood still, silent, listening again. The noise of falling coins tinkled through the darkness, followed by a muttered curse. Money was changing hands. The sound of the fallen coins suggested larger coins, rather than tiny copper ones. And enough had dropped that Rufinus was fairly sure it had been a *lot* of money changing hands.

The murmur went on for a while, and finally there was a silence again before footsteps echoed around the subterranean corridors once more. Rufinus pulled himself back into the alcove as the footsteps neared. Two sets, then two more as the soldiers fell in behind them. Aper and his companion were murmuring still, but the conversation died away now as they approached, and Rufinus silently cursed his luck.

He almost cried out in shock as the figures stopped right beside the alcove. It was pitch black here, but he could sense the figures, and knew they were so close. If he lifted his arm, he could almost touch them. He held his breath.

'Do you believe he's a man of his word?' asked an unfamiliar voice, deep and with an almost aristocratic Latin accent.

'When it happens you... *we*... will not be forgotten,' Aper replied confidently.

'Make sure of it.'

And then they were off again. Rufinus continued to hold his breath, lungs straining, as the two soldiers then passed by, and in moments the four were gone, back through the corridors and towards the light. Rufinus slowly let his breathing return, forcing it out slow and regular. He remained still in the alcove until he heard the footsteps climbing the stairs and even then, he counted them to be sure there were four sets before he moved.

Damn it but he wished he'd been able to see that second man. From the way they spoke it had been clear that the aristocratic voice was either Aper's superior or someone else who commanded respect. And whatever they had been up to it had been distinctly underhanded, else they would not have met behind trusted guards down here in these forgotten rooms.

Just in case, he retraced his route to leave the underground, making sure not to bump into the others, then removed his sash from his boots and disposed of it. Back above, he made his way to the hall beside the aula regia and there passed the time of day with one of his men, strolling around until he happened to bump into Aper in a corridor. Nodding a salute, he passed the man by.

All was normal, apparently.

But something was happening. Something was coming.

'When it happens,' the man had said. Something was definitely planned. Whatever it was, it was apparently not the work of Aper and his master, but they were involved in it somehow. And it was clearly something illegal.

Rufinus slapped his head. 'Do you think he's a man of his word,' the aristocrat had said. And money had changed hands. Only those two men and the guards had passed him, and he didn't remember hearing the distinctive shush and clink of a large number of coins as they passed. There had been someone else down there and Rufinus had left before him. Damn it, how could he be so stupid?

Trying not to run, still in sight of Aper until the man turned a corner, Rufinus hurried back towards that staircase down into the bowels of the hillside. He hissed and cursed at himself. There was no point in going back down there. The other person would undoubtedly have left now. He fretted and drummed his fingers on his hip.

Whoever it was would have to leave the palace. They were carrying a large amount of money, and that would hardly go unnoticed. As such, they would have to get out of here and take it home, or to their own boss. They would have to leave the palace and they would go through the least public exit. Almost slipping out like thieves, even. Rufinus quickly ran through every exit from the palace in his head. There were three that fitted the bill for someone wanting to leave with the minimum of fuss, but he could narrow it down to one with ease. Between the Palatine libraries and the grand triclinium stood a narrow corridor with one rarely used exit. Moreover, the fire that had ravaged Rome in the summer during Rufinus' rooftop fight had climbed the Palatine and threatened the palace before finally being extinguished. The libraries had been alight, and there had been serious damage to the triclinium. The door in between was a charred mess still. An easy exit. For security, of course, it was guarded, but by happy coincidence it was guarded by Rufinus' men.

He found the corridor and the two guardsmen there moments later and waved to his men.

'Did someone recently leave this way?'

'Yes, Centurion,' one of the men said, snapping off a salute.

'Did he have papers?'

A nod. 'He was a courier, sir, with the appropriate passes.'

A courier. Interesting. 'He had his satchel with him?'

'Yes, sir.'

'Did it by any chance look heavy? Did it bulge?'

The guard frowned oddly. 'As it happens, yes, sir.'

Rufinus nodded at the man. 'Don't tell anyone about this. I'll be back before shift change.'

With that he stepped past them and left the palace through the fire-blackened door. He would have to hope that neither of those men was anything to do with his enemies, given the trust he had just placed in them, but he was confident that since Aper had his four direct helpers in his own century, others in Rufinus' unit were less likely.

He emerged into an area of gardens and statues facing the great temple of Apollo, and there he stopped and looked around. There were few people about because of the cold weather, but he had no idea where to go. Scurrying across to the temple, he looked along the street that led across the Palatine heights. There were maybe twenty people in the street, and he peered intently at every one. Not one was carrying a bulging leather bag.

Turning, he hurried over to the top of the flight of steps that zigzagged down the Palatine's southern slope to the outer face of the Circus Maximus below. It took only moments to scour the various figures on the stairs, and he saw no leather bag.

Beginning to worry that he'd lost the man entirely, he instead ran over past the other temples and to the Scalae Caci, the ancient staircase that led down to the Velabrum. Here he paused once more and scoured the scene. He cursed the stairs that contained no courier, and almost by chance caught a glimpse of a bulging leather satchel on a distant figure some way across the street in the Velabrum before it disappeared around a corner.

He ran.

Twice he almost came to grief, slipping on the frosty steps in his nailed boots, and it was only clinging to the rail that saved him. Reach the bottom, he raced over past the corner and paused, looking about. He saw the man briefly, turning another corner, and was off again.

Another two streets, now below the towering Capitoline and the ancient Tarpeian Rock, he followed the courier, gradually closing on him, and as he turned that last corner, he saw his quarry dip into a door. Catching his breath, Rufinus clattered along the street until he neared the doorway through which the courier had gone. It was the door of a townhouse of reasonable quality, stores built along the front. Opposite, below the vertiginous Capitoline, a man with a large trestle table was selling utensils.

Rufinus wandered over to his table and examined the eating knives. He'd not replaced the one he lost on the Janiculum, and so he selected a nice one and paid the stall owner. As he handed over the coins, he thumbed back towards the door across the street as casually as he could.

'Do you know who lives there?'

The man found him a few small coins change and nodded. 'That's the house of Didius Nummius Albinus.'

Rufinus thanked him, put the knife and the coins back in his pouch and threw one last look at the closed door opposite before turning and making his way back towards the Palatine.

A new name. Didius Nummius Albinus. Not a Praetorian, this one, Rufinus believed. But tied to Aper and his master by a nefarious coming event and a sack full of coins. Rufinus was on the edge of something important here.

Aper was still the key. He had to get yet closer to the man.

IX – A SHIFT IN PERSPECTIVE

Rufinus stood at the frost-coated balcony with his arms folded, eyes ostensibly scanning the vista for trouble, though really seeing little as all his thoughts continually turned inwards. Briefly his gaze settled on the other occupants of the balcony, and he returned his concentration to the present, considering them.

The emperor, Commodus, golden prince of Rome and living Hercules, stood at the centre, arms raised and basking in the adulation of the people of Rome who filled the great circus. He would be among them soon enough, of course, in time for the parade of the chariots before the first race, but the emperor was a showman above all, and could hardly resist the opportunity to present himself to them in glory from the palace above the circus first. A taster for his glorious largesse to come. A larger than life figure as always.

Beside him and a single step behind, denoting her status, stood Marcia, the emperor's long-term mistress, who some said was more powerful than any empress in history. Certainly, there was a dangerous intelligence about her eyes, almost feral. Then there was Eclectus, the new chamberlain who'd followed the fallen Cleander into the position. A seemingly too humble man for his role, but then perhaps that was both deliberate and wise after Cleander. Laetus, the current single prefect of the Praetorians, stood next to Pertinax, the prefect of the Urban Cohorts. There Rufinus' gaze lingered. Pertinax was apparently in collusion with Severus to place the great general Pompeianus into the succession, yet there was in the powerful, full-bearded commander on the balcony a certain poise that suggested perhaps he saw himself as something more.

His gaze then slipped to the other Praetorian centurion at the far end. Aper stood straight and strong, mirroring Rufinus, while a contubernium of men from each of their centuries stood alert and impressive around the periphery. The man had hair and beard like black oil under a clouded midnight sky and a face that spoke of a wicked intelligence. Over the months, Rufinus kept thinking of the man as a character villain, but he was so much more, and none of that good. He was, for a start, unpleasantly likeable. It was very easy to become at ease and chatty in his presence. A man could find himself sinking into companionship with Aper and only at the moment of revealing the most personal secrets suddenly remember where he was. A dangerous man in so many ways.

Staying on Aper for a moment, Rufinus only pulled away his gaze when the other centurion turned. Aper was the hub of something important, or if not the hub, then at least some important working part in the machine.

Aper had a superior of unknown identity, but with a good Latin patrician accent. Between them, they were involved in, and waiting for, some important event from which they seemed poised to benefit. Whatever it was involved the payment of a large sum that had been delivered by courier to a house beside the Capitol.

Rufinus had approached the praefectus vehiculorum, the man who commanded the imperial courier service. The prefect had been an ally during that great plan to bring down Cleander, but it transpired that the man Rufinus managed to meet was someone quite different. His erstwhile helper had taken the expedient opportunity of a complete career change and a move to the provinces after the chamberlain's fall in case anything ever linked back to him. The new man in charge had no connection to Rufinus and despite his Praetorian status refused flatly to reveal any information about a private courier delivery without either the permission of someone involved or a direct order from the palace. With neither being likely, Rufinus had instead turned to Senova.

Within a day, he knew as much as there was to know, given his wife's familiarity with the administrative centres of Rome and her contacts there. Didius Nummius Albinus was an aedile with responsibility for public festivals held in the various entertainment venues of Rome, an important and influential position in these days when the emperor favoured such events and took a personal interest in them. The man was from an African family in origin, which piqued Rufinus' interest given both Pescennius Niger and Septimius Severus' origins, but there seemed to be no connection between the families, and this fellow's relations had been resident in Mediolanum in the north of Italia for generations.

The man seemed to have no connection to the Praetorian Guard and no link to Clodius Albinus. His contact with the emperor, with Cleander and with anyone of any importance had never gone beyond the minimal required for whatever role he was in. Nummius had been following a fairly standard career path for a man of position and wealth, with nothing whatsoever suspicious. Rufinus had fumed at the seeming dead end.

The family, though, went beyond just Didius Nummius himself. His parents were no more but had both died of natural causes after a seemingly blameless life. Nummius was the youngest of three sons. The middle one, Didius Proculus, currently commanded the Sixth 'Ironclad' Legion in Jewish lands, and despite his military might he seemed to have no important political connections. Moreover, the Sixth were not based in one of those regions that traditionally mattered in a push for the throne. Legions based in the lands of the Jews had enough on their plate, as history could attest time and time again, so the youngest brother seemed unlikely to be any kind of player of the game.

Rufinus had continued to fume over the lack of any obvious connection he could work with. The oldest of the three brothers, Marcus Didius Severus Julianus, currently served as the governor of Africa, having taken the role when Pertinax had left it for a new position in Rome. This governor had no apparent connection to Cleander and, indeed, had been one of those responsible for returning the steady grain flow to Rome after the recent disaster. Another uninvolved figure. What possible connection Didius Nummius might have that had led to the rogue Praetorian and his well-spoken master paying him off with gold, Rufinus simply could not fathom. Still, he kept all those names, positions and locations in mind now, waiting for a connection to arise.

The emperor was finished with his adoring public. As the crowds roared their approval once more and the emperor smiled like a benevolent father, the small imperial party retreated from the balcony, Rufinus' men holding open the door and moving through ahead to secure the exit, Aper's men following on.

They passed through the rooms and corridors of the palace and delivered the emperor safely into the hands of his next escort, two centuries from another cohort who would accompany him in the Circus Maximus. Duty safely done, the two centurions dispersed their men back to position only to hear moments later the call for the ninth hour. Even as Aper and Rufinus sent out the call for their men to prepare the next shift arrived, the centurions receiving the password from their predecessors and sending their men to assigned places. In a quarter of an hour, Rufinus and Aper had formed up their men and sent them back to the fortress.

Rufinus rubbed his eyes wearily.

'Busy day,' noted Aper, stretching.

'That it was. I'm for a rest. Maybe a time in the baths.'

Aper snorted. 'Time enough for baths later. *I'm* for wine.'

Rufinus laughed. 'Wine is tempting, I must admit.'

'Buy you a cup?'

Rufinus nodded, trying not to let the calculating look that flashed through him any time he saw an opportunity with the man show on his face. 'Why not.'

They departed the Palatine with a nod to their replacements and headed down into the city. Rufinus sucked his teeth. 'Where to? The best wine has to be the Falx and Gorgon on the Vicus Patricius.'

Aper shook his head. 'Unless I have reason to, I try to avoid anywhere the lads drink. Always looks good if a centurion can be seen to be a class apart from his men, I reckon.'

Rufinus nodded uncertainly. Personally, he thought there was considerably more value to being one of the men, but there was still a certain validity to that point of view, he supposed. 'Where to then?'

'Come with me.'

A short walk later they turned into the Vicus Statae Matris, a narrow thoroughfare on the edge of the massive sprawl of structures that served the great amphitheatre. Here the buildings rose to an impressive height on either side, giving the place more the impression of a brick-faced crevasse than a city street. Rufinus frowned. He'd been along the street once or twice, for sure, but never really lingered. It was not, to his knowledge, a street of bars and life, but one of squalor and trouble, hovering on the edge of a world of slaves and killers, wild beasts and greedy merchants, all of whom made their living by the spilling of blood on sand.

His surprise only increased as Aper turned into an unmarked passageway between two towering blocks, from which emerged the smell of animal excrement. Gingerly he stepped in the other centurion's wake, worrying about what he was treading in along the deep-shadowed passageway.

Then, suddenly, the odour changed entirely. The animal dung smell still lingered in the background, but it had been impressively overwhelmed with spicy, heady odours.

'What is this place?' Rufinus murmured as they approached an unmarked doorway from which the heady scent was emerging.

'Best kept secret in Rome,' Aper said slyly, and made his way inside.

For a moment, as he followed, Rufinus found himself choking in the thick odour. It was far better than animal dung, certainly, but was still rather overpowering. They emerged into a small room where two men who could probably have pulled the legs off a bull with one hand sat behind a small table. They gave Rufinus a Neanderthal once over, and he found himself not just planning how he would go about taking them on if the need occurred, but also on what kind of funeral urn he'd like to occupy afterwards. The men clearly knew Aper, though, and they waved the two centurions in.

They turned into another corridor and Rufinus stared. Ahead, there was a square of light ahead where the passage once more emerged into the cold outside world, but there were several doors off to either side. From some of those to the left great plumes of blueish smoke drifted and Rufinus found himself blinking in the scent.

'Caters for any pleasure, this place,' Aper grinned. 'You want women, girls, boys... even cast-off animals from the arena for your pleasure, you can get it. Knew a man a few years back who got his kicks buggering leopards. Costly habit, that one. Dangerous too.'

Rufinus stared, in shock at such revelations more than anything else.

'Ever do the Persian root?' Aper said.

'The what?'

'The stuff they burn in the booz rooz. That blue smoke. Smells like dreams, they say. Tried it once. Just made me cough a lot. Besides, it apparently does what far too much wine does, even in small quantities, and as Guard officers we can hardly afford to let our inhibitions go, eh?'

Rufinus nodded absently, still staring. Of course, Aper couldn't afford to get into such a state, not with the secrets *he* must hold. 'Look,' he said weakly, 'I'm not really into that kind of thing.'

Aper laughed. 'Oh, I didn't bring you here to hump a crocodile or stand in a smoke room, Rufinus. There's tamer pleasures here, too.'

Beckoning, the man strode on down the corridor and out into the light. Rufinus followed and was grateful as he approached that the smells dissipated, both the cloying smoky ones and the ones of animal dung. Better still, as he exited the corridor, he marvelled at what lay outside.

A wide patio was hemmed in by high featureless walls that kept the windows of neighbouring buildings away, and all around the edge flower beds were filled with the most beautifully scented plants. The place smelled like... he winced. In fact, the place smelled a lot like the family's villa garden back in Tarraco. He felt a momentary wrench as he registered once more that the villa had gone, a victim of his idiot father's desperate search for funds to climb the social ladder in Rome.

Trying to shove aside such angry memories, he looked around. There were a dozen tables around the patio, each with comfortable couches. Over by one wall, beside the flower bed, stood a large table beside an extensive rack. The table was stacked with cups and glasses and small dishes of rather tasty looking morsels. The rack was well stocked with amphorae, tilted for easy pouring, each with a lid on.

'What is this place?' he said again.

'Best bar in Rome. Self-service, but there's a reason for that. This is a place people come to do deals.'

Rufinus' ear pricked up at the words, and he tried to conceal his sudden interest.

'Traders and the like? Merchants for the arena?'

'And others. Only trusted patrons are allowed. No one here will ever speak of what they hear. That's why there are no slaves or servants. What is said here never leaves these walls but with the men who speak it.'

'How can such a thing be policed?' Rufinus frowned.

'It's well known what happens if you do. Two years ago, a gladiator by the name of Manatta overheard a rather juicy tale about a senator's wife.'

'I remember Manatta,' Rufinus said. 'He was a legend. One of the best.'

'Foolishly got drunk at a party and told the story. All they found of him was his face, wrapped around the marble face of a herm on the Fabrician Bridge. Rest of him disappeared, but that's the sort of thing that happens if you break the rules here. I'm a veteran with a good war record, Rufinus, and even I wouldn't fancy my chances if I talked too much.'

Rufinus shivered. What sort of people took off someone's face to make a statement? The answer was, of course, *this* sort of people.

'What do we do?'

'Help yourself. Whatever drinks or food you want. Price you pay is to come here, everything inside is free.'

Rufinus blinked. 'We didn't pay.'

'The owners and I have mutually beneficial arrangements. Help yourself.'

As Aper poured himself a glass of something and gathered up a plate of pastries, Rufinus looked along the amphorae, noting the inscriptions on each. He stared repeatedly and found himself pouring a glass of Chian from a vintage that he'd once had while in Severus' entourage out in Syria. Then, even close to the source and in the company of a powerful governor, the price had made Rufinus sweat. Here, it would cost *three* times that, at least.

Following Aper and taking a seat, he sipped the wine.

'Damn, that's good.'

'Everything here is. They only serve the best of everything. A bakery on the Esquiline devotes its entire working life purely to producing pastries for this establishment.'

Rufinus leaned back. 'I could get used to this.'

'Don't,' snorted Aper. 'This is a one-off treat. I pay dearly for this, and your wage wouldn't cover the cost.'

Rufinus found himself wondering, since they were paid the same, how Aper met such exorbitant costs. He wasn't about to ask, though, as the moment he considered it he also pictured his face wrapped around a statue on a bridge and shivered.

'Temperature's getting to me,' he muttered as Aper grinned at his apparent discomfort. 'Roman winters.'

'Well you may have to endure them alone, Rufinus.'

'Oh?'

'You can shiver in the ice, my friend. I am bound for warmer climes.'

Rufinus frowned. He'd heard of no such planned movements. 'Taking some leave?'

Aper laughed. 'Not at all. I'm being seconded as security detachment for a diplomatic mission.'

Rufinus' brow creased even more. 'But you're First Cohort. Palatine duty.'

'This is a little bit different, though. We're headed for Africa.'

Rufinus felt his heart drum out a tiny tattoo. Africa. Two pieces of his puzzle suddenly clicked into place. Didius Severus Julianus, the older brother of the very man to whom Aper and his master had sent money, ruled as governor of Africa. Rufinus felt a layer of the onion of mystery peel back to reveal the next innermost stratum. He tried not to let desperation or excitement show on his face.

'You lucky bastard,' he said. 'Africa. Good wine, good food, good weather.'

Aper laughed. 'Quite. A long way from the frosty marble of Rome eh? And we might be out there for some time.'

'You lucky, lucky bastard.'

They fell silent, each supping from their glasses, Rufinus almost quivering with the need to press this to action somehow. Finally, one of Aper's eyebrows lifted in interest.

'Two centuries are going. Carminius Clemens' unit too.'

Rufinus felt possibilities slipping from his grasp like sand. He tried to find some way to say what he needed to say. His difficulty

106

must have shown in his face, for Aper barked out a laugh. 'Gods, man, but you look like you're about to crap yourself. I take it you're somewhat disappointed to be staying behind while a social drooler like Carminius is coming.'

'And he's an even luckier bastard,' grunted Rufinus, taking a swig of wine.

'I don't really like Carminius,' Aper said levelly. 'He's a fart-faced pit of boredom. I'm not looking forwards to sharing his company for months.'

Months...

'But the officers decided it would be best to take centuries from different shifts, so as to spread the load, as it were. That being said, personally I see the value in simply detaching one shift and reducing the numbers of those with downtime in camp to make up the difference.'

Rufinus felt his pulse start to race again.

'Er...'

'I might be persuaded to having a word about assignments,' Aper said in a quiet voice. 'I'm fairly sure I could get Carminius reassigned.'

Rufinus tried not to leap out of his seat but allowed a look of hope to slide onto his face. Aper laughed again. 'Of course, you get nothing for nothing in this life.'

Rufinus looked about them around the patio. 'I'm not sure I can afford the price.'

Aper laughed again. 'You interested?'

'Of course I'm bloody interested,' Rufinus snorted. 'Africa for a few months or Rome in the cold?'

'You would owe me. You'd owe me big. And you need to know that I collect my debts, Rufinus. Are you willing to owe me?'

Rufinus felt another shiver run through him at the barely veiled threat in the words. In truth there was little he would like less, but this was it: this was the opportunity he'd been looking for. Months of hunting men who had peripheral connections to this lot, and finally he was close to the centre of the web and almost at the heart of their nefarious activities. How could he refuse?

'Hades, but yes,' Rufinus said.

They spent the next half hour in harmless discussion of the qualities of Africa compared with Rome in the winter and of the potential organisation required in such a mission. When they left, back through the heady smoke and the animal dung, Rufinus took another look at the two giants at the table. They were tough. He'd be willing to bet they had little trouble subduing anyone who broke the place's rules while some smaller, crueller employee with a love of torturing animals peeled bits off them.

He shivered.

Then they made their way back through town. At the amphitheatre, Rufinus gestured off to their left. 'I'd best go see the better half before I come back to camp.'

Aper laughed. 'You're going to be popular coming to Africa and leaving your woman in the cold.'

'I may have to buy her a new dress.'

Aper laughed again, waved goodbye and made his way back towards the Castra Praetoria. Rufinus turned and strode up the Caelian. He would certainly have to see Senova and be very, very apologetic. Hopefully she would see the necessity of the journey in terms of his duty and not simply assume it to be a perk. He wondered whether he should take Acheron with him. The hound was almost back to full mobility now, and the heat of an African sojourn would probably do him good. The only downside would be the journey. Not everyone would be keen on sharing a ship with the big black beast. Before he considered these things, though, he had something else in mind.

Passing his town house, he made his way to the Temple of Jupiter Redux just beyond the Castra Peregrina of the frumentarii. There he made his devotions to the smaller altar to the left-hand side, leaving a single gold coin as an offering. Exiting once more, he returned to their house, knocking at the door and being admitted in moments.

It transpired that Senova was out at the moment with several servants and a healthy bodyguard, and Rufinus braced himself as Acheron ran at him and almost knocked him from his feet, then removed the bulky toga and hung his sword and baldric on the wall. He sat in the triclinium with a glass of pomegranate juice and waited.

It didn't take long. A quarter of an hour later, Vibius Cestius appeared in the doorway with Naravas at his heel. The frumentarius officer flicked the gold coin back to Rufinus. 'I presume you have something important to report, then?'

Rufinus leaned back and nodded. 'Aper is being sent to Africa accompanying a delegation.'

'To the governor? Your Capitoline friend's big brother?'

'It seems likely,' Rufinus agreed. 'It fits.'

'And you need my help to get on board?'

'Oddly, no. Aper is going to secure my assignment with him.'

Cestius' eyes narrowed. 'Men like Aper don't do things like that for nothing.'

'No,' Rufinus admitted. 'He was very clear that I'm going to owe him one.'

Cestius chewed his lip. 'This sounds inordinately dangerous. You'll be a long way from any ally. Aper is not simply going to let you into whatever they're up to. There will be tests of your trustworthiness. You know this?'

Rufinus nodded. 'Yes, I can see I'm going to have to be careful.'

'More than that,' Cestius said. 'These are evil men, remember. I've found in my time that when you're deep in with bad men you sometimes have to make sacrifices that are... unpalatable.'

'I think I can cope with it.'

'I hope you can,' Cestius replied earnestly. 'There are some things I've done that haunt me even now, and you are a man of stronger principles than I, Rufinus.'

'I'll do what I have to. I have a sort of ally. My optio is on my side. I can trust him.'

'Trust him as far as you have to. No more. I will see to it that one of your men comes down with a temporary illness tonight. By the morning he'll have a replacement shipped in. A man by the name of Cassius Curio. Try to treat him like any other guardsman. Don't make him stand out, but he will be there if you need him.'

Rufinus nodded his gratitude. 'This could be it, Cestius. Whatever they're up to, I feel we're getting close. With luck, by the time we get back from Africa, I'll be ready to end this.'

'Just be damned careful.'

With just a little more discussion over organisation, Cestius bade his farewells and left, and Rufinus had only a short while to clear his racing thoughts before Senova returned.

'Good,' she said as she entered the triclinium, 'you're here.'

'Senova, I...'

'News on your friends,' she said, interrupting. 'This Didius Nummius Albinus held a grand dinner two months ago. I've got half the guest list so far, but what I've got already is rather telling.'

Rufinus hovered on the verge of interrupting but held his tongue. This sounded important too.

'I'll show you the names when I've unpacked and changed but I've been looking at them. They're not who you'd expect. Not senators and rich new men, but mid-range administrators. A weird collection. A few men from the command of the vigiles, several fiscal officers, a few priests, that sort of thing.'

'What on earth would he do with people like that?'

Senova gave him an arch look. 'Severus took a sailor, a grain commissioner, a master courier and a few others and brought down the most powerful man in the empire with them.'

Rufinus shivered. That was horribly accurate. Yes, if Didius Nummius was building a web of patronage that reached out at an unnoticed level into almost every sector of Roman society, what could he achieve? He straightened. 'Nummius has a lot of money now.'

'Yes,' Senova said. 'I wonder how quickly that gold is going to be distributed among administrators who are so miscellaneous that they're completely overlooked.'

Rufinus nodded. 'Everything is building to something. And I think I have the biggest lead yet, but you're not going to like it.'

Four days later, Rufinus stood at the dockside of the Navalia, watching the warship at the wharf as its crew dashed about on their various last-moment chores. Behind him stood his century, and over to the right Aper waited with his men, equally silent and still.

Acheron paced about, fidgeting, and sat heavily on the standard bearer's foot, causing the man to grunt in pain. The dog weighed a ton, and the man tried to lean away as best he could while in formation. Indeed, the entire century rippled to one side a little away from the hound, worried eyes locked on him. Acheron had been introduced to Rufinus' century a few times over the months, and he'd even taken to keeping him in the fortress with him sometimes, but still the men remained nervous around him. All except Gamburio. Oddly, the optio had immediately taken to Acheron and the dog had begun to fawn about Rufinus' deputy like a puppy. Gamburio had even taken to making sure he had a small supply of dog treats about his person. Rufinus had liked and trusted the optio from the outset, but Acheron's seal of approval had clinched it. The dog knew who to trust.

A blast of horns announced the arrival of the rest of the passengers, and Rufinus straightened a little. A small party made their way down the cleared space between the two centuries, towards the ship whose marines lined up neatly and whose sailors secured the boarding ramp and then cleared the way.

Rufinus turned to look at their leader as the group passed, and he frowned in surprise. He'd been expecting some sort of diplomat. A senator or a high-level imperial administrator or some such. He'd not expected to see the man striding between them, toga settled in the chill wind.

Tribune Tullius Crispinus, commander of the First Praetorian Cohort. The civilian dress might look impressive, but the two slaves behind him struggled under the weight of a chest that contained the man's armour and uniform. Tullius Crispinus was a soldier, not a politician. What in the name of all the gods he was doing leading a deputation to Africa, Rufinus couldn't imagine, but that at least explained why men of the First Cohort were being taken away from the Palatine for detached duty abroad.

Rufinus hadn't seen much of Crispinus since his transfer, and knew little about the man, but his world turned upside down once more as the ship's trierarch called out a polite greeting to the man he was taking to Africa, for when Tribune Crispinus replied it was in those same patrician tones Rufinus had heard in the belly of the palace.

Rufinus fought to keep his expression straight. Tribune Tullius Crispinus was Aper's superior, not only in his official cohort, but clearly in the speculatores or Cleander's web of criminals too. Crispinus was high up among Rufinus' targets, then, if not even at the apex. And the two men who'd exchanged gold with a man beneath the Palatine were now bound for Africa, where that same man's brother commanded as governor.

Everything was falling into place, and Rufinus was now at the heart of it.

Suddenly, he felt very alone, and Cestius' warnings rang in his ears.

Just be damned careful.

X – CARTHAGE

It had been an exceedingly odd and tense journey from Portus to Africa. The trireme, a heavy warship called *Aeternitas*, had been professionally handled, its crew busy and efficient, its marines stern and silent and watchful. But its passengers had been another thing entirely.

Rufinus had kept a close eye on all of them throughout the voyage, particularly on those of whom he suspected criminality. Tribune Crispinus had kept himself entirely separated from the soldiers of his cohort, shut away most of the time in his tent erected at the stern with his slave and his personal scribe, attending to administration. The only other person who spent any time with the tribune was the trierarch of the ship, apart from when he received reports from Rufinus and Aper or handed out orders to them. Had Rufinus not recognised the man's voice from that meeting in the cellars of the Palatine, he would never have guessed that the tribune was involved in this at all.

Aper, too, showed no sign of his true underhand nature, appearing to all intents and purposes to be a professional and loyal Praetorian centurion. The only connection between them he could think of would be those four men of Aper's century who the man used for his nefarious business. Rufinus occasionally saw one of them attending upon the tribune, though he couldn't see anything odd happening when they did.

Nothing showed as untoward, despite his alert behaviour. On the other hand, he suspected that from anyone else's point of view, he himself probably appeared rather suspicious. Quite apart from watching all the time, which he tried to explain away as a need to be at the rail for a long-standing bout of seasickness, there was the matter of his own century.

He still did not entirely trust his men. There was always the possibility that one or more of them was in league with these criminals, despite the lack of evidence to that effect thus far. This meant that he was almost as watchful over his own men as he was over Aper's. And the presence of Acheron did little to ease things. The dog snarled repeatedly at those he didn't like, which included the men Rufinus was trying to watch in particular, and veterans who had survived waves of screaming Marcomanni in the northern forests shrank away in nervous sweats when the big black hound paced past them glaring.

The big problem was that of optio Gamburio and the new surprise recruit Curio. Both men were entirely trustworthy as far as Rufinus was concerned. One had helped ease him into his position and had supported him in the role, despite knowing Rufinus' true loyalties, and the other had been sent to help him by the frumentarii. As such he had absolutely no need or reason to watch them, but only a few hours into the trip he realised that in not doing so, he was effectively singling out those two men. In being alert and watchful around the others he might make those two men stand out. Consequently, he began a strange balancing act of trying to seem exactly the same whether he was looking at someone he trusted, someone he suspected, or someone about whom he had no opinion either way.

By day two he had a permanent headache, which at least made feigning illness considerably easier. By the time they rounded the coast of Sicilia he was starving, having had little more than military *bucellatum* hard-tack biscuits throughout the voyage.

He had to admit now, though, to a minor thrill as the Aeternitas cut sharply through the aquamarine sea. The hills of Africa rose in staggered ranges above the most perfect waters, their heights varying shades of blue grey as the distance swallowed them up. *Africa.* One of the most exotic places he had ever been. A land as old as Rome, once home to the empire's greatest enemy and strongest threat, a land of deserts and mountains, yet of green fields and rolling rivers.

The walls of the ancient city that had once led Cato to declare to the senate 'Carthage must be destroyed' had long since been consumed by the city's growth. With little need to defend itself now that it was part of the empire, the city had become a great trade centre, the source of much of Rome's grain, and ancient defences were now knocked through and altered to become part of the huge warehouse and shipyard complex.

Still, Rufinus could just see the famous circular harbour structure over the roofs in between. Smoke rose from one area of the city in particular, where massive manufacturing and construction went on, while the ancient political and religious heart of Carthage rose towards the rear on a great hill, its solid palace towering over the city.

The Aeternitas slid towards the port's single great entrance, merchant ships and private vessels manoeuvring hurriedly out of the way of this great and powerful trireme bearing the sail of an imperial warship. Slipping past them all, the trierarch expertly rounded the man-made headland with its lighthouse and cut into the mouth of the harbour. Acheron padded over and joined him at the rail, tongue lolling, eyes scouring their destination.

Rufinus was less impressed initially than he'd expected. Carthage was famed for its port, after all, but this great rectangular basin with its jetties and wharves, warehouses and stackyard seemed a lesser version of the massive complex of Ostia and Portus rather than the ancient wonder of which Portus was said to be a pale reflection.

Then they passed through the narrower channel and away from the trade port into the military harbour, and he felt his breath torn away with the sight that greeted him. The narrow channel was even now watched from both sides by towers and walls, with ship-killing artillery atop them. Then the military harbour opened up before them.

Another man-made harbour formed the power centre of naval Carthage. A circular lake, surrounded by a great curved building divided into scores of great individual docks large enough for a massive warship, the whole thing covered with a roof, each bay supported by its own jetty and staff. And in the centre of that great circle of water stood another circular structure, an island made of shipyards and slipways where dozens of vessels at a time could be built or repaired.

It was a complex on a scale to match even those of Rome's greatest military architects, and looking at it, Rufinus wondered that Rome had ever bested Carthage at all. He tried not to boggle at it all as the ship was directed by a system of torches and guided to a dock. As the Aeternitas slid up to the jetty and was made fast, Aper and Rufinus both brought their men to attention in formation, Acheron pacing up and down along the line like a prefect on inspection day.

Once all was made ready and the ramp was run out, Rufinus took the rear, Aper and his men leading the way and securing the dock for the tribune. By the time the Roman contingent was on dry land once more and making their way towards the exit, an official party had arrived to meet them.

A rotund man in a rich looking damask tunic of saffron-yellow with a pattern of green flowers stood waiting, looking at one and the same time obsequious and self-important, a difficult combination to pull off. Behind him were two men of clearly southern descent, their leathery skin and tight-curled black hair stark against the archaic white linen thorax that protected their torso. Each bore a tall spear and a shield painted with a gorgon's head. Behind these three hovered a plethora of slaves and servants, gathered ready to help.

'Tribune Marcus Tullius Crispinus, it is my honour to welcome you to great and ancient Carthage. The governor has been expecting you and bids me tend to your every need before delivering you to the palace. Are you and your men hungry? Weary? We have the very best wines and we have a grand house set aside for you. Would you like to freshen up? The Antonine Baths of the city are a wonder of the modern world.'

Now dressed once more in the uniform and armour of his position, Crispinus threw the man a look that suggested he saw him as more of a rodent than a human and shook his head. 'None of this is necessary. Show me to Didius Julianus.'

The oiled functionary in the rich tunic looked only momentarily taken aback before managing a full and impressive recovery with a smile that was so slippery and false it looked like it might slide off his face at any moment.

'Certainly, Tribune. Would you wish a carriage? A litter? We have both available and it is a tiring walk to the palace.'

'A horse,' was the tribune's only reply.

'Of course, Domine.'

As the deputation busied themselves retrieving said horse from the traces of a carriage, Crispinus turned to Rufinus and Aper, his lip twitching slightly, eyes darting momentarily to the dog in distaste. 'These effete snobs with their private army are trying to impress. Make sure you outdo them at every turn.'

The centurions both saluted and passed the word down the line that any man with a hair out of place would draw latrine duties for a week. Moments later they were off, the tribune astride a black mare at the lead of the Roman contingent, the native deputation leading the way, having picked up half a dozen more of the soldiers with their gorgon head shields.

Carthage was a relatively flat and easy place with wide streets, a spicy odour and a gentle warmth despite the season. Gradually, though, as they passed between huge and impressive buildings and blocks of shops, bath houses and temples, the gradient changed, and they began to climb. Rufinus was sweating by the time they emerged from a street and around a corner and reached the base of a massive podium, three arcaded storeys high and with a grand structure built atop it. Climbing yet further, as they passed through a small square Rufinus took a momentary look back and was rewarded with an impressive view down to the ports and the blue-green sea beyond.

Around this massive complex they continued to climb until they reached the highest point, when they made their way through an enormous triumphal arch decorated with images of gods and of soldiers, of violent victories and kneeling slaves. Beyond the arch the forum opened up atop the hill, a massive paved square surrounded by basilicas and temples and offices. The obsequious local led them across the square, through another slightly less grand arch and past a temple grand enough to rival those in Rome, then to a second square. This one was smaller, though, and at one end the palace stood, a grand urban villa of impressive proportions. It seemed a bit much for a provincial governor, but Rufinus reminded himself that this city was as old as Rome and the palace atop its summit had held generations of kings in its time.

Those same guards from the medusa-wearing private army were in greater evidence here, and Rufinus urged his men once more into perfect lines as they approached the palace gate. They did well, especially considering they were generally all trying to be the furthest person away from the great hound trotting alongside. Acheron's fearsome reputation had been sealed when a guardsman on the ship had produced some salted pork to stave off hunger and Acheron had simply walked over to the seated man and stared at him, drooling onto his knee, until the man handed over the meat with a disappointed expression.

As the decorative bronze doors were thrown open, the rotund man led them inside, and Crispinus dismounted, handing the reins to one of the many local lackeys following them. With just a nod to the two centurions, Crispinus marched at a military pace into the great open hall of the palace lobby. Rufinus and Aper picked up the pace to follow, their men clacking and scraping on the rich and rare marbles of the palace floor. The fat native who had been swaggering ahead in his oddly self-important manner suddenly discovered that he had an entire force of Praetorians at his shoulder moving slightly faster than him, and he and his soldiers were forced to break into a speedy walk to stay ahead.

Rufinus almost grinned. It looked absurd, but Crispinus had clearly taken a dislike to this man and was determined to present an impressive face of Rome regardless of what the man did. The result was the Romans marching forwards at a mile-eating pace that seemed natural and easy, while the locals scurried ahead like rats from a flooding pipe.

The tribune knew exactly what he was doing, and it needed no command passed back to his men whenever the man guiding them turned or had a door opened for them, so that the Romans uniformly slowed for a pace or two to allow the man to continue scurrying ahead, since they still needed to be directed, after all.

A few moments later they reached another set of grand bronze doors, these ones bearing an oddly pre-Roman motif of a stylised woman in a dress with a crescent moon above. Rufinus found himself wondering just how old those doors were, and whether Hannibal had passed through them to march on Rome, or perhaps Scipio had passed the other way in victory before having the city razed.

This new room was an oddly African echo of the emperor's aula regia in Rome, a throne room of regal stature. It almost glowed with brightly coloured marbles, mosaics and painted walls, statues of the great and the good – or the great, at least – watching impassively from every niche.

Half a dozen more of those guards stood at the far end in an arc around the rear of the throne, beside which two men in rich tunics slouched at leisure. On the throne, like some eastern potentate, sat a man. Rufinus could almost feel the disapproval radiating from the tribune.

'Hail Tribune Tullius Crispinus,' the man said, lifting one hand lazily as though the effort was almost too much, his other hand busily collecting grapes from a bowl at his side.

'Governor,' Crispinus said in a rigid tone.

'You sound unhappy Tullius Crispinus?'

'You should dismiss everyone,' the tribune said flatly, as though speaking to an equal, rather than a superior.

'Why Crispinus, we have only this moment met and the business we have can wait. Surely an immediate greeting can be exchanged in the company of our men.'

Rufinus was surprised to see Crispinus' hand drop to rest meaningfully on the pommel of his sword. The medusa-clad guards in the room straightened ready for trouble.

'Your reputation, Governor,' the tribune barked, 'is one of ascetic nobility, much like your brothers. Yet I find you slouching in a throne as though you consider yourself a king of this land. It is both unseemly and dangerous and had I realised what sort of man I was considering working with I might have been tempted to change my mind from the start.'

The man in the throne went very still, eyes narrowing, grapes falling from his hand back into the bowl. He gestured with a broad sweep of his hand to the occupants of the room.

'Sophon, clear the room.'

The man at his elbow made his own gestures, and in a few heartbeats every lackey, slave and servant had departed.

'And your mercenaries,' the tribune said flatly.

'They stay. I'm sure you understand. And their loyalty is without question.'

As the doors closed and the two men were left alone with just soldiers, the governor slowly unfolded and rose from the seat. Suddenly, less slouched and straightening, he seemed a great deal more impressive. In many ways he reminded Rufinus of Severus, with a similar colouring and style, prominent brows over heavy-lidded eyes, thin severe lips almost hidden between a neat moustache and a well-tended, tightly curled beard. He was at least dressed in a tunic much like any senator of Rome might own, and not the gaudy damask of the courtiers.

'Not only do you insult me as a greeting,' the governor hissed, stepping forwards, 'but you do so in front of my people. Courtesy escapes you. Crispinus.'

'I warned you to dismiss them first. *Now* you begin to look like a Roman, Governor.'

'You are a soldier and not a politician, Crispinus. I do not expect you to understand, but just as the senators of Rome sneer at and degrade the emperor for not adopting their old-fashioned and staid manner, the rich and the important of Carthage respect shows of wealth and control. Had I appeared togate and stood at attention I would be out of place. A reminder that once upon a time, Carthage was a power and that togate men came and burned their civilisation to the ground. I have to control, tax and judge these people. To do so I have to ease them into thinking of me as one of them, and not as a ruler imposed upon them by a far-off land. So, before you begin to lecture me on my failings, do me the courtesy of attempting to discern the reason for them beforehand. Are we clear?'

Rufinus blinked in surprise. In his mind's eye he had already written off this man as a waste of flesh the moment he saw him, and now he found himself completely reappraising everything. The man was not only far from that, he was in fact clearly subtle and clever. Indeed, Crispinus was apparently undergoing the same shift in thinking, as his hand slid from the sword pommel and he nodded his head respectfully.

'My apologies, Governor. I have known your brother Didius Nummius for years now, and I should have expected this sort of wisdom. Forgive me. I am both out of sorts and tired by the voyage.'

Didius Julianus, governor of Africa, nodded easily. 'First impressions are easily formed and often difficult to amend, Tribune. Come, and we shall speak no more of this. Clearly, though, there is much to talk about, and we shall do so at length over a private dinner this evening.'

Crispinus simply nodded, and the governor stretched. 'Do you have any idea of timescale?'

The tribune shifted uncomfortably and glanced back momentarily at the Praetorians behind him before turning back to the governor. 'Things move ponderously. It will be a matter of months, I fear. I am certain we will at least see out the summer, and perhaps the autumn.'

Didius Julianus nodded. 'I suspected as much. I have property put aside for you all in the city. I will have someone lead you there shortly, so that you can relax before returning for the evening.'

The tribune nodded once more. 'We shall speak in more depth later,' he added. 'Farewell for now.'

At a barked command, the Praetorians turned and marched from the throne room once more, out into the open square, where a man in that same linen armour and shield as the governor's private army, but wearing a yellow cloak and a helmet with a high crest, walked over to join them, two soldiers at his back.

'Tribune, I am Ezena, commander of the governor's guard. If you will accompany me, I will show you to your accommodation.'

Crispinus nodded and in mere moments they were leaving the palace once more. For quarter of an hour they marched away through the forum and down the hill to the north before climbing another lower slope at the periphery of the city. To their left Rufinus could see two theatre buildings rising above the houses, and when they finally arrived at their destination, he could hardly believe his eyes.

A sizeable villa stood on this slope with carefully tended gardens. It was the property of a very rich man, or at least it *had* been. It was now equipped with a boundary wall of some height and a good solid gate. As they were shown around, the men of both centuries standing at attention just inside the gate, Rufinus found it hard not to stare. Crispinus and his entourage were clearly to live as well as any Roman senator here. A large structure at the upper edge of the grounds had clearly been converted to barrack rooms, and so the men would have quarters within the grounds. Rufinus and Aper were to have their own rooms in one of the villa's wings. The officers would have access to the villa's private *balneum*, while the soldiers would be using the massive bath complex of Antoninus which stood at the bottom of the hill beside the sea, visible from the villa's front door.

Half an hour later, Rufinus and Aper had settled their men and the tribune had retreated to his personal wing of the villa with his slaves and attendants. Rufinus considered using the baths but decided after his long day to instead take the rare opportunity for a lie down in the solitude of his chamber.

There, with Acheron curled up on a blanket, he mulled things over. Didius Julianus was an interesting man. Clearly, from his associations and the strange and oblique question he'd put to Crispinus, he was a villain too. Once more Rufinus had heard a reference to something they were waiting for, as he had in the Palatine cellars. Initially it had sounded as though what was to happen was not in the hands of Aper and Crispinus, and he had, during his journey, begun to suspect that the governor was somehow the one guiding that event. Now it seemed that was not the case. Indeed, it seemed as though Didius Julianus was also waiting for something to happen.

Something that would not happen for a while. Not for half a year or more from what he'd heard in the throne room. Were they to stay in Africa for all that time, and if so why? Every day here would be perilous for Rufinus, and every day Senova would be less and less impressed with the imposed distance between them.

It was all rather puzzling and frustrating.

He was not aware that he'd dozed off while considering the problem until he awoke to a rapping on his room's door. He was lying flat on his back on the comfortable bed, still in his military tunic, though at least he'd taken off his boots and armour. Groggily shaking his head to bring back his wits, he looked over at the door.

'Come.'

He was somewhat surprised when the door opened and Vectius Aper walked in, closing it behind him, but looking back and forth along the corridor outside first. With a nod to Rufinus and a wary eye at the hound curled up in the corner, he strolled across to the open window and looked out, again checking to either side before closing the shutters.

'I have had troubling news.'

Rufinus sat up, rubbing his hair. 'You have? From who? We only just got here.'

Aper turned a squinted look on him. 'I have sources of information and factors at work all over the empire Rufinus. Any man who wants to survive long enough and to go far enough in these troublesome days needs to do so. I have people in Africa, and one of them has now been brought to my attention.'

Rufinus frowned. He didn't like the sound of this. 'And you've come to me?'

'You owe me a favour, Rufinus, remember?'

His blood chilled at the realisation, and Cestius' warnings about what he might face in Africa came flooding back in. He tried to keep the worry and distaste from his expression, forcing it to remain neutral as he walked over, close to Aper.

'I remember. What do you want me to do?'

'I want a man killed.'

Even prepared as he was, Rufinus recoiled automatically. '*What*?'

'Don't look so shocked, man. You must have seen this coming. One of my former informants, I now learn, has been playing both sides in the same game for his own benefit. This sort of thing cannot be allowed to happen. The man has to be punished. Permanently.'

'Aper, we're men of the Guard. We can't just kill men at will.'

Aper's eyes narrowed. 'I seem to think differently. If I am not mistaken, you yourself have killed almost as many people as the Parthian plague. You have no issue with killing men who get in your way. Well this man is more deserving of the knife than most. If it makes you feel any better, the man has himself seen to the death of half a dozen good men, so you can think of him as a criminal if it suits your sensibilities.'

'Why me?'

Aper smiled nastily. 'Because I need to remain here. I have business here, while the man I want removed is to be found in the city of Zica, a day's ride to the south. And because I so want to trust you, Rufinus, but something about you just feels off. Simply because I *want* you to, Rufinus. Remember the consequences of betraying that little club I introduced you to? Our world is a world of duties and consequences. Borastes, the man in question, is expecting to meet me after nightfall three days' hence at the water temple in Zica, but it will not be I he meets. And I shall expect proof that you have completed the mission. I am not squeamish.'

Rufinus simply stared at the man.

'You have been seeking an in,' Aper said. 'I've watched you. But if you want in, you need to make it worthwhile. My friends could be in a *very* good position soon, but my enemies will be in a great deal of danger. Now is the time to decide whether you want to be a good little lad and run along home or whether you're ready to play stones with the big boys.'

Rufinus took a deep breath. He would have to think through the moral dimensions of this afterwards. For now, he simply had to agree. If he wanted to get any deeper and for all of this to not have been a massive waste of time and effort, he had to do it.

'I'm in. How will I recognise him?'

'You'll be bearing a scorpion shield. He'll find you, as long as you're in the water temple of Zica after nightfall.'

'You'll remember me when your friends are in this *good position*?' Rufinus pushed, making it sound as much as possible a matter of personal gain rather than moral dilemma.

'You scratch my back, Rufinus, and I won't be forced to put a knife in yours.'

Rufinus gave him a nod, and with a last, lingering look, Aper left.

Rufinus slept very badly that night.

When he awoke the next morning, he was no happier than he'd been when he'd retired. He had three days until he was expected to kill a man. Oh, he could guarantee that this Borastes would be a deserving target if he was one of Aper's informants, and especially if the man truly had killed people, but still it left a very unpleasant taste in his mouth. He couldn't think of a way around it, though. He had only two days before he needed to ride for Zica, and it might even be better if he went a day early, since he did not know the land and could hardly afford to get lost and be late. At least he would find it easy to disappear without trouble from his superiors, since they would be in on the reason for his disappearance.

That morning he left Acheron with Gamburio and took a stroll around the local area, quizzing as many natives as he could as to this city of Zica and its temple. It all seemed relatively straightforwards. There were good roads and plenty of small settlements in between. For a lot of the way the roads followed the aqueduct, since the water that flowed from the water temple in Zica was the same that emptied into the great cisterns of Carthage on the far side of the city. There was no logistical reason he could not achieve his goals, which did not help him one bit.

It took him a little while that afternoon to find Curio. He waited until the man was on duty rather than in his barracks with everyone else, and then took a short tour around the estate, checking in on his men like a good centurion. He found Curio standing leaning on his shield and peering off into the distance, over the hills, flatlands and salt marshes that lay between here and ancient Utica to the north. He came to a halt next to Curio and leaned on the wall, not looking at the man beside him.

'Centurion?'

'I have to kill a man, Curio.'

'I believe he won't be the first. Does he deserve it?'

'Probably. He works with this lot, so it seems a given really. Still doesn't sit well with me, though.'

'Is it important in unpicking all this shit we're in, sir?'

Rufinus sighed. 'Sadly, it's critical, I think.'

'Then it is not a choice. Sometimes sacrifices have to be made. You're sure this isn't a trap?'

Rufinus frowned. Oddly, that possibility hadn't occurred to him. 'I don't *think* so,' he replied, eventually.

'*Think* is a lot to stake your life on,' Curio noted. 'Bear in mind you have backup.'

'I suspect Aper will take a dim view of me heading out with a travelling companion.'

'Where are you bound?'

Rufinus sagged again. 'A place called the water temple in a city called Zica about a day's ride south.'

'I know the place.'

Rufinus turned now. 'You do?'

'I know Zica fairly well. I know the whole damned area, sir. Why do you think Cestius chose me? And I'm fairly confident I can get away without raising any great concern. I will be at Zica but be careful anyway.'

Rufinus nodded. 'Everyone keeps telling me to be careful, as though they somehow expect me to go blundering into danger waving a flag and blowing a horn.'

'Your reputation precedes you, sir,' grinned Curio.

Rufinus snorted. 'Does this sort of job ever get any easier?'

Curio laughed lightly. 'When it does, there'll be no need for us anyway.'

'That's something to look forward to, then.'

XI – AN INTERESTING MEETING

The journey south had been easier than Rufinus expected. The very name Africa had filled his imagination with great mountains of golden sand and exotic oases of palm trees and colourful birds, where dark-skinned traders in black robes would meet. In reality, it seemed that *this* Africa, within the region of Carthage at least, was actually a land of fertile fields and rolling green hills remarkably, and for Rufinus a little disappointingly, resembling the southern half of Italia.

He had travelled alone on a horse acquired from the governor's palace, and stopped at a small town for a lunch, where he had asked for half a roasted chicken and been somewhat bemused when the proprietor walked past with a struggling chicken and a cleaver. He'd been expecting the chicken to be halved afterwards, rather than first. He had left Acheron with Gamburio. The big hound was almost back at full strength now, but Rufinus had no idea what to expect from the journey, and Acheron was no longer a young dog. Making him trot across eighty miles of scrubland seemed a little unfair.

He'd approached the hill town of Zica as the sun was closing on the western peaks, sending golden rays across the green-brown land. The place was not large, not on the scale of Carthage by any means, but of a respectable size, brown-walled houses clustered together on a high plateau that lorded it above the plains and yet was dwarfed by high grey mountains behind, seemingly out of place in a land that was otherwise of green grass, abundant fields and rolling slopes.

The north-eastern approach to the town climbed the slope at its gentlest point, at the crest of which stood a grand looking triumphal arch with statues of Marcus Aurelius and Commodus in niches to each side, a carving of a bull's head with a wreath on the keystone. The head of the current emperor was proportionally a little on the small side for the body, and Rufinus suspected that until the accession of Commodus, it had probably been a statue of the old emperor's brother and co-ruler, Lucius Verus.

Beyond, the town was beginning to slow for the evening, a market packing up, carts leaving for farms. It did not take long to locate a likely looking tavern, beside which he hitched the borrowed horse to the rail. Inside, in the cavern-like gloomy interior, he purchased a cup of wine and watered it thoroughly, especially given its unusual rich and heavy character, and ordered a meal of lamb stew. When the man brought the food a quarter of an hour later, Rufinus asked him casually about the water temple. The man pattered off directions to it with a casual boredom, suggesting that he did this for tourists far too often.

Meal finished, Rufinus thanked the man and exited, climbing up onto the horse once more, passing through the town and out towards those peaks, now a dark silhouette against an indigo sky as the sun vanished. He was later than he'd intended to be. Perhaps that was simple bad planning. Perhaps it was more reluctance. He had absolutely no desire to kill a man he'd never met and knew nothing about, yet he could see no alternative.

He was beginning to see how Vectius Aper kept so completely clean as far as criminal evidence went. If the man did this sort of thing often, then he was essentially a criminal by proxy. And worst of all, people in Rufinus' position could do little about it. Aper was innocent of the killing, even if he had ordered it, but the actual tool of murder themselves could do nothing, for to officially tag Aper with the blame would be to reveal their own sordid part in it. Aper was sly and careful.

Exiting the town through its south-eastern side he climbed once more, heading up towards those peaks. He'd initially thought he would be able to follow the great aqueduct straight to its source at the temple of Zica, but if he'd thought more about it, he'd have realised that vast stretches of the channel would run underground and be impossible to follow. Such was the last section, approaching its source.

The temple was easy enough to spot, though, once he had left the streets of Zica. Clinging to the side of the mountains on a terrace of grand proportions and man-made design, it was breath-taking in many ways. The approach moved past several large basins of crystal-clear water, dancing with motes of light in the evening glow, and a small temple with no clear designation on the outside. Walking his horse past the basins and the temple, he looked up at the Temple of Water. A sloping construction slanting down from the complex had to be the vaulted roof of the aqueduct channel, flanked to each side by a wide, shallow staircase.

Rufinus walked the animal over to one of the trees at the periphery of the place, where scrubby grass abounded, and tethered her so she could graze. Then, heart in his mouth and hand on the pommel of his sword, he retrieved his scorpion-emblazoned Praetorian shield and climbed the steps.

The steps levelled out after only a short climb onto a narrow terrace below the main one. Above, the temple shone, white in the evening, reached again by narrow staircases to each side. Between these lay a pool shaped like a figure eight. As Rufinus watched, fascinated, he could see the waters in the basin moving. There was a constant flow as the torrent disappeared into that sloping pipe, beginning its twisting and winding eighty-mile journey to the thirsty metropolis of Carthage. Yet the basin remained full, and keen eyes could spot the eddies and bubbles where the water was constantly replenished from conduits beneath the ground, each fed by a spring in these mountains. It was an impressive piece of engineering. Still, he could not afford to distract himself from his grisly goal any further. Clenching his teeth against what was to come, he crossed to one of the staircases and continued on up, past that basin.

Above, the main terrace stood glorious. A 'U' shaped portico surrounded the paving, the two ends facing the view from the terrace and formed into almost triumphal-style arches. The whole thing had been whitewashed and virtually glowed in the evening. All around the walls within the portico, he could see niches filled with statues of a very high quality, and the greatest of them stood at the centre of the patio. A huge marble of Neptune, all muscled torso, wavy hair and wild beard, his eyes gleaming and wise, a bronze trident in hand as fish and all manner of exotic sea creatures cavorted about his feet.

At the rear of the 'U' stood what had to be the focus, the *cella* of the temple. A place for the worship of Neptune, whose waters were so important to this land, for though Rufinus had been surprised at its verdant nature, he knew still how close they were to those great seas of sand that had filled his imagination.

The thing that surprised him was how empty the place was. Not a figure moved. He had expected, if not a priest, then at least some slave busy sweeping or cleaning. Or just someone watching over the place. Nothing. The water temple was empty of life.

Frowning, he made his way to the edge of the terrace, overlooking that bubbling, figure eight-shaped basin. There he lowered his shield. It was really a little cumbersome to have brought up here, but Aper had said the man, this Borastes, would know him by his scorpion shield.

He leaned on the shield for a while, looking out across the rich landscape, feeling the weight of the mountain pressing down behind him almost as much as the weight of what he was here to do. Gradually, the last of the light slipped from the sky, and he almost leapt from his skin at the sudden sound of movement. Lurching around, hand back on the pommel of his sword, he felt his heart thunder and forced himself to calm at the realisation that he was not completely alone after all. A slave had emerged from that central temple doorway and was busy moving around the portico lighting lamps that gave the place a beautiful, if unearthly, glow. The slave gave him a nervous, polite nod as he went about his business.

Rufinus waved at him, and the slave paused.

'Is there anyone else here?' he asked.

The boy hurried over, making odd noises and as he came to a halt in front of Rufinus, mouth open as he mumbled, Rufinus realised with distaste that the slave had long ago had his tongue removed. He realised the slave was shaking his head and that this was as complete an answer as he was likely to get. He waved the boy away, and the slave finished lighting the lamps, then descended the stairs with his torch and began the same process on the narrow terrace around the pool, before hopping down to the lowest region and doing the same all around the temple and basins there. Soon the whole mountainside was aglow with golden light. Rufinus wondered what it must look like from Zica, which he could see a mile to the northeast and several hundred feet below. Glorious, he suspected.

He'd be enjoying himself more if he were not playing the assassin.

'I was expecting a *different* centurion,' a voice said, and Rufinus jumped again.

He turned, grasping his shield, hand back to sword yet again. For a long moment, he could not identify the source of the voice, then finally spotted a tiny movement. One of the statues in the niches around the colonnaded interior was moving, or rather the figure that had been behind it was. The man slipped down to the ground and padded out into the open. He wore a white tunic and his hair was an ash-blonde, which had helped hide him well within the whitewashed temple. Rufinus noted the sword buckled at his waist. The man might well be trained with it. There could be trouble.

'Aper sent me,' Rufinus said quietly in reply.

The man came forwards, stopping safely some distance from Rufinus. 'I was not expecting anyone else. Aper should be here.'

'You can speak to me. I will deliver your message to him,' Rufinus said.

The man frowned for a long moment. 'Tell him, then, that the new dies have reached the Carthage mint. All will be done in time.'

Rufinus felt a lurch in his heart. Coin dies? Images of poor Perennis leapt into his mind, Rufinus and his friends rushing back to the Palatine across that horrifying aqueduct bridge to deliver coin dies that were the only evidence that could save the man. He had failed, and Perennis had died.

Coin dies. With them, a man who had access to a mint could manufacture coins of any sort. Coins of an emperor? Could Didius Julianus already be minting coins with his face beneath the imperial slogans? Rufinus shivered. What had happened to the world to cram it so full of plotters, traitors and usurpers?

His fear and surprise must have shown in his expression, for Borastes' eyes narrowed in suspicion, and he took a step back. 'You're not from him, nor from the governor at all,' he said suddenly.

He withdrew two more steps, hand going to the sword at his side.

Rufinus felt the world slipping under his feet. Now was the time. He had no choice. He had to kill Borastes if he was to get any deeper with Aper, with Crispinus, with the governor, even. And undoubtedly this man was a criminal, if he was involved with illegal coinage, but that did not make the proposal any easier for Rufinus. Why hadn't he brought Acheron? Damn it!

Borastes was backing away from him now. The game was up. There was no way Rufinus was going to be able to recover his poise and pass for a fellow conspirator. On the bright side, Borastes was on the verge of either fighting or running. If he fought, then Rufinus was no longer an assassin, but a man defending himself, which would soothe his conscience considerably.

Rufinus ran through the situation in his mind in a heartbeat. Borastes was trapped. He could not run. The 'U' shaped portico had a solid outer wall with all those statued niches. At the centre stood the temple cella, but that would be a single rectangular room, with a side chamber or two at most, though probably not even that. There was no way out but the staircases down to the next level. Momentarily his gaze rose to the roof of the portico, but he quickly dismissed that. It was far too high for a man to simply jump up, and the man would have no time to climb. To do so would be to put him at Rufinus' mercy. No, down was the only way to go.

Sure enough, as he watched the man, he saw Borastes' eyes flick left and right, saw him settle upon a decision. Rufinus ripped his sword from its scabbard and moved simultaneously with his prey. As Borastes leapt towards the western stair, so Rufinus was there in his way. The blond-haired man now tore his own sword free and backed off once more. Rufinus watched him carefully.

The man ducked back to the great statue of Neptune and disappeared behind it. Rufinus could see him lurking there from the shadows flickering in the torchlight, but Borastes remained where he was. Rufinus had not picked up his shield, but that was fine. A large rectangular body shield was a useful thing on a battlefield but in a duel, when speed and agility meant everything, it could be more of an encumbrance than a boon.

Borastes ducked out of the other side of the statue, racing towards the eastern stair and Rufinus started to run, only to curse as the man immediately doubled back and ploughed west again. Rufinus spun on his heel with difficulty and hurtled back to cut the man off. He was not going to make it in time. He was strong and skilled, but Borastes was extremely fast. Rufinus gave it all he had, powering towards that stair in order to cut off this ridiculously swift man.

He was outmanoeuvred again. As he hurtled away, momentum now unstoppable, Borastes simply turned sharply once more, crossing Rufinus' path. The Praetorian stared in shock at the man's speed. He turned, stumbled, fell. Although he was back up on his feet and beginning to run once more a heartbeat later, Borastes had the advantage.

Rufinus saw him making for the other stairs again and realised that he had just once chance. If he let this man, fast as he was, get to that stairway and down it, he would outpace Rufinus. The Praetorian may have a horse down there, but straggly forest surrounded the complex and the light had all-but gone. A subtle man would be able to disappear among the trees and never be seen again.

He had to stop him now.

Rufinus leapt. He knew he couldn't outrun the man, so that was no longer his plan. As Borastes ran for the other staircase, Rufinus hurtled through the air. His left hand, free of weapons, reached out, desperately hoping to catch hold of the man's tunic and stop him. The man was too fast. Rufinus missed all his fluttering tunic and fell hard to the flagged ground, the breath knocked from his chest.

Fortuna was sheltering him, still, though.

Even as he fell, his stretched fingertips brushed the man's boot and his little finger hooked into the lip above the heel. It was far from a strong grip. He couldn't hope to hold Borastes back by one finger and indeed even that came away with a tearing of leather and a flash of pain through Rufinus' breaking finger.

But that finger had been enough. Borastes had been so fast and balanced, intent upon the stairs, that the momentary pull on his boot overbalanced him. With a cry of alarm, the conspirator tumbled, flailing, over the edge of the terrace.

Rufinus, pain lancing from his broken finger, lungs tortured and chest heaving, coughed and scraped himself up to his knees, using his sword, point down, to help lever him up, a move any legionary armourer or trainer would kick him six ways from market day for trying.

Coughing and heaving in breath, Rufinus made it to his knees and craned to look over the edge. It was not too far down to the next terrace – probably between ten and fifteen feet – but with a bad fall even that could easily break limbs or smash heads. He peered down to the next terrace in its golden glow. It was with an undecided mix of gratitude and disappointment that he realised Borastes had not died in his fall. Instead he was floundering in the figure eight basin, coughing madly where he had accidentally breathed in a little water.

Urgency took over once more. Rufinus had, against the odds, managed to stop his prey fleeing. Now he had to finish it. Staggering upright, he jumped.

He hit the water and disappeared under with surprise. The pool was deeper than he'd thought, at perhaps ten feet. Though he managed not to inhale any of it, he appreciated immediately how a man who'd fallen into it by accident might have struggled, for the current of the flow into the aqueduct and the many strong jets of water pumping into the basin created a dreadful series of currents that pushed and pulled a man in a dozen directions at once. It was only with difficulty that he broke the surface a moment later, heaving another breath into lungs that burned like fire.

As he trod water, sweeping his arms this way and that, looking for Borastes, he realised he had lost his sword somehow under the water. Borastes was trying to swim away, but the strong current was pulling at him, holding him back. Rufinus noted with grim satisfaction that the other man had also lost his sword in the rush.

He ploughed through the water after Borastes and soon caught up with the struggling man. At the sound of Rufinus' furious splashing, the conspirator turned and prepared to defend himself. Rufinus threw a powerful punch, but the man simply surrendered to the current, which helped pull him out of the way. The action sent Rufinus plunging down beneath the surface once more, and as he broke out into the air a moment later, drawing heavy breaths, Borastes made a swing back, arm slamming around in a relatively professional manner. Rufinus ducked aside, taking in a mouthful of water as he did so, and knocked away the blow with a forearm, once more adjusting his thinking on this man. Borastes was a boxer, Rufinus had no doubt. He would have his work cut out here.

Spinning with the current, he lashed out with an elbow, catching Borastes in the chest, though it did not wind or cripple him as it might have on dry land, but simply made him cough and lurch back in the water. Rufinus planned his next move urgently, treading water, and as his quarry came back for another blow, he kicked out under the water. His foot collided with Borastes' knee as hard as possible within the slowing flow of water, but at the same time, the man leapt, his forehead colliding with Rufinus' in a blinding flash of agony.

Both men recoiled in pain and disappeared beneath the water. There, under the surface, Rufinus considered the very real possibility that he was about to drown. The disorienting pain from the head-butt was preventing him from thinking even remotely straight, and he was flailing uselessly in water that pulled him in every direction but up.

He struggled and fought for life. He couldn't manage the strength and sense to swim upwards, and could feel his lungs bursting, forcing him to open his mouth and breathe in. When he did that, he was done for, and someone would find him floating face down in a sacred pool in the morning.

Something gripped him at the back of the neck, and he scrabbled at it in blind, disoriented panic. When his face broke free from the water's surface, he opened his mouth automatically and breathed long and deep. He was still struggling at the grip that held the tunic at the nape of his neck, but his wits were recovering fast now. He looked up, baffled, to see the face of his fellow guardsman, Curio, looking back down at him. He surrendered to the man, and the frumentarius hauled him up and over the edge of the basin, onto the stonework, where he coughed and heaved breaths.

Finally, as his eyes rolled and his chest pumped up and down, Rufinus realised what was happening and sat bolt upright.

'The man...'

'He's safe,' Curio said, as Rufinus went momentarily blind, spring water and blood running down from his scalp into his eyes. He blinked and rubbed it away to see the shape of his prey lying on his side a few feet away, coughing up water.

'Where were you... when I needed you?' Rufinus breathed in exhaustion.

'Right here,' Curio said. 'You seemed to have things under control, so I left you to it.'

'Thanks a bunch.'

The frumentarius laughed. 'Don't be so dramatic. Smile when you think that someone in Carthage in a few hours is going to be surprised by a cup of pink drinking water. We'll have to get that head wound looked at. There's a good native physician in Zica. I'll take you to him.'

'The man,' coughed Rufinus, pointing at the heaving figure a short distance away.

'Yes. Bloody lucky I got to you both in time, I'd say.'

'What?'

'I didn't realise it was Borastes you were here to kill.'

Rufinus blinked. Confusion was still in control of his brain, but this seemed more befuddling than the rest of it. 'You *know* him?'

'I told you, I know Africa. That's why I'm here. I'd have been mighty unhappy if you'd put a blade through him.'

'But he's Aper's man!'

'No, Rufinus, he isn't.'

A suspicion slid over Rufinus. 'He's not one of yours? One of ours?'

'No, not quite. In fact, Borastes is a private citizen.' He crossed to the heaving body and lifted the man's sleeve to display the upper arm to Rufinus. Rufinus focused slowly on the tattoo of a bull with a VII beneath it.

'Seventh Claudia?'

Curio nodded. '*Ex*-Seventh. Retired. But I was here for years and Borastes and I knew one another very well. He works for the former governor, Pertinax.'

Rufinus blinked, and Curio chuckled. 'Pertinax commanded the Seventh in Dacia some years back. A few of its veterans retired into his service when the campaign was over. Borastes here is Pertinax's man through and through.'

Rufinus shook his head. 'Not now. He works for the new governor, now.'

Borastes sat up, still coughing, wagging a finger. 'Wash your mouth out, Praetorian,' he breathed angrily.

'You don't work for Julianus? Or Aper?'

Borastes heaved in a breath, still shaking his head. 'Three of us were tasked with staying on when Pertinax returned to Rome. Africa is an important province, and in the general's words he 'didn't want some lunatic to come in and fuck everything up' when he left. I've stumbled into something pretty major, though.' He rubbed the bloody cut on his forehead. 'So, you work with Curio? You're a grain man?'

Rufinus nodded wearily. 'I'm investigating Aper and his master the Tribune Crispinus. They led me to governor Julianus.'

Borastes laughed. 'And I started from the other end, but it seems we've met in the middle.'

'It's a damn good job I didn't kill you,' Rufinus remarked.

'I suspect it was more likely to be the other way around,' Borastes snorted, 'but yes, I concede the point. What now?'

Rufinus sighed. 'Pool our resources, I suppose. I probably shouldn't speak of this outside the frumentarii?' He glanced at Curio, who nodded, so he began. 'The Guard is still infected with the filth of Cleander. His villains are everywhere, but especially in the former scout unit called the speculatores. It's taken me months of digging to unearth their upper echelon. Aper is one of them, as is the tribune. They seem to be in league with Didius Julianus, as well as with his brother back in Rome. A large amount of gold recently changed hands there, apparently to enable the other Didius to build a web of patronage throughout Rome. If I didn't know better, I'd say they were planning a move on the throne.'

Borastes nodded. 'I think it is distinctly possible that Julianus would do just that, and perhaps that was once his plan. It is my personal belief that Cleander's fate has made many a potential conspirator against the throne take a step back and rethink. No one is in a hurry to be the next head on a spike, but I think Julianus is getting ready to make a move when the time *is* right.'

'You mean when the emperor dies?'

Borastes shrugged. 'I may be stuck in the armpit of the empire here, but I hear things. The senate are against the emperor, and he's already had three Praetorian prefects and a sister betray him. I can't see him staying the course much longer, unless he manages to build a few bridges.'

Rufinus sagged. 'My people are of a similar opinion.'

'And Julianus will be a strong contender,' Borastes murmured. 'The gold of which you speak came from Africa. It was a test run, but the coin die was a poor copy, and there is a possibility that the fake coinage will be identified in Rome. The new dies that have been delivered to the Carthage mint will change all that. Julianus will be able to siphon off state resources and have new coins of an old issue created, indistinguishable from the real thing. He's already wealthy, but soon he'll be rich beyond measure.'

'And with a solid military and political background,' Curio added.

'And with the support of Cleander's speculatores and a large swathe of the Praetorians,' Rufinus grunted. 'Gods, but this is a mess. At least the Urban Cohorts won't be easily bought, since they're under Pertinax's command.' He paused, a thought occurring. 'Aper sent me here to kill you. Is it because he's discovered you're Pertinax's man, or is there some reason I'm missing?'

Borastes shrugged. 'Seems likely he's worked it out. Either that or someone along the lines of this blabbed. I tried to get word of the coins to Pertinax, but my courier was killed. It was me who arranged the imperfection in the original coin die. There are a dozen reasons Curio might decide I'm a problem. Looks like I'm going to have to disappear.'

Rufinus sagged again. 'The problem is, Curio expects proof.'

The three men sat in silence, just the gurgle of the sacred waters and the dripping from their bodies audible. 'Then you'll have to kill me,' Borastes said.

'What?'

'Oh, not like that. Come with me.'

Moments later they were descending the slope, rubbing sodden hair and nursing wounds. With Borastes leading them they picked up Rufinus' horse, then Curio's, which was hidden not far away among the trees. At the lowest end of the slope, they made their way to a small farm shed, where it seemed Borastes too had a horse. Rufinus followed with a brow folded in curiosity. Halfway to the town, they paused and turned aside from the road towards a strange brick structure like a cone rising from the ground.

'What is this place?' he muttered as they dismounted and tied their horses to the trees again.

'This is what the Persians call a *yakh chal*,' Borastes replied, 'an ancient thing they invented and that some desert dwellers still use.'

Rufinus followed him over to a door in the smooth, curved wall. The structure was at least five times Rufinus' height. He stared in surprise as Borastes pulled the door open and a draft of chilly air burst forth. 'It's an icehouse!'

'Of a sort.'

'Down here in hot Africa, close to the desert?'

'Where could you need one more?'

They followed Borastes inside and let their eyes slowly adjust to the gloom. Boxes and amphorae sat on shelves around the edge, but in the centre sat a small cart with the traces dropped to the floor. The shape of a body lay on the back of it.

'What in Hades' name?'

Borastes shrugged. 'I've been half expecting something like this to happen,' he admitted. 'Peril of the trade, I suppose. For the last week or so, since I heard Aper was coming, I've had something ready in case I needed to fake my own death.' He picked up the traces, and with ligneous creaks wheeled the cart out to the door, where the light caught it.

Rufinus stared down at the face of the body on the cart. If he wasn't standing next to Borastes, he would have sworn that the grey-faced body was him. 'Where did you get a dead man that looked like you?'

The man shrugged. 'Wasn't easy. Cost a bit too, but I consider my life worth it. Take my ring and his head back to Aper. That should be sufficient.'

Rufinus nodded, still slightly horrified that a man might be so prepared for trouble that he carted a dead lookalike around with him. 'And what will you do?'

'I have old friends in Hadrumetum. In two days, I can be on a ship to Rome under an assumed name. Pertinax will look after me when I get there.'

Rufinus nodded, still a little thrown by all of this. He turned to Curio. 'That's this solved, then. And when we get back to Carthage, I'd rather like a look at this mint.'

Curio sat back. 'You take the head and the ring and go back. I will follow on in a few days.'

'What?'

'I arranged for a duty to collect goods from a ship in Pupput. That's how I got away. I'll linger there until it arrives and then see you in Carthage. That way we do not return together and increase suspicion.'

Rufinus sighed. 'These men were so damned subtle, he felt he might never truly be one of them.'

XII – THE SECRETS OF CARTHAGE

Rufinus slipped from the horse and handed the reins to one of his men, removing two bags from his saddle and heaving them onto his shoulders as he made for his room. Acheron was sitting outside on a padded pallet that Gamburio must have acquired from somewhere, and as soon as Rufinus rounded the corner, the hound leapt up and hurried over, tail windmilling as he danced around Rufinus excitedly.

The Praetorian smiled as he pushed open his door and dumped his personal kit on his bed, but realised with a little irritation that it was not Rufinus' return that had Acheron so excited, as the big black hound suddenly grabbed the bag containing the grey-faced severed head in his powerful jaws.

'No!' Rufinus snapped, trying to pull the bag with the mouldering trophy out of the dog's grip hissing with pain as his broken finger, now bound to the next one, sent sharp though him. A few moments of struggle ensued and by the time Rufinus had the bag out of Acheron's reach, held high, he noted with dismay that it was covered in tooth marks and drool.

'You bugger. That's not going to look good,' he admonished.

Closing the door and with Acheron padding alongside, eyes constantly riveted on the raised head-bag, Rufinus moved out into the late afternoon sunlight that played across the peristyle of the grand villa, making for Aper's rooms.

He knocked on the centurion's door and at the call opened it and entered. Aper was seated at a small table by the window, where he had been writing. As he folded the vellum and slid it away, Rufinus wondered what it was, but soon dismissed it as unimportant. Aper was too clever by far to write down evidence of his crimes.

'It is done?'

Rufinus drew a deep breath and proffered the bag. Aper took it with no sign of emotion and opened the top. He looked inside. 'He's in a bit of a state.'

Rufinus nodded. 'He was well preserved until I got back, and Acheron decided it was a treat I'd brought him. Sorry. I presume you're not keeping it.'

Aper shook his head and took the small signet ring Rufinus now held forth.

'He went out with a fight, I see.'

Rufinus nodded, eyes rolling upwards as though he could see the cut on his forehead. 'He was fast and strong. Ex-legionary, clearly.'

'That he was. It was useful at one point. I have to say, Rufinus, that I was not at all sure you would do it. Your reputation in the Guard is a little too strait-laced, but odd rumours exist here and there that you are not quite the golden boy after all. Suffice it to say that I am content, for now. Consider your debt paid. I will ask no such thing of you again, in the foreseeable future, but I will say that the patronage of the tribune and myself can be very lucrative. Big things are on the horizon. Stick with me and the centurionate is just the start.'

Rufinus bowed his head. 'I could do with a bath, now.'

Aper nodded. 'Here,' he said, tossing the bag back. Rufinus caught it with distaste. 'For your dog,' the centurion added. Rufinus tried to keep his expression neutral as he took the bag and exited the room, Acheron padding along behind him. He took the head to the shed at the rear of the village where the food remains were kept for periodic disposal and slipped the bag in among the rest, much to Acheron's disappointment.

'What now?' Rufinus mused as he strolled back. It seemed they would be in Africa for some months, and now it looked as though he had finally managed to secure a place among the corrupt officers. The coming days would be ones of carefully watching and listening for anything he could use.

What he really wanted to do was to look into the Carthage mint, but he shelved that idea for a while. There would be guards on the mint, and watchful ones at that. He would need to carefully select his time and would feel better about it with an accomplice.

Thus, he spent that evening in the villa's baths, soaking and sweating away the dirt of the Zica escapade, waiting impatiently for the return of Curio, the one man upon whom he could absolutely rely.

He spent the next three days watching the tribune on the few short occasions the man deigned to show his face. The man spent most of his time closeted away with the governor, plotting whatever they were plotting, and Aper seemed to be playing the perfectly ordinary centurion to perfection, though it was an easy job here, with nothing to do but guard the estate. A cross between garrison life and a vacation, really.

One thing he occupied himself with was occasional trips through the town, each time making sure to pass the grand structure of the

Carthage mint on one side or the other. The smoke from the furnaces chugged from the roof during the hours of daylight, and Rufinus determined that work ceased at nightfall, presumably due to the need for good levels of light to be certain of correct coin striking. Poor light would inevitably lead to poor coins.

The protection of the mint lay in the hands of the Urban Cohorts. Rufinus had known that Rome's police force had counterparts in several provinces, but he'd not seen them in Carthage until he passed the mint. It seemed they held duties in the mint, the port, the forum and other official locations, but that the governor's private guards were more visibly evident.

During the hours of work, there seemed to be two contubernia of the cohort on duty at the mint, eight men inside and eight out. At the end of the day's work, each slave and worker was thoroughly searched before they were allowed to leave the building. Rufinus could imagine how tempting it must be for a man to try and sneak out money or precious metal. He wondered how thorough the guards were prepared to be, given that a coin could be secreted in some very personal places. Likely the punishment if found to be stealing from the mint would be horrifying enough to put off most would-be embezzlers.

During the night, there would only be one contubernium, Rufinus presumed, though he'd not toured the area at night. It seemed unlikely that soldiers would be set to patrol the inside. There were three places the mint was accessible: the main front entrance, a back gate where carts were admitted, and a small side door into an alley. All three would be watched. The mint adjoined only one other building, and that was the barracks of the local vigiles. No planner was going to be stupid enough to attach something like a public mint to a private house.

Rufinus fretted on a daily basis over how they would go about it, and took to sitting in the Tanit Tavern just off the forum while he mulled things over. He made sure people knew where to find him. It was good to have a regular haunt, especially when it came to alibis, and visiting the tavern was ostensibly his reason for such regular jaunts into town.

Curio returned three days later, leading a cart of goods and wares requested by Tribune Crispinus that had arrived in Pupput. Why it had been taken to a small fishing town and not brought straight to the harbour of Carthage had Rufinus intrigued at first, but as he watched the goods being unloaded, he realised that they were simply luxuries to make life in Africa a little more palatable for the senior officer.

Likely they had come through Pupput to avoid the exorbitant port fees and taxes, slipping in out of sight of the governor's administration. That was, after all, the sort of thing that kept rich men rich.

That afternoon, Rufinus found Curio checking through the century's armoury at the end of the barrack block and gestured for him to follow. He made his way across the gardens, between manicured hedges and neat flower beds, past basins of water and tinkling fountains, and out to the upper northern edge of the estate. Here, a small private belvedere sat surrounded by an arc of neat cypress trees that screened it from the rest of the estate, while the small domed structure looked out north over the hills and the countryside in the direction of ancient Utica. It was as secluded a place as was to be found on the estate, and was out of bounds as a guard post for the soldiers since one man had been found asleep on the bench, believing himself unobserved.

A quick peek between the trees to be certain they were alone, and Rufinus strolled across to the perimeter wall, Curio joining him.

'I think we could do with seeing what's happening in the Carthage mint, Curio.'

'Yes. Definitely. It will not be easy, though.'

Rufinus nodded. 'I can't see an easy way in.'

Curio drummed his fingers on the wall top. 'Three access points, each well-guarded, attached only to one building, which is itself full of armed men. Not easy. A distraction might do it.'

Rufinus frowned. 'The men of the Urban Cohorts aren't going to abandon their posts for anything short of an invasion or a major riot.'

'But the vigiles might,' Curio murmured. 'If they turn out of their barracks, we could get inside and use that building to get into the mint.'

Rufinus frowned. 'How?'

'The roofs are roughly at the same height. The vigiles' barracks are two storeys but have an observation tower an extra storey up to watch for fires in the area. That means there is ready access to the roof, and I know that there are roof windows in the mint. There need to be to give the best light possible for working, and they open to allow the furnace heat a little egress.'

Rufinus sighed. 'I keep forgetting you know Carthage so well.'

'I also know mints. I've been in several in my time. They get dark and hot, and so they're designed to admit as much air and light as possible. That can't happen at ground level for the sake of security, so it happens above. We distract the vigiles so they turn out, and we use their barracks to access the roof.'

Rufinus sagged. 'To get the whole unit out, we'd have to start quite a blaze. I'm not sure about that. I recently used a fire as a distraction for something similar and it burned half of Rome down. I didn't start it, mind,' he added hurriedly. 'I just took advantage of it.'

'Carthage is not as troublesome as Rome for that. Fewer tall, wooden buildings side by side. We just have to target it well. Leave the fire to me. You just watch the barracks and count the men to make sure they all leave.'

Rufinus still wasn't sure. 'When will we try?' he asked uncertainly.

'No time like the present. Tonight,' Curio said. 'We've both been absent a bit over the last few days, so being gone from the villa for an hour or two won't alert anyone.'

'And I've been frequenting the Tanit Tavern near the forum regularly, so everyone will assume I'm there.'

'Good,' Curio said. 'I'll meet you outside the Tanit Tavern at the third hour of the night.'

There seemed little else to discuss for now, and so the two men split up and went about their business. Rufinus spent the rest of the day fretting nervously. He desperately wanted to see inside the mint, but was not looking forwards to getting in. As nightfall approached, he prepared. He selected his caligae speculatoriae instead of the nailed boots, removed the jingling apron from his belt and all armlets, torcs and the like that might make noise. He changed into his 'going out' tunic, which was a dark blue, and kept only the pugio dagger at his side and his centurion's vine stick.

At the second hour of the night he left the villa, telling Gamburio only that he was going into town for a bit, and tasking the man to look after Acheron. Somehow, Rufinus didn't see his hound as being an asset when sneaking across roofs.

He made his way to the Tanit Tavern, the sign creaking in the breeze, showing the image of the ancient Punic goddess. Inside, he ordered a cup of wine and sat sipping it slowly, making it last. He eked out that one cup until the appointed hour, and then rose and strolled out into the city, stretching.

Curio was waiting at the end of the street and summoned him with just a nod. Moments later the two men were strolling through back streets towards the mint. They exchanged hardly a word as they approached, and Rufinus could feel the tension building in him as they closed on their target. Sure enough, men of the Carthage Cohort stood beside each door, two to an entrance, with one more strolling around on general patrol. Rufinus frowned.

'Seven. Unless they're under-strength, one must be inside.'

'We'll deal with that when we come across him. For now, we need to get inside. This is where we split up. You find a dark doorway and count the vigiles. There are twenty-five men inside.'

'How do you know that?'

'I enquired subtly this afternoon. Just make sure they're all out.'

Rufinus, still eyeing the Urban Cohort warily, found a shady archway opposite the barracks and stood there. He could see a man on the timber tower above the structure, looking this way and that around the streets. Lights flickered in the barrack house windows. He felt the nerves build continually with each passing moment.

When the alarm was sounded, he almost jumped from his skin. Atop the tower, the lookout cried out, pointing, and then shouting down into the building. Somewhere inside someone started to clang a bell furiously. In moments, men were pouring from the doorway, carrying poles with hooks, buckets, ropes and water bags. Another group burst from larger doors, wheeling their fire truck, a mobile water barrel with a hose and hand pump. Rufinus cursed himself as he lost count several times in the chaos. Then, as suddenly as it had started, the barrack house fell silent once more, its occupants all now out of sight, racing towards the conflagration, a man still ringing his bell as they ran through the city.

Rufinus jumped in panic once more as Curio appeared at his shoulder from the shadows, smelling faintly of smoke, and of mushrooms for some odd reason.

'Clear?'

'Probably,' Rufinus grunted. 'Lost count. Too chaotic.'

'Let's hope.'

Curio strode across the street, rather brazenly, and straight into the door of the vigiles' barracks. Heart pounding, Rufinus followed. He disappeared inside just as that patrolling soldier rounded the corner into sight next door. In the ground floor, he opened his mouth to hiss something to Curio, but stopped as the frumentarius put a finger to his lips and pointed upwards. Rufinus fell still and listened. They could hear two men in conversation above.

With surprising ease and clarity, Curio mimed overcoming other men, one each. He touched his dagger and shook his head, tapping the nightstick he'd brought. Rufinus nodded vigorously. He had no desire to fatally injure an innocent fireman.

With that, Curio moved to the stairs, his nightstick held up along the inside of his forearm, not exactly invisible, but not readily noticeable at first glance. Rufinus attempted something similar with his vitis, failing largely. They climbed the stairs, and Rufinus was surprised that Curio did so without any attempt to sneak.

'Vitalis?' called a voice from above.

'No,' Curio replied, emerging from the stairs onto the second floor. 'Message from the palace.'

The two men, seated at a table on either side of a game board, looked up, a little surprise on their face, but no other sign of alertness. Curio strolled over to them, and Rufinus hurried along behind.

'Who are you?' the man said, frowning.

Curio's answer came swiftly and accurately, the nightstick slipping down his forearm into his hand and then coming down on the fireman's head. Rufinus did something similar, with considerably less grace, and both men slumped forwards over their table.

'His head's bleeding,' Curio noted. 'You hit him too hard.'

'You've got a little stick; I've got a centurion's vitis. It's designed to hurt. I tried.'

'He'll live,' Curio replied, peering at the wound. 'He'll have a bad headache, but he'll live. Come on.'

Moments later they were climbing up the ladder onto the roof beneath the watch tower. Both buildings had low pitches to their tiles and there was little danger of falling, so both men stayed well back from the edge, out of view of the men below.

The roof of the mint was covered in wide windows, glazed with thick, green-ish hued glass. Rufinus suddenly remembered breaking into that warehouse back in Pannonia, years ago, and wondered how often in the course of a *normal* man's life he was given cause for such activity. Curio approached one of the windows and peered down through it. Shaking his head, he moved on, trying two more until he found the one he was looking for. Waving Rufinus over, he put his fingers under the edge and pulled gently. Rufinus lent a hand, keeping his broken finger out of the way, and the window opened with just the slightest squeak. Down below, something groaned, and Rufinus realised the window was attached to a pole, which was anchored to a post that ran all the way down to the ground so that a man down there could open and close the window. All the roof lights were thus equipped.

Curio had chosen well. This light was above a walkway that ran around one end of a large room.

Holding his breath, the frumentarius lowered himself through the gap and down to the walkway, then beckoned his companion. As Rufinus landed with more noise than he liked, the two men crouched. Rufinus peered this way and that, spotting the soldier easily. The man was guarding a door covered in locks, though not very well, since he appeared to be asleep in his chair.

'The metal store,' hissed Curio. 'Gold and silver in there.'

Rufinus nodded. 'I doubt there will be chests of coins waiting for us,' he whispered. 'What do we look for?'

Curio beckoned and began to pad along the walkway. Moments later they were out of sight of the sleeping guard and his precious door. 'If Julianus is doing something underhand,' Rufinus whispered, 'then he'll surely be doing it in a secure place?'

Curio shook his head. 'Depends on what he's doing. If they're just coins, then why hide it? Making coins is what a mint does, and most of the workers are illiterate slaves anyway. All they know is they're given a die and a hammer and told to make the coins. Even the civilian workers won't be too clever or cautious. No one wants clever and thoughtful men working on making money for them. Clever men will get ideas. It's my guess that this new work will be done out in plain sight as though it were perfectly legitimate.'

Rufinus sucked his teeth. 'How often are there new issues? New dies?'

'Not often. Annually is about the norm. Or after certain events. The last issue here was run by Pertinax when the new grain fleet was begun to celebrate Africa coming to Rome's aid after the famine.'

Rufinus smiled. 'So, the new coin die should be quite obvious from its scarce use thus far?'

'Yes, I would think so.'

'And all the coin dies will be kept in the same place.'

A nod. Then Curio was off again, hurrying to a stairway that led down to the ground floor. Alighting at the bottom, he padded lightly over to the wall. Here, in this side of the big L-shaped hall, there were numerous benches beside small circular tables where the slaves were seated to hammer out their days. Rufinus spotted it before Curio had to point it out. On the wall stood a shelf and upon that shelf was a box, riveted to the wall itself.

The container was around three feet long and narrow and short. It was made of iron, with a lid consisting of heavy metal grille running across the top, fastened at both ends with solid looking locks. Breaking into this thing would be hard and noisy.

143

Fortunately, as they stopped beside it and looked down, he realised they wouldn't have to. The coin dies were secured away to prevent their unauthorised use at times like this, some trusted overseer holding the keys. But thanks to the grille, inside he could see the coin dies lined up, all ones that were in use or recent enough that they might be called upon for reissue.

Curio began at one end, Rufinus the other, both examining one die after another and they had almost met in the middle when they both identified precisely what they were looking for. All the dies were grubby from constant use and with marks and flaws, except this one. It could not have been used more than a few score times. Rufinus squinted at it, wishing he had more light. As he peered, Curio produced a small lamp and vial, filled it with oil and struck a spark with his flint, casting light on the offending article.

'This is an old issue,' Rufinus muttered. 'A "Grain for Rome" denarius with the manned grain ship and the full modius. This is about five years old now, and it's not an African coin. It's a Rome design.'

'So, he's minting coins that look like they were made in Rome half a decade ago. Sneaky. Something that old will hardly be looked at twice. They'll just be taken at face value.'

'Which means,' Rufinus muttered, 'that they almost certainly don't *have* that value.'

Curio nodded, and they moved around carefully, listening out for the light snore of the guard by the door to change. It took a short while for them to find what they were looking for, and it was Curio that spotted it first, waving him over. A wooden bin at one end of the benches held the failed strikings, ready to be melted down and reused. They rifled through the box as quietly as they could by the light of Curio's small lamp, and Rufinus lifted the prize triumphantly.

A coin that looked very much like the five-year-old Roman coin, albeit badly off-centre and missing part of the inscription, where the die had slipped mid-strike. This was precisely what Didius Julianus' fake dies were being used to make. Rufinus held it up. It looked perfectly normal.

'Bring it with you,' Curio said, then fell still and waved to Rufinus.

The snoring had stopped.

'Shit.'

Curio blew out his lamp, tipped the spare oil into a corner and then slid it back into a pouch as the two men tip-toed back to the stairs and began to climb.

'Hey! You there!'

The guard from the door was hurrying across the room. Rufinus felt his heart lurch as he pounded up the stairs now, all care for stealth forgotten. Curio was still ahead and in moments they were up on that raised walkway. As they ran back around to where that access window lay, the angry guard was pounding up a set of stairs at the other end of the walkway, trying to cut them off.

'What do we do?' Rufinus hissed as they reached the open window above.

'We pray, we hope, and we run.'

With that he jumped, caught the lip of the window and pulled himself through. Rufinus watched the guard closing on them, shouting, and was up a moment later in the man's wake, hissing at the pain in his finger as he heaved. Pulling himself through and out onto the roof, he watched Curio kick the window closed, muffling the enraged shouts from below.

'That won't hold him for long.'

'Come on,' Rufinus barked, turning towards the vigiles' barracks, but he was greeted with the sight of a man standing on the lookout tower, who pointed at him and yelled for him to stop. Either those two vigiles had recovered quickly, or some of their mates had come back. Either way, that made descent through the barracks unpalatable.

'Shit. What now?'

'How's your long jump?'

Rufinus frowned. 'Hardly Olympian. Why?' His eyes widened. 'No. No, no, no.'

'Oh, yes,' Curio replied, rising and sprinting along the rooftop away from the vigiles' barracks. Rufinus, trapped and close to panic, followed, heart racing. He winced as Curio sped up, approaching the far end of the mint roof. The man did not stop. He sailed out from the roof, across the alley, the narrowest of the three roads surrounding the mint. He landed on the far roof heavily, almost missing, put pulling himself up.

Rufinus had the time neither to stop nor to question his actions, as he followed suit. He felt his feet leave the roof, and the terrifying, yawning gap beneath him. It came as a total surprise when he hit the far side rather than plummeting to a fate of broken legs far below.

Like Curio, he hit hard, and felt the breath knocked from him. Slowly, he straightened, recovering, and looked about.

Their pursuer was now on the mint roof, though he was slowing and showing no sign of mimicking their jump. He was shouting for his friends, though, and the soldiers in the street were pointing up at them.

'What now?'

'I think you were lucky, then,' Curio said. 'You're a bit heavy for things like that. I'll draw them off. You stay here and then head down through the building. Get that coin away safely.'

Rufinus nodded and felt a lurch of nerves as Curio was off, pounding along the roof and then leaping to the next one. Rufinus slipped down to his belly, out of sight, and listened as the men gave chase to the running frumentarius. He waited for sixty heartbeats and then rose gingerly, looking about. There was no movement.

Working his way across the roof, he found a trapdoor and let himself down into a winding stairwell. At the bottom, passing the entrances to three private apartments, he approached the outer door and carefully pushed it ajar, hand on the vine stick jammed under his armpit. Silence and stillness greeted him. He slipped from the door, looking this way and that, and then slid across the street and into another alley. From there, he began to move through streets with which he had familiarised himself over the past few days.

Somehow, he felt that running straight home might be a bad idea. If word of men breaking into the mint reached the villa or palace and more or less coincided with Rufinus arriving home, it would look very suspicious. Instead, he would head back to the Tanit Tavern and continue to establish an alibi of having been socialising in town.

Only one stop delayed him on the way back to the inn. He took a winding back route, constantly watching for the Urban Cohort and, as he moved through the street of the silversmiths, a thought occurred to him. Two of the places were still showing lights as they worked late, and he knocked upon the door of one with a Judean name on the sign. The door opened and a thin man with a leathery face and glittering eyes above a curled grey beard frowned out.

'Yes?'

'Might I ask your opinion on something?' Rufinus asked.

The man beckoned him inside, and Rufinus produced his badly-struck coin.

'This is a denarius. A fake one, I believe. I suspect it does not have anywhere near the silver content that it should. I would appreciate your professional opinion.'

The man nodded and took the coin. His gaze turned derisive as he examined it. 'It is badly made, but had the die been struck true it would be a very good fake,' he pronounced.

'But still a fake?'

'Yes. There is little silver in this at all. It is nine parts in ten of zinc. Better than most fakes, though, which limit themselves to that. The rest of this one appears to consist of lead and orichalcum in a mix, which gives it a more realistic colour and weight.'

'So, it's a good counterfeit?'

The man nodded. 'Almost the work of an artist. Only a man in the profession would readily spot the difference. To a man in the street, this would appear perfectly normal. Still, it is more or less worthless.'

'Except to a man who doesn't know,' Rufinus mused. 'Thank you, my friend.'

He opened his purse and handed over several coins. 'For your trouble.'

The man nodded his gratitude, seemingly happy over the validity of the other money. Moments later Rufinus was back out in the street, coin safely tucked away, heading for the tavern. So, Didius Julianus was manufacturing money not making him out to be emperor or any such foolish plan, but creating very good counterfeit coins that would appear to be ordinary money that had been circulating for years. He was literally making himself money. And unless someone had the coins tested, they would go unnoticed as Julianus amassed sufficient wealth to buy an empire.

Damn, but the rot he'd followed in the Guard had gone deep.

Reaching the Tanit Tavern, he bought a full jug of wine and took one of water and a cup, seating himself in a very visible place and leaning back, sipping his drink. It took an hour for the trouble to find him. Optio Gamburio and two other soldiers suddenly entered the tavern, looking this way and that until they spotted Rufinus, and then running over to him.

'What's up?' he asked, innocently.

'The city mint was broken into. The alarm has gone up. Aper sent me. It seems they caught the culprit.'

Rufinus swallowed nervously.

XIII – THE EXECUTIONER

All they knew for sure was that someone had been caught. That was the grand sum of information that had leaked out of the palace: someone had broken into the mint, which was, needless to say, an executable offence at the best of times. With the governor's dubious activities in there, execution was probably as much as the poor bastard could hope for.

Someone had been caught.

That was all *Aper* knew.

Rufinus knew more. He had got away from the mint only because Curio had drawn away their pursuers. He had bought Rufinus' escape, probably with his life. The worried Praetorian could picture the scene. While he'd snuck down through the building, Curio had gone on from roof to roof. The man knew the city and would probably have known where he could safely jump the narrower streets. Likely he had gradually come down to a place where he could get to ground once more.

But Carthage was full of soldiers, and the moment a whistle went up, others would answer the call. Undoubtedly Curio had headed south, away from Rufinus, the Tanit Tavern, and their villa – somewhere distant, drawing the pursuers that way. But everywhere he went, with men right on his tail, horns, whistles and bells would ring out and more men would join the hunt. Urban Cohorts from the walls and the port and anywhere they happened to be on duty, the vigiles from any regional barracks they passed, the governor's mercenary guard from the port. He would not have got far before his hunters numbered in the hundreds.

No wonder he'd been caught.

Moreover, he'd been overcome, probably suddenly and by surprise. One thing that had been drummed into Rufinus by his new frumentarius masters was that if an enemy closed in and there was no way out, a knife to the throat was your only path. Not only could you not afford to reveal what you knew, but facing the torturer's blade to reveal it was something no one wanted. Rufinus knew it well and it made him shudder. Even a poor torturer would succeed in the end, for it mattered not how strong a man was, his body could only take so much pain. Everyone talked in the end.

And that was what was troubling Rufinus most.

A 'grain man' took his chances. The job inherently involved risk. Curio knew what he was doing and had done so even as he'd sacrificed himself. Rufinus felt bad for him, but he knew that Curio would do the same again if faced with the same choice.

The problem was what Curio knew.

The man was privy to every secret Rufinus couldn't afford to let out. That Borastes was not dead. That he had been a spy for Pertinax and had escaped via Hadrumetum to Rome. That he and Rufinus had let the man go. That he and Rufinus were both frumentarii investigating Aper, Crispinus and the governor. That they knew about the coins and the meeting at the Palatine. That Gamburio was at least partially in on it. The name of Vibius Cestius, even. Most of all, though, Rufinus' true role. One too many strokes of the knife and Curio would sing Rufinus' name like a morning lark, which would in turn land Rufinus at that same choice: knife to his own throat or a torturer's blade to other parts.

It was a nail-biting situation.

The moment they had brought the man back to the palace, Aper had put the Guard on alert. He had left half his century under their optio guarding the villa and taken the rest, along with Rufinus' men, to the palace. Rufinus had been sent for and instead of going back to the villa had headed straight for the palace with Gamburio.

That had been in the middle of the night.

It was now just after dawn.

Rufinus had spent the night pacing nervously. Admittedly, he looked just like everyone else, for everyone was on tenterhooks over the situation, and only Rufinus knew that in his case it was panic over potential revelations. To add to his nerves, he still had a very incriminating coin about his person. He had not had the chance to hide it yet, since he had come straight from the tavern, and he could hardly afford to throw away such a critical piece of evidence. Yet having it hidden about his person right now carried immense danger.

The worst thing was that the Praetorians were hovering, alert, in the public areas of the palace, unaware of what was happening in the bowels of the place. Somewhere inside, Curio had to be being tortured. Aper was nowhere to be found, as were Crispinus and the governor himself. Without doubt they were all with Curio, listening to his final song. Rufinus shuddered again every time he thought about it, and his skin itched where the Syrian in the cellars of an imperial villa had cut, burned and branded him a decade ago.

Damn the world, but Curio didn't deserve that.

Rufinus sat heavily on a marble bench, rubbing his face.

'I'm surprised you didn't hear all the commotion, sir,' Gamburio said. He had been needling at Rufinus all night, probably suspicious. After all, he knew Rufinus to be frumentarius too, and must suspect that the two men had been together.

'I was in a tavern near the forum. From what I understand all the action took place in the southern region of the city. I was a long way away from it.'

'Of course.'

Gamburio was looking at him funnily, though. Probably weighing up his own position, Rufinus thought. He had supported Rufinus in his move into the century and was one of the good men. But faced with potentially being tied to Rufinus and Curio and the possibility of torture, he would even now be trying to decide what his honour was worth, and whether it might be expedient to sell Rufinus out for his own survival. Rufinus couldn't blame the man, but he would maintain his alibi as long as possible. No point in revealing anything prematurely.

'Funny, though, how…' Gamburio was cut off by the sound of approaching boots and a moment later the double doors crashed open. Aper strode in with his four minions at his back. Rufinus braced himself. He was at the far side of the room and had a very sharp pugio at his side. If the worst happened, he would have time to use it, like a defeated general of old. He would never allow himself to be tortured again.

He rose from the seat, fingers going to the dagger's pommel.

Aper came to a halt, brow low, eyes glowering, and looked about the room full of Praetorians.

'Rufinus, with me. The rest of you stay here.'

Rufinus swallowed but forced a mean, semi-disinterested expression onto his face. He could afford to show neither weakness nor fear right now. Still, his hand remained touching his dagger hilt. As they marched through the palace corridors, Aper's gaze turned on him. Appraising? Suspicious? Unreadable.

Rufinus' nerves began to seriously twang with worry as they descended a brick-lined staircase down into what could only be the cellars and substructures of the great building. Nothing good could come of this.

Along a lamp-lit corridor they trod; six men, Rufinus the only one not in uniform. Finally, as they rounded a corner, they slowed. Rufinus could see half a dozen more guardsmen standing in an antechamber, along with several of the governor's Medusa-head mercenaries. Rufinus swallowed the lump in his throat again. This was it.

The cluster of soldiers parted respectfully as the two centurions approached, and at a gesture from Aper, his men pulled open the door and stepped aside, allowing the officers to pass within. As they did so, two of those men stayed without, while the other pair followed their commander inside.

The second thing that hit Rufinus as they entered was the heat. The first was the smell. The moment the door opened, it hit him like a nauseating wall. It was the sort of smell you would only get in a place like this, and it was ten times worse than the stench of a battlefield. In battle you smelled blood and guts, shit and piss, vomit and filth.

You didn't smell roasted pork and burned hair into the bargain.

Rufinus winced, face lowered so that no one would see it. The smell alone told him everything he needed to know. His heart went out once more to Curio. The room was dimly lit and with the Tartaran red-gold glow of braziers, which also gave it the cloying heat that threatened to overwhelm him.

Finally, he steadied himself to take in the scene.

The governor was not here, which surprised him. Perhaps such base things were beneath him, though from memory of the practical, shrewd man he had met upstairs, he suspected otherwise. More likely, Didius Julianus had removed himself from the scene for the sake of deniability, knowing that his compatriots would do the job without him.

And they had.

Tribune Crispinus stood by the side wall, arms folded, an expression of disdain upon his face. Aper took a place close by. The rest of the room's occupants consisted of half a dozen more Praetorians and two of the governor's guards.

And the torturer.

And his victim.

The man was wearing an apron of leather which was stained, covered in blood and less mentionable matter. He was holding an eyeball by the root, which was swinging merrily back and forth and threatening to cause a re-emergence of Rufinus' dinner. The man was not smiling. He was not frowning. He had a calculating, interested expression. A professional, of course.

Curio was done for. They had clearly been working on him for half the night. Rufinus found himself wishing there was some kindly figure who might accidentally kill him as they had with Rufinus, to save him the worst. But no. Curio had suffered and witnessed it all during the night. He had been cut and burned, branded and rent, his nose and ears cut away and now one eye gone, the empty, raw red socket horrifying, like looking deep into the pit of Tartarus. His left arm was gone entirely apart from a small stump, and his legs were broken in many places, leaving him in a jellied heap on the floor.

'He yet lives, for his sins,' Aper said.

Rufinus shuddered. 'This is inhuman.' He hadn't meant to say it. It just sort of leaked out.

Aper simply shrugged. 'Sometimes we have to lower ourselves to the basest levels to achieve our goals. Do not pretend to be above such things, Rustius Rufinus. I have heard of some of the things *you* have done.'

Fear tremored through him once more. What had Curio said? He was dying to ask but dare not. He simply looked at Curio, who was looking back at him, mouth opening and closing silently, face ruined.

'This man and an accomplice were caught stealing from the city mint,' Aper said. 'Clearly, he was no common criminal, and the hot blade has revealed much to us. Curio is one of the grain men, hidden among our unit, one of the despised spies who ruin the military.'

Rufinus shivered.

'Curio was one of your men, Rufinus.'

Rufinus simply nodded, trying to keep his expression unreadable. Was it possible? Had Curio gone through all this and managed to keep Rufinus' name from spilling out?

'Tell us about him,' Aper said.

Rufinus shrugged. 'Gallus fell ill just before we were due to leave for Africa. He reported to the medicus and the next morning Curio was there. He'd been assigned through the headquarters, via the prefect, maybe. I never questioned it. He was just transferred to make up the numbers. Since then I've not noticed him do anything unusual. He was the one who went to Pupput to collect the tribune's cargo, though. He was gone for a few days.'

Aper nodded. 'The grain men are dangerously subtle. I would give good money to know what transpired in Pupput. Investigations will be made. However, something interesting has come from his rantings under the blade.'

Rufinus tensed, throwing an interested look at his fellow centurion. He couldn't trust his voice not to waver right now.

'It seems he is following you.'

Rufinus frowned. 'Me?'

'I understand that you have something of a history with the frumentarii. That the traitor Attius Sacratus, who abandoned his oath to the Guard and sold out his sword to the grain men, hunted you and tried to blackmail you for your ties to Cleander.'

Rufinus nodded, hoping against hope that those stories he had spread so carefully were finally paying dividends.

'It seems that Sacratus is not your only hunter, for this Curio had himself transferred to your century to follow you to Africa. It seems he is investigating you and therefore, by uncomfortable extension, us too. The tribune and I are uncertain both what to make of this, and what to do about it.'

Rufinus swallowed. Curio had not betrayed his identity. The man had suffered all this and kept his secrets. Incredible. But now, unless he wanted to be kneeling, one-eyed, beside his friend, Rufinus was going to have to deny him utterly.

'The devious bastards,' he said with bile. 'I thought I'd dealt with them after Sacratus. They've nothing on me. They can't have, because everything I did was ordered and for the empire, but I think they see me as their only clue. Their only lead to Cleander's clients.'

Gods, but how easy it was to turn his own investigation onto himself like that.

Aper nodded slowly, gesturing to the torturer with his eyeball. 'Our man here assures me that we will get nothing else from Curio; that he has spilled out all there is to spill. He is now past any use to us and cannot be allowed to go on.'

Rufinus had a sinking feeling. He felt sure he knew what was coming.

'You are the man they hunt,' Aper hissed. 'It is your honour to dispatch another of their kind. Perhaps if you kill two frumentarii, they will cut their losses and stop coming after you.'

Rufinus nodded absently. His gaze was on Curio. He would dearly love nothing more than to stop looking at his ruined friend, but he was searching what remained of the features for an answer. Then he saw it. The man's lips moved for just a moment, his eye locked on Rufinus. No one else would know, surely, for the lips barely moved, and Rufinus himself would have had no idea what the man had said had he not been waiting for those very words.

Kill me.

Curio had sanctioned it. He was silently begging Rufinus to finish it, and the Praetorian could understand entirely. In such a state there was nothing left to live for, and every new breath brought only hopelessness and agony. What was there to live for after such a night? Killing Curio would not be an onerous duty. It would be a mercy. A favour.

He stepped forwards, drawing his pugio. Many soldiers didn't bother much with their pugio. The majority of centurions ignored the dagger's existence. If you had to rely on the pugio in battle, the trainers said, then you'd already lost. As such, for a hundred years or more the pugio had been used for little more than shaving and cutting bread. And now, since beards were the norm, few people kept their dagger sharp enough to shave, either.

Rufinus kept *his* razor-sharp. Mind you, he was one of those rare few who kept their face clean-shaven anyway. But even had he a beard, he would still have kept the blade sharp. In his position, everything might turn into a life-saving weapon at a moment's notice.

He crouched before Curio, whose very expression urged him to speed, to end the pain. Rufinus had one thing he had to do, though. After what he had suffered, Curio deserved to go to peace and calm, not to be damned as a wandering spirit for all time.

He fished in his pouch, being very careful not to produce the evidence coin that was tucked into a side compartment. He removed a denarius and prised open Curio's mouth, slipping in the coin and then pushing the jaw closed. Then he counted down the man's ribs to the third. There, he placed the point of the dagger over the gap between the ribs, feeling his way to the depression through the waxy, ruined flesh.

Without delay, locking his gaze directly onto Curio's one good eye, he thrust.

The dagger punched into Curio's heart and he stiffened, a strange keening noise emanating from his lips. Rufinus kept his gaze in place. For so many years, since his brother's demise, he'd been unable to bring himself to watch a man's soul leave. Now, though, since that spell had been broken, he found himself willing it to happen, watching the light fade in Curio's remaining eye as he slumped back to the flagged floor, chest pulling away from Rufinus' blade with a dreadful sucking sound.

Curio was dead. Miraculously, Rufinus seemed to have got away with it.

'I think giving him the kindness of a coin for the crossing was a little too much,' Aper muttered from the wall.

Rufinus turned a neutral expression on him. 'Would *you* want him as a lemure, wandering the world and looking for vengeance?'

Aper snorted. 'I suppose not.' The centurion shared a look with the tribune, standing silent nearby, and the senior officer nodded. Aper turned back to Rufinus. 'You continually prove yourself. It is good to see, and I warm to you, Rufinus. Now there remains a loose end here. Curio was not alone. He had an accomplice at the mint. At the moment we have no information at all, though Curio described him as a 'branded man' and an 'orphan'. Not much to go on, but it would be a good idea to locate this man and deal with him. Given the fact that he may well be another frumentarius and similarly out to get you it seems both appropriate and expedient to give to you the task of hunting and removing him. Are you up to the job, Rufinus?'

Rufinus nodded, trying to keep the relief from his face. The second man had been a potential issue, for Aper and his men would investigate and inevitably the net would close on Rufinus, he was sure. But given the opportunity to shift blame, muddle the investigation and generally save his own skin, Rufinus felt certain he could turn his last great peril into a win instead. He felt sure he could concoct a good tale and load the blame upon some hapless member of the recently deceased, whose head he could bring back as proof. Something he had learned, oddly, from Borastes, a man he'd been sent to kill. All very neat.

'Good. Then from the next day, that is your task. We are at a loose end here for some months anyway, so I am content to leave this entirely in your hands. In the meantime, we have had no sleep this past night, and neither have you. If you are to hunt a grain man, you need to be rested. Go home and sleep.'

Rufinus nodded, sagging slightly, casting Curio a last glance. He was preparing to go, when Crispinus unfolded his arms. 'Before you retire, Centurion, do me the courtesy of joining me. I must report all of this to the governor, and perhaps it is time that you and I spoke more earnestly.'

Rufinus tried to look interested more than ecstatic, though the sight of Curio in a heap nearby helped there. He glanced momentarily at Aper, half expecting to see a touch of jealousy or dissatisfaction there, but in fact his fellow centurion seemed to radiate approval.

Leaving the rest to it, Rufinus waited patiently for the tribune to leave, then followed him from the grisly, hot, stinking room. The corridor outside, for all it was dank and musty, smelled like the sweetest of rose gardens by comparison and Rufinus breathed deeply as he made his way along the corridors in the tribune's wake.

'Such places displease you?' Crispinus said as they walked, his tone surprisingly neutral.

Rufinus coughed. 'It is not the reason, nor the values, Tribune. It is a bad memory that surfaces in me at such sights.'

The tribune nodded. 'It had slipped my mind that such a fate was once visited upon yourself.'

Rufinus flinched. Suddenly this quiet walk felt horribly like an interrogation. 'That is the problem, Tribune. It makes my blood run cold to be about such things now. Death and combat I can manage. I am no stranger to the blade, but the prolonged agony of the torturer I can no longer face. I have travelled that journey myself.'

Crispinus nodded. 'I can understand your position. Few men have been through such things and still walk to tell the tale. In that you are somewhat remarkable. You were wounded in the imperial villa at Tibur, I believe?'

Rufinus cleared his throat, nerves rising once more. 'Yes, sir.'

'You were assigned by Paternus to seek out treason against the emperor.'

'I was, sir. And I found it. I paid for my investigation, but I got the bitch in the end, sir'

He'd wondered about whether to lie over any of this, but clearly Crispinus knew enough of Rufinus' history to hold plenty of truths. 'You had, even then, a reputation as a man above any reproach. A man who held his oath to the emperor above all.'

Rufinus sagged a little. This was dangerous ground with a clever man like the tribune. 'Yes, sir. It is what it means to be Praetorian.'

'Yet you claim to have been sent on special missions by Cleander. I have heard conflicting reports. Many men served the chamberlain, and in fact it is true that there was such secrecy in the palace at the time that many of us did not know about one another. Something that still holds true to an extent.'

He stopped suddenly, and Rufinus almost walked into the back of him.

'It is difficult sometimes,' the tribune said, 'to look at a man and judge him without putting aside one's own biases, Centurion Rufinus. As such, I find I am taking time to warm to you, more so than Aper, who is usually very careful. That, though, may be my own prejudices preying upon me. As such, I also realise that the same may be true for you.'

Rufinus felt a weird lurch. He'd not expected to be spoken to on such level and so frankly by the man who seemed to be the leader of his enemies. He cleared his throat noisily.

'Tribune, I will state right now my position. I am from a patrician family, of low status admittedly. I am a loyal son of Rome. I took an oath to the emperor and will not break it. I am loyal to the emperor Commodus and I will not betray him. I saved him from his sister, but those around the emperor are both good and bad. I have served both, and I have fought both. The waters are often muddied, and sometimes those men who history will label heroes are in fact villains when it all comes down to it.'

Crispinus narrowed his eyes, but nodded.

'Know this, Rufinus: we are *all* loyal to the emperor. It is what follows him with which we concern ourselves. Some people served Cleander, some fought him, but all of us remain Commodus' men. Everything we do now is for the emperor and for the empire. Not treason, but preparation. Look past your muddied waters and realise this.

He started to march on and Rufinus fell in behind him. It was extremely hard to find fault with what the tribune had just said, and Rufinus had to remind himself that this man had sanctioned counterfeit coinage, the torture of a frumentarius and more, despite his honeyed words.

'What is your opinion of the emperor?' Crispinus said, suddenly. 'Not an official line. Your personal opinion with true permission to speak freely.'

Rufinus tensed. He didn't like the direction this was taking, but he should at least be able to say what the tribune wanted to hear without any lying involved.

'I have seen him only rarely, Tribune. Since his days serving with his father, he was always flamboyant and given to extremes. That still seems to be the case, and perhaps it is even worse now. The rumour is that he goes the way of the emperor Gaius, with whom he shares a birthday. That he is given to bouts of madness and that they get worse as time goes on.'

Crispinus nodded. 'It is not quite so black and white, but I have watched our blessed emperor up close, and there is more than an element of truth to that. So, what of the succession?'

Rufinus shivered. Here it went...

'The emperor has been unable to sire a boy with his wife, and it seems his mistress is having no greater luck. He is childless and seems likely to remain so. If a smooth succession is still to be achieved, then he must look to adoption as many of his predecessors have.'

It was flatly said, and all true, but it felt like a betrayal of his oath to spout it.

Crispinus, however, nodded as he walked. 'This is true. But the problem is that the emperor sees himself as the living Hercules. He has no intention of willing his throne to anyone less than a god. There will be no adoption. And given that it seems there will be no offspring, then the succession becomes a crisis. You understand what that means?'

Rufinus shivered. Pescennius Niger and Clodius Albinus both leapt into his mind's eye. 'Potentially civil war, Tribune.'

'Quite. If we are to avoid the events that succeeded Nero's demise, then we must be prepared for the time when the emperor dies. We must be ready to put another man on the throne without delay, before argument and war can begin.'

Rufinus shivered again. This sounded horribly like what Severus had said more than once.

'Who would *you* put on the throne?' Crispinus said suddenly.

Rufinus stumbled for a moment, then fell into step again. 'There are few men who could rule with the wisdom of Augustus and the authority of Trajan,' he said quietly. 'My choice would be the general Pompeianus,' he added, echoing the plan of Severus to test the water with this tribune.

'Pompeianus? The emperor's former brother-in-law?'

'Yes, sir. He is a consummate politician, a successful general, part of the imperial family and wise enough to have kept both his rank and his head throughout the past decade.'

Crispinus nodded slowly. 'Of course, Pompeianus would never accept. He is too clever to take the throne, for he would not get to sit on it for long. He is a provincial from a small family and will not suit too many in the senate. The senate may be an outdated institution full of old women, but it is odd how often they kill emperors. Gaius, Nero, Domitian...'

'Then who?'

'Can you not guess, Rufinus? The governor here. Marcus Didius Julianus. His family are old Italian stock, and he has the same credentials as your Pompeianus but without the stigma of provinciality. Mark my words, Julianus will be the next emperor, and with his avarice and simplicity of design, he will be easy to control; and those of us who help make it happen will reap the benefit. You are at a crossroads, Centurion. We are here in Africa while we watch the reign of our lord and emperor decline and fail, and when the time comes, we will march upon Rome with the banner of Julianus above us. You could be one of us. Or not. It is your choice.'

The man turned away. 'Now I am bound for the governor. Go and sleep and contemplate your future, Centurion Rufinus. Are you a man seeking stability and the guaranteed succession of Julianus? Think hard.'

And with that the tribune turned and marched off along a corridor. Rufinus found himself standing at a crossroads.

How symbolic...

XIV – THE SEASONS TURN

The rest of the year for Rufinus was characterised by putting plans into place, inveigling his way ever deeper into the confidence of the Praetorian officers in Africa and learning about the men he was investigating.

The warm winter evolved into a comfortable spring as Rufinus carried out his fake examination in Carthage. By Aprilis he drew his 'case' to a close with a brief journey to Sicilia. With the aid of trustworthy agents in the province that he identified through communiques with Cestius, he managed to manufacture evidence of a frumentarius who had been at imagined work in the city since Didius Julianus arrived and who had been tracking the coin dies, in collusion with Borastes. This imagined spy he named Mittius after a character in his favourite play, and he managed to provide 'evidence' that Mittius had fled the city past the many guards and took ship for Sicilia.

He was actually lauded by both Tribune Crispinus and the governor for not only his thorough investigation, but the fact that he followed this Mittius to Syracusae and there hunted him down, bringing back his head. The mouldering head that arrived in Crispinus' office in a sealed bag actually belonged to a carpenter called Pirias who had died in a scaffolding accident, but that minor fact would never arise.

In the course of all this, he also checked out Pupput, where Curio had had his sojourn watching the port for the tribune's shipment. There had been nothing untoward about the man's time there, of course, for he had done exactly as ordered, thus creating his alibi, but there was a small discrepancy in timing: the matter of a missing half day when he'd in truth travelled via Zica to support Rufinus. That, though, seemed such a small thing that it would almost certainly never arise, and so there was nothing to connect Curio to that non-murder at the water temple. All in all, the Pupput investigation turned up nothing.

Returning to Carthage at the end of spring, he then set himself the task of getting to know the men who worked directly for Aper, though all four were tight lipped, which made it hard work. He now knew the corrupt members of the Guard to be led by Crispinus and his centurion, but there would be others yet hidden back in the fortress in Rome, and it was time to become more familiar with anyone that might lead him to others. After all, somewhere among the First Cohort were the men who had shot Attius Sacratus with an arrow and tried to kill Rufinus the Lucus Furrina, and they were not men of either century in Africa, for those incidents had stopped when they left Rome. Another pocket of Cleander's killers remained, who seemingly did not report to Aper or Crispinus.

In a miscalculated move, he continued to play on those stories he had begun to spread in Rome when trying to find a way into Aper's confidence, and an awkward conversation revealed that one of the four men turned out to be a cousin of Appius Numerius, the optio Rufinus had been forced to kill all those months ago in Baia. Appius Silva, as this man was called, was the one man in Africa who continued to view Rufinus was narrow eyed suspicion, knowing that the centurion was in Baia when his cousin died. Thus, Rufinus began to back off from them in an effort to avoid conflict with the increasingly watchful Appius Silva.

Summer came around quickly with a dry heat that sucked all the energy out of the body.

Rufinus continued to play the loyal conspirator. Beneath his guise, though, he watched and listened at all times. As the height of summer came and went, he became increasingly frustrated. He had seemingly got as far as he was going to with the officers, and he dare not get closer to those four men for fear of alerting Appius Silva. Coded messages sent via a trusted factor in the port went to Cestius in Rome, telling the man what Rufinus had discovered and asking for his opinion.

As far as Rufinus was concerned, he told Cestius, he'd discovered all he felt he could about Aper, Crispinus and Didius Julianus. Charges of embezzlement, misappropriation of imperial funds, counterfeiting and even murder were possibilities. The governor could be linked with the coins, especially with the testimony of Borastes, who lived on somewhere in Rome. Crispinus and Aper could be charged with the murder of Curio and their own lesser involvement with the coins. Given the ever-decreasing chance of pinning further crimes on the trio, Rufinus asked permission to bring them to justice, along with Aper's four henchmen. He would require the city's Urban Cohort to help apprehend them, since they outranked him with his own men and outnumbered him otherwise, and that would require the intervention of Vibius Cestius back in Rome.

He sweated for half a month awaiting his reply. When it came it was terse and to the point. Cestius refused to allow Rufinus to arrest the men. Didius Julianus was powerful and rich and in virtual autonomy in Africa. He was also clever. He would have alibis and defences in place and could retain sufficient legal expertise that he would drift free of any charges they could level at this point. Rufinus was only to bring in the governor if he could provide solid evidence of direct involvement in a crime. As it was, everything had been done through third parties. Moreover, though he could arrest Aper and Crispinus, to do so would ruin any chances of investigating further, and there was clearly still criminal activity to uncover.

Aper would fall easily enough for the crimes Rufinus had noted, but Cestius felt certain that the tribune would be able to pin all blame on the centurion and avoid any culpability or punishment himself. However Rufinus played it, the most he could realistically hope for was Aper's fall. And he couldn't simply challenge and execute a tribune of high standing as he'd done with lesser criminals over the previous year.

In short, Cestius wanted Rufinus to keep watching the governor for any further nod to criminal activity and forbade him from doing anything official unless he acquired new and irrefutable evidence of wrongdoing. Moreover, Rufinus was to keep in with the two Praetorian officers. Though he had clearly identified the heart of the corruption in the Guard, there would still be plenty of rotten apples linked to the tribune. Rufinus' next step was to try and identify any more of their comrades within the Praetorians.

Rufinus grumbled to himself as he continued to live a tense but fruitless life in the African capital. There seemed no easy way to swing conversation around to reveal other names. Pressing Aper or the tribune would be dangerous, and the other four men tended to always be together. Given the fact that Appius Silva threw him openly hostile looks now and was almost certainly only held in check by their superior's orders, Rufinus didn't really think that was a safe route for further enquiry, either.

Nothing happened. Autumn rolled around, and Rufinus found himself having to play things ever more carefully. He took preparatory counter measures as best he could against Flavius Silva, hoping to split him off from the other three and give Rufinus a chance to get closer to them. He complained to Aper about the man, citing the soldier's suspicious and angry attitude, and warning Aper that he thought the man might just do something stupid, since he seemed to think Rufinus had something to do with his cousin's death, despite the fact that even witnesses said the optio was killed in a brawl with a Dacian.

Tense. Troubling.

Autumn turned back into winter, and Rufinus sent another communique to Cestius, exasperatedly telling the frumentarius that he could see no way of getting any more names while they were cooped up here in Africa. Perhaps when they were in Rome again Crispinus, Aper, or the four henchmen might lead Rufinus to others, but not while idly sitting and fanning themselves in Carthage. And a return did not seem to be on the cards until Didius Julianus saw an opportunity in the offing.

The reply, which came through as winter set in, was not encouraging. Cestius seemed tense and nervous in his literary manner. He said that things in Rome were constant trouble and that he and his people were constantly busy, but he would see what he could do to help. Rufinus could picture the issues with which the frumentarii would be dealing. If rumours were to be given credence, then the emperor was almost at war with his senate, who'd had their seats revoked at the games, while the emperor systematically went about renaming everything after himself and having statues of himself as Hercules raised on every street corner. It worried Rufinus.

Cestius' solution became apparent mere days later.

A letter arrived in Carthage by imperial courier with the seal of the Praetorian Prefect, Laetus. Rufinus never saw the message, which was taken straight to Tribune Crispinus, but the contents became clear almost immediately. The tribune called his two centurions into the office and informed them angrily that the commander of the Guard had ordered them back to Rome. It seemed that Crispinus had pulled strings to secure a long-term duty in Carthage, but the prefect had decided that enough was enough. He wanted the two centuries back in Rome where they belonged.

Rufinus privately exulted, for all the apparent disappointment he displayed among the others. Africa had been a means to an end, and he had achieved that end early on in the year. Dragging things out had done nothing really but make him nervous as he continued to maintain his façade without discovering anything else of use. Heading back to Rome would give him the chance to move on, to open up new paths in his investigation into the Guard, to identify other threads in Crispinus' web. Being removed from Didius Julianus' company would not impair any of his work after all. The governor was as corrupt as Clodius Albinus or Pescennius Niger, and like seemingly all men of rank and privilege he was jostling for position in an anticipated succession crisis. But being near him would uncover nothing new for Rufinus. Being back among the Guard might.

Thus, it was as the festivities for Saturnalia were being prepared around Carthage that the two centuries of Praetorians formed up in the port and took ship once more. Rufinus found himself a comfortable position towards the rear of the vessel, relatively secluded, and Acheron curled up beside him as they put to sea once more, Crispinus and Aper both fuming over their unexpected recall. Rufinus dearly hoped that Cestius had been careful in engineering this. The moment they arrived in Rome, the tribune would undoubtedly rush to the prefect and complain about his recall, hoping to return to Africa. If the trail of the decision led back to the frumentarii somehow there would be trouble.

He had to trust Cestius. The man was always careful.

The journey was slow. No one sailed the Mare Nostrum in winter unless they had urgent business, and the ship's trierarch had been distinctly unimpressed with the order to leave the safety of Carthage. Still, they had done so, risking the bad currents, the periodic storms and the general trouble of a winter sea. Twelve days it would take back to Rome.

The first day was uneventful, but then it had been a short hop across the bay from Carthage to the small harbour town of Hermaeum on Africa's eastern promontory. A hair raising day's sailing from there took them across the open channel to Sicilia, putting in at Lilybaeum for the night. While Rufinus and the others aboard the ship had had a bad enough time keeping their footing on the slippery, lurching decks, Acheron had slid and fallen about in a near panic, unable to stay stable, lacking the ability to grip onto things. Rufinus agreed then that for the rest of the journey, when aboard ship the hound would be placed at the rear of the cargo deck and tethered to the bulkhead for his own safety.

From Lilybaeum they spent two more days hugging the southern coast of Sicilia, staying at some port whose name escaped Rufinus before putting in at Messana in preparation for the worst leg. Tomorrow they would brave the straits of Messana to Regium. It was just a few short miles, but a dangerous enough stretch that the trierarch had set aside a whole day, for if they made it through safely then the crew would need the rest of the day in port to recover.

Rufinus had never done this journey in winter, but he remembered it plenty of times in better seasons, and in his time as prefect of the Misenum Fleet, the journey had been infamous. No one in their right mind did the strait in winter. Here was the place where Scylla and Charybdis had taken half a dozen of Odysseus' shipmates in the ancient tale, likely a rationalisation of their drowning in the treacherous waters.

As the ship sat at dock in Messana and the soldiers reported to the transit barracks at the edge of the port, Rufinus maintained his disgruntled expression, matching those of the other two officers who had no desire to return to the capital yet. They had been expecting to sit out the rest of the emperor's reign in Africa, assuming said reign to be nearing its end. Keeping up a sour face was not difficult, really, given the fact that each and every man on that ship, be they officer or soldier, sailor or Praetorian, lived in tense fear of the morning's sailing.

The transit barracks were the same as those elsewhere: a simple affair of timber and hard beds, cold and miserable, especially in the middle of winter. The tribune, of course, was given a room in the town, but Rufinus and Aper were appointed a barrack block each for they and their men. Just like the ones in a standard fort, the structure was split into rooms, each housing a contubernium of eight men in bunks, the room at the end given over to the centurion, the next to his optio and the unit's standard bearer.

Rufinus entered his room and sighed, shivering, dropping his kit bag on the bed. The days sailing around the Sicilian coast had been horrible, accompanied by bucking and rolling waves higher than a man and a constant drizzle that had gone largely unnoticed by the passengers and crew who had spent every hour soaked with seawater anyway.

Rufinus had rarely felt as cold or as wet in his life as he did now. He needed to warm up and get clean, scrubbing off the salt of the day's seawater. Knocking on Gamburio's door, he left Acheron with the optio for company and then popped back to his room. Stripping down to just tunic and boots and grabbing a spare garment from his kit bag, he locked his door and scurried across through the drizzle into the small balneum that occupied one corner of the compound. In the changing room, he grabbed a towel from the hook, shuffled out of his tunic and boots and slipped, shivering, into the warm bath.

There he lazed for half an hour, letting his body relax and recover from the day's trials and trying not to think of what was coming on the next leg of the trip. Inevitably his thoughts wandered back to what would happen when they returned to the Castra Praetoria in a few days. Presumably Aper and Crispinus would begin their machinations once more. In doing so, and with Rufinus now a trusted ally, he should be able to begin tracing their lines of patronage among the Guard, picking out the names of the other men Cleander had controlled.

He was comfortable, rested, and relatively happy with his plans when he emerged from the baths, dried himself and threw on the dry spare tunic. Bracing himself, he held the used wet tunic above his head to prevent too much exposure and hurried out into the rain once more, thudding across the courtyard and in among the barrack blocks, where he turned the last corner towards his own. He stopped suddenly, alert, as he caught sight of his door just in time to see a figure slip out of it and hurry away. The rain had increased, and there was now a dusky half-light, and all he could tell was that the figure was wearing a Praetorian tunic.

Heart racing once more, he ran along the barrack block and turned the corner, looking this way and that, trying to spot the man. All he could see was rainy empty alleyways. Then he spotted it. The door in the next barrack block bounced once, having been shut, hard, just as Rufinus rounded the corner.

He peered at the block. That was the barracks of Aper's century, and the room in question was the third along. Not Aper, then, nor his juniors. But there was no doubt in Rufinus' mind that the closest room would contain Aper's four henchmen.

One of them had been in his room while he was in the baths. Now he cursed himself for having left Acheron with the optio. He didn't like leaving the big hound on his own these days, since he was no young pup now, but had Acheron been in his room, no interloper would have got in.

There was no point in going any further. If he went inside that room, he would just alert the men that he was on to them. Besides, he felt certain that the individual responsible would have been Appius Silva, the suspicious cousin. Chewing on his lip, worried, he hurtled back to his own door and swung it open. The lock had been picked expertly, but the man had not dallied to refasten it, probably hearing Rufinus' approaching footsteps. He was lucky really that he'd returned when he had, else he might never have known about this.

His room looked just as he'd left it, which was to say barely touched. His armour and the bulky kit were still in storage on the ship with everyone else's. His kit bag with his personal effects, though, sat on the bed, along with his belt, sword, cloak, helmet and vine stick. With a sick sense of foreboding, he hurried over to the bag and delved inside. It had been put back well, with barely any sign it had been disturbed. Had he not been expecting it, he probably wouldn't have noticed the odd things slightly out of place.

His hand went straight to the one thing he felt sure had changed. His purse was the same size and weight, yet as he opened it and checked the side compartment within, the counterfeit coin from Carthage had gone.

Appius Silva had taken the evidence. Rufinus felt the edge of panic then. What should he do? Undoubtedly Silva would take the coin to Aper and denounce Rufinus. Rufinus forced himself to calm down. The centurion already knew that Rufinus was unpopular with this man. Rufinus had told Aper that he thought Silva was out to get him. He would continue to play that role. The moment Aper accused him of anything, he would shift the blame. He would deny all knowledge of the coin and claim that Silva was planting evidence to frame him. It sounded plausible. It sounded neat. He felt sure he could pull that off. With luck, the backlash would remove Silva from the equation entirely.

Satisfied that he could turn this around, he put the purse back and organised his room before calling next door, collecting Acheron and then locking his door and climbing into bed. He lay awake for two hours, waiting for the knock at the door announcing Aper's arrival to accuse him of something, but no knock came, and eventually sleep claimed him.

He rose with the buccina call early the next morning and dressed, nervous and tense, working through things in his head. It was possible that Silva had told Aper and Aper was only delaying dealing with the matter until he had seen the tribune. But another possibility had occurred to Rufinus during the night, and he felt it was more likely. Silva still suspected Rufinus of his cousin's death. He had evidence of Rufinus being involved in the mint issue, but selling Rufinus out would probably not satisfy the man's vengeance. He would want to deal with Rufinus personally. Silva was biding his time. He would come for Rufinus and then, after killing him, would be able to use the coin to justify his actions to the officers. Yes, that sounded more likely.

He would have to watch his back now.

The morning was cold and the air damp, but the rain had stopped during the night and the two centuries formed in the courtyard and there awaited the tribune's arrival. Rufinus felt his summation of the situation borne out as he stood there. Aper was not paying him any attention, clearly blissfully unaware of Rufinus' guilty possession.

Silva, on the other hand, was watching him carefully beneath lowered brows.

Rufinus tried not to look back at the man and was grateful when Crispinus arrived and the entire column moved out once more, down to the harbour and the jetty where the ship awaited. Rufinus elected, along with a few of the others, to travel below this time, in the cargo space, though not at the stern, where Acheron was already tethered. Most soldiers preferred not to be below, for during a storm a man can leap away from a ruined ship's deck, but if he was down below, he would sink with the vessel. The simple fact was, though, that Rufinus knew any man who went into the water in the straits in bad weather was as doomed as a man who drowned in the ship's hold.

The vessel put to sea and within half an hour of sliding out from the jetty, Rufinus was already feeling unwell. The ship bucked and dipped, rolling from side to side with every dreadful pull of the infamous currents, and he was far from the first man to throw up, even down here, among the cargo. For added stability, he wedged himself behind a pallet of waterproofed sacks, in a shadowed corner against the cold, damp hull, feet pressed against a wooden beam.

He could not say how long he sat there before it happened. It seemed like an eternity of being thrown about, coughing up bile and vomit, listening to wooden groans and ominous booming and crashing noises accompanied by the wails and cries of terrified men.

He almost died in an instant, so unprepared was he for any danger not of Neptune's doing. Silva was suddenly there, in his secluded corner of the cargo hold, sword lancing out as he leapt around the pile of roped-up sacks. In the instant he appeared and thrust, Rufinus let instinct take over, He simply relaxed his knees that had been braced against the timbers, and he sank away beneath the blow.

Silva's sword point slammed into the timber of the hull a hair's breadth from his target's neck.

Rufinus cried out in shock. His sword was sheathed, and the sheath had tangled up behind his legs as he dropped, leaving him unarmed and in a knot, unable to draw the blade. His left hand dropped to the other side of his belt and felt for the hilt of the pugio settled there even as his arm came up to ward off a blow as though it were a shield.

Silva pulled back his sword, issuing a feral snarl, and struck once more, this time chopping down with his blade. Rufinus, still concentrating on the fight, was vaguely aware that another figure had tottered and slipped into view across the other side of the hold, drawn by the noise.

'Help,' Rufinus shouted. 'He's gone mad!'

His forearm caught the downward strike of the sword, but because he had swept the arm up and out, he intercepted the blade before it could build up much momentum, and close to the hilt, so all he suffered was a painful thin cut and a blow that would blossom into an impressive bruise.

He found his knife but suddenly decided against it. If he had his blade out then culpability for this fight would be questionable, but if he was unarmed and the man across the way had seen as much, the whole thing would be seen as Silva's doing. Still, he couldn't let Silva get away. The man would never stop making attempts like this, and if he failed now, he would use the coin to shift the focus back to Rufinus.

Silva bellowed angrily as Rufinus, hissing with pain, deflected his strike. Then, having pulled his left hand away from the dagger hilt, he swung it upwards, turning it into an uppercut. His bunched fist connected with Silva's jaw, sending him sprawling back with a cry. Rufinus pulled himself to his feet, swaying about, partially with disorientation and partially with the rolling of the ship. He gave his attacker no time to recover. As Silva, still shouting oaths and curses through a painful jaw, raised his sword for another attack, Rufinus dived, hitting him in the midriff with a shoulder and barging him back, bringing him down to the timber with a crash and knocking the air from him. He was vaguely aware of several other figures now, watching in fascinated excitement.

Silva groaned, floundering beneath him.

Rufinus had an opportunity. Just the one. It had to look good. Like self-defence.

'Stay down, you mad bastard,' he shouted at Silva, and grabbed his hair, slamming his head back against the timbers. That was all the watchers would see. They did not see that, as the man's head smacked back down to the wood, Rufinus dropped with it and twisted the head until the neck cracked, and Silva gasped in fatal agony.

A broken neck. An accident. Obviously, Rufinus had been defending himself from the assault and had not meant to take it so far.

He staggered back away from the body, gasping for air and throwing up again. He waved a finger at the body, trying to maintain his fiction. 'Restrain the lunatic,' he shouted to the other men. As he gasped in air and peeled back his sodden tunic sleeve to examine the

169

damage to his aching arm, those men who had watched the fight in shock staggered over to the body of Silva.

'He's dead,' someone announced.

'What?' demanded Rufinus with feigned disbelief, rising one more.

'Broke his neck, the poor sod.'

'Poor sod, my arse,' Rufinus spat. 'The idiot attacked me.'

There was a chorus of noises signalling agreement among the men, and Rufinus straightened, struggling to stay on his feet. In moments there were approaching footsteps. Aper lurched across the rolling deck, closely followed by another of his four henchmen.

'What the fuck happened?' the centurion demanded angrily.

Rufinus was saved having to defend his actions as one of the witnesses stepped forwards. 'Appius Silva attacked the centurion, sir. Tried to cut him to pieces.'

Aper frowned, his glance going back and forth between the two men. Silva lay on the floor, his head at an unnatural angle now, wobbling about with the motion of the ship, his sword still gripped in his dead hand, blood on the edge. Rufinus stood panting, a red line across his forearm, weapons still sheathed, face bleak.

'What happened?' the centurion said again, this time directly to Rufinus.

'I told you this was going to happen,' Rufinus spat. 'This idiot's had it in for me for ages.'

Aper chewed his lip, looking back and forth between them again. Finally, he turned to the man behind him. 'Get him up top and remove his personal effects. Neptune can have the body.' Then he turned to Rufinus. 'Do you need a medicus? There might be one when we get to Regium.'

Rufinus shook his head. 'It's just a cut. Luckily the poor mad bastard's not very good with a sword either. I'll wrap it up for now and get it bandaged properly later. Other than that, it'll get better soon enough.'

And with that Aper nodded and departed. Four men manhandled the body back up to the deck above. Rufinus felt faintly irritated that the counterfeit coin he had kept as evidence was somewhere on the body and would now be lost among the other possessions. Still, he'd come out of this better than he'd hoped, his reputation intact and one less enemy on the horizon.

He sat wedged once more in his corner for the rest of the unpleasant crossing, a torn rag around the cut on his arm. It wasn't bad, but he could feel the bruising blossoming already. Still, he was grateful when they finally pulled into the protective arms of Regium's harbour and out of the terrible currents.

That night he bathed again, safe in the knowledge that Silva was no longer around to rummage through his things, his body somewhere back out in the sea. Still, this time he left Acheron in the room. After the bath, he dressed his cut properly and relaxed for the first time in days.

The remaining week of travel was relatively comfortable, travelling northwest along the Italian coast and stopping at a well-known town each night. Rufinus had almost begun to enjoy the voyage as they pulled into Portus on the morning of the eighth day out of Regium, and it was only as they slid up beside the jetty and he peered out across the great port that he realised the significance of the date. Garlands and streamers hung around the buildings and streets, celebrating both the god Aesculapius and the seeing in of a new year. It was the Kalends of Januarius, and the two new consuls were being seen into office this very day.

He smiled as they banged against the jetty and the ropes were thrown out, securing the ship. It was then that he realised something was wrong. There might be signs of festivity, but there was an odd dark undercurrent to the atmosphere in Portus. More than that, the place should still be busy, even in mid-winter and during a festival, but there were few souls to be seen.

The oddness of it all seemed to have sunk into the other travellers too, for as the crew busied themselves securing the ship, Tribune Crispinus strode over to the rail and waved at an official looking fellow who was deep in discussion with one of his workers.

'You there. Why is the port so empty? Where are the Guard detachment and all the workers?'

The official turned from his conversation and looked up at the tribune, his face pale and shocked.

'Have you not heard, soldier?'

'Of course not,' snapped Crispinus, 'we've been at sea. What is it?'

'The emperor,' the man shouted back. 'The emperor is dead!'

Part Three

Succession

Year of the Consulship of Sosius and Ericius

193 AD

Multi committunt eadem diuerso crimina fato: ille crucem sceleris pretium tulit, hic diadema.

(Many commit the same crime, yet with different results; for his reward one man will gain a cross, the other a crown)

- Juvenal, Satire XIII

XV – A DARK DAY

R ufinus rode like the wind, along with the small party of men, hurtling along the main road from Ostia-Portus to Rome. Slightly ahead of him Tribune Crispinus led the party, setting the pace, while half a dozen of his Praetorians who had confirmed that they were capable in a saddle came along behind as the escort.

The ship had docked in the wake of the bleak news, but the moment the tribune alighted, he'd sent the vessel straight back, despite the season, the weather, the dangers and the lack of turnaround time, heading for Carthage once more. Aper had unhappily remained on board with his century, making for the governor, Didius Julianus, hoping to be the one to break the news to the would-be successor.

The tribune had then commandeered horses from the courier station in Ostia and led Rufinus and the small group of mounted infantry back to the city. Optio Gamburio was following on aboard one of the barges up the Tiber with the rest of the century, and with Acheron too. The tribune was in no mood to wait, though. Time was now of the essence.

The emperor was dead. Rome was suffering a power vacuum and the succession far from certain. If Crispinus wanted his candidate on the throne he had to move fast and fill that vacuum. The alternative was either a different figure stepping into the breach and claiming the purple or that thing that no one wanted, no matter how rotten their soul: civil war.

As they travelled, passing small knots of people on the road, Rufinus found himself musing on the situation, darkly. Never trust what they say in the histories, he thought. When an emperor died, writers always made a big thing of the public reaction. In Rufinus' literary experience, the death of an emperor heralded one of two things: either wailing and gnashing of teeth as the public tore out their hair in grief for their beloved ruler, or angry glee as the despot was toppled, accompanied by merry looting, smashing of statues and the hailing of the first hapless idiot they could find hiding behind a curtain.

The truth was nothing like that, of course. Rufinus had watched the world when Marcus Aurelius died, and he was seeing it again now, on the death of a man, rather shockingly, younger than himself.

The people did not wail. They did not cheer. There were, in fact, two immediately visible symptoms of an emperor's passing. Confusion was one, bordering on panic. Everyone immediately worried about what would happen next. Would the following incumbent be set upon massacring those who cheered his predecessor? Would he, and this was *most* important for the people, raise taxes. The other thing was a weird and immediate consideration of how a person might profit from the situation. When Aurelius had died Rufinus had actually seen a stall in one street selling what purported to be fragments of the old emperor's fingernails. The incredible thing was that they had sold in droves. Rufinus could imagine that by the next dawn there would be small statues of Commodus available on every street corner to add to the household shrine.

How had it happened? That was something they were all still waiting to clear up. As they had gathered horses and prepared, the tribune had questioned officials in the port and people in the street. They had heard four different stories so far, and there would be a dozen more floating around yet. But they all agreed on certain things. The emperor had been assassinated. His mistress had been behind the plot and had dragged in several conspirators.

The name of Prefect Laetus cropped up as an assassin in two of the versions, and Rufinus prayed to every god he could name that this was not true. Laetus was a good man by all reputation. He had come in to heal Rome after the evils of Cleander. If he had now slid into a world of assassinations and wickedness, where would it end? It was bad enough Praetorians reneging on their oath of loyalty to the emperor, but for one of them, the *leader* of them even, to actively wield the assassin's blade was unthinkable. What use was it Rufinus cutting out the corruption within the Guard if even the best of them turned out to be rotten in the soul?

Fuming, he pulled his horse slightly forwards, bringing himself level with the tribune. They were going to break the beasts if they were not careful. They really should slow down, but that was not going to happen today. Crispinus became aware of the centurion coming alongside.

'What do we do now, sir?'

The tribune narrowed his eyes at the question in such an open location, but glancing back he could see only their own soldiers and even they were far enough back that they would hear little if anything. Besides, with what had now happened, speaking of

175

succession was hardly a treasonable offence. Everyone on every street corner would be speaking of it.

'It has been but a matter of hours. Nothing should have been decided yet. No one will make the mistake of pulling a dribbling uncle from behind a curtain and crowning him. The senate will be considering the situation carefully. There are no direct male relations ready to take the throne. Everything is wide open and every man who might claim the succession is currently at a distance, serving in the provinces.'

Rufinus tried not to compare the situation to a similar event in history and failed entirely. Right now, Didius Julianus was in Africa, Pescennius Niger in Syria, Clodius Albinus in Britannia and Severus in Pannonia. Over a century ago, when Nero had died, Galba had been in Hispania, Otho in Lusitania and Vespasian in Judea. No one wanted a second war of four emperors.

'You intend to address the senate, sir?'

Crispinus' lip lifted in a sneer. 'No. I intend to secure the support of the Guard for Julianus, and then give the senate an ultimatum. This is not a time for democracy. This is a time for decisive action.'

'Will the Guard support you, sir?' Rufinus probed. There would still be plenty of former agents of Cleander hidden among them, in league with Crispinus, but would they be enough to swing the whole Guard?

'I can convince the prefect. If it is true that he wielded the knife, then he will be desperate to be seen to be doing the right thing now. And the men? Well you know the men, centurion. Coin buys loyalty more than any oath. Chests of coins have been arriving from Africa for months now.'

Rufinus blinked. The coins from the Carthage mint were meant for the Guard? The tribune was actually going to feed his own men counterfeit coins just to secure Julianus' position? Insanity. He tried to keep his expression flat.

On they rode, closing on the city, and it was still only mid-morning when they arrived, passing through shocked and panicked streets and beneath the crumbling arch of the Porta Raudusculana. They did not slacken their pace as they entered the bounds of the city, clattering along the road down the Aventine valley, past the circus and the Palatine and on up the hills beyond.

Rufinus glanced only once at the imperial palace as they rode past. Somewhere up on those slopes lay Commodus, son of Marcus Aurelius, the only emperor ever born to the purple, the living

Hercules, beloved of his people. Rufinus shivered as they rode on. He'd never thought to see another emperor die.

At the crest of the hill, they passed beneath the fragmentary ruins of the Porta Viminalis and on to the great fortress of the Praetorians that loomed above the city. Rufinus swallowed nervously. He had to do something. Everything had happened so quickly. After months of waiting in Africa, impotent, watching these corrupt and criminal officers preparing for a succession he'd not truly believed was coming, suddenly it had happened, faster than any of them could have anticipated. And the ridiculous thing was that despite Julianus still being in Africa, he stood a better chance than many. As the tribune had pointed out, most of the contenders were very distant.

Rufinus had to do something, because right now he was on the cusp of being able to tear out the rot in the Guard, roots and leaves and all. But if Crispinus succeeded and Didius Julianus took the throne then those same corrupt men would more or less control the empire, their puppet on the throne owing them his position. That could not be allowed to happen.

Severus was going to be no help. He was too far away. And even if Rufinus wanted Albinus or Niger to ascend, they couldn't from where they were; not without civil war, anyway. Pertinax was in the city, for he was the prefect of the Urban Cohorts, but he did not seek the throne himself. If Severus spoke true, then Pertinax and he sought to put the great general Pompeianus on the throne. Where would that shrewd old man be? During all the years of trouble he had kept himself safely obscure in the hinterland. Likely he was still in a villa somewhere in Campania.

There would probably be no aid in the city. He wondered momentarily if the frumentarii could help, but quickly discarded that notion. He knew their duty, for he was one of them now. Their oath to the emperor was paramount, but the emperor was dead. The frumentarii would not involve themselves in the succession. They would sit back and wait and then take their oath to the next man on the throne, no matter who it was. That was what the frumentarii were. They could not afford to be politically biased. Neither, in truth, could the Praetorians. It was anathema to their whole purpose to kill and make emperors.

What could he do? He would have to play this by the moment, waiting for an opportunity to influence what was happening as it happened.

Before he knew it, they were passing beneath the arched gate of the Castra Praetoria. Straight to the headquarters building they went, and Rufinus was interested to see that at the grand entrance the standards and vexilla of several centuries and cohorts wavered. Something was obviously already happening. From Crispinus' narrow, suspicious eyes, the tribune had realised it too. Slowing and then halting, he dropped lightly from the saddle, Rufinus following suit. The tribune snapped his fingers and pointed at the standard of the First Cohort's eighth century.

'You. Go to the stores. Find the African shipments and bring them here as fast as you can.'

Rufinus' heart lurched. The 'African shipments' could only be Julianus' fake coins. Crispinus was going to buy the loyalty of the Guard, and he was going to do it now. Swallowing his nerves, Rufinus followed the man through the crowded arch and into the great courtyard.

Ironically a grand statue of Commodus glowered at them from one corner, a recent replacement for the one that had stood here for years, for in this representation the emperor wore a lion pelt and leaned on a great club. Minerva glared at him from the opposite corner.

As Crispinus and Rufinus entered from that gate they could see officers of the Guard filling the place, centurions and tribunes and a few of the more highly positioned lessers, all forming a circle at the centre of the courtyard where two men stood in hissed argument, angry arms gesturing. Prefect Laetus, the commander of the Guard and, if rumour was true, assassin of the emperor, stood face to face with Pertinax, the Urban Prefect, whose own men also occupied one corner of this very fortress.

As they moved to the gathering, Crispinus spotted one of his fellow tribunes and angled towards him. 'Are the rumours true?' he asked.

The other tribune, a man with a flat nose and high forehead, nodded. 'Drowned in his bath by his favourite wrestler.'

Rufinus blinked. This was nothing like any of the four rumours they'd heard.

'What?' snapped Crispinus, equally surprised.

'Apparently, he was about to turn the senate into a bloodbath, or so they say, and the prefect, the chamberlain and the emperor's own woman had the wrestler do him in.'

'What are they arguing about?'

The tribune shrugged. 'Laetus thinks the senate should take on the succession, as they did after Domitian. Pertinax has something else in mind but he's making us wait for something.'

'Since when did the Guard wait for the Urban Cohorts?' snorted Crispinus.

'Well, quite.'

And with that, Crispinus was pushing forwards again, ordering centurions out of the way as he reached the central ring. Rufinus remained at his shoulder, the hair at the nape of his neck bristling. He had that curious feeling of this being one of those great and momentous moments where history turned on the flip of a coin. He was almost holding his breath.

'The people cannot condone a vacuum,' Laetus was saying, wagging an angry finger at Pertinax. 'If we do not move now, then one of the dangerous governors with veteran legions will suddenly find himself wearing a purple cloak and marching on Rome. This needs to be settled now. The senate should debate and select a candidate.'

Pertinax was shaking his head. 'You're quite right, Laetus. It needs to be done now. Giving it to the damned senate will just delay the issue. Believe me, I've sat among their august number and it takes half a month just to decide who sits where.'

Laetus sagged. 'Publius, I respect you. We all respect you. There are few more successful generals and senators here, but no one man should be allowed to influence the succession, other than the emperor himself. This is a job for the senate.'

Rufinus chewed his lip. There was a commotion behind them, and he and half the crowd turned to see a small party of horsemen clattering through the archway. The various officers opened up a space before them and the group halted close by. Rufinus was surprised to see that they bore the uniforms of the Urban Cohort. Their presence would irritate many of the Praetorian officers, but then he noted the important thing; the one figure among them that mattered.

Tiberius Claudius Pompeianus.

The old general looked even older now. In fact, he had to be nearly seventy in Rufinus' estimation. He looked drawn and tired. His eyes were surrounded by black circles of exhaustion, and he sagged as he dropped from the horse, but all of that changed in a moment. Rufinus realised the man was tired beyond belief. He had been riding through the night, by the looks of it, yet the moment he stood, he straightened and shed years like a fighting bird sheds feathers. Straight and tall, he was dressed in the armour of a campaigning general, that same armour Rufinus remembered him in all those years ago in Marcomannia.

Rufinus felt a thrill of hope. This was a man who could rule and rule well. It had been Pompeianus who had guided Rufinus through his early days in Rome and taught him how to navigate the dangerous political currents of the court. A shrewd man, a good man, a respected general and former senator and, by marriage, a son-in-law of Marcus Aurelius. Who could argue against his succession?

Indeed, as Pompeianus strode like a conquering hero into that circle at the centre of the courtyard, Rufinus could see the respect in almost every face.

Almost.

Tribune Crispinus had a sour and angry expression.

Laetus turned, and Rufinus could see an instant shift from disbelief to acceptance. Pompeianus even suited him. There would be no civil war. No crisis. Everyone would accept the old general.

Pertinax stepped back.

'Tiberius,' he smiled and then shook the hand of the new arrival. Rufinus felt an odd thrill, watching two of Rome's greatest generals, both of whom he knew personally, preparing to place a worthy figure on the throne.

'Dragged from my bed in the middle of the night,' Pompeianus said loudly and with mock anger. 'It's almost as if there was a crisis.'

Men laughed. Even Pertinax and Laetus laughed.

Crispinus did not laugh. His lip was twitching, and he turned now, looking over his shoulder. Rufinus followed suit to see three carts being ushered in through the gate by men of the First Cohort. The African treasure. Rufinus felt his certainty slip away. Pompeianus was the obvious choice, but how far had the Guard fallen? Could their loyalty truly be bought so easily?

Trembling with anticipation, his head snapped back and forth between the approaching carts and the figures in the circle, settling on the latter as Pertinax addressed the assembled officers.

'There cannot be a vacuum in the palace. We cannot afford a civil war, nor the time it takes for the senate to choose a new candidate. The succession must be settled immediately and in a manner in which the entirety of Rome can enjoy confidence. There can be no other choice. Tiberius Claudius Pompeianus is the man to rule us. What say you?'

There were a variety of cheers and positive noises, and even Laetus was nodding, and it was only as the din began to abate that Rufinus realised Pompeianus had his hands in the air, trying to silence the crowd. When there was only the rumbling of the approaching carts, Pompeianus turned slowly.

'You seem of one accord,' he said. 'You appear to have considered all matters bar one.'

Laetus and Pertinax leaned forwards, frowning.

'You never asked me,' Pompeianus said simply, 'whether I want it.'

A shocked silence settled around the courtyard. Laetus and Pertinax exchanged baffled looks, and Pompeianus gave them both an oddly apologetic smile. 'I am truly sorry, my friends, but you have cast your lot in the wrong bag. I never sought the throne and even now, with no shiny arse to polish it, I am still not your man.'

'But you must be,' Pertinax said urgently. 'There is no one else. We need you.'

'There *is* someone else,' Crispinus announced loudly. Rufinus found himself being ushered aside as those three carts were brought forth and rumbled to a halt at the edge of the circle. Rufinus found himself willing the crowd to be better than this. To hold to their principles and not to agree to put a man on the throne for mere financial gain.

'A man,' Crispinus shouted, 'who already sends his largesse to a loyal Guard.'

He turned and gestured to the optio on the cart and Rufinus spun and looked up. The soldier's face was ashen grey. Rufinus frowned. The soldier cleared his throat nervously.

Tribune Crispinus waved at the man again. 'Go ahead.'

The optio winced.

'They're empty, Tribune.'

There was a strange, strangled silence. Rufinus turned his head back to the tribune, whose face was passing through a dozen different emotions in quick succession. It settled on an uneasy combination of disbelief and fury.

'What?'

'Empty, sir. All of them.'

'How?'

'I don't know, sir. They were full yesterday. We check them every few days as ordered.'

Rufinus had to fight to keep the triumph and glee from his expression. There was only one man who could arrange such a thing. A man who had managed to leave a purse of coins on Rufinus' bed without any sign he'd ever been in the camp.

Vibius Cestius. Only he and his frumentarii could have done this. Moreover, thanks to Rufinus' coded letters from Carthage, Cestius was the only man outside Crispinus' cronies who knew about the coins. Somehow, he had spirited them away.

The tribune stormed across to the nearest cart and pulled himself up to check, as though the optio might be lying.

'If your little performance is over, Crispinus,' Laetus said from the circle, 'we have matters of import.'

Rufinus simply didn't know where to look with all this going on around him, but when it came down to it the future of the empire had been taken out of Crispinus' hands with the stolen coins, and now it was being decided in that open circle at the heart of the Praetorian camp. He listened hard.

'You should have consulted me,' Pompeianus was saying defensively. 'I was not made to be emperor, my friends.'

'Then why did you come at my calling?' Pertinax said in exasperation. 'Why race through the night if you did not want the purple?'

Pompeianus snorted. 'The throne is a poisoned chalice, Pertinax. In my opinion only a fool actively seeks it. But there are men who can fill that role every bit as well as I. Why did I hurry to Rome, old friend? To laud you and to support you.'

The old general turned a slow circle, arms out like an orator addressing his audience. 'You all know Publius Helvius Pertinax. A man who started out commanding a cohort in Syria. A decorated hero of Parthia, of Marcomannia, of Raetia and Noricum. The man who quelled the British mutiny. The man who settled the Dacian disaster and regulated the gold flow from there. Senator of note. Twice consul. Who better to sit upon the throne?'

Whatever Laetus said next was lost in an eruption of positivity as the officers of the Guard threw their support behind Pertinax now. Whatever it was, it was itself positive, going by the look on his face. Pertinax turned slowly, Rufinus was glad to see what appeared to be genuine surprise, tinged with nerves, on the old general's face. He had truly not sought this. There were few better signs at this point than not having *sought* power. Rufinus wondered how Severus would react to the news.

Pertinax was shaking his head, not in denial but in wonder. Finally, he shrugged. 'If it is the will of you all, then I would be churlish to refuse.'

Another cheer erupted and was swiftly diminished as the new emperor waved his hands. 'But this is too important to simply decide here. I will abide by the will of the senate. If they confirm me then I shall accept. If not, then I shall bow out and they will select another.'

Rufinus could see the approval in Laetus' face, and this unexpected humility had gone down well with the gathered officers. Even Pompeianus was smiling.

Rufinus turned.

Crispinus was not smiling. Indeed, he and his cart-borne soldiers were the only ones not cheering. Their thunderous expressions portended terrible things. Rufinus had been careful throughout to keep his expression straight. He had to play the conspirator if he wanted to stay in with the tribune. And he did. Crispinus' plans to put his own man on the throne had failed, almost certainly due to Rufinus' timely warnings and the sneaky competence of Cestius' grain men, but this was not over.

The corrupt officers were still in the Guard and still powerful, and while Commodus, may the heavens accept his soul, had gone, Rufinus had a new emperor to protect. Pertinax was a good man, strong and wise but, in accepting the purple, Rufinus was fairly sure he had just made himself a target for those corrupt speculatores in the Guard. Pertinax would need protecting, and the machinations of the tribune and his men would go from strength to strength now, with a new foe on the throne.

He tried not to flinch as Crispinus dropped back down beside him and grabbed him by the shoulder, steering him round and away from the circle, to the edge of the courtyard, anger and shock radiating from him. As they reached the edge, Rufinus felt panic. Had the tribune decided he was behind this somehow?

Crispinus slammed him against the wall and jabbed a finger at his face. 'Rufinus, I have no idea how this has happened, and I am furious beyond reason. Months of work shattered in one moment. But we are not done. All is not lost. Aper is heading back for Africa and it will be a month at the least before he returns. Now *you* are my man on the Palatine. Make your way into Pertinax's favour. Stay close to him. Watch him like a hawk. Whatever Pertinax decides to do, I want to know about it before he has a chance to do it, you understand? His reign will be brief, I swear it.'

Before Rufinus could do more than nod hurriedly, the tribune let go of him and stormed away, out through the gate.

Rufinus stood, shaking.

The whole world had changed in one morning, and yet the same danger and the same mission remained.

The following two hours were some of the busiest in Rufinus' life. He and his few men present had to quickly change into fresh uniform and pristine toga and assemble with the rest of the First

Cohort outside the headquarters. From there they escorted the new emperor into the city, Prefect Laetus at their head alongside Pertinax, just behind them all the Guard's tribunes, with Crispinus wearing a carefully blank expression. They accompanied the emperor to the senate, though somehow word had gone ahead, and the entire gathering of Rome's fathers was there ready to welcome him. In moments they confirmed their approval of the new emperor, and Pertinax was turned about once more and hurried over to the Palatine.

There would be official ceremonies and parades, extraordinary meetings of the senate, sacrifices and money thrown to the people and so much more, but that would happen tomorrow. Such things took time to organise.

It felt strange walking into the palace. As long as he had been here, Rufinus had known this as Commodus' palace, and every step he took in the wake of the new emperor, he half expected the living Hercules to emerge through a door with a laugh and pronounce the whole thing a grand jest.

He would not. Commodus was gone. Rufinus wondered what had been done with the body. Where was the chamberlain? Where, indeed, was Commodus' vaunted and beautiful mistress? Where was the wrestler?

He shivered.

An hour later, hungry and having missed lunch, Rufinus was relieved at the palace and left for home. There would be much to do, and he had busy days coming. Crispinus would be at him constantly now, using him, demanding and commanding, and he would have to stay close to the emperor for a number of reasons. But for a few hours, it was time to see his wife.

Wearily, but despite everything overwhelmed with the excitement of returning home after so long, Rufinus hammered on the door and was admitted by the swarthy figure of Naravas, who grinned like a lunatic at the sight of his employer.

Rufinus hurried through the house and out into the peristyle, making for Senova's office. He stopped dead as he neared the door, surprised to see a figure standing within. He felt a mix of joy and irritation at the sight of Vibius Cestius. He wanted nothing more than to see his old friend... except private time with the woman he'd not seen for almost a year.

Despite the presence of the frumentarius, Senova rose from her chair with a cry and hurtled across the room into his arms, hitting him so hard and clasping tight that Rufinus almost fell backwards into the garden.

'Senova, my love,' he said softly, her reply lost in the folds of wool as she buried her face in his toga. He looked up, faintly embarrassed, at Cestius, who smiled broadly.

'Despite this being the blackest of days,' the frumentarius smiled, 'we do still find joy. Welcome home Rufinus.'

'Thank you, my friend. We narrowly avoided having Didius Julianus wearing the purple this morning. In the end the throne has gone to a worthy man, but I must admit to being astounded at the mysterious disappearance of nine chests of fake African coins. Tribune Crispinus was ready to tear men apart with his teeth.'

Cestius chuckled. 'It was not easy, I have to say. But the coins are safe. Within days they will be melted down once more and recast into a statue of the new emperor. I cannot think of a more fitting end for Julianus' imperial bid.'

Rufinus laughed. 'Quite. But it's not over.'

'No, of course not.'

'The same villains are in the same places still. They need to be brought down, and the tribune has already more or less told me that he intends to end Pertinax's reign prematurely. He will not rest until his own man is on the throne and he can control the empire through him. And they can always make more coins.'

'But we have bought time, Rufinus. At the most critical moment in Rome's history we have denied a villain and put a good man on the throne. Pertinax should do well, and he is an old friend. Now your mission has become two-fold.'

'Oh?'

'Excise the rot in the Guard still, but like a good Praetorian, protect your new emperor with your life.'

Cestius left politely shortly thereafter, and Rufinus and Senova retreated to their chamber. An hour later, as they lay in near darkness and Rufinus toyed with Senova's long, lustrous black hair, he sighed.

'I've much to tell you. I didn't want to risk letters from Africa. Even the important ones to Cestius I had to code and be careful with. This goes above Aper and the tribune. The governor of Africa is involved, and counterfeit coins, and so much more. Perhaps with Pertinax in control we can change things, but there's going to be more people to pull in yet among the Guard.'

Senova murmured and rolled over to face him. 'I've names for you. I can't tie them specifically to any of the events you're investigating, but I've put together over the months a list of names of people who *may* have been involved…' there was a catch in her voice, something that she wasn't saying, and Rufinus tensed.

'What is it?'

'They're watching the house, Gnaeus,' she said, her voice nervous and urgent. 'I'm fairly sure they've seen Cestius coming and going. Hurrius went to the market for me to buy food, and never came back. Officially he's a fugitivus, but you know as well as I that he's no slave. He's one of Severus' ex-legionaries sent to protect us. He had no reason to run.'

'Have you seen them?'

Senova nodded. 'Occasionally. There's just something about a soldier that shows up no matter what he wears or what he does. They're always in the streets around the house.'

Rufinus sighed. 'I knew there were others that were not connected with Aper and Crispinus. These people should know of each other, though, so it's only a matter of time before the two groups communicate, and then Crispinus and Aper will be on to me. We're going to have to deal with this. I'm going to have to treat it as a separate investigation. I shall stay at the house for now. The tribune won't question me wanting to spend time with my wife after Africa, but we're going to have to stop Cestius coming across.'

He scratched his chin. So now he needed to refocus on this secondary problem, but he couldn't afford to step away from the main issue. Crispinus wanted him glued to Pertinax and would expect reports. At least Aper was far away for now. That might buy him enough time to sort out those watchers.

He smiled encouragingly. 'Go to sleep. Rest. I'm home, and everything is going to be fine.'

XVI – THE NEW EMPEROR

Imperator Caesar Publius Helvius Pertinax Augustus sat on the throne, drumming his fingers on the arm. Rufinus found himself smiling at the sight. He had seen Marcus Aurelius and Commodus both on that throne. Aurelius had sat upon it like a father watching his children, wisdom and serenity enfolding him. Commodus had seemed to incorporate the throne like some other part of his imperial regalia. Both were innately imperial and looked to be in the very place the gods had designed for them.

Pertinax sat like a solider. He did not look comfortable, but more as though he were about to leap up and give commands. A low-born man with a military history, he was eminently qualified to rule after a life of public service, but pomp and civil ease did not come to him naturally. It was what Rufinus would have looked like on that seat, which further endeared the man to him.

Tribune Crispinus was absent. He had spent much of the last few days working in his office at the Castra Praetoria, presumably dealing with his plans to supplant this man with his own candidate. Rufinus was now the senior man on the Palatine and as such had set the duties and made sure that he was close to the emperor at all times. Crispinus would approve, since those was his orders anyway, but it also gave Rufinus the chance to be close enough for protection if required, given that there were few men in the Guard he trusted.

The room contained a few important figures. Eclectus, the chamberlain, was the big surprise. Though he had been implicated in the death of Commodus, just like the Praetorian Prefect, they had both retained their positions under the new emperor. Eclectus looked tired, and nervous. He had every right to, of course. It was said that he and the former emperor's mistress were now close. They would be a pair to watch.

Beside Eclectus, who stood close to the consul, Falco, present were the new Urban Prefect, Sulpicianus, the great general Pompeianus, and the senators Marius Maximus and Cassius Dio, both of whom were said to be former associates of the emperor. The rest of the room was dotted with Rufinus' men, while he stood close to the throne.

187

'Thank you for attending, gentlemen,' Pertinax said briskly. 'I want to keep you abreast of certain matters and to clear the air and quash rumours before they begin.'

There were a series of nods at this.

'Firstly, the senate calls for the body of my predecessor. They want Commodus damned in the public eye, and they want him disgraced and ruined, torn limb from limb and shown to the people as a dismembered and broken despot.'

There was an uncomfortable silence. Dio, Falco and Marius were almost certainly among those men who had bayed for the former emperor's damning. Commodus and the senate had never been close, but the stories Rufinus had heard since his return to Rome were hair raising. The god-emperor had clearly spent his last year or more deliberately riling and humiliating the senators, who had made more than one attempt on his life in retaliation. No wonder the great men of the empire had been preparing for a succession no one else had expected. In retrospect even Rufinus might have prepared himself.

Finally, Pertinax broke the silence. 'I have a mind to compromise. I am well aware that the rift between the senate and my predecessor had widened to an uncrossable width and, as a former senator myself, I wish only good relations with that body, but I also remember Commodus the golden child of Rome, and while the *senate* might despise his memory, he remains popular with the army and with the people.'

Rufinus felt a tiny thrill of pride in his new emperor at that. It was all too easy at a time like this to bow to the powerful. That Pertinax was not simply doing so spoke volumes.

'You will not have him damned, Domine?' asked Falco, an edge to his voice. If rumours were true, then the emperor had been planning to execute both Falco and his fellow consul on the morning after his assassination. The man had more interest than most in the former emperor's damning.

'I will,' Pertinax replied. 'Commodus will be prevented from taking his place among the gods. His desire to be seen as one of them while he yet lived is at much of the root of this trouble, and so I fear angering the gods if we send him among them. Commodus will be damned, and his name struck. His greatest works will be undone and the self-important monuments he imposed upon the city reworked or destroyed.'

Rufinus felt a shiver. What sort of compromise was this?

'But,' Pertinax said, leaning forwards and jabbing a finger at them, 'an official damnation is all the humiliation he will receive.

The body will not be ruined and torn in public. Indeed, I have had those closest to him…' a glance at Eclectus here, 'spirit away the body and inter it with honour and respect in a secret place. You will not make sport of his remains.'

Another thrill of pride. It *was* a good compromise. Worthy of Aurelius himself.

The senators and the consul looked uncertain for a long moment, but then shared glances, and nodded their understanding and acceptance.

'Those responsible for Commodus' death are the only ones other than myself who know of his burial site. Each of them remains in position with no prosecution for their actions.' Another look at Eclectus. 'The moment that information becomes public, there will be proscriptions. I hope that is understood. I will not have Commodus so dishonoured in that way. Let this be the rule and let the senate be satisfied.'

Another silence.

'On to more pleasant matters,' the new emperor said. 'It is customary for a new emperor to pay donatives to the army and the mob. I have been through the imperial accounts and find that there is something of a dearth of funds.'

'Your predecessor spent it all on games for that same mob, Domine,' Falco muttered.

'That is where you are wrong, Falco. My predecessor made grand decisions, yes, but the minutiae were always left to his freedmen.' Yet another glance here at Eclectus, himself a freedman and a killer of emperors. 'In my mind it is those freedmen who managed the administration for him who are at fault for leaving us a bankrupt empire. I have dismissed the bulk of the palace freedmen and replaced them with traditional imperial slaves. There will henceforth be restrictions placed upon the power a freedman can hold.'

The senators and the consul all nodded their approval of the measure. Eclectus had the wisdom to lower his gaze and not state his position.

'There will be an auction,' Pertinax announced. 'At the next kalends let all those men of wealth come to Rome and bid for the most exquisite and impressive things. I will sell the great collections of Commodus. All his personal wealth, a number of his villas, his slaves and more. What Commodus acquired as the empire's treasury emptied will be sold to replace it. And when the funds are once more there, every citizen shall receive a donative, and the army shall be paid a bonus, the Praetorians receiving the lion's share as always. A sum shall be set aside for public buildings, and the treasury kept healthy.'

There was an odd clearing of throat and Rufinus looked across at the new Urban Prefect. Sulpicianus was Pertinax's father-in-law, he remembered. The emperor chuckled. 'Yes, Titus, the Urban Cohorts will also receive an increased donative. And while I have a mind to favour my former unit, I want you to prepare the Urban Cohorts for a move. It is no longer feasible for them to share a barracks with the Praetorians. The tensions between the two units have caused many issues over the years. The Castra Nova that Commodus had built in the north of the city for the visiting forces of allies and clients will now be turned over to you as a permanent Castra Urbana.'

Rufinus nodded his own approval this time. To separate the two argumentative forces was simple sense and such a move was long overdue.

'I do believe that is all I have to impart at this time,' the new emperor said. 'You may go about your duties and business and inform all who this concern of my decisions. Official edicts will follow, of course, but in the interest of good relations, I wanted all to be aware of these matters before they became public knowledge.'

As the men filed out, Rufinus watched them leave, mostly satisfied with the conclusion. When the man by the entrance closed the door behind them, Pertinax sagged a little in the throne.

'I do declare that this seat was designed for a man with an enormous behind. It leaves much to be desired in terms of comfort.'

Rufinus chuckled.

'You're amused, Rufinus?'

'The throne has had to accommodate some grand arses in its time, Domine,'

Pertinax let out a roar of laughter, and then leaned back. 'In this time of trouble, it is refreshing to be able to laugh. Thank you.'

'Might I speak with you, Domine?' Rufinus said suddenly. He'd not planned on it, but it had sort of slipped out anyway.

'Of course. I have a short interval before the next lot of grasping hands and wagging tongues seeks me out.'

'Priscus,' Rufinus addressed his most senior soldier. 'Take the others out to the vestibule.' He turned to the emperor. 'With your permission, Domine?'

Pertinax nodded. 'Go on.'

The Praetorians filed out and as the door shut, leaving the two men alone, Pertinax turned to Rufinus. 'It is most unusual for an emperor to give a private audience to a soldier. It's a terrible precedent to set. Your prefect was responsible for my predecessor's death, after all.'

Rufinus swallowed noisily. 'I am aware of that Domine, and I can only assure you that...'

'Relax, Rufinus. I have known you since I was a simple senator and you a war hero taken under Pompeianus' wing. In that we share a spiritual father. It was Pompeianus who secured me my position as a cavalry tribune, and I learned much from him. In an odd way, we are martial brothers of the same stoic father. If I believed for even a moment that you were capable of deceit and murder, then I would have thought twice, but we both know better, eh?'

Rufinus felt a chill run through him. Ten years ago, that would have described him perfectly. What had he become since then? Still, in this case at least it was true. He was loyal to this man, and always would be. Pertinax was as much his long-term ally as Severus or even Pompeianus.

'I have concerns, Domine. Ones of which I cannot speak too openly.'

Pertinax frowned. 'Go on.'

'I have spent much of the past two years attempting to identify those men whom Cleander had bought in the Guard, who had murdered citizens and stolen land on his orders. When the chamberlain fell, much of his corrupt web remained in place. The Praetorians are infected with this rot. I have several names already and am working on uncovering more.'

'I see. Go on.'

'I have been ordered by the frumentarii not to bring certain men to justice as it might impede further investigation, but I believe there are enough leads to go on without at least their head. If I produce a written affidavit concerning the crimes of a certain senior officer, would you have them dealt with through imperial channels, Domine? If the charges do not come from me, then I can continue to work my investigations, while the danger to the throne is diminished.'

Pertinax nodded seriously. 'I understand, of course,' he replied. 'But I have set a precedent with those who conspired against Commodus. I succeeded the throne only through popular acceptance. I have no innate claim to it, Rufinus. In truth, you have as much right to sit here as I do. That being the case, I need to maintain good relations with everyone until I am properly secure. I have done what I can to alleviate the financial issues solely so that I can pay each and every man what he expects. Remember that Galba, a century ago, came to grief after just seven months because he failed to pay the soldiers what he'd promised.'

He sagged back again. 'The worst possible way for an emperor to start his reign is with proscriptions and executions. No matter how much such men might deserve death, they all have similarly powerful supporters and relations, and every single death creates a dozen more enemies. So no, I will not have any officer arrested and executed at this time. Perhaps in the future, when I am settled and it is not seen as paranoia or revenge, I will consider it.'

Rufinus took a deep breath. 'In this case, Domine, I worry for your ongoing safety. I strongly suspect these men of already conspiring against you.'

'Then you have done sterling work, Rufinus. Continue to do so. You are, after all, the emperor's bodyguard. My safety is your concern.'

Rufinus huffed. 'Domine...'

'No, Rufinus. But I *will* do this: my predecessor granted a certain latitude to the Guard that allowed them to far exceed their remit. As such, I will undo that work. I will have Commodus' various favours he bestowed upon them withdrawn. The Praetorians have become a political animal, and that is not their intended role. The Guard will be restored to a military model. That, I suspect, will seriously inhibit conspirators and aid you in your investigations.'

Rufinus nodded. It was not what he'd hoped for, but he could understand the new emperor's position. Even Commodus, who'd had every right to the throne, had been immediately at risk from his sister's attempted coup. That Pertinax wanted to see his reign settled before attempting anything risky was neither surprising nor stupid. At least if he planned to curb the powers of the Guard's officers, he would place limits on the ability of men like Crispinus to stand against him.

'Thank you, Domine.'

'I may never get used to being spoken to so,' smiled Pertinax.

Rufinus bowed and retreated to the door, opening it and admitting his men once more. As he left, he cast one last glance at Pertinax. Rufinus had been loyal to Commodus. Liked him. Respected him. Much the same, he could already say for this low-born ruler, a new Vespasian. He left in relatively high spirits.

The remaining hour of his shift passed in peace, and he then departed the Palatine with his men, leading them back to the Castra Praetoria before dismissing them and leaving the extremely capable Gamburio in charge. Steeling himself, he strode from the barracks out to the main street and then along to the row of large peristyle houses that housed the Guard's tribunes. While it made him twitch to do so, reporting to Crispinus was his duty. He'd done so after every shift so far, although before today the new emperor had been busy and locked away, and Rufinus had had little to report.

Today was different. He had much to report and was struggling to decide how much of it to repeat. Tribune Crispinus' house was neat and severe, and a knock had the door opened by a German slave with a broken nose. The décor here was out of date and cold, the altar to the household gods plain and minimal. No tromp l'oeil or fancy paintings here, and those busts in evidence, clearly relations and forebears, were every bit as miserable looking as the tribune himself.

Crispinus was in his office, and as Rufinus stepped out into the peristyle, the big German held out a restraining hand and hurried over to the office. When he came back, he held up a hand telling Rufinus to wait, and made odd noises with a tongueless mouth. He stood quietly, trying to listen. There was low conversation in the tribune's office, but too muffled and quiet for him to hear anything.

Finally, a figure emerged from the door and stepped out into the open sunlight, blinking and straightening his belts where he had been sat and they had become twisted. Rufinus frowned. This man was another tribune, judging by the stripe on his tunic, though not one Rufinus recognised. As the man stepped out across the gravelled path, Crispinus now appeared in the doorway.

'Remember,' he called to the other officer, 'two months. Just two.'

The second tribune turned and nodded, and something unspoken passed between them that Rufinus saw revealed in their eyes. He shuddered at the sight and forced himself to stay still and expressionless. The second tribune gave him just a momentary glance as he strode past and out of the house.

Two months… what would happen at the end of Martius?

'Rufinus,' Crispinus said, 'good. Come in.'

With that the tribune retreated into his office. Rufinus followed him inside and stood at attention, waiting for the officer to speak first.

'No word as yet of Aper,' the tribune said finally, sinking into his seat.

'He will almost certainly not arrive in Carthage for several days yet, sir,' Rufinus replied. 'Even if they have smooth sailing and he and the governor immediately embark and return on the same tide it will be half a month, sir.'

Crispinus nodded in irritation. 'You are correct, of course. I am being impatient. It is the simple matter of spending so long putting things in place only to have them swept from beneath one's feet. As yet I have had no success in uncovering what happened to the coins from Carthage. Given that they were safely locked away in the fortress, guilt can only lie in one of three places. Either other members of the Guard work against us, perhaps in support of their own goals, or the Urban Cohorts managed some devious activity, given that their commander has just been named emperor. My money is on the grain men, though. They have long been investigating certain activities within the Guard. You should appreciate that, since I'm told they are watching you also.'

Rufinus made affirmative noises.

'So, you still have nothing to report?' the tribune grumbled wearily.

'The emperor met with several senior functionaries and senators this morning, sir. He intends to organise an auction of Commodus' wealth in order to fill the treasury and pay donatives to the military. He plans to pay the Guard well, and his former unit, the Urban Cohort, too.'

'If he believes that it will buy him security, then he is sadly mistaken,' Crispinus snapped.

'Yes, sir. He also plans to move the Urban Cohort out to their own barracks.'

'Now *that* is a sensible decision.'

'And he intends to curb the powers of the Guard. He plans to undo Commodus' various grants and restore us to the state we were in under Aurelius.'

Crispinus turned a frown on him. 'He said this? Openly?'

'No, sir. This was his private musing, but I believe we can expect public announcements to follow.'

The tribune's mouth curved up into a smile that contained not an ounce of humour. 'Well done, Rufinus. This is precisely what I need. Useful information before anyone else knows it. This is ammunition beyond compare.'

Rufinus felt a jolt of worry. Perhaps he should have kept that to himself?

'If ever there could be something guaranteed to turn the Guard against its master, it is being disenfranchised and stripped of privileges. When word of this leaks out, as it surely must now, even the staunchest men loyal to this new usurper will turn against him. Our strength grows. Better still, he seems now to favour the Urban

Cohorts, giving them an increased donative and their own fortress. Men long passive will soon be up in arms. This is extraordinarily well done, Rufinus. Now we can begin to sow discord before the announcement, increasing the damage tenfold.'

Rufinus twitched. Damn it, but why had he opened his mouth? He had been the only person to hear it, and he should have kept it to himself. Would the increased favour of Crispinus this would buy really be enough to outweigh the damage he might just have done the new emperor?

He remained in position, expressionless, until a cruelly gleeful Tribune Crispinus dismissed him, and then made his way from the house, back across the fortress, into the city and away. Before noon, he was striding up the street to his domus, his eyes flicking to the walls of the Castra Peregrina across the road. He had sent a message via subtle channels to Cestius to stay away from the house. He would soon have to think of a way to stay in touch with the frumentarius, although knowing Cestius he had probably already planned such a thing.

As he rounded the corner, his gaze flicked momentarily around the populace. Since Senova had mentioned the watchers, he'd kept his eyes open as he approached or left the house, and he'd soon seen what she meant. Rome had plenty of ex-soldiers in its streets, of course, but to see them so regularly up here, away from the centre, seemed unlikely.

This time, they were either getting bored and playing with their role, or they had become lax and let themselves go. There was a beggar across the street, sitting in the gutter with a wooden cup waiting for coins. He was an old solder like so many of Rome's beggars, but he was so clearly a fake one. Nine beggars in ten who came from a military background were missing an eye, an arm or a leg. Thus, they had been released from service without the requisite pension. *This* man was whole. But unlike those other unfortunates of the sort he was aping, this man had not fallen into poverty and ruin, for he had the frame of a healthy and well-fed man. Moreover, while he may be lightly coated in dust, Rufinus had seen enough beggars to know that they were a lot filthier than that, usually with a hint of old urine, for the city baths would not permit them entry.

He looked at the scarred man and dropped a copper coin in the cup, committing the face to memory even as the fake beggar thanked him.

Inside, he made his way straight to Senova's office.

'They're there again. They must not be sure of me, still. If they knew for a fact I was a frumentarius or working against them, they would have tried to kill me again this past few days. That they continue to just watch suggests that they are compiling information on me.'

'Then you need to be careful.'

'What do you know about the Praetorian tribunes?' he said. 'Are any of them on your list?'

Senova frowned. 'After a fashion. I presume you are not talking about Crispinus?'

'No.'

'One man might fit your bill then. Titus Flavius Genialis. Tribune of the Fifth Cohort. According to records he was on the sick list on the day that Cleander died, when the Praetorians were busily cutting their way through the people of Rome, and yet I managed to secure records from the Castra Praetoria's hospital and he is not logged there.'

Rufinus sucked his teeth. 'It's not conclusive. He could have simply signed himself off and stayed home. Or if he had medical attention, since he's a senior officer, it might have been from a private medicus.'

'Or he might have been covering his tracks and hiding his involvement in the butchery of citizens.'

'True.'

'Is it likely that more than one tribune could have been in league with Cleander?'

Rufinus nodded, remembering the look the two tribunes had shared. 'It's at least possible.' He scratched his head. 'The man who gave me Aper's name at the mill was not one of Aper's men. He seemed to intimate that Aper would not know about me. That's how I know there's others in the Guard not connected to Aper and Crispinus. What if even at risk of his life he gave me Aper's name to divert me? To throw me off track and send me looking elsewhere?'

'You think he worked for this Genialis?'

'I wouldn't be at all surprised. It should be easy enough to find out. Three men died that night, probably all from the same century, let alone cohort. If you can track them down and link them to Genialis, I will bet you that he's our man.' A thought struck him. 'And if he is, we need to deal with it straight away. If Genialis decides I'm a threat and says as much to Crispinus, then I'm done for.'

Senova straightened in her chair. 'Then I'd best check that connection for you.'

'And I'd best check on our friendly watchers.'

Things were closing in again, and this time, Rufinus didn't believe he could rely upon the frumentarii for help.

XVII – WATCHERS

Rufinus hovered outside the room, pacing back and forth in just his centurion's tunic, belt, and boots. Not even a knife in evidence. His fingers drummed on his elbows, arms crossed, until the door opened and Senova stepped out with the bundle in her arms.

'It's ready?'

She nodded. 'Bear in mind, Gnaeus, that I'm no seamstress. I've only ever done a little mending and alteration, and not even that since the days I served the empress. I think it looks fine, and it's modelled on your spare kit, so it should fit, but it might not stand up to close scrutiny.'

'I have a recognisable face, Senova. If they get that close the game's up anyway.'

When did she become so Roman? he mused to himself, remembering when she'd had trouble with words like 'dog' and would think 'scrutiny' was something you did to someone that caused a lot of pain.

She proffered the pile and Rufinus took it, three garments carefully folded and pressed. He tried not to sigh. He needed to blend in, not look so neat that he stood out. Still, he smiled and took them.

'I'll be back soon. Usual rules apply. Only Naravas opens the door, and only to me or someone we know.'

'I know the routine, Gnaeus. Good luck, try not to hurt yourself, and pass on my greetings.'

With a last smile, Rufinus turned and strode through the house, hobnailed military boots clacking on the marble. There was a moment of unexpected quiet as he crossed the great thick sheepskin mat that now lay on one side of the atrium, half covering an expensive mosaic. You could take the woman out of Britannia, but you clearly couldn't take Britannia out of the woman.

In the alcove by the door, Naravas nodded at him and produced the leather satchel. It was a miscellaneous looking thing, much like any other used by a courier, a medic, or anyone else with bulky gear to carry. He opened it and looked inside. The sackcloth bag was screwed up inside. Good. Stuffing the clothes into the satchel such that it bulged, he fastened and shouldered it, and Naravas opened the door so he could step out into the street.

By the time he'd gone a hundred paces he could already feel that he was being followed. He'd come to the conclusion that there were two sets of eyes on the house at all times, so that one could follow anyone who left while the other could maintain their vigil. Idly, he wondered how the soldiers engaged in this clandestine task accounted for their duty hours back in the fortress. Undoubtedly Genialis or one of his pet centurions covered their trail.

He walked as normally as he could, doing an excellent impression of a man going about his daily business unaware that he was being followed. Turning left, he entered the valley of the Nymphs and the sacred gardens. Between well-tended groves and box-hedged gardens he passed, alongside elegant ponds and fountains, in a small oasis of beauty and peace amid the stink and press of the city. Here and there he could see members of the vigiles on one of their more favoured duties: keeping vagrants and criminals from ruining the park for the better class of citizen.

His boots had gone from the clacking of nails on stone flags to the crunch of gravel, and the crowds here were thinner and quieter, with no beggars or hawkers, the vigiles on guard at all times. Rufinus forced himself to walk steadily and not even once look back to identify his pursuer. It was enough that he was sure there was one. That made this tiresome subterfuge worthwhile. He could hear the gentle crunch of many light-booted footsteps on the gravel, but by the time he was halfway through the gardens he'd isolated one set that stayed at a constant volume, and therefore a constant distance from him.

At the far side of the gardens stood the monumental arcaded front of the Baths of Mercury, and Rufinus made his way inside. Once in the apodyterium, he crossed to one of the alcoves and put his satchel in it. There he undid it and faced the door, watching. No one entered. Satisfied that the pursuer was waiting outside for him, he hurriedly stripped off his breeches and tunic. Equally swiftly, he slipped into the new tunic from the satchel, pulling on the fresh breeches, fastening his belt and throwing the cloak about his shoulders. Yes, she'd done an excellent job. The clothes had been made a perfect fit.

Now, he removed the sack from inside the leather bag, shook it out and put the satchel and his other rolled up clothes into it. He then slung the sack over his left shoulder and walked over to the bronze plaque on the wall that served as a mirror.

Light blue breeches, slightly faded, darker blue tunic and a grey cloak. With the military boots and belt and the kit bag thrown over his shoulder, he looked like any other sailor of the Roman fleet, as he knew from the experience of working in their barracks in Rome for a year. He faffed for a while with his hair, making it a little more unruly and spiked, while he waited for a trio of youths to emerge from the baths and dry and dress themselves.

Once they were ready, the three lads made for the exit, and Rufinus fell in behind them. He kept his face down a little, and the moment he emerged out into the sunshine, he turned right, the bag over his shoulder between him and any position a watchful enemy might occupy.

It was as neatly done as he could manage, and he felt a tiny swell of smugness that this was the sort of thing the frumentarii were known for. Walking purposefully but not over-fast, he headed south for the edge of the gardens and there stepped out into a street again. He crossed to a small tavern and ordered a cup of wine, seating himself at a table near the door where he could see the street. He spent a quarter of an hour there until he was satisfied that the pursuer remained outside the baths and had lost his trail. Out once more into the street, he moved at pace up the slope to the gate of the Castra Peregrina.

He did not have the passwords, of course, due to his current enforced separation from the frumentarii, but he did have a fibula brooch with the silver pilum of the unit in his pouch, which he surreptitiously produced, and which granted him entry. Inside, a man in a nondescript brown tunic intercepted him and led him off to the left.

The Castra Peregrina was a dual-purpose fortress within the city. Its prime, and official, purpose was as a transit barracks for any units passing through the city. As such there were permanently legionaries, sailors and auxiliaries from all over the empire temporarily housed there, in numbers anywhere from single travellers to entire centuries.

The frumentarii occupied one part of the barracks, kept aside from the rest. It suited their purpose, for it was a simple job to slip in among a visiting unit that way and depart for hidden service somewhere across the empire without anyone realising they had joined, such was the high traffic of servicemen through the barracks.

Rufinus was led to the building where Vibius Cestius had his office, and once inside was left to his own devices. There was no need for him to give individual identification. The men who worked in this building full time knew by sight those with authorised access. Up the stairs and along a corridor, he made his way to the office of Cestius. A brief knock and he was admitted.

The frumentarius officer was seated behind his desk, engaged in a discussion with a swarthy looking Syrian archer who had his conical helmet tucked beneath his arm. The man thanked Cestius and left the room with just a professional nod at Rufinus, who wondered momentarily where the man was going.

His inquisitiveness must have shown on his face, for as he shut the door and approached the desk, Cestius gave him a sly smile. 'Pescennius Niger. The time has come to keep a close watch on our friends in the provinces. Consessus has just retired from a unit in northern Britannia and is heading back to his homeland where Niger now happens to be governor.'

Rufinus nodded. He didn't envy the man delving into Niger's works, though it would certainly be no more dangerous than what Rufinus was doing.

'What can I do for you, sailor?'

Rufinus snorted and dropped his bag before sinking into the seat.

'The lengths you have to go to when you're being watched.'

'Nice job, though. Your disguises would be more convincing if you grew out a beard like most soldiers.'

'Too itchy. I need your advice.'

Cestius, humour put aside, leaned forwards over his desk, steepling his fingers. Rufinus folded his arms.

'I'm at something of an impasse, and I cannot decide what my next move should be. There are now two distinct problems I have.'

'Tell me.'

'Well, you know about Crispinus. Here's the situation: Aper is in Africa with his thugs, readying to being Didius Julianus back to the city. Once he's here, I'm fairly sure that Crispinus intends to engineer a coup and remove Pertinax from the throne, replacing him with the grateful and pliable Julianus. I may have inadvertently given him a little ammunition when I reported that Pertinax intended to curb the Guard's excesses.'

'I can see how that might rile some Praetorians, yes, but on the bright side such information would reach him sooner or later, and your being the man to do so early increases your value to the tribune. This is how covert appointments work.'

'There will be more men in the Guard who report to Aper and Crispinus,' Rufinus grumbled, 'but the effort and time it will take to root out those men has to take second place to the main problem, which is preventing a coup by Crispinus and his men.'

'Agreed.'

'The problem is that I spoke to the emperor directly and he is unwilling to do anything about these men. In my opinion, we could remove Crispinus by imperial authority, leaving all of us out of the chain of command, and that would diminish Julianus' chances. Aper does not have enough authority and influence in the Guard on his own to raise them against the emperor.'

'I would generally advise against moving on just one conspirator, but given the situation, you might be right. The removal of Crispinus could be advantageous now. The emperor refused?'

Rufinus nodded. 'He says he won't start a reign with proscriptions.'

Cestius leaned back. 'He could just... *disappear*, of course.'

Rufinus shook his head. 'No. If we're to cut out the cancer among the Guard it has to be done properly. He needs to be arrested and interrogated, leading to further arrests, not grabbed off the street and tortured in secret. That's not the way.'

'Sometimes, Rufinus, I think your morals get in the way of your common sense. Alright, so you've got a situation building with Crispinus, and it might just explode when the governor of Africa arrives in Rome. What else?'

'There is an entirely different group of criminals within the Guard, almost certainly also former members of Cleander's web of informants and killers. It's my theory that when Cleander fell, the entire web split and went their own ways, or at least in small groups, in order to prevent precisely what we're doing. The bonus is that in that way they are less well informed, for they do not necessarily share information. This second group seems to be within the Fifth Cohort and controlled by another tribune, Titus Flavius Genialis. The fact that his men are following me and my people and even attacking me, while Crispinus considers me one of his own, suggests to me that the two tribunes are not talking to one another.'

'Yet.'

'Exactly.'

Cestius frowned. 'Of course, if they are so separate that they are not even sharing information, then it is entirely plausible that they do not share goals either.'

'I hadn't thought of that. Perhaps Genialis is not in on the Didius Julianus thing.'

'Again, *yet*. If Crispinus is planning to turn the Praetorians against the emperor, he will need the support of tribunes and perhaps even the prefect. One cohort might be able to do it, but all it would take was for the rest of the Guard to say no and Crispinus' coup would fail before it started. It's only a matter of time before your friend speaks to this Genialis and the two compare notes.'

'And then I'm screwed six ways from kalends.'

'Quite. It would seem you are caught between two enemy units and they are coming together, squeezing you. You have limited choices, I think.'

'Oh?'

'If the emperor will not sanction the arrest of Crispinus, then the only way to stop what is coming is to tend to him ourselves. In this very short timeframe, you have to deal with either one or both tribunes. You cannot afford for them to join forces. If you won't move on Crispinus, you need to move on Genialis.'

Rufinus sighed. 'Something Severus once said to me struck me as insanity at the time. That perhaps the only way to save the Guard is to completely destroy it and start again. The more I delve, the more I'm starting to think he was on to something. A year and a half ago I was of the opinion that there were a few bad apples in the barrel that needed to be removed before they ruin the lot. I'm starting to think that only the ones on the surface were ever good and that underneath the whole barrel is rotten.'

'Do you need help?'

Rufinus was startled. He'd not thought about it. Cestius never seemed to offer. The man just turned up when you needed him. He mulled it over for a moment. 'I don't think so. I don't think bringing anyone else in will help. I would need to find a way to bring them into the fold with Crispinus and that would be difficult. And after what happened to Curio, I'm not comfortable having another man's life in my hands like that.'

Cestius nodded. 'The life of a grain man is no stroll in the garden. Shall I give you advice, then?'

Rufinus nodded eagerly.

'Deal with your second problem. That one has a time limit, and the constant surveillance is hampering your abilities to work. You need to clear that problem completely, right up to this second tribune, if you can. Then, with no danger of being uncovered, you can concentrate once more on Julianus.'

Rufinus straightened. 'You're right, of course. Thank you. And I think I need to do it quickly. No careful pulling of strings. A direct confrontation.'

'Perhaps. But remain wary. You do not want to bring Crispinus back against you. I will have men in place at the various ports. We'll have ample warning when Didius Julianus is on the way.

Concentrate on your immediate problem but never forget the bigger picture while you're doing it. Will you need a change of clothes?'

'No. I won't need a disguise again. It's time to end this. I'll report in again once this is done.'

Cestius nodded and wished him good luck. Rufinus thanked his friend and made his way from the room once more, back through the fortress. Exiting through the main gate, still dressed as a member of the Misenum Fleet, he strode back towards the house. He had to draw Genialis and his men out. He did not have time to unpick their net. Straight to the top. And if he wanted to do that, he had to catch their attention.

As he approached the house once more, his gaze raked the street. A trader had set up a stall selling brooches and imported Gaulish clothing accessories across from Rufinus' door. He was a thin and reedy man and had, like many traders who were selling more costly wares, brought his own muscle to protect the stall. Such types were often ex-soldiers, but there was something about the big man standing there. He was paying too little attention to the stall to be genuine, and his gaze kept flicking up across the street at Rufinus' house.

This was it. Rufinus strode towards the stall and came to a halt in front of it. The surprise in the big soldier's face was apparent. He'd not expected the man he was surveilling to come over to him, clearly. Rufinus smiled at the trader. 'Apologies, my friend, but I need to borrow your guard here.'

The trader looked baffled and a little unhappy, but the big soldier turned a frown on Rufinus, the unspoken mutual understanding hovering in the air. 'I'll be back shortly,' the man said to his trader boss, who looked for a moment as though he might argue until he took in the two muscular figures at his stall and the air of seething danger growing between them.

'Don't be long,' he said nervously to the big man in a Hispanic accent.

'This won't take long,' the guard replied, still narrow eyed.

'Follow me,' Rufinus said, turning and marching back out onto the Vicus Capitis Africae. Taking a left on the large thoroughfare, he marched down through the great arch in the aqueduct and took a narrow alley a block further on. Here, the ancient mouldering city walls still stood and they formed, along with the insulae on the other side, a narrow, deep and very shadowed alley. Rufinus walked far enough along the alley to be unnoticed by the casual passer-by on the main street and between branching lanes. The most subdued and shady place he could think of close by at short notice.

He stopped then, threw his bag down near the wall, and turned to the big man who'd followed him.

'I've a message for your lot and your favourite tribune.'

'Yeah?' grunted the big soldier as he flexed his muscles.

'Tell Genialis and any goat-buggering half-wit centurion between you and him that I'm done playing this game. Either he backs off and pulls you lot away to some other pointless mission, or I will devote my days and nights to making sure that your cohort suffers repeated losses in the Caelian region. Do you get my drift?'

The soldier sneered. 'You've a reputation, Rufinus. And you made a mistake when you took down two of our friends. We shouldn't be watching your *house*. We should be watching your funeral pyre.'

'Brave threats.'

He'd been watching the man since they stopped, and listening to his movements before that, so he was ready. The man was bulky across the shoulders and had that mode of movement with his arms that suggested he was used to wearing segmented armour, which limited the angles an arm could be comfortably raised at. He favoured his left leg, which was slightly heavier and more muscular than his right. Conversely, his right arm showed no difference in bulk to his left.

The man was a front-liner in combat. He was used to planting his left foot and bracing with his right, pushing his left shoulder into the shield to take a charge. Had he been a man from the next few rows the difference in bulk would be more visible in his arms, where his right would be stronger from the throwing of the pilum over the front lines.

If he was a front-liner, that meant he was inordinately strong. His punch would be enough to floor most people and being charged by him would be painful. But it also meant he was trained for a slow and gradual expense of immense strength, rather than speed.

Advantages like that were where boxers won out.

The man flexed his shoulders and cracked his knuckles. 'I'm assuming you brought us somewhere quiet so you could face me down. Bad news, Rufinus: I'm no wilting lily. You'll regret this.'

Rufinus noted a tiny flicker in the man's eyes and realised immediately that they were not alone. He began to adjust his thinking. The second man must have given up at the baths. He'd headed back towards the house and been somewhere in that street, following them here.

He ran through anything he could remember in his head. The footsteps he'd heard on the gravel in the gardens had been light. He'd heard maybe a dozen people, but none of them had the heavy crunch of a front-liner. This man was smaller. Lighter. Probably faster. And wearing soft soles, not nailed boots. At the moment, the second man could not be aware that Rufinus knew about him.

Another advantage.

He kept his eyes on the man in front, not giving away his suspicions.

'The tribune would be upset with me if I killed you,' the big man said, 'but I don't think he'd mind a few lumps and bruises at all.'

Rufinus heard a faint shuffling of feet behind him, as quiet as possible, but clear when you knew the man was there. He prepared. Take the big man down in one move. It wouldn't be enough to keep him down but would buy time to deal with the quick one before returning to him.

The man favoured his left...

Rufinus took a single step forwards and was matched by the big man. There was the faint sound of the smaller fellow behind creeping forwards too.

'Do I have to deliver the message in blood?' Rufinus said as he slowly and barely-noticeably put all his weight on his right foot. 'There's still time for you to walk away.'

'I'm not scared of you,' the big man grunted.

'Then you're stupider than you look, and that beggars belief.'

He grinned and, sure enough, goaded by the insult, the big man leapt, closing the gap. On instinct bred from so many years bracing in the shieldwall, the man slammed his left foot down and swung a right hook, his big, meaty ham-joint of a hand coming at speed, a glinting ring bearing the image of Mars on the middle finger.

The man was used to concentrating on his upper half, his lower protected by the shield, and also by a greave that guarded his leading leg. A greave he was not wearing now.

Rufinus pivoted on his right foot, dropping low as he swung the kick. As the big man's hand swept over him close enough to ruffle his hair, Rufinus' hobnailed boot connected with the man's shin. He was rewarded with a cry of pain as the worn and jagged iron studs tore two dozen shreds across the man's leg, combined with a weighty kick that damn near broke the bone.

Big man fell to the ground with a shocked bellow, and now Rufinus ignored him. Instead, he continued to spin, dropping back to two feet in a crouch and facing the slighter, swarthy man behind him.

'What about you?' he murmured threateningly. 'You feel like walking away from this?'

The man did, to his credit, look considerably less sure of himself, but he came on another step and his fists came up ready. Rufinus watched him carefully, gaze locked on the man's eyes, peripherally aware of his movements.

He saw the flicker as the man made his initial move. As the left fist came out in a swift jab, Rufinus brought his forearms up to block, taking the blow on the fleshiest part. His counterattack was instant, arms dropping, right punching out forwards, aiming for the man's chin. His hit was blocked, and then suddenly the pair were in a melee, locked in a flurry of blows as fists pounded and flew, blocked and jabbed.

Rufinus felt a sharp pain in his cheek below the right ear, and a couple of blows to the chest, but he also knew that he'd delivered much the same to the man. The flurry ended as they pulled apart, both men testing their jaws and blinking. It had been brutal, and this man knew what he was doing, but there was one thing he could do nothing about that Rufinus had spotted in the press.

Rufinus was bigger. His arms were just that little longer than his opponents, and such a thing could make a big difference in the ring. He peered at the man's arms and tried to estimate the difference. The man seemed to take this as Rufinus delaying and suddenly came on, fist swinging. Rufinus danced one single step back and slammed out with his own fist.

Both blows connected, but Rufinus' estimate had been good. The difference in reach had robbed the man of power, but not done that to Rufinus. The man's blow was well aimed and struck Rufinus full in the face, causing a good deal of pain and disorientation, but the return blow was something else entirely. Rufinus' big fist connected with the man's jaw and there was the crack of breaking bone.

The lithe boxer shrieked and fell.

Rufinus turned slowly, blinking away pain. He thought that perhaps he had a broken nose, and certainly he could taste blood, but there was nothing that would put him out of commission or cause permanent damage. His opponent with the broken jaw, however...

The big man was clambering up to his feet again now. He had a wary look about him, and a grudging respect that had been missing before. Rufinus took everything in as he wiped the blood from his face.

They had an audience now. Several windows and balconies showed excited faces, and a small knot of people had gathered at the end of the street.

Rufinus gestured to the big man. 'Your friend here's up for a medical discharge now. He'll never talk properly again. So far, you've got a grazed shin. Are you mad enough to ante-up for more, or happy to walk away with my message before the medicus has to pronounce the same verdict over you?'

He watched the man weighing up his chances and was in many ways relieved when the man stepped back, straightened with a hiss of pain, and nodded.

'This is done,' Rufinus said. 'Next time I find one of Genialis' men outside my house he'll end up in a bag in the Tiber. I don't make false threats. Now piss off and don't come back.'

The big man paused for just a moment, considering slinging a final insult, and then turned and limped away. There was a distinct air of disappointment all around him as the impromptu audience groaned, cheated of further entertainment.

Rufinus waited until the big man had gone, turned his back on the other, who was still lying on the ground and whimpering, and then strode away down the alley, testing his nose and swearing at the pain. It did not click. No actual break, but it might be a little bit flatter anyway now. He'd had worse. One of his teeth felt loose, which was more worrying, but even that could have been far worse. He sucked the iron tang from that tooth and swallowed before spitting out the rest of the blood and stalking away.

He turned away from his domus, though. Half an hour later, he rapped on the door of the modest town house that had been his father's. It was answered by a small but bulky pale doorman with Celtic tattoos. 'Yes?'

'Please tell Publius that his brother is here.'

As the man closed the door and disappeared inside, Rufinus took a look up and down the street. As he expected, he could see another soldier-like figure watching the house. It almost made him smile as he turned to the small candle shop opposite and saw an almost imperceptible nod from the man behind the counter. Genialis might have a man watching the house of the Marcii, but so did Cestius. It was the only reason Rufinus had not been concerned for his brother before.

The northerner appeared at the door again and beckoned for Rufinus to follow. The door closing behind them, he followed the man into Publius' triclinium. His brother looked well. A little bit older and more settled, his dress of good quality. Several slaves bustled around the place, and the house looked a lot higher quality than he remembered.

'You've redecorated.'

Publius shook his head, not in denial but at the sight of his brother. 'Have you been chasing parked carts?'

Rufinus gave an awkward chuckle. 'You should see the other fellow.'

'Problems at work?'

'Publius, I think something big is building and, while I know you're capable of taking care of yourself, especially with your slaves, I think it might be a good idea if you came and stayed with us for a while.'

Publius' eyes narrowed. 'Is it bad?'

'Potentially disastrous. If things go wrong, which they very well might, there could be a whole bunch of angry and dangerous people coming after both me and anyone who means anything to me. Thus far it's been a possibility, but I'd say it's moving into a probability. I'd feel better if you were with us. Plus, it would make it easier for me, since I wouldn't have to worry about the security of two houses at once.'

Publius nodded slowly. 'What you just did... this is going to bring people to your door?'

'It's very likely. I've sent a challenge to a very important man. He's either going to bow down to me or rise to the challenge.'

'You never know when to quit, do you, Gnaeus?'

'I'll quit when it's done. For now, it becomes a waiting game.'

XVIII – THE SECOND THREAD

He became aware of the danger only too late. This narrow street stood not far from the strange inn that Aper had once led him to when they first met, a far from salubrious part of the city. It served him right, he reflected, for taking shortcuts back from his house to the Castra Praetoria through the seedier end of the amphitheatre valley.

It was late evening, and no one respectable was around in the streets. Of course, in these particular streets no one respectable was around at *any* time of day, but the moment the two figures stepped out from a side alley ahead, Rufinus knew he was in trouble. He didn't have to turn around to know there were two more. That was how it worked: snare the prey and then tighten the noose.

The buildings to either side were tall, perhaps four storeys of crumbling brick and fire-damaged timber. There were no side alleys, for the four men had chosen their positions to seal him off between them. There were a few darkened doorways, each leading into stairwells that would grant access to the upper floor apartments of the residents. Nothing else in the street but the occasional piles of refuse and the legs of a man jutting from a doorway – a drunk or a beggar. Or both, of course.

There would be no help and there would be no escape. The only ways off the street led to places where he could be further trapped. Still, at least in those places he would not be quite so exposed.

He focused in the gloom, trying to pick out details.

The two men were of a height, average-sized but moving with the steady, confident but slow pace of a wary hunter. If they were Praetorians, then they were from the more subtle end of the scale. He could hear the same slow pacing behind. Similar men.

A gleam revealed that at least one of the men in front had a blade, and if one was armed, then almost certainly all of them were. They were within the pomerium, the ancient sacred boundary, and to be found with weapons of war here was a criminal offence, but then these would not be the sort of men to worry about such niceties. Praetorians traditionally looked down on both the Urban Cohorts and the vigiles and would laugh at any attempt to arrest them. Moreover, they were only just inside the pomerium and could easily get from here back to the fortress without incident.

Rufinus had only his centurion's vine stick. He'd never flaunted the pomerium law unless it was a matter of life and death or sanctioned from above, and being off-duty and heading back to barracks did not count.

He eyed the men warily. He was good. He *knew* he was good. With fists or weapons, he had been good ten years ago as a legionary. Now, with the most brutal experience under his belt, he was even better, and few men could match him one on one. Two on one was more problematic. That required a small amount of planning and tactics not to fall foul. Three on one was asking for trouble. It was just about possible to fight one man down while avoiding another while a third figure added a level of unknown. And a fourth? Fatality.

Oh, he'd dealt with numbers before, but only when he'd had plenty of time to plan and the initiative and ground were both to his advantage. Now, he'd been surprised, outnumbered and was facing superior armament. To fight these four on their terms would be fatal. Rufinus gave himself one chance in ten of getting out of here alive, let alone victorious.

He edged towards his right, taking the chance to glance over his shoulder and confirm what he had suspected. Two more men, much the same as their friends and both armed. All four were here to kill, and that was clear. He'd brought it on himself, of course, provoking Tribune Genialis and inviting attack. Perhaps he had been rash after all.

All the insulae were similar, but there were three advantages to the one he'd chosen. Firstly, it was equidistant between the two pairs and therefore bought him the most time. Secondly it happened to be the one with the drunk or beggar in the door, and when being chased it was always worth having potential obstacles to work with. Thirdly, if the worst came to the worst, two floors up, the residents of the facing blocks had run out a line across the alleyway to dry their clothes. If he could get to it in enough time, he could use it to either hand-over-hand to the other side, or perhaps drop to the ground. This was not about winning, but about escaping.

Without warning, he broke into a run. He was peripherally aware of them leaping into speedy pursuit, but his concentration now was on what was in front of him. He made straight for that darkened doorway. As he reached it, he leapt, passing over the slumped figure in the archway, but his right hand dropped, holding the vitis stick, which caught the slumbering figure a light blow in passing.

By the time he was at the staircase and heading up, he could hear the drunken indignant mumblings of the man he'd struck, and as he reached the first landing and turned into the second flight, he could see the unsteady figure rising in the doorway. He was rewarded as he climbed by the angry shouts of the four men as the struggled to pull the man out of the way while he flailed angrily at them. A small pang of guilt passed through him and he hoped they hadn't simply gutted the poor man as they passed.

He had his own problems, though.

Second landing. The small space was lit by an open window out onto the street. A door led off either side into private apartments. He didn't bother trying the doors. Both would be locked, latched or barred, given the dangerous region they inhabited. Instead, he turned into the next staircase and stopped dead in his tracks.

A large sleek hound that bore a resemblance to Aegyptian dog-god statues he'd seen was chained at the next landing, and it looked neither friendly nor welcoming. It snarled and roared, saliva dripping from its jaws as it strained towards him. Clearly the residents of the next floor were well aware how dangerous their neighbourhood was.

For a moment, he dithered. Was it worse to face the four men below or the dog above?

He chewed his lip, listening to the thumping boot steps on the stairs. No, he knew how to fight men, but if the last decade had taught him anything it was that attacking an enraged dog was begging for trouble. Besides, he'd done what he could. Only one man at a time could come at him here unless they managed to spill out onto the landing.

He took a deep breath and stepped back to where the staircase emerged just as the first of his pursuers rounded it. The man slowed, realising that their prey was now waiting for them. Rufinus gave his vine stick an experimental swish. There was not a lot of room. Not enough to get up much of a swing, except from above, which would open him up to blows from even a half-competent swordsman.

The second pursuer came round the corner now, and the first was advancing slowly, measured pace one step at a time. Rufinus prepared himself. At least they would be equally hampered by the space.

The first man ripped his scarf from his neck, the brooch that held it tinkling away down the stairs, and wrapped it around the knuckles of his left hand as a makeshift shield. Rufinus would make him regret that. If the man was prepared to do such a thing, then he was going to lunge with his blade and parry with his knuckles, thinking that a scarf would be adequate against a stick.

Dodge and strike was the clear response.

Rufinus stood poised. He had to be careful to maintain his balance here at the top of the stairs. He lifted his stick in his right hand, the tip over his left shoulder, but he also reached out with his left, cradling the fingertips against the brick of the wall, giving him a little better balance, or at least appearing to. In fact, he put no weight on it. The whole purpose of that left arm up was to supply an opening, an easy target for the swordsman. Rufinus had to draw the man into a move that would help him.

Sure enough as his arm came up, the left side exposed, with that all-important armpit bared, the man stabbed out with his blade, attempting to put an end to Rufinus straight away. As the blade lanced out, though, Rufinus ducked right, away from it, and brought down the vine stick with as much force as he could manage in the press.

His aim was accurate, and he heard the smashing of bones in the man's hand, despite the protection of the scarf. The attacker screamed, staggering with the momentum of his lunge, wobbling as he tried to fall neither forward onto his face at Rufinus' feet, nor backwards and down the stairs into his friends.

Rufinus drew back his vitis and used it like a gladius, stabbing out. The tip of the age-hardened vine stick slammed into the man's solar plexus and he was rewarded with the noise of air rushing out of the man's lungs as he was all-but paralysed by the blow, still screaming in pain at his broken hand.

Rufinus glared over the top of the ruined man at the remaining three on the stairs.

'I sell my life dearly,' he snarled, then put his boot against the staggering attacker and heaved, pushing him back down the stairs. The three men behind him would be more prepared, knowing their limitations and what they faced, and they all stepped lithely aside as the body of their friend thumped and clonked down the stairs past them, accompanied by further wheezed cries of pain.

Rufinus prepared himself for the next assault. Try not to get cocky, he reminded himself. He had started to think that perhaps he was the lucky one here, despite the numbers, and that sort of thing made people complacent and got them killed. He watched the eyes and hand of the next man. The sword moved from his right to his left, and Rufinus' eyes narrowed. Was he ambidextrous? If so,

Rufinus was less well prepared. Fighting a man against the offhand was something the legions were not trained for.

Testing the water for a moment, he stepped back with his left leg, stick lifted ready to strike, almost gifting the man his right leg as a target. To his credit, the man didn't fall for the bait, lessons learned from his broken friend.

Rufinus struck out, instead taking advantage of the man's hesitance. His vine stick swept down at the man's left shoulder, hoping to put the arm out of commission. The man was waiting for the blow and dodged to his right, the stick connecting but only as a glancing blow. Even as Rufinus rocked back on his feet, trying to regain his poise and bringing his stick back, the man suddenly threw himself forwards.

Rufinus was taken by surprise by the unexpectedly suicidal move, and the man hit him hard. The attacker was a foot lower than Rufinus and the barge would not wind, but it did overbalance him, and he and Rufinus went down together in a pile.

Desperation gripped him now, as he realised his advantage had just gone and the remaining two men were coming. In increasing fear, he lashed out with his feet, though the struggling man was on top of him, and he only caught another glancing blow. He was rewarded with hisses of pain as hobnails tore shreds from the man's legs as they struggled. The attacker now had his sword back in his right hand and was fighting to slam it down into Rufinus, but there was inadequate room to get much of a build-up, and Rufinus was succeeding in keeping the blade away by swatting it aside with his stick.

It was a struggle this way and that, neither man achieving any advantage, but that couldn't hold for long, and Rufinus knew he was in trouble. The other two men were coming up past them now, emerging out onto the landing. The moment they found an opening, Rufinus would be lying on his back with three armed men above him, and the end would be inevitable.

Fights were often won with a moment of unexpected advantage, and it was with some surprise that Rufinus discovered he had open space around his knee. The man was still on top of him, and that suggested one thing above all others. Hoping he was right, as he clattered the blade aside again, he brought his knee up as hard as he could. There was an unpleasant crunching sound, and the man on top of him stiffened, eyes widening. The descending sword wavered and fell aside and as the man began to open his mouth, the most unearthly keening sound emerging, Rufinus took the opportunity to head-butt his opponent, smashing him as hard as he could.

The attacker was done for. His privates were mangled, and now his head was swimming in confusion. His sword fell away with a metallic clatter, and Rufinus heard it bouncing end over end down the stairs to the next landing. With immense effort, he heaved the man away, until the body went down the stairs after his sword.

He lifted his vine stick, ready to face the next disaster, but he was still on the floor, and a military boot caught him a painful blow on the wrist. His hand flexed automatically with the pain, and with dismay he saw his stick fall away and heard it clatter down the stairs after the rest.

He shuffled backwards against the wall.

He was unarmed, his head thumping and a little swimmy from the head-butt, and now he was in real trouble. There were still two of them and he was entirely unarmed. Moreover, they were both on the landing with him now, and with space to make it two on one.

Rufinus pulled himself upright as the two men took a step forwards, nodding at one another. The unfortunate result of Rufinus scurrying backwards was that he was now trapped. The two men were between him and the stairs down, and that damn dog was still snarling, straining at the leash above. He liked to think himself a dog person, and the fierce Acheron – oh how he wished the dog was here now – had taken to him instantly, but he had a feeling that any attempt to come near the beast on the next landing was asking for a painful bite.

Up was out, then, and so was down. Had he the urgent desire to throw himself from an upper window, that was out too, since the aperture was behind one of the men. They had blades. He had nothing.

The miracle was more unexpected than anything that had happened that night. He never heard it coming, and clearly neither did the two attackers. One suddenly made an 'oof' sound and staggered a step forwards, face folding into a frown of consternation. He bent and lurched to one side, and Rufinus stared in surprise at the arrow jutting from the man's back.

It was lucky, really, that the shock had struck the other fellow just as much, for had he taken advantage of the moment, he could quite easily have run Rufinus through. The beleaguered and unarmed centurion recovered first, and reached out, grabbing the sword from the arrow-struck man's hand. Plucking it free, he turned and faced the last man.

The fourth attacker recovered, but his eyes were full of fear now, rather than sureness, as they both saw out of the corner of their eyes the man with the arrow lodged in his spine stagger into the corner making a hollow moaning noise, and then collapse in a heap, shuddering.

Rufinus took the chance to step back into the open.

One on one was more like it. Equally armed, too.

In a heartbeat he had gone from being trapped between the dog and the two attackers to trapping the last man against the dog. The soldier's worried gaze turned to the slavering animal at the top of the stair, whose eyes rolled madly as it snarled, then back to Rufinus, who nodded slowly. 'This isn't how you saw the night panning out, is it?'

To his surprise the man made no attempt at threat or negotiation, but instead went for a sudden swing of the blade. Rufinus pulled himself back away from the blow, the tip of the sword shearing through the fabric of his tunic before clanging into the brick wall.

Rufinus stabbed him. There was no grace or finesse to the blow. He was too tired and angry for anything fancy. His sword found the man's ribs, slid to a gap between them, and he pushed the blade in, heaving it deeper and deeper a little at a time, gasps emerging from the man's lips with each push.

As the tip broke out from the man's back and he staggered away, transfixed, blood emerging on his lips and his eyes wide, Rufinus simply let go.

Turning away from the doomed attacker, he picked his way between the bodies and then gingerly down the stairs past the man with the ruined testicles, pausing on the next landing to gather up his vine stick.

Breathing heavily, he emerged from the doorway back into the street. The drunk had long gone, driven away by the fighting. Three men stood in the street. Two had nightsticks out, and the third a bow, which he was busy re-slinging across his shoulder. They were Praetorians, as he could see from their tunics, but he didn't recognise them. Under any other circumstance he would now be on his guard, presuming them to be his enemy's backup. He didn't think so, though.

An arrow shot up two storeys, through a dark window and into a man's spine was a good shot. The archer was clearly an expert, and anyone capable of that wasn't going to make the mistake of hitting the wrong person. That meant the shot had been deliberate, and not meant for Rufinus, which made them, against all odds, his allies.

'Thank you,' he managed, and then broke into a prolonged fit of coughing from the effort of the past quarter hour.

'Follow us,' one of the men said, and they turned and strode along the street. Rufinus, relieved at the sudden change in his fortunes and exhausted from his efforts, simply nodded and followed. The three men led him along the valley of the amphitheatre and up onto the lower slopes of the Esquiline. Rufinus noted how they were moving steadily into a much higher-class area and soon the drab alleys gave way to wider streets and walled estates. On a higher-class commercial street running parallel to the Via Labicana, the men drew to a halt outside a tavern that was open and from which the gentle sounds of a lyre and female vocal accompaniment emerged. This was no soldier tavern, but one frequented by the wealthy locals.

Rufinus frowned at his escort, one of whom nodded at the door.

Taking a deep breath and wedging his stick under his arm, Rufinus made his way inside.

The place was much nicer than the dives to which he was accustomed, and he noted that the wealthy patrons were generally secreted in booths, where they chatted with their friends. No gambling here, and no foaming Gaulish beers. Here were good quality wines and empire-changing conversations.

A man stood at the bar, leaning there with a cup, and his rank was made clear despite his civilian clothes, for just like Rufinus he had a vitis under his arm. The man pointed to the rear of the inn. Rufinus nodded and walked into the shadowed recesses.

Half a dozen of the booths back here were empty, but the rearmost one was occupied. The man sitting within was thin and neat with a chiselled face covered with a neatly clipped beard, his hair naturally curled, reminiscent of the Hadrianic fashion. He wore a tunic with a thick stripe, and Rufinus made a leap in assumption. This man was a Praetorian tribune, and that almost certainly made him Flavius Genialis, the very man at the top of the hierarchy of villains that had been watching Rufinus' house.

'Gnaeus,' the man said with unexpected warmth and even a touch of good humour. 'Might I call you Gnaeus? Please, sit. I have good wine. And water, if you so desire.'

Rufinus' eyes narrowed. Did the man know about his love/hate history with alcohol? Few did.

He slipped into a seat opposite the man and poured himself a small glass of wine, cutting it with four parts water. Genialis nodded.

'I see you ran into some trouble.'

Rufinus nodded. 'I would have assumed them to be yours, had it not been your men who came to my rescue. And that opens up more questions than it answers, Tribune. Not that I'm not grateful,' he added.

Genialis chuckled. 'I thought it was time we met. You see I know a great deal about you, Centurion Rufinus. More, I suspect, than you even think you know about me.'

'I know you were one of Cleander's men.'

Genialis sighed. 'Half of *Rome* were Cleander's men, Gnaeus. In fact, were we to level accusations, one might even be tempted to label yourself similar.' He held up a placating hand at the sudden flash of anger in Rufinus' face. 'I mean no insult. I merely make the point that while it might have been because the chamberlain held your brother, you did his bidding for a time. When you accuse his former associates, be prepared to consider that not every man is a villain merely through association.'

Rufinus nodded slowly. 'I'll grant you that. I might, however, cite your men attacking me and mine.'

Genialis winced. 'Early days and poor judgement, I'm afraid. You see, I am one of the best-informed men in Rome, and it came to my attention that you were investigating and removing those in the Guard associated with Cleander. A number of men you dealt with disappeared or turned up dead, and a little investigation produced strong links with the frumentarii. The thing is, Gnaeus, that I might not be one of Cleander's killers, but I am a man who has long taught himself to survive this dangerous political world and, when I identify men who are inevitably going to come across my name and hunt me down, it seems prudent to act first.'

'And yet now you offer me wine and your men save my life. A turnabout from the killers on the Janiculum? The gladiator at the nymphaeum of Nero? What has changed?'

Genialis chuckled again and poured himself another drink. 'As I said, Gnaeus, I am a survivor. I have had my cart tethered to Paternus, to Perennis and to Cleander, and each of those three men has met with a grisly end leading to proscriptions. I have not been one of those affected, and I have no wish to start now.'

'This is about Crispinus?' Rufinus said, eyes narrowing again.

'Crispinus is driven and narrowly-focused,' Genialis said dismissively. 'He seeks to hitch his cart to Didius Julianus and whip the man into line, even if he is emperor. He does not think outside his own little corner of the world, and that will undoubtedly be his undoing.'

'And you want to help me bring down Crispinus?' Rufinus muttered. 'In order to save your own hide?'

'Oh, Gnaeus, don't be so naïve. You can turn Rome upside down and inside out, but you will never find a scrap of evidence linking me to a crime. Largely, because I try to stay *clear* of crime. It tends to stick like tar. And partially because if I have regrettably become involved in anything I find disagreeable, I am exceedingly careful not to leave any trail. However, I can provide you with half a dozen pieces of evidence that will help you with Crispinus and Aper when the time comes. Evidence that ties them to the murder of senators and even members of the extended imperial family. But I have no intention of doing so, as yet.'

'Why? Why approach me, then?'

'Because it is becoming clear that while you infiltrate and investigate Crispinus, you are also targeting my people. Now you are aware that I have not only called off my people, but set them to your active protection. There is, however, still the possibility that Crispinus will succeed and control the next emperor, and if he does, I will be there to sing his praises. I have no intention of setting myself against the men who may soon control the empire. I am loyal to Pertinax as I was to Commodus, and I will not intrigue against him, but I'm not so lacking in foresight that I will make an enemy of the man who might next be on the throne.'

'So, you're playing both sides. Hedging your bets.'

'Of course. How do you think I've survived the fall of three of the most infamous figures in generations? I simply want you to understand that if Crispinus wins out, then I'm afraid any alliance between us will be worthless, but that until then, I might be inclined to offer you aid against the possibility that you come out of this victorious.'

'That's very big of you,' Rufinus grunted.

'I thought you knew how this game was played, Gnaeus. Your history with Pompeianus suggests so.'

'You know a lot.'

'I do. I told you I was well informed. Would you like to know where your wife's old house was? She might sing you a song of rural and wild Britannia, but her family still occupy a small house behind a potter's shop in some provincial hole called Isurium.'

Rufinus felt his heart skip a beat. Even he didn't know that. Moreover, in a moment of self-loathing, he realised he'd never enquired as to whether she had surviving family.

'I bet you would love to know who owns your family's villa in Hispania, wouldn't you?'

Another lurch. This man was far too well informed. And dangerous. Rufinus suddenly realised that this man was far more dangerous in many ways than Crispinus. His level of criminality was yet to be revealed, but Rufinus had to admit that it would be more than advantageous to have this man on his side, for now. He nodded slowly.

'I might be tempted to accept that there is more to you than simply being one of Cleander's agents,' he said. 'But I want to know something.'

'Go ahead.'

'Who were those men who attacked me? In fact,' he added, thoughts racing, 'there are several things that don't add up for me. The man who shot Attius Sacratus on the roof of his house wore a blue feather crest and I'd assumed him to be one of Aper's men, but he couldn't be, could he? Aper is unaware of my frumentarius connections. So, he was one of yours?'

Genialis smiled apologetically. 'He was supposed to remove Sacratus. Any move he made on you was unauthorised. I am, however, far from remorseful over the episode. Frumentarii are bad enough in principle, hiding among the legions and reporting infractions to their masters, but one who had come from our own ranks and with knowledge of us all? He deserved what he got, Gnaeus.'

'Undoubtedly. So, you have men in the First Cohort too.'

'I have men everywhere. That's how to survive in this game.'

'So who were the four in the alley today if not yours?'

Genialis took a sip of his wine. 'If I am not much mistaken you will find in the morning that they are missing from muster in the First Cohort, Fifth Century. Not all of Aper's eyes and ears are in his own century. It may be that Aper is already on to you. Or it may be that your somewhat unsubtle activities since your return to Rome have brought you to their attention. No doubt we will learn this when Aper returns to our shores. Whatever the case, I strongly advise you to play the good little villain for now and stop causing ripples to spread.'

Rufinus nodded. 'I do not trust you, Tribune Genialis.'

The man laughed. 'An attitude that does you credit. You would be foolish to do so. As long as our goals do not come into conflict, however, I will call off all but the most subtle of my observers and you need fear no violence. Let us have a pact to our mutual advantage.'

Rufinus nodded slowly. He couldn't escape the feeling that he had somehow entered into a deal with the enemy, but the logic of it made sense. Until now he had been facing two groups of loosely connected enemies. To achieve a temporary alliance with one would allow him to concentrate on the other.

'You have a deal,' Rufinus said. 'You wish it sworn on an altar of Apollo?'

Genialis laughed again. 'Hardly worth it. Deals are made with the rigidity of a spider's thread in this world. But I appreciate the offer.' He sighed and stretched. 'It is time you went back to barracks, for I have another meeting shortly.'

Rufinus nodded cautiously and rose. Today had been an eye-opener. Useful, but far too unsettling to be a good thing.

XIX – THE GOVERNOR

ROME, EARLY MARTIUS

Rufinus stomped through the streets with half his century, face contorted into a mix of anticipation and dread. There had been rain during the night and small puddles lay all about the roadways and pavements, mixing with the ever-present ordure to form a sludge that deadened the sounds of hobnails on stone.

All around, in the morning's weak and watery sun, people were busy taking down garlands from the Matronalia festival the previous day and tidying up the inevitable debris. The people of Rome loved a festival, and they rarely had to wait a handful of days between even the more important ones.

The Esquiline hill had been raucous last night as the centre of the festival, but even here, in the Campus Martius, things had clearly got out of hand at times. The century veered out like the swerve of a snake in sand to avoid the legs of a partygoer who remained prostrate at the roadside, alternately coughing and giggling.

Rufinus' thoughts wandered back to last night. Senova had insisted on having a little soiree at their townhouse. She had invited a few of the less vapid women in her circle of brainless noblewomen, along with their avaricious and underhanded husbands. He had made sure to invite Mercator and Icarion to maintain a conversational level throughout the night.

It had been a costly affair. Tradition had the household's staff being given the day off, and the lady of the house preparing a meal for them. Senova having all the culinary ability of a cabbage, she had delegated the responsibility to a caterer she found. A caterer, moreover, who came with a good reputation and who cost a small fortune to take the place of the house's staff for the day, especially since they were in demand for the festival and therefore trebled their rates for the duration.

With the influx of temporary staff, while the house's 'servants' and 'slaves' might have taken the night off, they remained in evidence around the domus, watching the new arrivals like hawks. They were not about to let an assassin slip into the house so easily.

As it happened, nothing untoward had happened. Rufinus had not expected it to, given the strange truce he now had with Tribune Genialis, and the continued absence of Aper, though he could not rule it out, given what had happened in the street that day.

Before the guests arrived, Rufinus had given Senova her gift, for husbands and children always gave gifts to the household's mother figure on Matronalia. The dark-haired Briton had opened the package, weighing it first, and had lifted the contents to examine it, one eyebrow cocked quizzically. It was not the reaction he'd hoped for, but then he'd never been very good with presents.

It was a knife. He'd had it made especially by a craftsman down near the Ludus Gallicus. It was of the sort used by a retiarius in the arena, like a military pugio though narrower and straighter and more lightweight. The man had been good and the cost extortionate, and the hilt was engraved on one side with an image of Senova's favoured goddess, Brigantia. In actual fact it was Minerva, but the man had labelled it BRIG, and Senova would only see her own goddess in it. The other side had a stylised outline of Britannia that Rufinus had hastily copied down from one of Ptolemy's maps held in the tabularium.

'Times are dangerous,' he'd said. 'It's time you had something of your own.'

'Thank you,' she'd said, and he couldn't read in her voice how she felt about the gift, though her expression suggested she might have preferred clothing or jewellery. Women were complicated, he'd concluded, and he had then settled in for the evening.

Mercator had been in high spirits and had been mysterious. Annoyingly so. He kept mentioning his business deals and his acquisitions. He was due his honesta missio in two years, and Rufinus had always assumed he would just reenlist, though he was clearly wrong. Icarion and Mercator had joined together fourteen years ago and were looking forwards to retirement.

Icarion was trying to decide whether to stay in Rome and live off his pension or to return to his family's lands in the east. Praetorians were still largely drawn from the home country, from the regions around Rome, but there were exceptions, and Icarion was one. Connections with a leading senator at the time had seem him acquire Praetorian white even from his distant Greek estates.

Mercator, though, was looking forwards immensely to becoming a man of leisure. He would be, he said happily, a very wealthy man. He might even buy himself into the equestrian order and see how far he could go politically. He had dabbled for more than a decade in various markets, increasing his purse continually until he was able to acquire land. Now, he had numerous estates producing wine, oil, fruit and more. A magnate. A new Crassus in the making.

Rufinus had considered his own estate and been a little jealous as he noted the huge difference between the two. Mercator had laughed and hinted that he would see Rufinus right. He had one investment in particular that would be of interest to Rufinus but was consistently coy and evasive when pressed on it. Irritating man. Good job he was a friend.

The party had wound down before midnight, disappointing the various rich idiots Senova had invited, but Rufinus had been adamant, given that the Praetorians would all need to be safely in barracks in time to sleep before shifts. Particularly given what was happening today.

The Navalia came into view ahead, and Rufinus took a steadying breath. A courier had reached Rome two days ago, informing Tribune Tullius Crispinus that the governor and his retinue were en route. The courier had been sent up the Via Appia from an overnight stop at Formiae with advance notice, and with no horrible storms to delay the ships, today would be the day of their arrival.

He could see ships now, settled in against the dock of the Navalia. Damn it, but they looked like African ships from the colours. He'd assumed the governor's retinue would arrive in the afternoon, but it seemed that they must have overnighted at Portus and just sailed upriver this morning to Rome. He was late.

In fairness, it shouldn't really matter. The African governor would have Aper and his century with him anyway. It was only a matter of courtesy that Crispinus had sent Rufinus with an escort, but it would still have looked better if they had been awaiting the ships' arrival rather than hurrying to catch up.

As they passed into the great square of the Navalia, he could see that the ships had only just arrived. To his relief, he spotted Aper forming up his men on the stone flags, while Didius Julianus and his retinue faffed and argued still aboard their ship, and all his luxuries and worldly goods were unloaded from the ship behind.

Rufinus passed the orders to his signifer and veered away from his men as they fell in at attention roughly halfway between their sister century and the Navalia gates. Rufinus, however, strode across to the newly arrived Praetorians as Aper stepped away from them to intercept him.

'How was the journey?' he asked.

Aper's lip wrinkled. 'Hate winter travel, even this late in the season. Time is becoming an issue, though. The governor felt the need to be on hand.'

Rufinus thought he detected something in the man's voice that sounded like more than mere travel irritations. He cleared his throat. 'I can understand that. Things continue to move apace. How has the governor arranged his return? Wasn't he due for recall to Rome at the end of the year?'

Aper nodded. 'The governor's brother has raised a case in the courts contesting the will of an uncle. In truth, I don't think either of them really care about the pitiful inheritance, especially given how wealthy they now are, but it was an adequate excuse for him to set aside the governance of Africa and return to Rome to deal with family matters.'

Rufinus chewed his lip. 'The timing might look suspicious,' he suggested.

'That cannot be helped. He has appropriate permissions to return and lay down his baton, and no one will argue. Messages from the tribune have been vague by necessity.' The centurion looked about to make sure no one was listening in, and led Rufinus across to a portico filled with crates and coiled ropes, far from open ears. 'Tell me what's happening.'

Rufinus scratched at his neck. 'The emperor's position grows ever more tenuous. The senate are still wholly in support of him, and the mob cheer for him, but you know the people of Rome. They'd cheer a donkey if you put a purple cloak on him.'

A nod. 'Go on.'

'Word is that he has the tentative support of the military. There have been no open moves against him, and all legions have taken their oath.'

'But?'

'But we know that Albinus is in Britannia with three legions, and he considers himself a contender for the throne. The same can be said of Niger in Syria with his two legions. Lupus and Geminus in Germania are unknown quantities, but they have a great deal of military strength. Whoever they throw their support behind will be a strong candidate. So officially, the army supports him, but it's a house made of glass, and one thrown stone could see the whole thing shatter.'

'Do not forget Severus,' Aper murmured.

Rufinus' heart lurched. 'What?'

'Septimius Severus. Governor of Pannonia. He can call in four legions through direct or indirect control, and he's a strong man. An ambitious one. He's as dangerous as Albinus or Niger.'

Rufinus frowned, shaking his head. 'I have it on good authority that Severus is a solid supporter of Pertinax. It seems that when Pertinax tried to persuade Pompeianus to take the throne, that was Severus' doing too. I don't think he's a threat to Pertinax.'

'Perhaps,' Aper replied, eyes narrowing. 'I would be interested to know where you get your information. What of the Guard?'

Rufinus scratched again. 'There the emperor is on very shaky ground. He's undone all the grants of Commodus, withdrawing numerous privileges and reinstating a more legionary-style administration and rule. Some of the men approve, but the majority have seen a reduction in pay scale, free time, and general quality of life, and an increase in shifts, duties and restrictions. The number of men on sick lists, applying for leave or simply seeking early retirement are the highest in Guard history. The emperor has not made himself popular.'

'And what of the prefect?'

Rufinus shivered. This was all true. Pertinax had responded to the threat of corruption in the Guard not by excising it, but by restricting their capabilities and authority. Far from making them less of a threat, this course had turned against him men who might otherwise have been ardent supporters of the new regime. Moreover, Tribune Crispinus had been at work, spreading dissent like a plague, often using Rufinus in the process, something that he hated to do yet had to in order to maintain his fictional allegiance.

The men were easily swayed, from Rufinus' recent experience. Men were readily bought with matters of finance and luxury. But the officers were a different matter. The majority of the centurions seemed to be of the opinion that any restrictions or impositions would gradually ease as the new reign continued and that they simply needed to ride it out. Moreover, the tribunes were not turned from Pertinax. They were in a very favourable and lucrative position, and each of them knew that they could be made or broken with a single word from the emperor. Their continued wellbeing relied upon his good favour.

The major coup for Crispinus, though, had been the Praetorian Prefect: Laetus. The prefect, who persistent rumour said was the man behind the plot against Commodus, had been a grudging accepter of Pertinax. His initial support had waned, though, as the new emperor imposed his list of restrictions and changes upon the Praetorians.

Still, he had a reputation as a solid man despite his involvement in the recent imperial demise, and he would almost certainly have remained loyal to Pertinax had Crispinus' honeyed words not worked their poison into the man's ears over the past month, continually eroding ardent support. The tribune had advised Rufinus that the time for action was near. Even if he did not lend his weight to change, the prefect was unlikely to stand in the way when it happened. And two of the tribunes and several centurions were in, along with a sizeable portion of the general soldiery.

Rufinus could feel it coming, and the arrival of Didius Julianus in Rome would be a catalyst for sure. He'd managed a single, brief clandestine meeting with Vibius Cestius, pressing the matter. Cestius had shared his concerns, but had advised him that even the frumentarii, who were the emperor's staunchest allies, had been unable to persuade Pertinax away from his course, of the danger it posed to him. And so Rufinus had watched the plots sliding into place.

He'd even been tempted to do something about it himself, despite being advised, and even ordered, against it by both Cestius and Pertinax. But at this stage, he reasoned, it would be fruitless. He could perhaps bring down Crispinus, and maybe even Aper too, but it was too late now to stop what was looming. With the prefect dissatisfied and others in the Guard turning against the emperor despite having nothing to do with Rufinus' investigation, the loss of Aper and his master would probably be little more than a bump in the road to the runaway cart of Praetorian disobedience. It was yet another indication that the rot Rufinus had set out to cure in the Guard went far deeper and was more widespread than anyone could have guessed. It was hard to imagine the Guard under Perennis having been so pliable and corrupt. Cleander's influence had seemingly ruined the Praetorians for good.

He'd even tried to arrange another audience with the emperor. It was not a common thing for a mere centurion, but given their history he felt that Pertinax might well agree. Sadly, the new emperor was so busy with affairs of state this early in his reign that he could not find the time, continually putting Rufinus off with hazy promises of a meeting to be scheduled when time allowed

And so Rufinus stood in the metaphorical street and watched that metaphorical cart of treason rattling down the hill towards the emperor who stood with his back to it. Julianus was here in the city now with his fellow conspirators, and the emperor might be aware of the danger, but he still refused to act sufficiently to stop it. There was just one hope left for Rufinus. Perhaps, just perhaps, Pertinax would hear the rumble of the cart wheels as it approached in sufficient time to step aside. Then the cart could crash harmlessly into a wall and those aboard could be dealt with.

In other words, what with Rufinus and the frumentarii keeping an eye on building events and fruitlessly reporting them to the emperor, when a move was finally made hopefully Pertinax would be prepared enough to counter it and grant Rufinus and his ilk the authority to deal with it.

It was a worrying hope. Things would be a little too close to the line by that time.

He took a breath and turned back to Aper. 'The prefect is mostly, if not wholly, in Crispinus' purse now. The Guard wavers. Men in position back us.'

Aper nodded and Rufinus once more caught something in his eye, just for a moment before the centurion turned away. Something subtle and worrying. Suspicion?

He shivered.

The two men returned to their units as Didius Julianus, former governor of Africa, stepped down the boarding ramp and onto the dock side. There was the inevitable quarter hour wait as the man's entourage readied itself, almost enough pomp for a consul, or even an emperor. Finally, as six lictors stepped into position, the entire procession was ready. Rufinus wondered at the presumption of the man. A governor was entitled to lictors, yes, but Julianus had resigned his governorship to come home. Doubtless no one would argue that he should no longer have his lictors, but by rights they should now have stepped down.

Aper's century positioned themselves as the vanguard and peripheral protection, leaving Rufinus and his half century to bring up the rear. A litter was brought forward and Julianus helped into it. Finally, with everything ready, they departed. As they left the Navalia the rain began once more, initially as only a light shower, but as they passed across the Campus Martius and began to climb the slopes, it gradually became heavier until it settled into a thunderous downpour.

Up the slopes of the Quirinalis they moved until they took a side street and approached a large house with an impressive enclosed acreage of gardens. There, the Praetorians delivered the former governor to his Roman town house.

Julianus was in Rome, awaiting his chance, and his chance looked like it might come worryingly soon.

As the last of the entourage was seen into the domus, the century and a half of Praetorians turned and marched away, heading for the Castra Praetoria. As they marched, the two centurions side by side and their men tromping along, sodden and weighed down behind them, they moved in silence, but Rufinus was becoming increasingly concerned by the aura emanating from his fellow officer.

The occasional looks he caught from Aper were less than encouraging, and there was a definite air of suspicion. Had it been there from the start? Had Aper already been considering Rufinus' loyalty when he arrived, or had he accidentally let something slip in that short conversation at the Navalia? He couldn't remember dropping anything dangerous into it, but Aper was clever and cautious, after all.

Up the hill they clomped, the rain running down the street beneath their feet, carrying a brown-grey torrent of slurry as it went. Every man in the unit would be cleaning his boots tonight. It came as something of a relief when the gate of the Praetorian fortress came into view, for the tension in him had been building throughout the march. He couldn't say for sure whether the tension was all within him, or whether it was perhaps also coming from Aper.

In the camp, once Rufinus had given the watchword and secured them access, Aper dismissed his century, sending them back to their barracks for the first time in over a year. Rufinus did the same, and walked slowly after them, keeping a peripheral eye on his fellow centurion. He'd assumed that the first thing Aper would do was report to his tribune, and so it came as something of a surprise when the centurion walked straight past the headquarters building and off towards the granaries and the fortress stores.

Suspicion building, Rufinus hurried after his men and passed his helmet and shield to one of them to take back to barracks, then pulled the hood of his cloak up over his head against the rain and made off at speed. Ahead he could see Aper stomping away through the rain. The man did not turn to look back, but Rufinus played it safe anyway. Hurrying along the barrack blocks, he made his way to one of the streets that ran parallel with that along which Aper walked. He ran for a short time until he caught up with his prey and there the two centurions walked, parallel but one block apart. Rufinus, just cloaked and without his identifying blue shield or blue crest, would look like any other soldier, especially through the torrential rain.

Finally, he passed a barrack block and glanced left to see that Aper had turned away. Keeping his distance, Rufinus followed. The man had passed the granaries and was in the area of storehouses.

What was he up to? Slowing to match the centurion's speed, he walked on, head lowered, looking up from under his hood to keep a watch on his prey.

Aper stopped at the door of a storehouse, a plain, windowless block much the same as all the others in the area, and he pulled open the door and stepped inside. As Rufinus approached, slowing further, three guardsmen emerged from the building into the rain, hastily throwing cloaks over themselves. Aper had thrown them out. Clearly, he sought privacy. Was he alone now, or was he in there with some conspirator?

The door to the storehouse closed and the three men dispersed. Feeling free of the danger of discovery, Rufinus picked up his pace once more, first to a fast walk and then to a jog. Moments later, he was at the block. Chewing his lip, he looked around. There were precious few folk about. Unless men had urgent business, they would be inside, hiding from the downpour. Here among the storehouses there were few visitors generally, and in this weather Rufinus was alone. He wanted to know what was going on inside that hut but could not work out how to do so.

Opening the door was clearly out. There were no windows or roof lights. Some of the storehouses had them, but others, containing the more important stores, and especially the armoury, did not sport such apertures. This place wasn't the armoury. What did it contain, he wondered?

Holding his breath, he crept close to the door and listened as hard as he could. He could hear nothing. The solid walls of the block, added to the thunder of torrential rain on stone and on tile roof, drowned out any hope of hearing conversation within. Fretting and fidgeting, he circled the building once more. He couldn't hear what was going on. He couldn't open the door, and that was the only entrance. There were no windows on any other wall or on the roof. No way in.

A thought striking him, his gaze dropped to the ground.

Like many of the stores, and the granaries in particular, this block had been built on raised supports with narrow channels to allow circulation of air that would both prevent rot settling in from beneath on any perishable goods, and go some way to stopping rats nesting among the stores. He frowned at the narrow gaps.

Could he fit?

Crouching, he measured the gap. He could probably squeeze in there. It would be tight and far from comfortable, and it was a damned good job he was wearing his chain shirt, as segmented body armour would never fit. He tried to picture the storehouses from the various times he'd been in them in the past. They were pretty uniform in design. Aper had been in there long enough already.

Hurrying back along the building and checking to make sure he was unobserved, Rufinus dropped to the ground, discarding his cloak carelessly and pulling himself into the gap. It was claustrophobic, unpleasant, and very smelly, but by wriggling, he could pull himself along beneath the building. After a few moments, he reasoned he should be somewhere beneath the desk. He wriggled to a halt, the sound of the rain now muffled in these horrible confines. He turned his head to angle his ear upwards and found himself face to face with the long dead eye sockets of a mummified stray cat. He felt his gorge rise and fought it down as he focused on the muffled voices from above.

He could just hear them. Just make out most of the words through the floorboards and over the drumming of the rain back out from the air duct.

'…what the fuck happened to them?'

He couldn't hear the reply enough to make it out. There was a second voice that sounded halfway between accusation and apology. Rufinus frowned. Another of Aper's men. A man in charge of a storeroom. He had to be talking about the four men who had attacked Rufinus in the street recently. That meant they were probably all Fifth Century. He suddenly remembered that day they had arrived back in the fortress in the wake of the emperor's demise. Men of the First Cohort had brought Crispinus' empty chests out to the headquarters. Rufinus would be willing to bet a great deal of money that the four men who attacked him in the street had been among those on the carts that day, and that the man to whom Aper was now talking had also been with them. This secure store had been the one where the African coins had been kept.

'You don't know who?' Aper demanded angrily. Rufinus realised that if he crawled across the cat's desiccated body to the next channel, he might be able to hear the other man better. But then he would risk being heard from above, and then he might not be able to hear Aper anyway.

Resigned to only one side of the conversation, he listened to the centurion.

'I think I know who,' Aper snapped. 'Pull back the rest of your men. Leave it to me now.'

There was a muffled and quite long reply, and Rufinus chewed his lip, which tasted of dust. And long dead cat.

'I don't trust him either,' Aper grunted, and Rufinus knew now that it was him about whom the man spoke. That explained those suspicious looks as they walked. 'No, I *can't* do anything about him,' snapped the centurion loudly. 'He's been useful to the tribune, supplying information. He's Crispinus' new golden boy. I've been out of the loop so long that Rufinus has become his go-to. I need proof if I want to deal with him. I can't even think of bad-mouthing the tribune's new favourite until I can prove his treachery.'

Another muffled and long-winded reply. Rufinus felt his heart racing. Aper suspected him, especially after the death of those four men, but Crispinus did not. As long as Aper had nothing on him, nothing would happen, but the moment Aper had proof, Rufinus would be in for it.

'He has important friends,' the centurion said now. 'He had the patronage of Severus, the governor of Pannonia for a while. He was in Dacia with Niger and Albinus on Cleander's orders, so gods-alone know what deals he might have made with those two snakes out on the edge of the empire. More than that he seems to have some connection with Pertinax, though I can't ascertain how.'

More muffled replies.

'No, that's another reason I cannot move on him without proof. No matter how tenuous his hold on power, Pertinax is still emperor for now, and I can hardly move on one of his old friends without risking everything.'

More replies.

'Severus, Albinus, Niger and Pertinax. And he's definitely got connections to old Pompeianus.' Muffled words and then the reply. 'No, Pompeianus is far from harmless. He may have refused the throne and settled into a supportive role, but he's of the extended family of Marcus Aurelius and popular with both the senate and the army. One word from him would turn a dozen legions against us. And he seems to be closely linked to Rufinus. The bastard lived with him for a while at the empress' villa before her attempt at a coup. Jove, he's married to a Briton who Pompeianus used to *own*. No, he's too well connected to deal with directly.'

Rufinus shivered. There was more than an element of threat at the end there.

'No, we can't,' Aper said in reply to his friend again. 'But keep a wary eye out. And I'll needle and damage Rufinus again and again until I goad him into doing something stupid. I'll make him betray himself soon enough, and then we can all move.'

More conversation.

'No, nothing will happen for a few days, but I reckon the end will come before the month is out, and I'll have Rufinus reveal his true colours to the tribune by then.'

There was a further muffled exchange, and then heavy footsteps as Aper marched towards the door and left the building. Rufinus lay still for a long moment, aware that the centurion might pause as he departed. Giving it a count of three hundred to be sure, Rufinus began to pull himself forwards once more. It was no good reversing out the way he'd come. If Aper, or indeed any other casual observer, happened to be in the road, they would notice the legs emerge from the channel. Instead he pulled himself from the far side of the building and emerged into the empty street there, heaving in sodden but relatively clean air. His lungs felt full of dust and dead cat, and he coughed as he hurried around the building until he collected his cloak.

Checking that Aper had truly gone, he trudged steadily and slowly back to his barracks and opened the door to his room with a great deal of relief. His quarters were empty and seemingly undisturbed.

Aper was on to him. He could prove nothing, fortunately, and wouldn't move against him until he could. That meant that Rufinus had to keep his nose totally clean from now on. Tribune Crispinus trusted him, and he had to do everything he could to maintain that trust. He had to be more useful to the villain than ever. Could he call in the other tribune, Genialis? No, the man might have struck up an uneasy temporary alliance with Rufinus, but he had made it perfectly clear that he was out for himself and would not move against anyone that endangered his future.

But Aper was out for blood now. He was going to push and prod Rufinus until he broke and did something. There were people in the city about whom Rufinus cared a great deal, and if the centurion could not go after him directly, it seemed logical that he would next turn on those to whom Rufinus was close. Cestius could look after himself and was all-but untouchable. Then there were Mercator and Icarion. He would have to warn them. They would probably be alright, but in the absence of easier targets, Aper might move on them. The prime concerns, though, remained Publius and Senova. Both were already on alert and in the same house, and both were protected by a small force of ex-legionaries chosen by both Cestius and Severus. Yet still, Rufinus worried for them. He would have to warn them of the increased danger, and perhaps supplement their staff with even more men.

He would not let the bastard get to his loved ones, but the noose was tightening.

Within the month, Aper had said.

XX – DARK OMENS

ROME, LATE MARTIUS

Rufinus reflected grimly how fast a month raced past when every day of it counted. He had spent much of that time watching Aper carefully, being extremely helpful to Crispinus wherever possible, failing to achieve a private meeting with the emperor, and checking up on his loved ones.

In the latter he was at least satisfied. Aper had said he would make Rufinus break by needling him, and yet over the days since that conversation nothing like that had happened. But then Aper would have needed god-like powers to get to any of them now. He had persuaded Mercator and Icarion to secure a temporary assignment which took them across the water into Pannonia. Not only would that keep them far from Aper's clutches, it was land under Severus' control, and the centurion would have little influence there. They were as safe as he could make them. Cestius he had not spoken to, but the Castra Peregrina was as safe from Praetorian moves as anywhere in the empire.

And the townhouse of the Marcii was a fortress in itself. Rufinus had visited the barracks of the Misenum Fleet and spoken to his old adjutant, Philip. The man was a Christian and a man rigidly bound to the fleet, and one flash of Rufinus' new frumentarius insignia was enough to secure his loyalty. Philip was a man Rufinus trusted above most, and a man who had no connection with either Cleander or the Praetorians. Philip had arranged for a courtesy posting of three contubernia of burly and hardened veteran marines, who Rufinus had put in the house, stationing them also at any approach to the place. Even the most rapacious enemy would think twice about taking on a house protected by twelve legionaries and eighteen marines. Senova and Publius had been safe, though both were forced to live a somewhat insular life, unable to leave the safety of the house.

The fact was, though, that they had got through most of Martius without incident. He could see in Aper the impotent irritation, though he said nothing. The centurion was unaware that Rufinus knew of his suspicions or his plans, and it was better to keep it that way. But

Aper was seething over his failure to get to Rufinus, who cleaved ever closer to their tribune commander.

Now was the fifth day before the kalends of Aprilis, and the month was almost over. Given that the centurion had been convinced that their plot would culminate before the month was out, Rufinus' tension levels had built constantly to the point where he was almost twanging.

He looked around at the soldiers with him. They were on the alert as much as Praetorians ever were in their emperor's company, but he would have liked them even more prepared, in truth. If he could have found a way to suggest to optio Gamburio and the rest of the century that he had good information that a plot against the emperor was already underway, he would have done so, but to suggest that would risk too much. He had to rely on their professionalism. At least Gamburio and the others remained loyal to their oath and seemed not to have succumbed to the infection of dissatisfaction that pervaded the Guard now.

The emperor stood at the altar in front of the Temple of Jupiter, accompanied by priests and attendants and senators. The white lamb lay still on the marble surface, blood already collected in the bowl and running down the ornate white block. Eighty Praetorians stood around the edge of the open square before the temple, each man watching every movement of those present, the people of Rome gathered in the forum below.

This was the sort of place an attack on the emperor could easily be made. Public and open. Rufinus was determined that his men would prevent any trouble. Other than that, the palace would be the place to worry about. The Palatine was guarded by Praetorians, but how much use was that when it was those same Praetorians who posed the danger.

He chewed his lip, eyes darting back and forth, and when a bark of worried consternation arose from the small crowd at the altar his hand went straight to the hilt of his sword. Spinning to face the emperor, he loosened his grip again. No mad assassins rushed at him. No arrows whirred from the shadows. Something had gone wrong with the sacrifice, though.

That in itself was a worry, of course, but a lesser one than Rufinus' main concerns.

'Where is the heart?' he heard the emperor stutter in shock. 'Where is the heart? Where is the liver?'

'The beast was whole, Domine,' breathed a priest. 'It walked to the altar.'

'They must be hiding in the gut now,' Pertinax grunted, rummaging in the animal's innards.

'Domine, it is a bad omen.'

The emperor grunted. 'It's a sign that I was too rough with my sacrifice and accidentally shifted its organs about when I went in is all.'

But the damage had been done. A voice towards the rear of the group suddenly called out in a panicked voice. 'The heart of Rome is missing! Rome is dying!'

Rufinus knew how fast such rumours spread, and he pointed at Gamburio. 'Shut that man up.'

Half a dozen Praetorians wrestled the speaker to the ground, silencing him, but it was too late. The story of the sacrifice missing a heart was racing through the crowd like wildfire. Pertinax irritably shouted 'Here they are. They were out of place.' But it was too late. The word had gone out.

The emperor looked about. Men stood ashen faced, and the crowd down in the forum let forth groans and moans of dismay. It would be the work of days putting the facts right and stamping down that rumour. Damn the man with the big mouth.

Pertinax straightened, face angry, snarling. 'This is done. See that Jove is given his dues. We return to the palace. I must clean up before the performance this afternoon.'

Leaving the attendants to their work, the Praetorians formed up around the emperor and his entourage, the lictors out front, and escorted him from the Capitol. With a sigh of relief that once more nothing had happened, they delivered Pertinax to the Palatine, saw him safely into the palace under the watchful eyes of the Second Century, none of whom Rufinus had any specific concerns about, and then withdrew and returned to the Castra Praetoria.

As they made their way through the main city-facing gate of the fortress, Rufinus dismissed the century, and Gamburio took the men back to their barracks. Rufinus stood for a moment in the cold air, grateful that the rain of the past few weeks had finally abated, and tried to decide what to do next. The emperor would spend a few hours in the palace getting himself ready, and then the relatively trustworthy Second Century would escort him to the Athenaeum for the poetry reading. He was as safe as he could be for now.

Time to work on Tribune Crispinus then, to see if he could identify any advance in their plans. He had been focused on Aper this past month but had spent plenty of time with Crispinus. The man had been closeted away with Laetus on occasion, had been visiting

Didius Julianus at his house on the Quirinalis, and had spent much of the rest of the time in his office. Rufinus had the feeling the tribune was moving things along, but not openly, and Rufinus had seen nothing of it. He only hoped that Aper had not changed his mind and spoken of his concerns to the tribune. It seemed the most likely reason for Rufinus' exclusion from the plan. But then, if that were the case, he would more likely be languishing in a cellar than worrying about it all.

Likely Aper, frustrated in his attempts to get at Rufinus, had turned instead to ingratiating himself once more with the tribune. Rufinus squared his shoulders and turned, striding towards the headquarters building. He paused beneath the grand archway, a frown folding his brow at the sound of sudden military mobilisation. Ducking back against the wall into the shadow, he peered out along the street.

His heart leapt into his mouth as a mass of Praetorians emerged from a side street, armed and armoured for war. He recognised Aper leading them, and the centurion of the Fifth who was in the man's pay. A third centurion he didn't recognise was there too, and some three hundred men, bearing such an array of shields and crests that they had to have been drawn from more than a dozen different units. This was no official patrol. This was a mob, drawn from all over the Guard and led by Aper.

Surely the tribune's plan had been more subtle than this?

He watched them move. They did not march together, and they kept no formation. This was an angry mob of soldiers with murder in mind. Gods, but the plan did not *need* to be subtle. That was why Crispinus had not been working his plot. He had already put everything in place weeks ago, and had then just waited for it to boil over. Rufinus wondered for a moment what had triggered it. Some dispute over pay perhaps? A man being refused leave? Something small and innocuous, certainly, but which had been the final blow that had collapsed the wall, and now the anger of the Guard that had been building for two months and more flowed out.

Rufinus wondered if the men of the Second Century at the Palatine would be able to stop them. Would they be *willing* to do so, he suddenly thought with a catch in his throat?

He stared as the force passed. Fortunately, Aper was intent enough on goading his mob that he failed to notice Rufinus lurking in the archway. Heart racing, he watched them stomping towards the gate. By rights they should not be permitted to leave the fortress, not without official duty and certainly not in this form. It confirmed one of two things when the gates opened readily for them: either the gate guards were in on it, or the dissatisfaction within the Guard was so all-pervasive that it had reached almost every man.

What should he do? Panic began to settle in. His duty as a Praetorian, as a frumentarius, and simply as a loyal Roman citizen, was to warn the emperor and attempt to stop this. His ongoing investigation, though, demanded that he remain seemingly part of Crispinus' cadre. Shaking, he fumed with indecision. His eyes strayed back across the inside of the headquarters, towards the tribunes' offices, and he was surprised to spot Tribune Genialis standing close to the statue of Minerva. The man gave an almost imperceptible small shake of the head that sent a cold shiver through him once more. Genialis could not be relied upon to help.

Damn it.

He had to do something. Watching the gate close behind the mob, he turned and ran. Not towards the gate. Not towards his own block. Certainly not to Crispinus' office. He made for the stables. Bursting in at one end of the familiar complex, he hurried along to Atalanta's stall. A slave was busy polishing his saddle and recoiled in shock as Rufinus ripped it from his hands and kicked open the stall door, breaking the lock.

'Open it up,' he barked, pointing to the main doors that led out onto the road beyond, as he threw his blanket over the horse's back and then dropped the saddle in place, cinching it. He glanced at his bridle and reins but decided that time was of the essence. He was no cavalryman, but he was passing competent at guiding the mare with just his knees.

By the time the slave had unbolted the large doors and pulled them back, Rufinus was mounted, and clattered out past him a moment later. Out in the street, he made for the southeast gate. No good using the same gate as the others and getting too close to Aper. He had no idea what he was going to do, but he had to at least try and maintain a fiction of still working for the tribune. Not being seen by that angry mob was important.

He slowed as he approached the gate. The optio on duty called out to him, demanding to know his business. Rufinus simply bit back his retort and answered with the password.

'Carthago delenda est. Now open the damn gate.'

The soldier frowned at him, but he was a centurion with the appropriate password, and a moment later he was through the gate and clattering off down the street. He knew the city well, and knew the roads taken by the Guard to get from one place to another. Aper and his men would be marching along the Vicus Patricius now, the most direct route to the Palatine. They would move fast, for the centurion could not afford to slacken the pace and risk his angry mob cooling their blood to the point of reconsidering. There would be his conspirators among them, of course, but the bulk would be simply soldiers who had lost their temper and gone with the flow.

They would be fast, but they were still on foot. He was taking a longer route, but Atalanta would give him sufficient edge. Racing down the Vicus Macellum Liviae, he crossed the Esquiline. All the time as he rode, he tried to plan ahead, but he simply could see no easy way to do this. Whether or not he blew his cover or even sacrificed his life, though, the critical thing was to warn the emperor.

Past the corner of the Baths of Trajan he hurtled, shouting for panicked citizens to get out of the way. All along the street he had left a wake of staring Romans, and women scooped their children out of the way of the hurtling mounted Praetorian. Past the great amphitheatre he now thundered, and into the Via Triumphalis. Aper and his men would be somewhere approaching the forum, making straight for the palace's main entrance.

Passing beneath the lofty arches of the Aqua Claudia, he climbed the hill. Past imposing buildings, he turned onto the next terrace and rode back along the side of the hill, climbing as he went, then close to the end of the palace, where the aqueduct reached the hilltop, he reined in and threw himself from the saddle. Not even bothering to tether the reins to anything, he trusted Atalanta's good sense and left her standing in the street as he ran over to the small postern door that marked one of the lesser entrances to the palace, hammering on the timber loudly.

The door was pulled open a couple of handbreadths and a suspicious face appeared.

'Yes?' asked a neatly attired Praetorian, one of the Second Century.

'Centurion Rustius Rufinus, First Cohort Third Century. Let me in.'

'Password?'

'Omnia Vincit,' Rufinus breathed, 'now open the door.'

The guardsman did so, and Rufinus burst in past him, running off through the rooms at the end of the stadium garden. Past surprised looking slaves, freedmen and Praetorians he ran, through the peristyle with the pond and towards the imperial apartments. The emperor had no official business until the poetry reading and would be preparing himself in the private rooms.

At the door that divided the public areas from the private ones, Rufinus saw two men on guard. He recognised neither. They could be Aper's men, or simply ordinary guards. He had no way of telling. But he had to get inside, so he was going to have to trust to luck and the will of the gods. Running over to them, he waved a hand.

'Let me in.'

'The emperor is not to be disturbed.'

'This is a matter of life and death. Let me in or I'll see you transferred to the Arabian desert frontier within the week.'

The two men shared a look built from uncertainty and panic. One nodded and they stepped aside. Rufinus gave them a glare. 'No one else comes in, got it?'

They saluted and he ran on inside. They would, of course, admit any other Praetorian officer who threatened them, but it had to be worth a try. Hurrying through the rooms and corridors, Rufinus found a slave he recognised as one often seen with Pertinax.

'Where is the emperor?'

'In his study, Domine.'

Rufinus ran on past, making for the room that looked out over the circus valley that Pertinax, like his predecessor, used as a private office. Another soldier stood outside the office, and Rufinus came to a breathless halt before him.

'Announce me. Centurion Rufinus.'

The guardsman frowned in confusion.

'Do it!'

Swallowing nervously at the strength in the officer's voice, the man rapped quietly on the door and at a murmur from inside, entered. A moment later, he re-emerged and stepped aside. Rufinus moved to the doorway. Pertinax, emperor of Rome, had risen from his desk and turned.

'Rufinus?'

'Domine, an armed mob of Praetorians closes on the palace with the intent of treason.'

Pertinax frowned. 'You jest, surely?'

Rufinus shook his head. 'Dissatisfaction in the Guard is just too much. Your austerity measures, Domine. Villains who worked for Cleander work against you now and rouse the Guard to dethrone you. You must gather what men you trust and withdraw. Make for the Villa of the Sessorium. The guards there are threaded with men from the frumentarii and will hold true.'

'You *do* jest if you see me as the sort of man who backs down from a threat, Rufinus.'

241

'Domine, this is crucial!'

'As is my reputation. I will not cower like Nero. Come.'

Rolling his shoulders, Rufinus followed the emperor from the room. As they moved through the imperial apartments and made their way into the public area, a distant din became noticeable.

'They're in the palace, Domine,' Rufinus said urgently. 'You must get out.'

'No. Not this time.' Pertinax, exuding the aura of a lion among his pride, strode for a door, and Rufinus swallowed nervously as he realised where they were. That door led to the Palatine office of the Praetorian Prefect. Laetus. Gods, no.

'Domine, you cannot trust the prefect.'

Pertinax frowned at him. 'Laetus helped lay the purple on my shoulders, Rufinus.'

'Domine…' Rufinus hissed urgently, but the emperor was already knocking on the prefect's door. Rufinus, suddenly aware that he was at the absolute centre of it all, and yet so far remained unnoticed by the enemy, heard the door handle go and on instinct ducked back around the corner. Breathing shallowly, standing just out of sight, he heard the prefect's voice.

'Domine?'

'I understand that some of the men under your command are coming to reckon with me. Do your duty, Laetus, and make them stand down.'

Rufinus held his breath, half expecting to hear Laetus sheath his sword in the emperor. The man had already killed his predecessor, after all. He was relieved when he heard an affirmative and the sound of the prefect's boots marching away. Perhaps Laetus could not survive another imperial death with his reputation intact, perhaps he realised that this emperor was also a soldier, or perhaps he simply did not wish to commit when he could yet sit on the fence as Genialis did. Whatever the case, he had not directly attacked the emperor, but Rufinus had no confidence that the commander had any intention of stopping what was coming.

Once he knew they were alone again, he stepped back out.

'Domine, Laetus will not stop them. He might even join them, but he certainly won't stop them.'

Pertinax's eyes narrowed. 'You sound convinced.'

'I am.'

'Then let's do this properly. In the aula regia and from the throne. If they are here because of grievances, I will talk them down.'

Rufinus winced. 'I'm not sure that's possible, Domine.'

'You say I have enemies, but that these men are dissatisfied. Then let's solve their problems and bring order back to the Guard.'

Rufinus shivered. Was it possible? Could it be done? He remembered Pertinax of old. There were few men in Rome who might be capable of it, but Pertinax was certainly one of them. A famed general, beloved of his armies, respected by the senate. A man who had played the great game for two generations. Maybe he could?

He hurried along in the emperor's wake, past the libraries and towards the great hall of state, and there, at the entrance to the peristyle garden and the state banqueting hall, they met the fleeing imperial staff. Eclectus, the imperial chamberlain and another man said to be implicit in the death of Commodus, was hurrying towards them across the gardens, wide-eyed and white-faced, half a dozen other court functionaries and slaves with him. Rufinus looked about. There were no Praetorians around. He'd have at least expected the occasional one on duty, but they had gone. He had to pray they'd mobilised to meet the insurgent mob and not simply walked away as he suspected Laetus had.

They were on their own, with just one sword between them.

'Domine, I do not think you can talk them down.'

'Rufinus get back. Get away.'

'Domine?' Rufinus' heart thundered in his chest.

'I shall face them down and settle this, but if you are right – if there is no way to resolve this – then one sword is not going to save me. Find my wife. Find my son and daughter. If the worst happens, get them away, to safety.'

Rufinus stared. It was about time that history stopped replaying itself around him. He was suddenly horribly reminded of being given the same orders by Perennis all those years ago. *Save my family.* A desperate plea from a doomed man. Gods, but was that what Pertinax was? Doomed like Perennis?

'Sir...'

'Go, Rufinus.'

Still he dithered, and finally, unhappily, stepped back out into the corridor. As he left, just as he turned the corner, he saw Pertinax pull himself up to his full height, all imperial power and strength. The emperor stepped up onto the wide stair of the banqueting hall, where he could look down at anyone just as the doors to the aula regia across the gardens burst open.

Rufinus' mouth dried in an instant. Hundreds of men, all still angry, all still armed. With them now were members of the Second

243

Century who had been guarding the palace. With them too were some of the palace freedman, also angry at their disenfranchisement. Disaster loomed. Rufinus knew he had two choices now. He could do what he *should*: step out and join Pertinax, who had not even a blade, let alone a bodyguard, and protect him to the end. Or he could do what he had been *ordered* to do and spirit away the emperor's family, out of danger. In the event, he could do neither, frozen to the spot by cold dismay. From the shadowy corner of the corridor, he watched the garden. He could not see the emperor and his civilian companions, but he could see the Praetorian invaders well enough. They poured from the three doors, flooding the garden.

'Be still,' bellowed Pertinax, and such was the power and authority in his tone that the entire mass of angry soldiers did precisely that, stumbling to a halt halfway across the garden. Rufinus stared in astonishment. He'd known Pertinax was good, but he'd not truly believed the man could stop this happening. Now, watching the emperor at work, he was beginning to change his mind. Maybe it could yet be halted.

The entire mob of men, blades already unsheathed, milled and murmured on the lawn, faced down by the emperor's powerful manner.

'The title "Praetorian" has always been one of honour,' Pertinax announced like an ancient orator. There was a murmur among the gathered guardsmen again now, but the tone was slightly different. The man's approach seemed to be working.

'When I had the purple thrust upon me,' he went on, 'an honour I did not seek, in truth, the Guard was still reeling and in disarray in the aftermath of my predecessor. There was chaos and corruption. I sought to heal this. My measures, no matter how they have been received, were not put in place with the intent of limiting the Guard, but of helping them rediscover their strength and their honour. To make you the men who took the field against the Marcomanni in Pannonia once again. To drive out the ghosts that have arisen throughout the reign of Commodus and to remake the Guard in their traditional image, as the elite among the elite.'

Rufinus stared. Men were nodding. The emperor had touched a nerve, appealing to their pride, and pride had always been a great part of the Guard's attitude. Rufinus began to breathe again. He'd done it. They were backing down. He even saw men sheathing their blades. Men were standing with horror-stricken expressions at what they had done.

The emperor had *stopped* them.

Rufinus swallowed now, relieved. Now Pertinax knew what they were up against. He would have to sanction legal moves against those behind this rebellion, once it was truly dispersed and no longer a danger. Aper was among them, and he would connect to Crispinus, who would link to the rest. The whole thing would come tumbling down now and Rufinus' job would be complete. And with Pertinax surviving this dreadful event, he suspected that Tribune Genialis would suddenly be all aid and support. Everything would be good.

His head snapped round.

He couldn't say what it was that drew his attention, for it was definitely not something shouted, and all the movement he could see was simple embarrassed and remorseful milling about. *Something* had made him look, though.

He spotted Aper when it was too late. The centurion was at the crowd's periphery, where he'd been deep in whispered conversation with a burly guardsman. A moment later he pulled away, and Rufinus watched with a sinking feeling as that big soldier stepped away from the crowd, out into the open garden. His hand came up. He was holding a pilum.

Gods, no...

Rufinus was rooted to the spot. There was nothing he could do in time. The guardsman roared defiance and cast his missile, an expert throw. Rufinus didn't see it hit, but he did hear the pained bellow of the emperor. As if they had been waiting for this trigger, the mob burst into life once more. To their credit, three quarters of the gathered crowd were departing, refusing to be part of it, but a full century's worth of men suddenly howled their anger and, brandishing swords, raced for the emperor and his companions on the banquet hall steps. Rufinus began to step back, face aghast, eyes wide.

They had been so close.

It had almost worked.

He heard the sickening sounds of butchery, accompanied by the screams of every figure on those stairs. The emperor had been murdered. Two emperors in three months, now. Pertinax was gone. And there was little doubt in Rufinus' mind what was about to happen. Crispinus would have his pet emperor ready for action.

Still backing away, Rufinus turned and hurtled through the palace, away from the chaos. Aper couldn't yet know he was here. Rufinus still had a chance to see his own way out of this even if it was too late for the emperor. He had to save the family, though.

Moments later he was at the imperial apartments again. The emperor's wife, the lady Flavia Titiana, was seated in the sunken peristyle on a marble bench, as her two children cavorted around the gardens. Rufinus swallowed nervously. Gods, but how could he say this?

'Domina?'

She looked up, and as she caught the look on his face, her easy smile slid away. 'My husband?'

Rufinus nodded. 'I am so sorry.'

She simply stared at him, her face blank.

'Domina, it was your husband's last command that you be taken away from this place to safety. Please. We must move now if we are to stay ahead of the mob.'

He could see the horror and the panic rise in her only to be pushed back down by generations of implacable equestrian breeding. She nodded, turning, the only sign of her misery the slight crack in his voice as she spoke.

'Children, come. We are going on an adventure.'

Rufinus breathed deeply and beckoned, hurrying away through the palace, checking every corner they approached and finding no one. The three fugitives scurried along behind him, the children laughing, as yet entirely unaware of why they were leaving. Where to, though? He had to get them out of danger, and there was only one place.

He half expected to have to overcome the guard at that postern door, but as he rounded the last corner even that man was no longer there. A distant roar suggested that the angry mob of soldiers was even now surging through the palace looking for anyone else upon whom they needed to take out their anger. They would soon reach the imperial apartments and find them empty.

There was only one place the trio would be safe.

Outside, to his immense relief, Atalanta walked around aimlessly, waiting for her master. With no attempt at propriety, Rufinus pointed at the horse. 'Get on.'

She mounted with difficulty and with Rufinus' help. Women did not ride, after all, but once she was wedged in the saddle, he lifted the children up one after the other.

'Where will we go?' she asked, her voice hollow.

Rufinus rubbed Atalanta on the nose. He would lead her. Even without reins, his mare would follow him obediently, he knew. He looked up at the stricken empress and her blissfully unaware children.

246

'As far from this hill as we can get for now. Then we will double back past the Aventine and the docks, through the markets and around the poorer districts of the Campus Martius. Everywhere we are away from the centre and any real chance of meeting Praetorians.'

'And then where?'

'To the only place you will be safe. Your father, the emperor's father-in-law, commands the Urban Cohort. Sulpicianus will protect you.'

XXI – NADIR

The Castra Urbana was a mess. Until very recently it had been used only by visiting forces, and for the past month the Urban Cohorts had begun to settle in as the permanent garrison, but there was still alteration work to be done and blocks were covered in scaffolding and half-finished, piles of building materials in evidence all over the place and some units still living in neat tent lines like a campaigning legion while they waited for a barrack block of their own.

Two soldiers demanded the password as Rufinus approached and their expressions settled into distrust and even belligerence as they spotted the Praetorian whites he wore, but the revelation that the woman and the two children on the horse he led were their commander's daughter and grandchildren gained him admittance without further delay.

The soldiers led him to a half-demolished and part-reconstructed headquarters, where a third man on guard rapped on an office door and informed the prefect that his family were here. The door opened and Titus Flavius Claudius Sulpicianus emerged into the daylight, his brow wrinkled into a frown. He was a tall man, and lean, with a faintly Greek look, his hair and beard tightly curled in the Antonine manner. His gaze fell upon the horse's occupants and he smiled as the two children yelped with delight and slid from the horse, shouting for their grandfather. Rufinus and one of the soldiers nearby had to rush over to catch the children as they jumped, and the soldier even gave Rufinus a smile as they watched the boy and the girl rush over and embrace the prefect.

The older man nodded at the empress on the horse and then the frown returned as he turned to Rufinus. 'You are about to explain?'

Rufinus took a deep breath, eyeing the children. They shouldn't hear about their father like this. He chewed his lip as he searched for the right words.

'There has been a change in the wearer of the purple,' he said.

Sulpicianus' frown deepened, and he patted the two children on the head and bent over them. 'Go with Tiberius here and he will find you some honey cakes.'

With squeals of delight, the children hurried away after the soldier who had been guarding the office. Once they were gone, the prefect jabbed a thumb at his office. 'Come.'

The other soldiers helped the empress from the horse and Rufinus followed the prefect into his office, the lady padding over in his wake and the door shutting behind the three of them. Sulpicianus stood behind his desk, steepling his fingers.

'Tell me everything.'

Rufinus took a deep breath. Perhaps not *everything*, but there was still so much to tell. 'I fear that the common story that will emerge is that a mob of dissatisfied Praetorians attacked the Palatine and cut down the emperor in his own palace,' he said flatly, wincing at the look on the lady's face. Sulpicianus nodded grimly, reaching out to squeeze his daughter's shoulder.

Rufinus steadied himself to continue. 'The emperor made a rather heroic attempt to talk them down, refusing to flee. He almost had them, too. I saw it with my own eyes.'

'And yet you stand here alive?' prompted the prefect.

'He ordered me to protect his family and escort them from the palace. Hence, we find ourselves here. There is more, Prefect. There are powerful men in the Guard who were behind much of this trouble. Without their corrupt influence, this might very well not have happened. These same men seek not only to bring about the fall of Pertinax, but also the ratification of their own candidate as his successor. An emperor in the debt of his own Praetorians. Their power would become unmatched if they had control of their own emperor.'

Sulpicianus nodded again. 'Laetus?'

'A willing accomplice, I think,' Rufinus confirmed. 'But not one of the prime movers and not one of those who took an active part. The danger lies with his senior subordinates. I…' Just how much should he tell this man? He swallowed. 'I have been investigating these villains for some months. I had reported the danger to the emperor more than once, but he continued on his course regardless. These men have been planning the accession of Didius Julianus, the former governor of Africa, for some time. They even contrived to have him return to Rome earlier this month in preparation.'

Sulpicianus breathed heavily and folded his arms. 'It is almost too brazen to believe. How do these men believe they will succeed in placing Julianus on the throne? I have met the man from time to time. He is a passing competent general and has carried himself well as a governor several times. Gods, but the man has even been consul, but he was implicated in one of the plots against Commodus, and he has no ties to the Antonine family, nor to Pertinax. The senate will not approve.'

Rufinus shook his head sadly. 'I do not believe these people care what the senate thinks. They are of the opinion that an emperor can be made by the Guard just as he can clearly be broken by them. Sadly, I fear they are correct. If the Guard settle on a man and throw their support behind him, the senate will fall in line, I suspect, out of the fear of further bloodshed and potential civil war.'

Sulpicianus dropped into his seat. 'How will these villains secure the full support of the Guard?'

'With gold. Julianus and his allies have been minting fake coins in Africa for a year now. He is rich enough to buy the Guard out. It matters little that the coins are counterfeit. They are good fakes, and no one will notice until it is too late. Julianus and his allies will offer coin to the Guard, and they will support him. Thusly will the enemy gain the throne.'

Sulpicianus' eyes narrowed. 'Perhaps there is a better candidate? Someone whose very strength counts for more than money?'

Rufinus sighed. 'Sadly, I think we are past that stage. Pompeianus would have made a great emperor, but with clear foresight he turned it down. Albinus and Niger both covet the throne, but I have met them personally, and I would rather not picture them wearing the purple, for they are as much villains as these men.' He took a deep breath again. 'I would raise my standard for Septimius Severus, but he is too far from Rome right now to do anything, just like Niger and Albinus. No, there is no one in Rome who can match Julianus for the Guard, I think.'

'You believe him unstoppable?'

'I hope not, but I fear so.'

'Then we do what we can,' Sulpicianus said firmly. 'Come with me.' He turned to his daughter. 'Stay here with the children. If I do not return by nightfall, Tiberius will escort you from here to one of the country estates, where you will be safe.'

'*Will* they be safe?' Rufinus murmured. 'If they pose even the slightest threat...'

'My son-in-law was a thoughtful man, soldier. He had the foresight upon taking the purple to carefully keep his family out of the way. None of them were voted imperial titles. The children will not be considered heirs to the throne. They will be safely anonymous.'

Rufinus deflated a little. At least they should survive this, then. 'What will we do, Prefect?'

'What will we do? We will outbid Julianus. I have estates and funds of my own. Perhaps not to the sum Julianus might produce, but mine will be true silver and legitimate coin.'

Rufinus frowned. Sulpicianus? It was worth a try. The man was the emperor's father-in-law, after all. The senate would approve. And he had as much appropriate history as Julianus. It might just work.

'Prefect, I cannot afford to go with you. My investigation into these people continues, and if I stand against them, I will fall before I can do anything about them.'

Sulpicianus considered him for a moment, and then nodded. 'Very well. I am indebted to you for both the timely warnings and the survival of my family. Fare you well. With luck we shall meet in better circumstances very soon.'

Rufinus nodded his acceptance, saluted the prefect, and then left the building. One of the soldiers escorted him to the camp gate leading the horse, where Rufinus mounted Atalanta and angled away to make his way up the hills back towards the Castra Praetoria.

What could he do? "Nothing" was the answer. It was too late now to bring down Crispinus and Aper. In a matter of hours there would be a new emperor – the third incumbent to sit upon the throne in as many months, he thought, his lip wrinkling at the thought. Unless Sulpicianus could do something, it would be Didius Julianus who won the day, and then there would be no stopping the bastards. The rot in the Guard would bloom and become total.

Turning onto the Vicus Patricius not far from the Castra Praetoria, Rufinus steeled himself. Then, as he climbed the last slope, the street filled with shocked voices as the news of the emperor's murder spread, the gate of the fortress opened and a small force of Praetorians emerged, clad in togas. Rufinus on instinct dropped from Atalanta and dipped into an alley. There he lurked in the shadows. His caution was rewarded as the small unit passed him by a moment later. Aper and Florianus, that centurion from the Fifth Century who'd guarded the gold store, led a small togate force of Praetorians. Their expressions were halfway between determination and triumph.

Rufinus watched them, narrow eyed, as they turned off the Vicus Patricius close to his hiding place. He pictured the route to Julianus' domus and that clinched it. They were heading to the man's house to collect him. He chewed his lip. It would be something of a race. If Julianus got to the fortress first, little Sulpicianus could do would make a difference. Once they were safely out of sight, Rufinus ducked back out of the alley and leapt up onto the horse once more, riding for the gate.

There was nothing he could do now. In a perfect world he would find Cestius and seek his advice. In a perfect world Pompeianus would have accepted the throne. In a perfect world Severus would be here to impose his strong will on the situation.

It was not a perfect world.

A minor villain with the support of major villains was coming to be acclaimed emperor. Rufinus had done all he could by saving the empress and her children and by giving Sulpicianus sufficient warning to do something about it. All he could do now was wait, watch, and see how the dice fell.

Moments later he was passing through the fortress gate and riding for the stable. There he handed Atalanta over to the same slave from whom he'd taken her earlier and hurried to his barracks. He quickly changed and kitted himself out in armour, with his blue shield and full regalia. Any time now there would be a new emperor, and whether it was the dangerous Julianus or the stoic Sulpicianus, he would need to be ready.

Fully prepared, he returned to the gate and climbed the stairs in the tower, emerging onto the wall walk above. He did not know the centurion who nodded at him from across the gate top, but these days that did not mean he could trust him. Rufinus nodded back, then leant upon the parapet, chewing his lip, tense as he waited for the world to change.

His already failing good humour took another knock shortly thereafter, when the tribunes Crispinus and Genialis appeared from the stairwell, each with a serious, expectant look on his face. Crispinus gave Rufinus a knowing nod and found a place to lean on the gate parapet. Genialis was as unreadable as ever, but was clearly prepared to throw his lot in with his fellow tribune.

As if the entire fortress knew that something was about to happen, the number of officers and men on the wall top gradually increased as time passed, and those without the authority or reason to be on the parapet began to gather down below, inside the gate. Had word spread so fast or was this another part of Crispinus' preparations unveiling itself?

Rufinus gripped the battlements so tight he feared his fingers might crumble the brick, his knuckles white with the pressure. He almost exploded with relief when he spotted them and had to keep a tight rein on himself lest those with him on the wall pay him undue and unhelpful attention.

Sulpicianus emerged from a side street and strode manfully towards the gate. He had changed from the very military ensemble in which Rufinus had last seen him, and was now attired in a tunic displaying the broad stripe that marked his status beneath a traditional toga. As a nod to his military position, he had continued to wear his soldier's boots. He looked every inch the imperial Roman. Just togate enough to be senatorial, not displaying his position in the Urban Cohorts, which would rile many Praetorians, yet the boots would resound with them, marking him as a kindred spirit in some way. It was masterfully done. Better still was the fact that he had come on foot, not in a carriage or litter like a pampered civilian, yet also not on a horse like a conquering general. Best of all, he was not accompanied by men of his cohort, despite the danger, travelling with only two equally austere companions.

The men were dressed likewise in togas, and their features were well known across the city, especially in higher circles. Falco, a senator who had been vocal and important during the reign of Commodus, but also during both the accession and the reign of Pertinax, would lend a great deal of weight to Sulpicianus' position, as would the other senator at his opposite shoulder, Cassius Dio.

There was a weird, expectant hush across the wall top. For a long moment Rufinus kept his eyes on the man, trying hard not to cheer or at least look relieved, then finally he turned towards Crispinus. The tribune had a face like thunder, glaring out at the man approaching, who was clearly not his own candidate. It really was hard not to smile as Crispinus watched the same disaster repeating itself for the tribune. He had been a hair's breadth from putting Julianus on the throne three months ago and had just been beaten to it by Pertinax. Here again he was just waiting for Julianus to arrive, but Sulpicianus had beaten him to it.

Genialis' face was openly blank, registering neither joy nor anger at this turn of events, but Rufinus felt he knew the man well enough now to believe that he would be running through every possibility in his mind, calculating his chances depending upon how the dice fell this time. He was a clever one, Genialis.

Rufinus turned back to the approaching figure of Sulpicianus, who came to a halt far enough from the walls that he was easily visible, but close enough to be within arrow shot, sending a clear message of strength and confidence. Rufinus found himself admiring the old man all the more with every turn. Perhaps he would make a good emperor, despite the unexpectedness of his standing.

'What is your business here?' called out the duty centurion.

'To see that the empire continues to run smoothly, soldier,' Sulpicianus replied in a clear voice.

'Sir?'

Sulpicianus spread his arms. 'My son-in-law, the emperor of Rome, is cruelly slain less than three months since his succession, and so as yet he has no heir in place to inherit the throne. Rome's great aula regia stands empty. There is a hole in her heart that must be filled.'

'And you would stand in your son-in-law's place, Titus Sulpicianus?' demanded Genialis now from the wall top.

'Who else?' the prefect asked, waving his spread arms to indicate the empty street around him. 'I am the only adult male relation of the emperor. I have served the empire as a consul, a governor and a general in the field. I have already sought senatorial support and received appropriate promises of ratification from these two esteemed gentlemen. All I ask is the similar support of the Guard and then with appropriate gratitude I will take my unfortunate and lamented son-in-law's place.'

There was an odd pause, which was broken by the voice of some soldier along the wall.

'How *much* gratitude?'

Rufinus' lip curled in distaste. He'd found corruption and rot in the Guard over the past two years and had hoped to trace it to its roots so that he could pluck it out and dispose of it. The conclusion to which he was now coming, though, was that there *was* no thread of corruption in the Guard. The entire Guard was corrupt. That even an ordinary soldier felt confident in demanding a bribe from a former consul in the open said it all.

Everything had changed. He could not cut out the rot. The Guard was no longer worth saving.

To his surprise, relief and even distaste, all in one, Sulpicianus calmly replied to the soldier.

'Five thousand sesterces apiece,' Sulpicianus said.

Rufinus blinked as a stunned silence settled a across the wall top. Pertinax, just three months ago, had promised three thousand a piece to the Guard as a donative, and that had been extortionate. Commodus himself had paid them less than two thousand in his time, and that had been enough to make them deliriously happy. Five thousand was too much. It was almost a joke.

As the impact of the gesture settled into all those atop the wall, and avarice shone like a beacon from the eyes of many, Genialis looked sideways at Crispinus. The tribune had gone so pale he was almost white.

'What say you?' Genialis asked his fellow officer. 'Is five thousand enough to buy your loyalty?'

Crispinus was twitching, a tic pulling at his cheek.

'I suspect five thousand is enough to buy the loyalty of all those around us,' Genialis pressed. 'Just how much is Julianus worth to you?'

Rufinus realised he was holding his breath and forced himself to exhale as he watched and listened.

'Will you escort me to the senate for ratification?' Sulpicianus asked up at the wall.

'Never,' bellowed a new voice, and Rufinus felt his spirits sink as a second group appeared in the street. Didius Julianus rode a white mare, surrounded by togate Praetorians, Aper and his fellow centurion close by his side.

'What is this?' the duty centurion demanded.

'The loyalty of the Praetorians is worth far more than five thousand sesterces,' shouted Julianus as he rode to a position parallel with Sulpicianus and dismounted with minimal help. He waved away his escort and in but a moment he was standing as a mirror image of Sulpicianus, with just the two centurions, one at each shoulder.

'You offer more, Didius Julianus?' Tribune Genialis prompted.

'*Six* thousand apiece,' Julianus announced, throwing out his hands to accentuate his generosity.

'Seven thousand,' replied the prefect off to his left, quietly and calmly, not once looking at the new arrival, but keeping his eyes on the wall top.

Rufinus could feel the disbelief and the greed rising from the soldiers all around him, flooding the wall like an avaricious tide, flowing all around them. He was disgusted. He was angry at Laetus for having ended the legitimate emperor, Commodus. He was furious at Crispinus for arranging the fall of Pertinax and bringing Julianus to this point. He was angry at the former governor for so blatantly attempting to buy power. He was angry at Aper for many, many things. But he was utterly sickened by the attitude of the soldiers around him.

He had swelled with pride the day he was raised from the legions to the Guard but now, just ten years later, it was clear to him that the Praetorian oath no longer meant anything.

'You think our honour can be bought so easily, sir?' called a voice from source unseen somewhere on the walls, and Rufinus' twitch intensified. He couldn't decide whether the man had been thinking along the same lines as Rufinus, or whether he felt he hadn't been offered enough.

'*Nine* thousand,' barked Didius Julianus.

The hush descended upon the wall again. That was ridiculous. Three times as much as Pertinax had agreed. This was madness. Was the throne something to sell at an auction? Rufinus almost stomped away from the wall, and only morbid fascination kept him in place. How far were Julianus and Sulpicianus prepared to go? Nine thousand sesterces was already almost four years' wages for a guardsman. Of course, Julianus' money was almost worthless in truth, but still...

'Ten thousand,' shouted Sulpicianus.

Rufinus winced. The man could probably pay that, but it would take much of his family's finances to do so.

'Twelve,' countered Julianus.

'Fourteen.'

'Sixteen.'

The tension along the wall top was nearing breaking point. The soldiers could hardly believe their ears. Their wildest avaricious dreams were coming true. Crispinus' face was a picture. He could scarce countenance that Sulpicianus was matching his own candidate.

'Eighteen,' bellowed Sulpicianus.

'Nineteen,' said Julianus, and there was something in his voice that drew Rufinus' attention. He focused on the man. There was uncertainty there now. He wondered whether perhaps even with his fake African coins, Julianus was at the edge of his capabilities. Could Sulpicianus truly win the throne this way?

'Twenty,' said the prefect, his tone confident and strong. Rufinus might have laughed again, as he saw Julianus break into a sweat. He saw the man turn his head, seeking Crispinus along the wall top. Rufinus spun in time to see the tribune give his pet governor a small nod.

'Twenty-five thousand sesterces per man,' Julianus announced, his voice cracking slightly with nerves.

Rufinus stared. They all did. *Ten years' wages for every man in the Guard.* That was beyond simple extravagance. And he would have to pay a lesser donative to both the Urban Cohort and the Vigiles, too, not to mention the legions as a whole. And while he might get away with his fake coins to begin with, he would still have to empty the treasury to secure what he'd offered.

'What my esteemed friend the former governor of Africa here is not telling you,' announced Sulpicianus, 'is that much of his wealth is counterfeit coinage and is worth little or nothing.'

'I shall see you gutted for that lie,' snapped Julianus, though the sweat continued to pour from his brow. The composed and shrewd governor Rufinus remembered from Carthage seemed to be unravelling with the tension and the danger.

'I offer every man here twenty thousand,' Sulpicianus said flatly, 'and no more. But every coin of mine is true, and the value goes beyond money, for I offer you self-respect.'

Rufinus listened to the susurration of muted conversation all around him on the wall. It was hard to make out too much, but one thing was clear. The name 'Julianus' was on the lips of most men.

'I don't like it,' someone said quietly, a few paces away. 'What use are fake coins?'

'They won't be fake,' another grunted.

'But what if they are?' demanded a third.

Rufinus watched, still sickened by the whole display. He almost jumped as Tribune Crispinus' voice cut through the murmur.

'While you are all thinking with your purses, perhaps you might consider a more important factor here.'

The conversation faded and all eyes along the wall top turned to the tribune.

'Remember who Sulpicianus is. Remember who his son-in-law was and remember how he died. Will you pin your futures and even your lives upon the goodwill of a man whose kin your fellow soldiers murdered in cold blood in his palace mere hours ago? I for one say no.'

Rufinus felt a chill as this fact sank into every man on the walkway. Sulpicianus had almost had them with his honesty, but if there was one thing that would affect the men on the wall more than greed, it was fear. Again and again, when a ruler of Rome died those men responsible had been hunted down and executed for their pains. From the assassins of Julius Caesar onward, this was the case. Marcus Antonius and the future emperor Augustus had fought wars the length and breadth of the empire to revenge themselves upon those responsible for Caesar's assassination.

The atmosphere changed in but a moment.

'Julianus!' the bellowed cheer came from far along the wall, from some ordinary soldier who'd finally been swayed. The name was taken up by others, and in moments the cry had become a chant that rose from the Castra Praetoria like a war cry.

Rufinus felt cold. Disgusted. Horrified. The Praetorians he'd thought to save were gone. All that remained now was a gaggle of greedy would-be kingmakers led by villains and fools. His mission had failed. There was no cutting the corruption out of the Guard, for the Guard was corrupt in its entirety.

He turned to look down at the defeated Sulpicianus and was at least pleased to note that the man continued to hold himself proud, his face unchanged, while Julianus had passed from his cold sweat into a grin of elation. Rufinus shivered. Someone gave an order and the fortress gates were opened. Aper and his fellow centurion escorted the new emperor of Rome into the Castra Praetoria. Rufinus felt hollow. He did not doubt for a moment that even if Dio and Falco down there continued to throw their support behind Sulpicianus, the senate would now ratify Julianus. The man would be emperor before the day was out.

Crispinus and his criminals had won.

He continued to watch, keeping his face carefully neutral, as Didius Julianus was brought up the staircase to the gate top, and the great timber doors were shut on the Urban Prefect and his two senators. As the new emperor emerged, looking at once both relieved and extremely angry, soldiers melted out of his way. Rufinus shuffled just a little closer as the man approached the tribunes.

'Thank you for your support, gentlemen,' the emperor said. 'Since your prefect can clearly not be trusted and does not even consider these events worthy of his presence, one of my first acts will be to dismiss Laetus into quiet retirement and to see the two of you promoted to his place, as joint prefects.'

Rufinus was pleased to note a little irritation in Crispinus' expression as his fellow tribune was made his equal once more, but it passed in a moment as the emperor turned and smiled warmly at Aper and his fellow centurion. 'That will leave me short of two tribunes in the Guard, of course. Aper and Florianus, you will need to attend the palace as I make arrangements for your advancement.'

There was an almost jubilant air atop the wall, though Rufinus could feel the icy chill settle in the middle of it upon the new emperor as he turned and looked down into the street. In low, leaden tones, gesturing to Crispinus, the man pointed at his rival outside. 'Kill him,' Julianus commanded.

Genialis suddenly stepped forwards even as guardsmen hefted pila ready to comply. 'No, Domine. Do not do that.'

'What? He will become a usurper. He and his brood are a threat to my security.'

The tribune still shook his head. 'No. He is with two respected senators, and he has done nothing that you yourself have not done. If you kill him, what message do you send the senate?'

Crispinus, who had clearly been struggling with this, finally nodded his grudging agreement. 'He is right, Domine. Moreover, Sulpicianus is the Urban Prefect. Killing him risks opening up a civil war on the streets of Rome, Praetorians against the Cohort. He is no threat to you now. Leave him.'

Rufinus turned to look outside and noticed soldiers of the Urban Cohorts emerging from side streets to surround their commander. Sulpicianus gave Rufinus one brief look tinged with sadness, and then turned and walked away with the senators and his men.

Rufinus swallowed. The bastards had won after all. Despite everything he had achieved, they had won. And he could do nothing further against them, not with Julianus on the throne. The Guard had fallen as low as it was possible to fall, and there was no recovering from it. He was done.

He turned. He was done with the Guard. He had to walk away. He had to see Vibius Cestius.

Most of all, he had to get away from this nightmare.

Part Four

Resolution

Year of the Consulship of Sosius and Ericius

193 AD

Iniqua nunquam regna perpetuo manent.

(Unjust rule cannot last)

- Seneca: Medea

XXII – IMPERIAL MAJESTY

R ufinus slunk from the scene, heart hollow and face grim. His sole intention now was to report to Cestius and abandon his investigation, then to resign his commission from the military altogether and perhaps move to a quiet province somewhere with Senova and wait out the current political mess. For the first time in his life, he began to wonder what Senova's homeland was really like? Could it be as cold, wet and uncultured as he'd naturally assumed? Of course, a noble barbarian would surely be better than a corrupt patrician any day.

He was halfway to the postern gate, to which he presumed nobody would be paying any attention, when he became vaguely aware of his name being called. Pausing, he turned to see optio Gamburio hurrying his way.

'What?' snapped Rufinus, rather unkindly. Gamburio had done nothing wrong and it was extremely unfair to load Rufinus' current bad mood onto him, but still he couldn't help it.

'Tribune Genialis is looking for you.'

'Good luck to him. If he finds me, it will be a thousand years too soon.'

Gamburio shook his head. 'I'm serious. The new emperor needs to visit the senate. They have to ratify him if he's to be legitimate for the people. The tribunes are assembling the bodyguard to escort him from the fortress. That's Aper's century and yours.'

Rufinus' lip lifted in a sneer. 'I would rather smack him over the head with a mattock and tip him in the latrines than save him from an angry mob. *You* do it. You were in line for this job until I barged in anyway. I'm done. I'm gone. Congratulations, Centurion Gamburio.'

He turned and began to walk away.

'Oh no you bloody don't,' barked the optio, and his restraining hand landed on Rufinus' shoulder. Before he'd really considered what he was doing, Rufinus instinctively spun and lashed out. His balled fist, filled with months of impotent fury, connected with Gamburio's cheek and sent him staggering, blinking.

Rufinus stared at his hand as though it had disobeyed him. Something in his mind slipped, readjusted. He couldn't quite form the words over what he'd just done, but his throat was making pathetic, apologetic noises.

He held out his hands plaintively. He really did not want to hurt or anger this man who'd had his back for over a year now. Gamburio straightened. His expression was sharp and angry, but when he spoke, his voice was soft and controlled.

'I'll give you that one for free, Rufinus. You've had a pisser of a year, and I know that this feels like you've failed. But that's the only one you get. Now straighten up and follow me.'

'But I...' began Rufinus.

'No you fucking don't,' snapped Gamburio, stepping so close he was almost in Rufinus' face. 'I was in line for a promotion I'd waited for for years. One I deserved. I'm good at what I do. And I was blissfully unaware of all this corrupt shit going on around me because I was a soldier, and my century were soldiers. Then along you come and change everything. You've turned our world upside down and put us in endless danger. And if half what you say about these people is true, then walking away won't help anyway. They'll just quietly dispose of you later, and anyone you worked with will be investigated. I'll end up on a torturer's table in the bowels of the palace. You know why? Because the men who do that nasty business for the emperor... you know where they come from? They're what happened to the speculatores. That's why they were never fully disbanded. So, you walk away, and we *all* suffer.'

Rufinus blinked at the barrage of words, and at the realisation that Gamburio was right and had made the connection between the palace's torturers and the secretive speculatores where Rufinus had completely missed it, but Gamburio was not finished.

'This isn't over, Rufinus. You think you've lost, but this is a single step on the staircase. Pertinax was strong and respected and he lasted less than three months. This Julianus is weak and disliked. How long do you think *he's* going to last? Your job isn't over. They have won a battle, not the war. Your job just got more important than ever.'

Rufinus sighed. 'Gamburio, Aper is onto me. I've not got long before he makes a move. And Tribune Genialis knows about me. Now that he's thrown in his lot with the others, he can end my investigation any time he feels like by just revealing the truth. The situation is no longer tenable.'

'If Genialis wanted you dead, he wouldn't have sent for you for the escort. Rufinus, you've opened my eyes. I'm loyal to my Praetorian oath, but I've not *taken* an oath to Julianus yet, and I'm damned if I'll do it. I can't stand back and let these things happen now that I know about them. You owe me this, Rufinus. Now get back there and lead us into the city.'

Rufinus made to argue, but the optio's face was implacable, and the worst thing was that Rufinus knew the man was right. The Guard may be lost as a unit, but there were still good men in it. Slowly, he nodded. 'Did you know that now there are precisely three people in the Guard I trust. For years there have only been two. Thank you.'

At a nod from the optio, they marched back to the gate, where two centuries of men in blue and white were assembling. Aper was busy with two of his cronies, and Crispinus was in quiet conversation with the new emperor, while slaves fawned around him adjusting the hang of his toga. Tribune Genialis stood nearby, arms folded, observing the scene. Rufinus nudged Gamburio. 'Form the men. I'll be there in a moment.'

Veering off, he strode over to the solitary tribune and, judging that the ambient noise level combined with their distance from events would allow freedom of speech, he took a breath and stopped in front of Genialis.

'I cannot understand why you have not already given me up.'

Genialis pursed his lips. 'What good would that do? What would I gain? I already have everything I need, but the problem is that I can see how tenuous that "everything" is. No, I'm not done with our little alliance, Centurion. I suspect that you and I will find we stand shoulder to shoulder yet.'

'Why?'

Genialis removed his helmet and cupped a hand around his ear. 'Can you hear that?'

Rufinus frowned and followed suit, listening as hard as he could. 'Hear what?'

'Block out this mess here and listen to the city, Rufinus. Tell me what you hear beneath it all.'

Rufinus did so. It was extremely hard to blot out the orders and the sound of men falling into lines, and even when he did it took some time before he realised what he was hearing.'

'Nothing.'

'Quite,' Genialis confirmed. 'The city is silent. I remember Aurelius taking the purple, and Verus after him. I remember Commodus coming home when his father died. I remember poor brief heroic Pertinax. One thing links them all: celebration.'

Rufinus frowned.

'A new emperor is a cause for celebration,' Genialis went on. 'Even if they're mourning the last one, the people love a new emperor. The start of a reign is time for hope and promise. Moments after the announcement people are clamouring. With Pertinax he'd barely got out of the gate before people were throwing flowers. It's been perhaps a quarter of an hour since Julianus won his throne, and it was horribly public, right in front of the fortress gates. People watched it. By now every neighbourhood as far as the river has heard the news. Where then is the cheering?'

Rufinus shivered. 'The people don't like him.'

'I'm not sure whether it's him or just the way he came to power, but something is very wrong. The city is silent. It would be a foolish man indeed, I think, who hitched his cart to this particular horse.'

'And so once more,' Rufinus snorted, 'you look after yourself.'

'If I don't, who *will*, Centurion? The fact remains that despite Julianus and Crispinus believing they've won, I think it's a very hollow victory. I do not think it will last.'

Rufinus frowned. That almost echoed Gamburio's earlier words. 'What do we do, then?'

'Until something happens, he is the emperor now. We do our duty, but we are watchful. And we wait to see what comes next.'

'To the senate, then.'

'To the senate,' the tribune agreed, 'and be prepared for trouble.'

By the time Rufinus fell in with his century, horns were blowing, and standards were raised. There were no lictors here to escort the emperor, but twenty-four of the men from the Fourth Century had donned togas and hastily bundled sticks together to create makeshift fasces. They looked the part sufficiently for the public. The gates of the camp creaked open.

At a command from Crispinus, half of Aper's century formed the van and led the way, the other half lining the left flank. Rufinus was given the right flank and the rear-guard. Sending Gamburio at the head, he formed up at the rear with his men, and winced as they left the gate, emerging into the city. Gods, but Genialis had been sharp, noticing what he had.

Crowds lined the street leading away from the Castra Praetoria. Their faces were grim. Not one petal was thrown. Not one voice called out in celebration. Even funerals saw more sympathy than this. Rufinus shivered. If ever a reign had got off to a bad start...

They marched through the silent, angry crowds, and as they turned onto the Vicus Patricius, Rufinus became aware that there were voices here and there in the crowd. What he heard was not encouraging. The name of Sulpicianus was being spoken openly. The exchanges at the gate of the fortress were a matter of public knowledge, and clearly the favour of the crowd had come down in support of the man who'd been bested and sent away.

He became aware of tension building among the men close to him. As centurion, his place was to lead from the front, but with this particular formation it had seemed sensible to command the rear-guard. Now he realised that he was wandering along at the back, behind his men, carrying his vine stick but no shield, and the angry faces of the people they passed suggested that they'd like nothing more than to see him fall.

How things had changed. They passed the arcade of the portico that fronted the baths of Novatus now, closing on the lower land towards the amphitheatre and the forum, and that was where it happened. A voice somewhere off in the shelter and shadow of the portico bellowed a word that could not be allowed.

Usurper.

Rufinus tensed. This was how riots started. Even as he urged his men to be ready, other words were rising from the crowd beside the street. Thief. Murderer. Crook.

He could not see the emperor, living embodiment of Rome, father of his country, Didius Julianus from here, which was a shame, because he'd have given money to see the look on the man's face.

Then a missile came. A half-brick, probably prised from some crumbling wall in the area, hurtled at the procession. Two of Rufinus' men leapt into action, lifting their shields and protecting the emperor's entourage, the brick clattering harmlessly against the linden boards. The single missile was a trigger, and in moments things were being cast at them from both sides. This was not an organised protest or attack, though, and the missiles were formed of whatever came readily to hand.

Matter of all kinds struck the column now, and Rufinus winced at the sight of rotten food, the carcasses of small animals gathered from the gutter and even faecal missiles, battering against blue shields and spraying the white of the Praetorians.

It was only when he himself was struck with a broken cooking pot that he realised his all-too-open position and accepted the gesture from his men to push his way in among those with shields. The barrage kept up all the way down the Vicus Patricius, and eventually someone at the front gave the order for an increased pace. It was, to Rufinus' mind, about as undignified as an emperor could be, being made to half-jog as his entourage was pelted with shit.

It did do one thing positive for Rufinus, though: it confirmed what both Genialis and Gamburio had said. This was not a popular accession. Something was very wrong, and that meant that Rufinus' job was not yet over. There was still a chance to turn this around. Somehow, he could still win. What he needed now was an official reason to stand against Julianus. A standard for the right-thinking to rally behind.

Now he had to see Vibius Cestius more than ever.

They passed into a square and the barrage let up. The procession slowed once more to a stately pace and proceeded along the Via Sacra into the forum. As they passed beneath Titus' triumphal arch, he glanced across at the procession carved into the stone, showing that popular war hero's victorious army marching into Rome carrying the spoils of the Jewish War. A journey far removed from the one they undertook this day. Not a man among them had escaped the barrage and the whites of both soldiers and lictors were stained with a dozen different colours, none of them pleasant.

The crowd had gathered in the forum, too and, taking advantage of the current lack of missiles, Rufinus stepped out of the unit to one side. Ahead, he could see the senate house. The statue Commodus had placed out front as a joke, of himself as Hercules the archer, bow nocked and arrow pointed at the senators in the doorway, had been smashed to pieces, only the lower legs remaining. Rufinus felt sick at the sight. How those senators must be kicking themselves over their glee at Commodus' fall now that they saw what was to come after.

Senators in white togas stood outside the building, but at the approach of the group they vanished inside. A low murmur of discontent echoed across the forum. As they approached the curia, Crispinus barked out orders, and Rufinus felt his lip curl once more at the instructions. This was not how things were supposed to happen. As The lictors and the new emperor strode purposefully towards the door, the two centuries of Praetorians were deployed in a circle around the building. *That* had been done before. In times of crisis, when the senate and the emperor had summoned emergency meetings to resolve issues, either Praetorians or the Urban Cohort had been deployed to protect them, keeping the public from getting to the curia.

Not this time, though. This time, the Praetorians were deployed *facing* the building, their back to the people. The message this sent to the senate was blunt and underlined for Rufinus how tenuous was Julianus' hold on power. If an emperor had to threaten his senate into accepting him, his reign was not off to an auspicious start.

As the men fell into position, Rufinus settled at the nominal front of his unit, close to the curia's great bronze doors. The two tribunes had gone inside with the man, along with the lictors, which was strictly against protocol, and further bolstered the message of control. What was being said inside was inaudible out here, but Rufinus could picture it. The demands from Julianus that he be confirmed as the senate's choice. That he be granted the traditional titles that went with the position. That his family be raised too, probably. Whether or not the new emperor would announce anything else yet he couldn't say. Probably not. Crispinus would want time to work through the list with his pet emperor before it happened. Thus far everything had happened too quickly.

He felt eyes boring into him and turned instinctively. Aper was close by, at the head of his own men. The centurion's eyes were hot coals of hatred now as they burned into Rufinus. The man was close to abandoning all pretence of brotherhood. Rufinus tried not to meet his gaze. Aper was on the edge. Any time now he would break and something bad would happen.

He waited uneasily for the next half hour, and finally the curia doors opened once more and the emperor emerged, an air of satisfaction about him as he gathered his lictors. The tribunes had the Praetorians fall in as escort units once more, but before they moved off, three men emerged from the curia and strode over to the rostrum, climbing the steps to stand on that most important of all public stages, fronted by decorative arches and adorned with the prows of ancient ships captured by Rome. Rufinus stared. Two of the senators he did not know, but the central one was Falco, the very man who had stood beside Sulpicianus recently outside the fortress.

'People of Rome,' Falco said, his voice clear and strong, a born orator, trained in the art over decades of Roman authority. The crowd fell silent, every ear straining to hear his words. 'People of Rome, it is my duty to inform you…'

– not 'pleasure to announce', Rufinus noted –

'… that Marcus Didius Severus Julianus has been granted, by the recognition of the senate of Rome, the titles Augustus, Father of his Country, and High Priest, with the additional honour of the Proconsulate, Tribunician power and membership of the patrician order. Praise Jove, we have an emperor.'

It was delivered with an air of disgruntled acceptance, and Rufinus wondered just what threats had been levelled within the curia to persuade Falco to make such an announcement. Even then, the brave senator had connived to deliver the information in such a manner that it did nothing to improve Julianus' appeal and spread no encouragement into the crowd

Rufinus endured Aper's hateful glares for a moment longer until the entire column turned and began to escort the emperor to the Capitol for the expected sacrifice. Even then, he could feel the centurion's glare on him again as they attended the officiation. For now, Aper was still a centurion, and his master still a tribune despite the promotions promised them. Julianus could not promote or dismiss until he had been ratified by both the senate and the gods, but by the end of the day those orders would be pushed through. Rufinus wondered how much more trouble Aper was going to be able to cause once he had become a tribune. It did not bear thinking about.

He suffered the entire proceedings in silence, thinking about his next moves, and was somehow disappointed when Jupiter did not choose that day to have his temple fall down upon the head of the would-be emperor. By the time they delivered Didius Julianus to the palace that would now be his and handed over to the next shift, he was thoroughly dejected.

Once the duty was done, he led his century back to the Castra Praetoria, where he changed and collected Acheron, who lay curled up on the bed, waiting for him. He was once more attired as a civilian, and yet despite the ancient rules of the city, he retained the sword at his side beneath his cloak as he left the fortress once more with Acheron trotting along happily at his side.

He passed through the city, continually aware that the populace was less than content with their new ruler. The murmur of dissatisfaction was palpable, and he became more and more convinced by what he'd been told. Julianus was a clever politician, but he would have to call upon every ounce of his skill to pull himself out of this mire of public discontent.

Struggling still with his plans, Rufinus climbed the hill beside the Neronian nymphaeum, instinctively keeping a wary eye on its statuary now since that day he had been attacked from within its depths. Finally, he turned into the side street where his house stood.

He saw nothing, but a low growl arose from Acheron, warning him that something was amiss. The street was empty, and it took him a moment to recognise that this in itself was another warning. There was always life here, from street hawkers to beggars the place was never entirely empty. He walked on calmly as though nothing was wrong. Until he knew precisely what he was seeing, he could not afford to alert any enemy to the fact that he knew something was amiss.

Looking down to his left he saw Acheron, still growling, glance up at him and then focus once more. The hound was looking ahead and left, somewhere just past Rufinus' house. There was an archway there that led into the yard of a small potter's shop where the owner kept his delivery cart. The gate was open, even though the shop had now shut for the day.

Rufinus lifted his hand and adjusted the hang of his cloak, incidentally freeing the sword underneath from the mouth of its scabbard. With his other hand his shifted his grip on the vine stick in readiness. Someone was lurking in the shadow of that arched gate which should, by all rights, be shut.

He turned slightly, as though making for his front door, and at the last moment spun once more and marched at speed for the arch, hand going to the sword and pulling it free of its sheath. There would be no back entrance from the yard, and he was now close enough that no one could escape along the street.

He heard the shuffle of someone moving away in the darkness. Grimly, he marched on into the shadowy archway. As he approached, he narrowed his eyes to slits, cutting out the late afternoon sunlight so that once he entered the shadow there was little adjustment to make to the gloom. He spotted the figure back across the yard, ducking down behind the cart that stood there full of empty amphorae.

'There's no way out,' he said. 'Come out.'

The figure did not move. 'Then you are not from one of my allies. And I know that Genialis is keeping his men back. Crispinus is as yet my commander, and so you are one of Aper's men. And if you are his and you are here, then you are my enemy.'

He stepped into the yard, angling to the right to make his way around the cart. As he neared the rear of the yard, he heard the figure move away again, trying to slip out around the far side and make for the gate. The man's plan fell foul instantly, as Rufinus could hear from the snarl of Acheron, who had gone around the other side of the cart.

'No escape that way,' he said, menacingly. 'My blade will be faster than his jaws, and a lot less painful, believe me.'

He almost laughed as he heard the man scramble back behind the cart once more, trapped. The cart's handles were on the large blocks, the whole thing tipped back to prevent the amphorae from sliding off, but because of the blocks no one could crawl underneath. There was no way out.

'I can make a deal,' hissed a voice from behind the cart.

'No deals,' Rufinus said. 'I know who my enemies are and there is nothing you can give me.'

'I have information.'

Rufinus frowned for just a moment, but then shook his head. The voice had a pleading, desperate edge to it, not a confident, calculating one. This was a frantic man pleading for his life. He had nothing of value.

'Sadly, even if I believed you, which I don't, I cannot let you leave. Aper will not gain the upper hand now.'

The figure shifted and there was a sudden snarl and the snap of jaws. A howl of pain accompanied the figure as he burst from the cart, shaking his left hand, which sprayed droplets of blood from the bite wound in it. He saw Rufinus now, panic filling him. Acheron slunk out from behind the cart after him, and Rufinus was waiting with sword and vitis.

'You bastard,' grunted the man, who lunged with his sword. Rufinus parried it easily with his stick and drew back his own blade ready but was beaten to it as Acheron sank his teeth into the man's hamstrings, tearing them whole from the back of his knee. The man screamed as he fell, sword forgotten.

Rufinus glared at Acheron. 'I could have done it, you know?'

Acheron's lips pulled back over red teeth and Rufinus could have sworn the dog was laughing at him. Taking a breath, he stepped forwards and delivered a killing blow, mercifully putting Aper's agent out of his misery. As he did so, he registered the man's face and realised it was one of the four soldiers from Aper's century who'd been close to him back in Africa. That confirmed it, at least.

Looking around, he wondered what to do with the body. Better that the man didn't show up too soon. When he heard the gurgle of water, he smiled grimly. A sewer or drain ran along the rear of the property, and now he could see where the red and brown stains of clay slip had poured from the workshop, mixed with cleansing water where it dropped into the drain. Lifting a section of grating, he looked down into the flow. It was wider than a man's shoulders and the smell confirmed that it carried away waste. A few moments later he'd dropped the body in and watched it slide away. There was just enough give to let the flow take the man. He probably wouldn't get as far as the cloaca maxima or the river and would end up jammed at a bend until the drain overflowed and the authorities were called to deal with it. That would buy him a few days, though, and in the meantime Aper would fume and fret about what had happened to his missing man.

Crossing the road, Rufinus rapped on his door. Naravas pulled the door open with a suspicious look, hand tight on his club, and when he saw Rufinus relief flooded him and he stepped back.

'Trouble?' he murmured, noting the blood on Acheron as he trotted past.

'A little. Nothing much.'

'You have a visitor,' the doorman said. 'In the domina's office.'

Rufinus frowned and strode through the house and to his wife's office. As he entered, he spotted his brother and Senova sitting close together near the desk and was immediately on his guard at the sight of a wizened old man in a doctor's robe. As the man turned, Rufinus boggled. His eyes adjusted with the knowledge of what he was seeing and Vibius Cestius unfolded from his guise.

'Gods, but how do you do that?'

The frumentarius gave him an infuriating smile. 'I was just delivering a gift to your wife.'

Rufinus turned to Senova, who lifted the burden from her knee. It was the robes of a priestess. 'What?'

Senova smiled. 'I have been appointed to the Augustales. I am to serve at the temple of the empress Faustina.'

'Why?' Rufinus said, turning to Cestius, whose work this had to be.

'Because it gives her certain immunities and protections. Your rank protects you, and physically you are both safeguarded in the house, but despite your informal arrangement, you are not officially married, and so Senova has no legal protection. It is only a matter of time before your enemies realise this and use it against you. It seemed prudent to arrange some legal protection. And the position is prestigious. It will certainly do Senova's reputation no harm.'

Rufinus glanced back at Senova and she nodded. He turned back to Cestius. 'Thank you. It is something I had not thought of. Soon we will have to address this situation and make things official. For now, though, we have an enemy on the throne who is subservient to his own Praetorians. Aper is out to get me, and Crispinus has become the most powerful man in Rome. Julianus' position is still shaky, though. What do we do? How do we topple him from his precarious throne?'

Cestius shook his head. 'We don't.'

'What?'

'You are a Praetorian. Your oath is of allegiance to the emperor above all, and Julianus is now your emperor. I am frumentarius, like you also. We are loyal to whoever sits on the throne, no matter who they are. We do not move against our lawful master.'

'But that...'

'Until he is no longer our lawful master.'

'What?' snapped Rufinus again.

'It has happened before, Gnaeus. Especially in reigns of tenuous control. Something will turn the people against an emperor and the senate will take action, declaring him an enemy of Rome. It happened to Nero, remember. It will happen to Julianus. All it takes is something to shake him enough, to turn the senate against him. Something like a preferable and stronger candidate making himself known.'

Rufinus' brow furrowed. 'But we cannot afford Albinus or Niger to...'

'And that is why I sent a private dispatch to the governor of Pannonia at first light before all this started.'

Rufinus blinked. *Severus?*

He pictured that speech from Falco on the rostrum. The faces of the crowd throwing rubbish at emperor in the street. It would not take much for a strong candidate to turn Rome against this man.

Gods, but yes. *Severus...*

XXIII – RECKONING

The last day of Martius came around, with the kalends of Aprilis hovering in the wings. The military season had begun, and despite the fact that there was no grand imperial campaign planned for the year, recent days had seen the streets around Rufinus' house and around the Castra Praetoria ever busier. Units of the Guard heading out to provincial duties and the Castra Peregrina of the frumentarii seeing a constant flow of soldiers, both regular and undercover, coming and going.

Rufinus left the barracks, yawning from the long shift protecting a man he loathed, as he headed home, Acheron padding along at his side. The streets were busy as ever, with the aftermath of the festival of Luna blending into the preparations for the Veneralia, and street hawkers, whores and thieves abounded, making the most of the busy streets. As Rufinus descended from the hills into the amphitheatre valley and then climbed once more across the Caelian, he noted four separate incidents being dealt with by vigiles or members of the Urban Cohort, the latter casting him baleful glares as he passed. The enmity between that unit and the Praetorians which had simmered for more than a century had never been closer to becoming all-out war, since the Praetorians had snubbed their noble prefect and placed their own man on the throne above him.

He gave the men a weak smile which they sneered at, and then marched on home. A good old-fashioned punch-up was taking place in the street close to the gate of the Castra, and Rufinus gave it a professional eye as he passed and approached his door.

At his knock the door was pulled open. He frowned at the sight of Hemda, the gardener, standing there with the doorman's club, and made his way inside, the big black hound at his heel. Acheron seemed to be sensing something. He looked and sounded tense and unsettled.

'Where is Naravas?' he asked, his tone polite rather than commanding. Though officially every member of the house's staff was a slave, in truth almost all of them were ex-soldiers of the Danubian or African legions, assigned by Severus or Cestius. None of them were really slaves and even this gardener, not the bulkiest or youngest of the domus staff, bore the tattoo of his legion and scars that suggested he'd made a name for himself against the desert nomads in Africa.

Hemda shrugged. 'Naravas is with the domina.'

Rufinus relaxed. 'Alright, where are they? In the office?' he asked, stepping further in and shrugging off his cloak.

'No, Domine. In the city.'

Rufinus blinked. 'What?'

'The domina is at her temple, sir.'

'What? Why?'

'It was required, sir. Something to do with the Latin festival and foreign visitors, sir.'

Rufinus felt his blood begin to race. 'She's not supposed to leave the house at the moment. It's too damned dangerous out there. Aper's got eyes on this place all the time again. Her sacred position was only supposed to give her legal protections, not duties.'

Publius appeared through the atrium. 'She was insistent. It seems she takes her gods very seriously. I made her take the three strongest men we have with her, though, and Naravas is good.'

Rufinus shivered. 'But is he good enough. When did they leave?'

'About an hour ago.'

Rufinus wracked his brains, thinking back. When had he last seen Aper and his twin menaces? Certainly more than an hour ago. Perhaps *three* hours, in fact, on the Palatine. Aper had not been with his men when they were dismissed after shift, and Rufinus had a horrible feeling now that he knew why. At the time he'd just been glad the man wasn't there but hadn't given much thought to where he could be.

'Stay here,' he jabbed a finger at Publius. 'Don't go outside and don't open the door except to one of our own.'

'I know the drill, Gnaeus. So does Senova, but she knows her own mind better.'

Damn the woman, Rufinus thought as he turned and tore open the door once more. He was halfway down the street at a fast jog before he realised he'd removed the cloak which had been covering the sword belted to his side. He had to hope no one was inclined to arrest him for an infraction of one of Rome's oldest and most sacred laws. Having Acheron with him was often enough to keep people away.

Still, as he passed a pair of men from the Urban Cohort, he made sure to keep the sword as hidden as possible on the far side of his body. Fortunately, they had their sights set on something else and so he ran on, down the slope, past the nymphaeum and around beneath the terrace of Claudius' temple. The square beside the great amphitheatre was busy, people gathered at the meta sudans and cupping the fresh bubbling water in chilled hands as they washed away the dust of a late spring day in the city.

The forum was equally crowded as he ran up past the arch of Titus and along the Via Sacra. Over the rise he descended into the forum proper, and as he did so his heart lurched. While the forum was busy in general, there was a concentration of folk close to the temple of Antoninus and Faustina. Fearing the worst, he ran on, heading straight for that gathering. Acheron was alert once more, and as he reached the gathering, the people closest suddenly noticed the armed man with his giant savage-looking hound and melted away.

'What is it?' Rufinus demanded, pushing his way in among them. The tone of authority seemed to cut through the hubbub, and eyes tracked his way. The crowd parted to allow him access to what they were examining, and his pulse began to pound faster once more at the sight that awaited him.

Three bodies lay in a large pool of gore. All three he knew well, from months at the domus. Three ex-legionaries, each a strong and competent man. They had been armed with clubs and nightsticks, which still lay on the ground around them. They'd done well all things considered, but they could only last for so long against blades. All three had been hacked and stabbed half a dozen times, and the slashes to their forearms made it clear that they had desperately tried to defend themselves to the end.

'What happened?' he snapped. 'Who saw it?'

'A fight,' someone helpful replied.

'Details, you fool.'

An older woman gestured to him. 'They were escorting a priestess to the temple and they got attacked by men in white tunics and in grey. They took her.'

Rufinus shivered, ice in his heart. White tunics could only mean Praetorians, while grey could be anyone. Aper had Senova. He'd tried to deal with things subtly, and Rufinus had stopped him, 'disappearing' his latest observer. Now, he'd decided to do something more direct. It was incredibly brazen, attacking in broad daylight in the crowded city centre.

'Where?' Rufinus asked urgently.

The old woman turned and pointed past the curia and up at the slope of the Capitoline hill. The Gemonian Stair rose from the forum past the tabularium and the great temple of Juno. It took him a moment to realise why what he was looking at seemed wrong, and then he felt that lurch of nerves all over again. The Capitol was usually nearly as busy as the forum, and that great ancient staircase that connected the two was rarely to be seen without people making their way up and down.

Now, it was empty.

'Hey,' shouted someone as Rufinus tore his forbidden sword from its sheath and began to jog along the colonnade at the front of the portico of the Caesars. He ignored them and ran. Somewhere up there Aper had Senova. Why? What had he planned? If it was murder, he could easily have killed her with the other three, so that was something to cling on to. She had to still be alive, then. Why did he want her? Awful notions like Aper sending her back a piece at a time leapt to mind, and he pushed them aside, refusing to believe them.

Aper wanted him to break. Despite the fact that the scum was now a tribune and outranked Rufinus he couldn't directly attack him, because Rufinus was still closely tied to Crispinus and Genialis, both of whom were now in command of the entire Guard, and who, since they more or less controlled the emperor, were the two most powerful men in the world. And so the man was living up to his threat and attacking those to whom Rufinus was close.

They'd been carefully looked after thus far. None of his friends had been exposed enough to attack, frustrating the man. Finally, though, Senova had broken cover and Aper had seized his chance. It would likely be the only one he got, so he would make the most of it. How would Aper use Senova against him?

Halfway up the stairs, with Acheron pattering along beside him, a voice called out. Four men emerged from the door of the carcer, the prison where political prisoners were kept while awaiting their sentence. There was almost always a small unit of the Urban Cohort based there. The four men had their nightsticks out and were waving at him angrily. He remembered now that he was brandishing a naked blade in the most forbidden area of the city.

'Stop,' snarled one of the men, pointing at him.

'No,' shouted Rufinus, ducking slightly to the left. They fanned out ahead to fill the stairs.

'Acheron, go,' commanded Rufinus, pointing up the stair as he ran. The great black hound leapt ahead, still huge and fast despite his years. While the four men of the Cohort had been more than prepared to line up and stop a hated Praetorian who flaunted the ancient laws by carrying a weapon of war to the Capitol, they were apparently a lot less inclined to stand in the way of two hundred pounds of muscle and claws and bared teeth all wrapped up in a snarling black bundle.

Acheron burst through the line as the men dived out of the way, and Rufinus ran on behind him, through the gap he'd opened up. As he pounded, breath coming heavily, sweat pouring from his brow, Acheron racing on ahead, he was aware of the four soldiers recovering and coming on in his wake. Good. They might actually be useful.

At the top of the stairs, he paused for a moment, heaving in air as he looked this way and that. There were remarkably few people about, and those he could see were hurrying in through doorways into the various temples and governmental buildings that occupied these sacred heights. His attention was drawn by a distant murmur of voices, and he jogged ahead, peering around the corner of the Temple of Jupiter the Thunderer. A small gathering of people was standing at the edge of the open area in front of the Arch of Calpurnius and hemmed in with small temples.

As Rufinus started to jog once more, heading in that direction, he could see what they were watching. Five men were standing in a line across the open thoroughfare, sealing it off. Two were in white and three in grey, and even from this distance, Rufinus could see that the two Praetorians were Aper's remaining cronies. The other three he couldn't identify, but they would almost certainly be hirelings, probably ex-soldiers or former gladiators.

He couldn't see beyond without getting past them and rounding the corner, but he felt he knew who would be there.

One of the white clad figures, Volcatius Cilo, if he remembered correctly, seemed to be peering at him in consternation, and a thought occurred. He turned his head. Sure enough, as well as the snarling shape of Acheron pounding along and keeping pace at his heel, four tired but extremely angry men of the Urban Cohort were in close pursuit. He knew they were chasing him, but to Cilo it probably looked as though they were all together. He grinned wickedly.

'Take the grey tunics,' he shouted an instruction to the men chasing him, 'the whites are mine!'

He could imagine the confusion now in the men chasing him. He was a Praetorian they hated, and illegally carrying a blade, and now he seemed to be suggesting they were his to command, while they ran at two more Praetorians and three hoodlums, all also with blades. Whatever they said was lost beneath a surge of excited noise from the spectators nearby.

He was getting close now and could see the faces of the men waiting for him.

'Go on,' bellowed Volcatius Cilo, gesturing at him with a gladius. 'He's waiting for you, but you gotta go alone.'

Rufinus shook his head as he ran. His blood was up now. He waved the fingers of his left hand at Acheron and then pointed at Cilo's companion, the other white clad Praetorian.

'Kill.'

It was all the urging the hound needed. In a heartbeat he was racing ahead, angling at the second white figure. Cilo stared at Rufinus, wide-eyed.

He could hear the men behind him now, shouting conflicting instructions, trying to decide what to do even as they ran out of time on their approach. They had been intent on arresting one Praetorian armed with a sword, but now there were two more armed Praetorians, and the three seemed determined to fight among themselves. The argument resolved in a moment. Whoever the Praetorians were and whatever they were up to, the three in grey were ordinary citizens breaking the law, and there would be no retaliation for dealing with them.

The line crumbled in stages. Firstly, the second Praetorian braced himself, sword held shakily in both hands as a huge black ball of fur and fangs hurtled at him. Then, just before Acheron leapt, he lowered the sword, shouted 'fuck this,' and tried to run. He was too late. Acheron had him. Barely had he managed to turn his back before the great hound hit him at full speed, throwing him to the ground.

Just as the man screamed and vanished under the horrifying shape of Acheron, the men of the Urban Cohorts bellowed orders to drop swords and made, as one, for the grey-tunics. Men whose only loyalty was to their purse are ever willing to go only so far, and weighing up their chances, even with swords against nightsticks, they decided that discretion was the better part of valour.

The three broke and ran. The men of the Cohort, satisfied now that they were arresting actual criminals and had the upper hand, gave chase. They might catch them, they might not. It mattered little to Rufinus. What really mattered was that they were out of the picture.

He gave his nastiest smile to Volcatius Cilo.

'And then there was one.'

Cilo's nervous eyes flicked left, to where he could see two soldiers disappearing around a corner after their grey clad prey, while the other two merrily kicked the shit out of the one they had caught. His gaze then snapped right, to where the shaking form of his friend was dancing a weird horizontal dance of agony as a dog ate his face. Then back to Rufinus, who had slowed to a menacing step, sword held out to the side. As he stomped forwards, he pulled his vine stick from his belt in his left hand.

Cilo wavered for a moment, and then began to step backwards.

Rufinus sped up a little.

So did Cilo. His eyes were wild and his face pale, as well they might be as he listened to the revolting sounds of Acheron's fury. He broke. He ran.

Rufinus charged after him in an instant, but as he passed the corner of one of the temples, his roving eye found a new and more important target, and he slewed to a halt. Cilo raced away into the shadows of another building, fleeing the scene, but Rufinus let him go. He could wait. He was relatively unimportant. The figure Rufinus could now see in the open square was all that mattered.

The newly-stripe-tunic'd Tribune Aper stood on the rich paving not far from the edge of the hill, where a low balustrade afforded a magnificent view across the Velabrum to the Palatine. Senova was held tight by a handful of her long black hair, her wrists bound behind her. In Aper's other hand was his sword.

'I thought you'd never come,' snarled Aper.

'Let her go and this doesn't have to end too badly.'

Various noises insisted upon him as he strode towards them, and he glanced around to see that the spectators had closed on them now, no longer held at bay by men with swords. Acheron was with him too, now, padding along close by, black fur glistening and matted with Praetorian blood.

'Keep that thing away,' Aper warned, pointing at Acheron with his sword.

Rufinus shook his head. 'I'm more inclined to let him eat you.'

Aper jerked his hand around, and Senova yelped as some of her hair was pulled out, but his hold was tight, and she was hauled back to the balustrade, where she danced desperately in his grip.

'Aper…'

'Better stop there, Rufinus. Your mutt too. Don't want to see how long it takes for the splat, do you?'

Rufinus, eyes narrowing dangerously, slowed to a halt, Acheron still close by.

'You've messed up, Aper. This is too open. Too public. It's idiotic. Even if you got away, and you won't, there are plenty of witnesses to half a dozen crimes being committed even now. Your men have been chased away and the Urban Cohort are on their tail. You can't win.'

Aper snorted. 'You don't know me as well as you seem to think, Rufinus, if you believe for even a moment that I'm worried about the police monkeys. They wouldn't dare arrest a Praetorian tribune, especially one with ties to both his prefect and the man who rules the world. I'm more or less untouchable. I can wriggle out of anything that comes from this, but she'll still be dead.'

'You can still walk away,' Rufinus said quietly.

'Do you realise what this is?' Aper murmured, glancing over the edge, and dragging Senova just a little closer. 'This is the Tarpeian Rock. Long before heads rolled down the Gemonian Stair, this was the place where traitors died. This is where slaves who committed crimes were executed. Rather fitting, don't you think? This slave girl who had ideas far above her station, and a Praetorian who wormed his way into our midst and then started to pull us apart from inside, just like the insidious grain man you have to be.'

Rufinus took another step forwards.

'Ah, ah, ah...' cautioned Aper, and with impressive strength, pulled Senova up by the hair so that she leaned over the balustrade.

'Eighty-six feet,' he said. 'Eighty-six. Imagine the ground she'll cover when she hits. Of course, she might be dead before she lands, as there are some nasty jagged bits of rock to bounce off on the way down.'

'What do you want?' Rufinus snapped. 'You have to know that if you throw her, I'll kill you moments later.'

'But you know me, Rufinus. You have to know I'll still do it. Here's the deal: I need you. I want your head. Preferably on a stick, but I'm not that fussy. And I need your truth revealing. You're going to go to Prefect Crispinus, you're going to give him the frumentarii insignia I'm sure you have hidden away somewhere. You're going to tell him what you've been doing all these months when he thought you were his man. And when he accepts the truth and you are condemned, then I'll be happy.'

'There's not a lot in this deal for me,' Rufinus said.

'I'm no fool, Rufinus. There could yet be repercussions if I start executing all your friends and family. So, you have my word, and the basic logic of it, that when you fall, I will forget all about your woman, your family and your friends. It's a very simple question, Rufinus. You or them, and you get to decide.'

Rufinus took another step and Aper jerked Senova out over the drop, so that her centre of gravity was now at the balustrade top. If he let go now, she might just fall anyway. Certainly, a little push and she would go.

Rufinus chewed his lip. What could he do? If he went any closer, Aper might just do it. He was clearly capable of it. But if Rufinus agreed and bought himself some time, walking away, Aper would take Senova and who knew what he might do then? Perhaps he could head back and call on the Urban Cohort, but that would be equally disastrous. If they came, then Aper might just throw Senova away, and the bastard was right in that even in these circumstances the men of the Cohort would at least think twice before arresting a man of his rank and connections.

Aper's sword came up and back, point hovering at waist height around a foot from Senova. 'Think fast, Rufinus.'

Damn it. What to do?

Had he blinked then, he would have missed it. Senova's bound hands had found her belt while Aper's attention had been on Rufinus, and had pulled from it that knife he had given her for Matronalia. He stared. She couldn't do much with it, her hands bound behind her back. But she was doing something. Fighting back. He realised he had to keep Aper's attention on him.

'You're down to one helper now, you know? I killed one on the ship on the way back from Africa, and another in the potter's yard opposite my house. Now Acheron's eaten a third. Only Cilo remains, and he deserted you just now. You may think you have power, but all your support is diminishing. And you might believe that the patronage of Crispinus and the emperor will protect you, but I think you've got a shock coming. You've seen how popular the *Imperator* Didius Julianus is. Even the peasants hate him, let alone the senators. If he didn't have Praetorian backing, he'd be dead already. How long do you think he's going to last?'

Aper was simply glaring at him, silent.

'And who comes next do you suppose? I don't know the answer to that, but I can tell you one thing: if he wants to be popular in Rome, he's going to distance himself from Julianus, and every little criminal shithead who helped him along the way is going to fall far and hard.'

Aper opened his mouth to spit a reply, but at that moment Senova moved. She had managed to turn, unnoticed, just enough that she could see what she was doing. The bound hands lashed out as far as they could. The knife jabbed into Aper's chest, not far from the armpit.

He bellowed in pain and surprise, and everything happened at once. It had not been a serious wound, for she had not the strength in her position to strike a powerful blow, but it had shocked her captor. In his surprise and pain, instinct kicked in and he let go.

As he staggered a pace back, grunting, looking down at the red bloom growing on his white tunic, Senova pitched forwards over the balustrade with a shriek. Rufinus moved, throwing down his sword and vitis, blood thundering in his ears as he leapt forwards.

Senova had gone over the balustrade and with her hands bound she grab nothing, but somehow even as she'd fallen, she'd managed to jam her foot in the narrow gap between two of the balusters on the stone rail. As she'd gone over it had wrenched, and he could see with panic that she had clearly broken her leg as she went, her continued howling illustrating how agonising it must be to be held up only by a wedged foot at the end of a broken leg.

He reached her a moment later and grabbed at her, pulling her back away from the drop over which she lolled. She shrieked with every movement and he worried that her leg might tear away entirely, but as he lifted her back to safety, the foot came loose from the railing, dangling at an unnatural angle.

He took the opportunity to glance around. Aper had been backing away, but Acheron had begun to circle him, as though rounding up sheep, and now had him pinned against the balustrade a little further along. The hound was snarling fit to release Tartarus itself, and Aper was hissing in pain at the minor wound in his chest, but he still held his sword tight, the tip out towards Acheron. If the dog leapt, both might well die in the ensuing mess.

Rufinus looked about him desperately. The crowd of oohing and ahhing observers had come closer now, getting their fill of the entertainment. Rufinus gently lowered Senova to the ground and gestured to the crowd. 'Get a board of some kind and lift her onto it.'

No one moved.

'Do it,' bellowed Rufinus furiously, and several onlookers suddenly burst into life, rushing around, doing what they could. He crouched beside Senova. 'It'll be alright. I'll make sure. Let them help you. I'll be back in moments.'

She nodded, her face pallid and waxy and, grasping his fallen sword and vine stick, he rose, turning back to the cornered Praetorian.

'That's it, Aper. You're finished.'

'Don't do anything rash, Rufinus. Your woman might only lose a leg, and you've got brothers and friends yet.'

Rufinus began to step forwards slowly.

'You'll not touch them. You'll not touch anyone ever again, Aper.'

'Very sure of yourself, aren't you. Rufinus? I'm good with this, you know?' he waggled the sword and then steadied it at Acheron once more.

'Acheron, heel.'

Reluctantly, snarling as he came, Acheron backed off, away from Aper towards his master. A quick glance back confirmed that people were trying to help Senova. It was all he could do right now.

Lifting his sword, he advanced on Aper. The tribune shifted his grip on his own blade. As he neared, Rufinus broke into a run. When he reached Aper, he swiped with his vitis, and stabbed with his gladius, two simultaneous attacks.

Aper, even though he had been prepared for the attack, could only hope to block one of the strikes. His sword parried that of Rufinus with a nerve-jangling shriek of metal edges scraping along one another, and he managed to lean left just enough to avoid the worst of the second hit, but the vitis did catch him a glancing blow on the shoulder.

The man grunted as he returned the favour, his sword coming fast. Rufinus blocked it in turn, but realised too late that it was a feint, just as the reason for the distraction became clear. Aper's other hand was now gripping his vitis. The gnarled ancient wood was too solid to break by far, but it was useless when gripped by both combatants, one at each end. As the stick jerked this way and that, both pulling hard, the swords came round and down again and again, striking and parrying, striking and parrying.

They were more or less evenly matched, Rufinus realised then. How could he overcome the man? Scenarios leapt into his mind in quick succession even as they struggled and fought. He settled on an idea and even then struggled with it for a moment. Pride demanded that he beat Aper fairly. But, he decided with a grim set of the lips, pride could go hang on this occasion.

'Acheron. Kill.'

Even as the struggle back and forth with the vitis continued and the swords clanged together once again, Acheron jumped forwards, his jaws closing on Aper's lower leg. The Praetorian screamed at the pain, though he continued to fight with Rufinus and did not drop the weapons. The three of them remained there for a weird moment, locked in battle, swords pushing against one another, vine stick grasped in both hands and Acheron savaging the man's ankle.

Then Rufinus ended it.

Letting go of the vine stick so that Aper's hand shot backwards with the vitis still gripped, he lifted that hand and simply shoved at the Praetorian's bloodied tunic. Aper had not realised how close to the balustrade he'd come during the fight, and as he fell back, his eyes widened with realisation.

At the last moment, Acheron let go, and Aper, accompanied by a blood-curdling shriek, disappeared backwards over the eighty-six-foot drop of the Tarpeian Rock. The ancient place of execution for traitors. How appropriate indeed.

With a sigh, Rufinus blinked away sweat, and then stepped forwards to look over the edge. Aper was a long way down, but he'd been right. He covered a surprising area down there. Rufinus wondered if he would ever find his vitis. He could draw a new one from stores of course, but he knew that one well now, and had got used to all the knobs and lumps on it. He sighed. Best not to get arrested now as he tried to save Senova. With another tinge of regret he removed his scabbard and dropped it and the sword over the edge after his victim.

He turned and ran back over to Senova who had been laid flat on a wooden board that had recently been a grocer's stall judging by the stains and smells. For a heart-stopping moment, he panicked that she was dead, but then realised that she had passed out, probably through the pain.

'I know a good physician,' he said close to her ear and he cupped her cheek in his hand. 'He saved Acheron. I know he can save you.'

XXIV – AN OLD HAUNT

R ufinus cast a glance back at his front door. He did not like to leave right now, but there were things that needed doing, and he was of no use here other than company and moral support. The days after Aper's death had been complicated and worrying.

Senova had been brought back to the house on her board stretcher, and that same Greek physician who had saved Acheron, Alexios, had been sent for courtesy of one of the more helpful members of the gathered crowd. Rufinus had been delayed only briefly by his following encounter with the Urban Cohort. They had caught two of the three grey clad men and were confident that they would track down the third with the 'help' of the other two. They had been less than worried about the death of Aper. A Praetorian officer was nothing to them, and the fact that he'd broken the law so blatantly made the death a simple thing to deal with. There would be no repercussions for them. There had been a brief interrogation of Rufinus, but with no weapon about his person and the supportive testimony of a large number of onlookers, there was really no case to pursue. The villains had been dealt with, and so Rufinus was released.

By the time he got home, Senova was locked away in a room with the medicus. Even Publius had been thrown out of the room while the man worked. Rufinus was allowed in to see his wife briefly following the initial medical investigation. She was still pale and in a great deal of pain, though even as he spoke to her that began to ease, for Alexios had fed her some concoction that took away the pain, along with much of her wit and sense.

Leaving her to the medicus once more, he had stood with Publius in the atrium and fretted. It was late into the night when the Greek finally emerged properly, rubbing tired eyes.

'What news?' Rufinus begged urgently.

'With the will of the gods and sufficient care, the news is good, I would say.'

Rufinus felt a burst of tension released as Publius patted him comfortingly on the shoulder.

'The break was very clean,' Alexios continued. 'The leg must have jerked hard and fast to split so straight. There will be hardly a hairline mark on it when it sets, if all goes well. She has also broken several bones in her foot, as well as damage to the various cords and muscles that bind the whole together.'

'But she will live? She will keep the leg?'

Alexios gave a tentative nod. 'Gods willing. The leg is set, bound and splinted. She must not be moved at all until I give you the word, with the exception of using the latrine, of course, and then she must be supported and helped every step of the way, the leg touching nothing. I will return daily to check up on her. She will be in a great deal of pain for some time, though I can ameliorate that problem. My only real concern now is infection. If rot sets in, and to allay your fears there is little chance of that, then we may have to look at the loss of a leg. But if infection does not take hold then all is simply a matter of time.'

'And then she will walk again.'

'Probably. There is much other damage than the simple break, and I cannot for certain say what effects that will have until we can get her standing. I would be very surprised if she heals without a sign of the damage. Very likely she will walk with a noticeable limp for the rest of her days.'

Rufinus nodded. A limp he could deal with.

And so Alexios had left and the days had set in, with the medicus arriving every morning to check on his patient and Senova largely unable to make any kind of social interaction thanks to the concoction that kept her sleepy and dreamlike, but which swept away the pain. Periodically, Rufinus would slip away and visit the temple of Aesculapius on the Tiber Island, giving whatever he could afford to draw the goodwill of the healing god. He even surreptitiously asked that image of Brigantia in his hallway for her help, arranging for a painter to come and touch up where he'd damaged the work, oddly worried that in his earlier insults of the British deity he had somehow contributed to Senova's predicament.

By the third day, Rufinus went back to work. He'd sent a missive explaining that he had suffered an injury within his familia and begged a few days. He'd not explained that it was his wife, although that was still a somewhat complex subject, for he was not officially allowed a wife while serving. The Guard had granted him a matter of days leave.

When he'd returned, his first port of call had been the new prefects of the Guard. Crispinus had been angry and suspicious. His two right hand men had been involved in a public altercation, resulting in the death of one of them. Rufinus had spun a most plausible lie about Aper, claiming a resentment that had been present ever since the journey back from Africa, and seething jealousy arising from Rufinus' increased importance while Aper languished in Africa. It all sounded very likely, especially given that even Crispinus had to admit to an increased reliance upon Rufinus over recent months, and a slight overlooking of his former favourite.

Disaster smoothed over, Rufinus had set upon his next task. One of the last few conspirators of whom he knew the name: Volcatius Cilo. Before the year was out, he had vowed, the Guard would be cleared one way or another. He would deal with Genialis at the end, for the man at least had been of some use and might be able to redeem himself, and Crispinus' time was coming. For now, Aper's last henchman was his target. Cilo had been one of those men who had snatched Senova off the street and killed Rufinus' people, and was by extension therefore responsible for his wife lying in a chamber with a ruined leg. Cilo's number was up.

The problem was that Cilo knew he was being hunted now. While Rufinus had spent a few days overseeing his wife's healing, Cilo had made use of his time. He had, presumably by calling in favours and using his speculatore connections, secured a transfer to the protection detail of the emperor's brother, that same Didius Nummius Albinus who Rufinus had found involved in bribery way back at the start of this all. Nummius had been granted ownership of one of the imperial estates, and Rufinus had had trouble finding out which one. Had Senova been her usual self, undoubtedly she would have known within the hour, but he was less competent at the administration of investigation.

Finally, several days later, he found the records he needed and noted with grim satisfaction that Nummius had been granted that same palace close to Tibur where Rufinus had worked undercover ten years ago to bring down a different emperor's sister.

He'd returned to his house and given instructions. Their level of security was to continue. With Aper gone, the threat had diminished seriously. There were probably no watchers now, and the last of Aper's close henchmen had left the city. Still, with Genialis and Crispinus around they should watch out. There would still be other men in the guard, after all, including those men under Florianus who had once guarded the African gold. Publius was to look after things for the day and keep Senova in good spirits.

He hated leaving them, but the time had come. A man had to die.

He tore his gaze from the house and pulled himself up into Atalanta's saddle. He was dressed in a simple brown tunic and cloak, and had not shaved for several days, allowing his stubble to grow out. He wore his caligae speculatoriae, not for their connections and meaning, but for the simple fact that they were boots designed specifically for hunting. He'd bought a new sword in the days following the disaster, and that was now slung at his side. He would not be entering the city's pomerium with the blade this time, for his destination lay elsewhere.

The ride out to Tibur took only a few hours. Rufinus had arranged his shifts at the palace such that he had no need to be on duty until nightfall the next day, and anyone with any interest in him would assume him to be at home with his injured wife.

He stopped at the mansio on the Tibur road that stood close to the drive leading down to the imperial villa and ate and drank at a table in the corner, listening out to conversation. The new resident of the villa was not overly popular with the locals by the sound of things, but there was nothing particularly untoward he heard, and so after eating, he moved on. It did not take him long to find the clearing where so long ago Acheron's brother had died. Good job he'd left the hound at home guarding Senova. Memories of this place were bad enough for Rufinus. How would they affect Acheron? But this was a job for subtlety, and Acheron might be many things but subtle was not one of them.

On the assumption the system still worked the same here as it had when he'd guarded the villa, this was too far out on the estate to be patrolled. He also suspected that the Guard assigned to Nummius Albinus would not be large, so they would be stretched thin. As the sun began to slide down behind the hills Rufinus moved to a viewpoint where he could see the ruined southern theatre where he'd passed many a cold day on guard. It did not take long before he spotted a man in white walking around the perimeter. Shuffling closer, careful to move quietly and not send up wildlife, he reached a position where he could make out more detail. It was not Cilo. He had to assume that each man would have an area of the villa to cover. Of course, it was entirely possible that Cilo was currently off-duty and hidden inside somewhere, in which case Rufinus would have to make several circuits, investigate the assigned guards and perhaps come back another day. He could probably have learned more and worked out a better plan to begin with, but without Senova's mind on the job it would have been more difficult. Besides, the urge to put this bastard in the ground had grown exponentially every time he'd looked at Senova lying injured in her room.

No, Cilo had to die now.

Rufinus moved on carefully, along tracks of which he had only hazy memories. He spotted the long terrace and the summer house at the eastern perimeter, and along their lines he found two more guards patrolling, neither of whom turned out to be Volcatius Cilo.

On he went now, following the eastern terrace from a distance so that he could see the figure wandering along the top of it. Past the circular temple, around the golden house, with two more men who were not Cilo. Below the amphitheatre walls and along the imperial perambulatory. Rounding the end of the next set of terraces, he was beginning to lose hope that tonight would see an end to things, when a familiar face suddenly hoved into view. He ducked back around the terrace corner and then peeked once more.

It was Cilo, he was fairly sure. The light was now getting very low, and he had to strain to make out details. There was a *chance* he was mistaken, but he didn't think so. By now that face was so ingrained in his memory, he would probably know the man even in pitch darkness.

The terrace ran along to the left, following the valley's contour. Off some way to the right stood the low, sprawling complex of the palaestra and the gymnasium, with the great theatre beyond, and in the recess at the end, between palaestra and terrace wall, stood the temple of Venus. A semi-circular space of rich marble floor, surrounded by a porticoed building, with a small circular tholos-style temple at the centre, the complex to one of Hadrian's favoured deities rose upon a high storey of brick substructures.

The figure in white on that half-moon courtyard that surrounded the tholos disappeared into one of the doorways on the right. Rufinus wracked his brains, trying to remember the layout of the place, but it had not been one of his regular haunts when he'd served here, and he couldn't quite recall much of it.

He turned the corner and immediately ducked back once more, for the guard on duty at the palaestra suddenly put in an appearance, wandering along the wall before disappearing again. Rufinus dipped out for another look and, satisfied that no one could see him, began to jog along the edge of the terrace retaining wall. There was probably a man atop that wall too, but with Rufinus right at the bottom of it, he would go unaware unless he leaned out to look down. Moreover, in his light hunter's boots, Rufinus was making precious little noise on the soft grass.

In moments he had reached the base of the temple's substructure. The next move was not daunting in itself, for the brick had long since lost much of its mortar and any man with good grip and strength would have little difficulty in climbing it. The heart-pounding came from the risk of discovery.

Undoing his cloak and letting it fall to the grass, he jabbed his fingers into the gap between two bricks and began to climb. It was some twelve feet to the set of ornamental niches that had been built along the wall to give it pleasing form from a distance, and he was grateful when his hand grasped the lip of one of them. A noise made him stop dead, and he turned his head slowly.

The guards at the palaestra and above the terrace wall had chanced to spot one another across the gap and were calling to each other, laughing over something. Rufinus clung to the brick, fingers shaking, worrying that he could hardly stay here forever, but aware that movement could draw their attention even if it was near dark and he was wearing brown against a brick background.

When the two men moved on, he heaved a sigh of relief, pulling himself up into the niche. Taking a breather, he flexed his fingers and prepared to move on. Grasping the wall to his left, he climbed once more. Over and over, up the brick wall he hauled himself, every now and then wincing as his sword came loose and clattered against the surface.

He felt a tiny thrill as his fingertips reached the top, and as his muscles screamed and his fingers ached, he slowly pulled himself up so that he could peer over the edge. The edge of the wide half-moon patio was lined with a low wall just two bricks high, punctured with drain spouts all along. Even as he looked about, one of the doors opened off to the left, and he dropped back out of sight, holding his breath. He heard the clack of nailed boots across the marble. As he hung there, wishing he could relieve the pressure on his aching fingers, he heard the man cross the patio and come to a stop somewhere to his left. He gritted his teeth as he heard fumbling, then a curse and finally a sigh as a jet of urine arced out over the edge and down to the grass below. He thanked the gods he'd not chosen that position to climb the wall. Still, he was close to falling, his fingers straining and his eyes watering by the time that jet stopped with a couple of extra spurts and the footsteps clacked away to the right. When they disappeared through a door, Rufinus took his chance, pulling himself up and over the edge.

Breathing heavily, he lay there for a moment. Gripping and straightening his fingers over and over to push life and warmth back into them, he rose to his feet and padded across the rich marble. The circular temple at the heart of the complex was perhaps fifty feet across, its conical roof supported by columns all around the outside.

The temple was dark and clearly unused now, and Rufinus hurried to the nearest edge. There he tested several of the spaces between the columns until he found the best one, which was hidden from every door in the surrounding porticoed arc. He would be partially visible to the guard at the palaestra but only from a long distance, and would be aided in his hiding by the ever-increasing shadow.

He was as invisible as he was likely to get, and Cilo would have to walk past him to tour the edge of the drop, which he had done twice while Rufinus watched, and from which he'd stopped to pee. Slowly, carefully, Rufinus now slid his sword from its sheath. Gripping it tight, his breath slowed, and he relaxed.

He was as ready as he could be when he heard the door off to his right open. The clack of nails on marble approached and Rufinus prayed he'd been right. If this *wasn't* Cilo then he would have a thousand miles of atonement to crawl along for what he was about to do. The figure came closer and closer, reaching the edge and then walking along it. As he neared the circular temple, Rufinus lifted his blade, gripped tight.

Cilo stepped into view completely oblivious to what awaited him. One moment he was sauntering quietly along a peaceful patrol route. The next he had stepped past the temple columns and the tip of a gladius jammed itself into his neck just above the plates of his segmented armour. As he gurgled, eyes widening in shock, unable to scream around the thick steel blade that had passed through his windpipe and throat, the man in the shadows pushed hard, driving the blade deep into his victim's neck until there was a crack. Cilo stiffened. Finally, the blood put in an appearance, initially soaked up by the man's scarf. Now it bloomed and spurted around Rufinus' sword.

There was nothing Rufinus could do about it He simply accepted that the blood was going to cover him. Once he was satisfied that Cilo was finished, he leaned close, blood spattered across his face.

'That was for my wife, you bastard.'

Then he yanked his blade free and pushed the man, watching as Cilo toppled from the edge to land with a subdued thump on the turf below. Rufinus looked down at his blade. It was soaked with crimson. Slamming that into the sheath would glue it in for good, but he could hardly climb with it. Sighing, he dropped the sword over the edge and pulled himself back into the shadows just in time for the palaestra guard to put in another appearance.

The man strolled about for a moment and then disappeared once more, oblivious to the death of his fellow soldier. Once he was gone,

Rufinus lowered himself over the edge again and rapidly descended the brick wall, with one or two hair raising moments brought on by his blood-coated, slippery fingers.

Reaching the ground once more, Rufinus felt around, retrieved his sword and cloak, and then hurried back along the terrace wall. Rounding the corner, he heaved a sigh of relief. It would probably be some time before a change of shift brought to light Cilo's absence, and it might well be morning light before his fate was known. Plenty of time.

Quarter of an hour later, Rufinus was down among the farmers' fields at the tree-lined edge of the estate, and hurried around the perimeter until he reached the forested area once more. In all it was just less than an hour before he reached the clearing and found Atalanta patiently waiting where he had tethered her. Unwilling to ruin his saddle with all this sticky blood, he walked away from the estate, leading the mare by the reins.

A mile and a half from the villa he reached the banks of the Anio, where he left Atalanta to graze while he threw himself bodily into the river, scrubbing and rubbing by moonlight in the cold water until he was content that he'd removed enough of the coating of blood spatter to pass casual inspection. Once he was content, he checked and sheathed his sword and mounted once more, beginning the ride back to Rome.

It was still several hours before dawn when he turned into the street where his house lay. He approached wearily and rapped on the door, looking around and noting contentedly that no one seemed to be watching his home now. The door was opened by Diogenes, the newly appointed doorman who had served with the Fourteenth Gemina in Pannonia.

'Can you take Atalanta round the back?' Rufinus muttered in a tired voice.

Diogenes looked him up and down. 'Wet, and still bloodstained. A successful evening, Domine?'

Rufinus snorted. 'You could say that. Is the bath furnace still warm?'

'Always at the moment, sir. The medicus believes the heat to be of benefit, and so the Domina is in there whenever she wakes lucid, which can be any time of the day or night.'

Rufinus nodded wearily. 'I could use a warm dip myself. The River Anio doesn't cut it as a relaxing bath.'

'Before you do, you have a visitor.'

Rufinus frowned. 'Can't see visitors like this.'

'You can, sir,' Diogenes smiled. 'It's the baker.'

Rufinus' frown deepened. The *baker* was the household's codename for Vibius Cestius, playing on his position as a frumentarius, or grain man.

'In the office?'

Diogenes nodded as he passed Rufinus and took the reins of Atalanta, ready to lead her round to the rarely unbolted rear door of the house which had access to the ancillary quarters, stable, store house and more. Rufinus watched him go, took a last look up and down the street, and then slipped inside and bolted his front door.

Strolling through the house, he paused twice to pay respects to the household gods and to Brigantia, asking again for their favour in Senova's recovery. Briefly, he paused at the door to the room where she slept. He could hear the gentle sound of her breathing, almost a snore but not quite, relaxed and calm. She was asleep, so he did not try the door. Instead, he passed on through the house and out to the office.

Vibius Cestius awaited him, dressed normally.

'No old man disguises or anything?' Rufinus muttered.

'I suspect there is little need now that you've sent Aper off to the underworld. I gather from the state of your attire that you've finished the job. Publius told me you'd gone to Tibur.'

Rufinus nodded. 'The immediate problem is dealt with. There are still plenty of villains. I think we could probably safely deal with Crispinus now. Genialis will side with us if it suits him, and he's certainly unlikely to stand against us in favour of Crispinus. And I don't need Crispinus around to continue excising the rotten core of the Guard, as I know that the new tribune Florianus from the Fifth Century is in with them, and so are some of his men.'

'You are still determined to finish the job, then?'

'More than ever. My only worry is that the rot is now so deep that by the time I've finished the Praetorian Guard will be so empty they won't be able to field a full century of men. The corruption seems almost total now.'

Cestius leaned back and folded his arms. 'Then my tidings might come as something of a relief to you.'

'Oh?'

'This is restricted information right now. If will become public sometime over the next day or perhaps two, but our people often manage to intercept tidings before they reach the general populace. You would be astonished at some of the news we have prevented becoming public.'

'What is it?' Rufinus murmured, intrigued now.

'We've had a man in the Fourteenth at Carnuntum for some time. He went with Severus when the man took command of Pannonia. Our man returned last evening. He is riding perhaps a day ahead of the official word that comes by courier.'

'Word of what?'

Cestius smiled enigmatically. 'Your friend Lucius Septimius Severus has been proclaimed emperor by his legions on the Danubius.'

Rufinus blinked.

'You seem surprised?'

'I am,' Rufinus replied. 'I mean, I kind of half anticipated it, but it's one of those things you come to expect, but deep in your heart you don't believe will actually happen. This is accurate? It's true?'

'Our man was there. Severus has become a rebel against the emperor. The problem is that a large proportion of the empire already see Julianus as a usurper, so Severus is by extension lent a certain legitimacy.'

'You sent him a letter, warning him about Julianus. Did you urge him to take the throne?'

'You should know by now, Rufinus, that I am a lot more subtle than that. Let's say that I was content with what Severus' reaction would be.'

'What will Julianus do?'

'Therein lies one important question,' Cestius replied quietly. 'But there is more from our Carnuntum man.'

'Oh?'

'It appears that Severus is not alone.'

Rufinus frowned. 'Who?'

'It seems that the Syrian legions had already proclaimed Pescennius Niger as their emperor. News has not reached Rome, because the courier that bore it never made it.'

'Severus?'

'Let's just say that one of our operatives thought it would be prudent to delay matters so that Severus could announce his claim first.

'You people are too damned devious,' Rufinus sighed. 'I'll never fit in. What of Albinus? If Severus and Niger have both claimed the throne, Clodius Albinus is hardly likely to stand aside.'

Cestius nodded. 'Fortunately, Albinus is the most remote of them. News of Julianus will have reached him last. To pre-empt any issues, Severus has sent him an offer. If Albinus supports him, Severus will name Clodius Albinus his junior co-emperor, like Verus was for Aurelius.'

Rufinus frowned. 'Severus *hates* Albinus. Doesn't trust him.'

'But it's always better to have a predator leashed by your side than out there hunting you. This way, he can keep Albinus under control while he deals with Julianus and Niger.'

'What a bloody mess,' Rufinus grunted. 'It's like the death of Nero all over again. So what do we do?'

'We... that is, the frumentarii, do nothing. We are the emperor's eyes and ears. We will pass on all tidings we have received when the time is right, and in the best order for the safety of Rome. You, as a Praetorian, will likely be mobilised to protect your emperor against this flurry of usurpers.'

'Protect Julianus?'

'Like us, you are oath-bound. You may hate the man, but if you do not do your duty to him, how are you any different from the men you hunt? He's your emperor. You're his bodyguard. But times are changing. This entire matter crescendos, and as Crispinus' right hand man, you will be at the very heart of it. You will never be in a better position to change the world than in the coming days, Rufinus.'

'But... protect Julianus?'

'Until the day he dies, or until the senate votes to remove his status and strip him of the purple.'

'And you still think that will happen?'

Cestius smiled again. 'Rumour is one thing. Wait until the senate know that Severus marches his armies on Rome and watch how quick they change their tune.'

XXV – A WORLD PREPARES

Maius came with a flurry of organisation. Rome was abuzz with panic. The empire had seen usurpers come and go over the generations, with men like Cassius in the east rising against Marcus Aurelius, but they had always been short lived and very distant affairs. The last time civil war had come close to home had been over a century ago, following the death of Nero. In those hated and feared days, legions had marched on Rome from Hispania, from Germania, from Judea. Bloody battles between men who might be brothers had been fought in Italia itself, a stone's throw from the capital, and troops had mustered in the streets to defend whichever emperor had managed to grasp the throne at the time.

No one wanted to see a return to those old days, but the possibility was now beginning to loom in men's minds. Hot on the heels of the information that Severus had been proclaimed emperor by his Danubian legions came the news that Pescennius Niger had been similarly raised by his Syrian forces. Rufinus waited twitchily for the third of the three lions to announce his claim, but no word came from Albinus in Britannia. Had Severus succeeded in buying him off for now?

The emperor had given orders to muster at Rome every man within reach, to defend the 'legitimate emperor, *chosen by the senate*', from these usurpers. No one, of course, dared point out that the senate had only ratified Julianus at sword point and in any other circumstances would likely have thrown him from the building. Still, Julianus knew where his powers of persuasion lay, and so here they were once more at the curia for an extraordinary meeting of the senate.

Rufinus stood just inside the door, close to Crispinus. Florianus, the tribune who had been Aper's colleague and another of the corrupt web, stood at the far door and his narrowed, suspicious eyes were not on the proceedings, but upon Rufinus, as they had been since the day Aper died. Rufinus sighed. In ridding himself finally of Aper and his men, he had simply transferred the enmity to this other officer. If ever there were proof that the Guard suffered such rot to its very core, this could be it.

Worse still was what they were now being asked to do.

The senators sat around three sides of the chamber, facing the open floor where speakers would address them, and around the outer wall of the room, neatly penning them in, stood a second U shape of white togate men, though these latter bore the familiar bulge of swords beneath their armpits. Once again, the emperor's bodyguard were being used to bully the senate.

His attention was drawn to the click and creak of an opening door, and the emperor entered the curia. Rufinus looked at Didius Julianus. Folk murmured when they thought no official ear listened that he was not long for the throne now, even not long for this world. Certainly, Rufinus had noted changes in the man since that day he'd first met Julianus in Carthage.

In that beginning time, the man had seemed shrewd and strong, putting Crispinus in his place and commanding his province with aplomb. There had been a shift when the man came to Rome, though. He might have come here to become the most powerful man in the world, but there was something changed in him then, something a short step from snapping at all times. He'd known that he owed everything to his praetorian prefects, and his authority was gone, now that he needed them more than they needed him. Still he had played the role of emperor, in a lesser manner than he'd played governor of Africa.

Now, though, he'd changed again. Rufinus had difficulty looking into the man's eyes, for they were constantly flicking this way and that, as though watching for assassins in every corner. They were hard dark coals, his eyes, sunken in red-rimmed orbits in a waxy, sweating face. The ruler of the world was hardly sleeping, waking in fear when he did and imagining an end to his reign around every corner. He was probably right to do so, but his image would not instil confidence in anyone.

The emperor cleared his throat and began before stuttering to a stop and looking confused. A quick glance at Crispinus and he nodded and straightened.

'Conscript fathers of Rome, I beseech you now, in this time of dire emergency, to further support your emperor. Base usurpers rise and march against us, and in the great traditions of Rome... according to the *mos maiorum*... I seek the will of the senate in facing them.'

Silence greeted his words, where a cheer would have been expected in other circumstances. His sweating increased. His eyes danced a little more wildly.

'I ask the senate to declare these usurpers, Pescennius Niger and Septimius Severus, enemies of Rome, so that we might deal with them accordingly. What say you, great fathers of Rome?'

Again, silence.

'What say you?' he asked again, his voice cracking.

At a gesture from Crispinus, the men close by jerked their swords a handbreadth from the sheath, the metallic scraping of the blade against the scabbard mouth making a horrible rasping sound that cut through the soul of every man in the building. Men all around the outside of the curia followed suit, so that the rasp went on for some time, making the situation clear for the trapped senators. Rufinus noted here and there men doing as they were bade reluctantly, pulling free their swords with a grimace of distaste. There were still men in the Guard who disapproved, but sadly another sign of the endemic rot was how few they were by comparison.

'You had best condemn the rest then,' snapped a voice from the white clad ranks of senators. Falco. The man who had opposed Julianus from the start but had been forced to recognise him.

'What?'

'You ask us to make Severus and Niger enemies of Rome. What of Clodius Albinus in Britannia, who has tacitly declared for Severus? What of Severus' own brother who commands the legions of Moesia, and who undoubtedly has already mobilised in his support? What of Claudius Candidus, war hero and respected senator who commands the Tenth Gemina and who personally draped the purple upon Severus, we are told? Should we be condemning the prefect of the vigiles, Plautianus? He is Severus' uncle, after all.'

Julianus was going paler and paler with every name, his lip twitching. He started to say something to Falco, but though his mouth moved the only sounds came from the outspoken senator's mouth instead.

'What of Aemilianus, the proconsul of Asia? He has not declared for your enemy, but he is the one man who stands on Niger's border and who should be stamping on Niger's neck now if he supported you, yet his men remain unmustered and languishing in their camps.'

At a nod from Crispinus those men close by suddenly pulled their blades free entirely with a metallic din that echoed around the chamber.

'I ask you humbly to accede to my wishes,' the emperor said in a tone that would have dripped with malice had it not also warbled with nervousness.

299

Falco opened his mouth, but something happened at the far side of the room, there was a yelp of pain, and suddenly the senators were shouting their support, damning Severus and Niger as usurpers. Falco turned amid the shouting of the frightened, pliable senators and fixed Crispinus with a withering glare. He was a brave man, Rufinus decided. *Foolish*, but brave.

Rufinus felt the disgust rising as he slid his blade home. The job had been done. The senate had condemned the emperor's enemies, where Rufinus had hoped they would *support* Severus and condemn Julianus.

The following days saw ever increasing disdain from Rufinus. As far as necessary he remained with Crispinus, but as much as possible he spent his time at home, where Senova had passed through the worst time of her injury without the dreaded signs of infection. She had stopped taking the strong medication the physician had prescribed and took only a small draught of poppy brew, measured carefully by Rufinus, who knew how horribly addictive the drug could be. She was becoming mobile on her crutches now, but it would be some time before the Greek would let her put any weight upon the leg to test its strength.

And while he served Crispinus where he must and accompanied Senova where he could, Rufinus watched Rome change. After that horrible incident at the senate house, he held out a brief hope that there might be a revolution, for the more vocal elements among the Praetorians began to argue about why they were supporting a man who had bought them with counterfeit coins. For a shaky day or two it looked as though the Guard might finally rebel and turn on the emperor, but Julianus dealt with it the only way he knew. He threw more money at them, and like the corrupt institution it had become, the Guard took the money and sealed their lips, encouraged at every turn by Crispinus.

And so, the Praetorians were mobilised for war. It had been thirteen years since they had seen action, and only the older veterans now remained from that time when the Guard had fought for Rome across the Danubius. The vast majority of the Praetorians had never seen more action than the training palus in the fortress yards. They *looked* good, and probably gave Julianus hope, for he was no soldier and no judge of warriors. They marched well, and they gleamed in their top-quality equipment, but Rufinus had seen *real* legions in times of war, and he was under no illusion that if the Guard met

Severus' veteran Danubian legions in the field right now they would be trampled and gutted to a man.

The Urban Cohort were a little more professional. Sulpicianus had been removed from their command quietly and assigned to some provincial role, and his successor had neither the will nor the desire to stand against the emperor. Consequently, the Cohort mobilised alongside the Guard, their cooperation frosty and uncomfortable. They appeared to Rufinus to be the better soldiers by far, which made him feel disgusted at the unit of which he'd once been so proud. Even the vigiles, who had dropped their buckets and taken up the sword as part of Julianus' hasty force, seemed more the veteran soldier than many of the Praetorians.

All these three city units, though, were shown up by the fourth force who the emperor had brought into the city to help build his army against the advance of Severus: the Misenum Fleet. The sailors who had always been seen as a sort of second-class military by the army, who Rufinus had come to respect over his year as their commander, were now formed like legions within the city.

And as this weird mishmash of an army drilled in the outskirts of Rome, they began to erect a new temporary defence around the city. The ancient walls from the time of the early republic were little more than crumbling vestiges poking up from between buildings, far from the edge of the modern city. Now houses were pulled down and reformed into makeshift ramparts, and streets were hacked to pieces to make ditches. Rome was becoming a vast army camp for this odd force

And the unspoken thought among the few wary veterans like Rufinus was how futile it all was. With every day of preparation, the quality of Julianus' force improved but little, while Severus' hardened northern legions marched every closer. Word had them approaching the edge of Pannonia now, having been bolstered by men from Severus' brother in Moesia, the massed force closing on the border of Italia itself.

It became almost laughable when Julianus even had the elephants that were used in parades and festivals brought out of their vivaria and adorned with small towers for archers after the eastern fashion. These elephants, though, were no creatures of war, and panicked at the things being placed upon their backs, trampling their handlers and numerous soldiers about them before breaking through gates and running amok and finally having to be penned and put away once more.

If anyone might *not* suspect the emperor of an increased state of paranoia, that changed when on a whim, fearing that those who had already murdered one emperor might do the same again, had Laetus, the former Praetorian Prefect, and Marcia, who had been Commodus' mistress, put to death without public accusation.

Things were falling apart

How long Crispinus thought he could hold Rome together for his pet emperor, Rufinus could not imagine. Then, as Maius dragged on and reports of Severus' implacable advance continued to come, the emperor finally seemed to withdraw from public. To Rufinus abject shock, he reported for duty at the Palatine one morning to discover the Urban Cohort fortifying the place. Whether Julianus saw the Palatine as some last redoubt if the city fell, or whether perhaps he feared attack from within the city now, Rufinus couldn't say. But the fact was that men were busy attaching metal grilles over every window, bricking up doors and fitting positions for archers about the palace, such that it could be defended as its own citadel.

Oh, how the senate must be missing Commodus and the security of an Antonine dynasty now.

Finishing his shift there with a wrinkled lip of distaste, Rufinus returned to the Castra Praetoria to put away his equipment and return home to check on Senova, only to find a message awaiting him, ordering him to attend upon Prefect Crispinus at the headquarters.

As he marched across the courtyard and towards the office, Rufinus could see through the window more than one figure inside. Angling his approach to get a better view, he spotted the figures of the other prefect, Genialis, and of Florianus, former centurion of the Fifth and now tribune.

His breath caught in his throat. All his remaining known enemies in one place boded ill. He prepared himself, straightening, and rapped on the door. At a call from Crispinus he stepped inside and closed the door behind him. Those three were the only other figures in the room.

'Rufinus, good,' said Crispinus in a business-like tone. 'I find myself in something of a difficult position. Since the loss of Aper, I have come to rely somewhat heavily upon my two remaining confidantes: yourself and Florianus here. The problem is that with the world being torn in two and legions marching against legions, with Rome in chaos and being pulled apart and forces that hate one another barracked together again, I simply cannot afford to have division in my own ranks.'

Rufinus turned his head to find Florianus glaring at him.

'The tribune here is insistent that there is something fishy about the death of Aper. He seems convinced that you are not what you seem, and so in the interest of continued security, I have summoned you to answer to him in front of us all. Defend yourself.'

Rufinus frowned. 'Sir, I have been through this. I have at no point attacked, or threatened to attack, Aper. The man seems to have suffered a growing resentment against me, which I put down to his confinement back in Africa with the emperor while I tended to matters here for you. He attacked my house, took my woman, and tried to throw her from the Tarpeian Rock. He told me flatly that he intended to do the same to my brother and to anyone about whom I cared. I can provide dozens of witnesses to all of this, for a crowd had gathered on the Capitol, and even the men of the Urban Cohort were present. I have no idea what Florianus believes, but Aper is the architect of his own fate, not I.'

'And what of Aper's men?' snapped Florianus.

Crispinus turned a puzzled frown upon Rufinus now. 'True, there have been four shady losses among my most trusted men. Can you explain this?'

Rufinus nodded. 'As far as possible. One, when we were in Africa, had already taken against me for some personal reason. He attacked me aboard ship, and I did kill him, but only in defending myself.'

An oddly reminiscent story,' growled Florianus. 'I wonder what it is about you that sets off both these men working against you?'

'I wish I could say,' Rufinus replied with a cold glare. 'One of the others was with Aper on the Capitol, and I have no regret that my dog savaged him, for he helped Aper kidnap my wife... my *woman...* in broad daylight.'

'Another man who took against you for no reason?' snorted Florianus.

'Or just on Aper's orders,' Rufinus responded just as harshly. 'Of the other two I know nothing. One disappeared some time ago. The other is on seconded duty serving the emperor's brother if I am not mistaken.'

Crispinus shook his head. 'That last man was butchered at the imperial villa near Tibur at the turn of the month.

'At which time I was attending upon Senova night and day when I was not on duty, since she broke her leg during Aper's unwarranted attack.'

Genialis nodded. 'I have checked the records, and this does indeed match up. I have also spoken to those men I have in place at the imperial villa and in various positions in Rome, and it would appear that Rufinus was nowhere near Tibur when this happened.'

Rufinus frowned, then as the others argued for a moment, he shot a questioning look at Genialis, who could surely have noted that Rufinus had time to get to Tibur and back even if his men at the villa were unaware, and yet who had said nothing, defending Rufinus from potential disaster.

'And what of the other?' Florianus demanded. 'His body was found wedged at a bend in the sewers. He was a mess. We tried to determine from where he had come, but he was found at a major junction in the passages, and it was impossible to tell. Can you tell us you had nothing to do with that?'

'Unless you can tell me where or when it happened,' Rufinus snapped angrily, 'I fail to see how in the name of all the gods I can defend myself against your accusations. No, I had nothing to do with it. Once upon a time my word was enough. It's all I have right now.'

Crispinus nodded slowly, then exchanged a look with Genialis, who nodded, judiciously avoiding meeting Rufinus' gaze. The prefect spoke with a heavy sigh. 'There must be something going on, I agree, but there is no sign of wrongdoing on Rufinus' part, Florianus. More than that, Rufinus has been invaluable to me in those days when we positioned the emperor for his accession. He has not once displayed a hint of opposition or treachery. As such, I will accept no more bad blood between you. You will work with Rufinus as you have worked with Aper, and if your continued enmity becomes a problem, I will have you transferred to a provincial duty rather than you join Aper's ilk and go for Rufinus' family.'

'I still want to know what happened to them,' grumbled Florianus.

Rufinus turned to his accuser. 'If you want someone to blame for your man in the sewer and your man at Tibur, I suggest you look no further than the frumentarii. They have hounded me before now, and they will ever look closely and suspiciously at those men who served Cleander. Moreover, in my time I have served at that same villa of which you speak, when the empress Lucilla was in residence, and I can tell you that there were frumentarii at work there even then. I would be extremely surprised to learn there was not a grain man assigned to Tibur while the emperor's brother is there. Therein, I suspect, we can find your killer. Now stop weighing me down with your suspicions and your threats. We are in enough peril with usurpers all over the empire.'

'Quite,' agreed Crispinus. 'Let that be an end to it.'

Florianus continued to glare at Rufinus but gave a sullen nod. Finally, he took a deep breath and turned back to the prefect. 'So what do we do with these boys?'

'Boys?' asked Rufinus, startled at the weird question and the sudden change of subject.

Crispinus sighed. 'Twenty Pannonian slaves the emperor has called for.'

'What in Apollo's name does the emperor want with twenty Pannonian slave boys?'

The prefect's face folded into a frown of disapproval. 'The emperor has consulted auguries about the peril he faces. Some weird Gaulish lunatic has convinced him that war can be stopped. All he has to do is sacrifice twenty Pannonian boys and twenty Syrian and the armies can be prevented from marching from those provinces against Rome.'

Rufinus' eyes bulged. 'That's insane.'

'Mildly so, I agree,' murmured Crispinus.

'And so Florianus here has been to the slave markets this morning,' Genialis said in tones thick with distaste, 'and rounded up twenty Pannonian boys. The Syrians are proving harder to acquire, but then the Syrian threat is further away and less urgent.'

'Surely you're not going to let the emperor perform human sacrifices?' Rufinus boggled. 'What are we, Punic barbarians?'

'It has been done before, Rufinus,' Crispinus replied in resigned tones.

'I know,' Rufinus said sharply. 'At Sarmizegetusa in Dacia. I've stood at the place it happened, and the place is a land of ghosts. The echo of that horror is still with the people there, even the legions, nearly a century after it happened. No good comes of human sacrifice. It is not the Roman way. Did Caesar and Plautius and Suetonius Paulinus stamp out the child-murdering druids just so that we could become their successors?'

Crispinus turned a raised eyebrow to him. 'Something of an impassioned plea, Rufinus? I had no idea you were so squeamish.'

Rufinus shook his head. 'This is not squeamishness. I will kill a man when I have to, and I will not cry over his corpse, Prefect, but I cannot condone the mass murder of children on the altar of insanity. And nor should you.'

The prefect's brow lowered a little. 'They are slaves, Rufinus.'

'My woman Senova was once a slave. I am not for liberating the slaves, mind you, like some altruistic idiot, but they are still more than sides of meat to be butchered to order.'

Crispinus' brow unknotted a little more. 'I take your point. And I do not like it myself. But it is an imperial command.'

'An insane one.'

'But a command no less.'

'The emperor will not wish to bloody his hands personally,' Rufinus said. 'He must know that if he is said to have done this thing it will be the end of his failing reputation in Rome. The people will turn against him. Save his reputation. Free the slaves and tell the emperor the sacrifice is done.'

Crispinus leaned back in his seat. 'And if the Gaulish augur speaks true, and the death of these boys could stop Severus advancing? And what of angering the gods by withholding a sacrifice?'

Rufinus snorted. 'You do not believe any more than I that the death of twenty snotty children would stop Severus marching on Rome. It is madness, and nothing good can come of it. Severus and his legions are coming, and I will not raise a blade to a child to stop them. And the gods? You think the gods really want the heart and liver of twenty Pannonian boys? If you want to keep the gods happy release the boys and kill a white bull. *That's* a sacrifice.'

Crispinus chewed on his lip.

'What do I do with all these slaves?' Florianus said again.

It was Genialis who answered, though. 'Send them to the paedagogium on the Palatine. Have them assigned as palace slaves.' And when Crispinus shot him a look, his fellow prefect shrugged. 'Rufinus is right. You don't believe this crap any more than I do, and I will sink to most levels, but sacrificing children is beneath even me.'

Finally, Crispinus nodded. 'Do it. Have them distributed among the imperial slaves. I will find a way to inform the emperor that his will has been done. It might make me itch to lie to the emperor, but this wasn't right.'

Even Florianus looked a little relieved.

'Alright,' Crispinus said, rising from his chair. 'We know that the force we have assembled in Rome is insufficient to fight off the usurpers. However, thanks to the emperor's largesse at least those men we have are loyal and will fight. The Third Augusta is on its way from Africa, along with numerous units of auxiliary cavalry, which will swell our numbers and give us more of a fighting chance. With luck, Niger and Severus will both be marching and will meet on the way, which might well see the end of one or both of them and would certainly weaken them and buy us time. The emperor has sent to the governors of the Germanies to seek their support and asked them to send legions, and demanded the few auxiliary units active in Hispania too. Things look bleak, but with sufficient time we can gather enough of a force to fight off Severus or make his legions waver until we can re-secure their loyalty.'

'That's a lot of ifs,' Rufinus said, wincing.

'And that is why there is another plan,' Crispinus said. 'The emperor and I are in the final stages of hashing out the idea, but bid your woman a short farewell, Rufinus, and gather your kit. Tomorrow we are bound for the provinces.'

Rufinus shivered with worried anticipation, but saluted, and left the office. So much to think on. He'd diverted suspicion yet again, but he doubted Florianus would let it rest no matter what the prefect said. The man was going to become a problem, and simply making him disappear was going to be far too suspicious now after this discussion. That was a problem to ponder. And then there was Crispinus and the emperor's plan. They were being sent somewhere, and to Rufinus' mind there was only one possible place they could be going. What could they hope to achieve in Pannonia?

He was still mulling things over unhappily when he arrived at his room in the barrack blocks. Unlocking the door, he stepped inside, Acheron opening a lazy eye from his blankets beside the bed.

'Looks like we're going on another trip, lad.'

He turned to shut the door and leapt back as a hand grasped it and pulled it open again. As he instinctively reached for his sword, Prefect Genialis stepped into the room.

'Prefect?'

'Rufinus.' Genialis looked this way and that along the street and then shut the door.

'What can...' Rufinus began but fell silent as Genialis put a finger to his lips. They listened in silence for some time, and finally Genialis seemed happy.

'You still report to Vibius Cestius?'

Rufinus flinched. 'I still have the connections,' he said evasively.

'My time of sitting upon the fence is at an end, Rufinus,' the prefect said.

'Sorry?'

'Crispinus is marching into oblivion and dragging us all along in his wake. The emperor is mad, Rufinus. His mind has broken with the pressure. He wants to murder *children*, for Jove's sake. The time has come. All I ask is amnesty for past acts. I want to be off your list.

In return you have my total support against the madman Julianus and against my esteemed and suicidal colleague.'

'Do you know what Julianus and Crispinus plan?'

Genialis shook his head. 'Not yet, but I could hazard a guess. The Pannonian legions march under the banner of Septimius Severus. He is a lion while Julianus is a toad. But if Severus were to perish, then there is a chance the whole thing will crumble. Certainly, there is a better chance of buying the loyalty of those renegade legions.'

Rufinus winced. 'You think they mean to assassinate Severus?'

Genialis nodded. 'I would imagine assassins have already been sent more than once. In fact, I have circumstantial evidence to that effect, and to men being sent for Niger too, but it would appear that all such attempts thus far have come to naught. I suspect that with the failure of underlings, Crispinus and the emperor have decided that it if you want something done right you should do it yourself.'

Rufinus shivered. If Genialis was right, then tomorrow morning he and the prefect would be riding out to assassinate Rufinus' patron.

'Will Rome be prepared for the enemy when we fail?' Rufinus muttered.

'Doubtful,' Genialis replied. 'Rome is poorly defended, and the emperor is doomed. If Severus and his army continue to come, Julianus will fall. And the African forces will not arrive to save him.'

'Why not?'

Genialis gave him a wicked smile. 'Because I was given the task of summoning them, and the letter never left my office.'

Rufinus sighed. 'Then things are coming to a close.'

'I believe so.'

'And whether you protest the righteousness of your sudden attack of conscience or not,' Rufinus said, eyes narrowed, 'it is interesting that with your coming onside with Severus once more you set yourself up in the best position to profit.'

Genialis laughed. 'Happy coincidence follows me, Rufinus. Now let us hope it follows *you* on the morrow.'

XXVI – THE LION OF LEPTIS

R ufinus chewed his lip as he rode, keeping his gaze on the seemingly endless flat salt pans stretching to either side of the road, careful not to let the nervous habit show to his fellow officers. Prefect Crispinus rode at the head of the column in his best regalia, which now looked *past* its best after six days of riding northeast across the peninsula, especially with the last stretch being in a region where the very air carried corrosive sea salt. A column of two turma of Praetorian cavalry followed on, along with Rufinus and Florianus on horseback accompanying the prefect. Every man was bedecked in his finest kit, now salt-marked, and the scorpion standards gleamed with pitted glory in the Maius sun.

Ravenna lay ahead, its stout grey walls rising above the flat fields and salt pans, red roofs invisible behind them. The azure sea lapped against a thin beach before the city way off to their right, and ships passed in and out of the harbour mouth between the moles upon which sat lighthouses. Here was the home of Rome's other great navy. Provincial fleets were based around the empire in scattered locations, but the vast majority of Rome's naval power lay in the two Praetorian fleets, one in Misenum that Rufinus had commanded for a time, and the other here, at Ravenna.

Any strategist in Rome would consider the loss of the Ravenna fleet to enemy forces a terrible blow, and the fact that Severus had not had to draw a sword to secure it was perhaps a sign of where public and military favour lay outside the capital. For Severus had crossed into Italia, seizing vital Aquileia and marching around the coast to secure Ravenna, and all without a blade being drawn. Rumour had it that when the army had reached Aquileia, the gates had been thrown open for the supposed usurper, and rose petals cascaded over the commanders as they entered the city.

Now, Severus had paused briefly at Ravenna in his advance to await further forces joining him from across the sea. Rufinus felt horribly exposed with this small column of less than a hundred riders as he looked out across those salt pans.

Outside the walls of Ravenna lay the largest concentration of military in one place that Rufinus had seen since the wars across the Danubius fifteen years earlier. Seemingly infinite rows of tents behind sudis-stake fences, with vexilla and standards gleaming and fluttering in the sea breeze and the late spring sunshine. From here he couldn't see the individual banners, but there was no doubt who they would be. Pannonia held four legions alone, the First and Second Adiutrix, and the Tenth and Eleventh Gemina, and Severus' brother's province of Moesia could field the First Italica, Fourth Flavia, and the Seventh and Eleventh Claudia. Even if the Severan governors had left half their forces in garrison, that meant that four legions now sat encamped outside Ravenna, along with sundry auxiliaries. Upward of thirty thousand men were ready to march on Rome, not to mention whatever further forces they still awaited at the great port city.

Rufinus shivered. He'd seen Julianus' slightly insane preparations in Rome. Even if Genialis had not blocked the call up of the African legion, the army in Rome would present little more than a hurdle for this vast gathering of veteran killers.

Still, Crispinus looked confident.

What was his plan?

It nagged at Rufinus that he was being kept in the dark, though at least the same could be said for Florianus, as his sour expression confirmed. All Crispinus had told them was that he carried an offer for Severus. Nothing else. What the offer was, Rufinus had conjectured silently over and over throughout the ride, but whatever it was, it was unlikely to buy off Severus, and Crispinus had to know that, so if he was still intent on his task then there was more to all of this than just his mysterious offer.

As they neared the city, a force of legionaries spilled out from the gate to line the road at either side. Enough to swamp this cavalry unit ten times over, Rufinus noted. Severus was no fool. He was further dismayed to note the standards of the Tenth Gemina among them. His old legion was here to greet him as an enemy. It had been thirteen years, but there would be veterans among them who would remember Rufinus from the days of the war. He hoped he'd aged enough to be unrecognisable. Any meeting with old compatriots would be at the very least uncomfortable.

As they slowed, approaching the city, Rufinus' eye climbed the solid walls to the parapet, where ballistae and onagers were slowly turning, tracking the approach of the mounted column. He couldn't see them closely, of course, but had no doubt whatsoever that they were primed.

Not an auspicious start.

No group of officers or dignitaries emerged from the open maw of a gate that lay between those lines of hard-looking soldiers and beneath the weapons of war. This was no parley. The deputation from the beleaguered emperor Didius Julianus was not to be received with dignity. They were to walk into the lion's mouth.

Rufinus braced himself. *He* knew that these men were his allies. He knew that Severus would not deliberately place him in danger, and he had friends here. Gods knew that there were almost certainly agents of the frumentarii among them. But he was officially a member of this enemy force, and if the worst happened and violence broke out, there would be little chance of his being saved in the chaos of brutality.

He kept his face down a little, just in case old friends happened to line the road, and held his breath as the lead units passed between those rows of disapproving murderous eyes and into the deep shadow of the gate house.

Ravenna was a neat city of brick walls and red tile roofs. It presumably suffered the same problem of shitty, detritus-filled streets as any other urban sprawl, and yet as they made their way through the streets, he could see only clean thoroughfares and smell only the aromas of food and shops and workshops, all overlaid with the ever-present tang of salt. Ravenna, he decided, was a pleasant place. Shame he had to visit it in the least pleasant of circumstances.

It came as no surprise that the threatening military presence did not end at the gate. Every crossroads or corner was occupied by a contubernium of grizzled veterans in full battle array, and as the column moved on into the city, they each turned and began to march alongside, keeping pace, joining up with the next as they moved, so that the closer to the centre the Praetorians moved, the stronger their escort became.

It was something of a relief to emerge into the forum with its clear paving, wide open space and room to breathe. Despite the military presence, the locals did not seem to be put out by their visitors, as was so often the case. Indeed, the looks on the face of every civilian they saw carried awe and respect for the men garrisoned temporarily in their city, and disdain and disapproval for the white clad new arrivals.

It was a distinctly uncomfortable trip.

The city's basilica sat on the longer side of the forum, opposite three great ornate temples, and flanked by victory columns topped with statues of great admirals and sailors both recent and ancient. More soldiers stood on guard outside the basilica, and as they approached across the square between edgy lines of enemy troops, the first official they had seen hoved into view.

The man who emerged from the basilica doorway wore the uniform and armour of a senior officer, with the knotted belt around his middle that marked him as a commander in the field. He was a legatus, most certainly, commanding one of the legions that lay outside the walls, and as the man close by had another vexillum of the Tenth Gemina raised, that suggested he was their commander. Tiberius Claudius Candidus, a veteran officer of the Marcomannic wars.

The man did not look any more welcoming than the rest.

Crispinus held up his hand for the column to halt as he neared the officer who stood with his arms folded.

'Greetings. I am Gaius Tullius Crispinus, Prefect of the Praetorian Guard and envoy of the emperor of Rome, Marcus Didius Julianus Augustus. I seek an audience with Lucius Septimius Severus, Governor of Pannonia.'

The legate's lip curled. 'The emperor will see you, with a personal entourage of no more than four men. Follow me.'

With that, Candidus spun on his heel and marched back into the door without waiting for them to follow. There was such an insulting edge to his manner that had this been a true parley it would probably have caused a political incident. Even now, as Crispinus swung from his saddle and dropped to the ground, his own cheek twitched with annoyance. He pointed at Florianus and Rufinus and then stomped off in the wake of the legate.

Rufinus hurriedly dropped from the saddle and handed Atalanta's reins to one of the waiting soldiers from the Tenth, fortunately far too young to remember a time when Rufinus had been one of them. He and Florianus hurried inside, catching up with Crispinus. They entered the wide hallway of the basilica and Rufinus glanced apprehensively up at the far end.

Septimius Severus sat on a curule chair on a dais so that he was head and shoulders above the visitors. To one side stood a small knot of officers in senior uniforms, and to the other a small huddle of civilians, presumably local dignitaries. They were surrounded by an arc of legionaries kitted for war.

This was unlikely to be a pleasant meeting, Rufinus decided. As they clacked across the marble floor behind the legatus who had so curtly greeted them outside, Rufinus frowned. Crispinus reached down to his belt and slipped on a calfskin glove that had been tucked into it. Just the one, on his right hand. Rufinus had never seen the man wear gloves at all, let alone a single one, which seemed an odd affectation. What was the man up to?

As he reached the dais, Legate Candidus saluted his master and then turned to one side and fell into position with the other officers. Six legates, Rufinus estimated, and mentally adjusted upwards the size of the force outside the city. Severus and his brother, who stood among those officers and was plainly identifiable by his family resemblance, had left only one legion in each province. Either they planned on a show of strength unmatched in Roman history when they reached Rome, or they truly intended to make war.

Rufinus shivered again.

The prefect stopped eight paces from the dais and was forced to look up at the usurper. Florianus and Rufinus fell in alongside him at each shoulder. Never had Rufinus felt in a less tenable position than now.

Severus was clever. His gaze moved from Crispinus to the men at each shoulder but did not linger on Rufinus or make any sign that he noted the presence of his erstwhile colleague. Rufinus tried not to tremble at the momentousness of the meeting. His eyes played across the gathered great men in the room, from Severus to his brother, to the legates, to the town's decurions, to the other officers, and then to the arc of men.

His heart skipped a beat as his gaze alighted upon familiar faces. Two men in the uniforms of legionary centurions standing close to the emperor, but men who he had always seen in white before. Mercator and Icarion had seemingly thrown in their lot with the rival emperor, preferring to take up regular army commissions for this man than to serve in the Guard for Julianus. Rufinus could hardly blame them. Still, he made sure not to draw attention to them as his gaze moved on, though both men registered their recognition with just their eyes. Severus had clearly organised all this very carefully and briefed them all in advance.

'Say your piece, Prefect,' Severus commanded in an emotionless, cold tone.

Crispinus straightened. 'I come from...'

'We know who you come from. Get to the point.'

The prefect's twitch intensified.

'Marcus Didius Julianus Augustus, Emperor of Rome and father...'

'The *point*, Prefect.'

The twitch was making Crispinus' cheek jump now.

'The emperor seeks an end to this dangerous situation and to avert the possibility of a new civil war that could ravage Rome and kill thousands.'

'I expect he does, given that he will lose it.'

'I am here with an offer. I heartily urge you to accept it. Didius Julianus was acclaimed emperor in Rome by the Guard and by the senate. He has political, military and popular support, and is the legitimate emperor of Rome, having risen to than position through the correct channels and having been responsible for no murders or usurpations.'

'That I will grant,' Severus said quietly. 'Though I would hardly think him innocent of muddying the imperial waters, and I fear that the words popular support might be stretching it a little for the senate and the people of Rome, don't you?'

Crispinus almost snarled his next words. 'Whereas *you*, Lucius Septimius Severus, Governor of Pannonia, are a usurper and nothing more. The senate have declared you an enemy of Rome. You are as far removed from the legitimacy of power as a man bedecked in purple can be.'

'And yet I *do* enjoy popular support, and I seem to have all the advantages. And for some reason wherever I go the cities of Rome throw open their gates to me and shower me with petals. Odd, don't you think?'

There was a derisive ripple of laughter among the gathered dignitaries that did nothing to settle the twitch in the prefect's cheek.

'Despite his legitimacy and your savage and illegal seizure of power, the emperor recognises your value, Severus, and your long history of service. He is willing to overlook your recent crimes and to welcome you back to the capital as his junior colleague. He offers you the consulship and a supporting role in the office of imperator. His son has been named as his successor, but he is yet very young, and the emperor seeks your support as his co-emperor at least until the boy comes of age.'

There was an odd and very uncomfortable silence.

'You are a criminal, and he an emperor,' Crispinus said with a sneer. 'This offer is beyond all hope for you, as it grants you legitimacy that in my opinion you do not deserve. Accept the offer and disband your army.'

Severus sat silent for a long moment, and then suddenly burst out laughing, which spread throughout the gathered officers and men, and which made the prefect yet more angry. When his mirth finally subsided, Severus leaned forwards in his seat.

'I find it baffling not only that Didius Julianus thinks I might be bought by the offer of something worth less than that which I already have, but that you would have the brazen, crazed courage to come here and deliver that offer.'

'Then your answer is no?' Crispinus spat.

'No is too small a word, Prefect. I would rather be an enemy of Rome than a colleague of the serpent Didius Julianus. I refuse his offer. Please return to your master with these words and bid him step aside and run as fast as his feeble legs will carry him, for no army will stop me peeling him from that throne and casting him into the Tiber to float away with all the other shit.'

Crispinus was actually shaking now. Rufinus saw his eyes narrow – a decision privately made. The prefect reached down to the bag slung at his side and as he opened it, he removed a scroll case. Lifting it in his gloved hand, he turned it over a couple of times, looking at it.

Rufinus thought he caught a waft of something from the bag as it opened. Radishes? A sharp but small and subtle odour, for sure. He knew it from somewhere.

The prefect stepped forwards and lifted the scroll case, proffering it to Severus. 'I shall do as you bid, Governor, but I am bound to deliver you the terms regardless, else my task is incomplete.'

Rufinus peered at the case as Crispinus stepped forwards again and Severus leaned further forwards.

Why the glove? What was wrong with the scroll case? The smell he'd smelled, which was like radishes... Aconite? Yes, it was aconite, the poisonous herb he'd seen and smelled growing in abundance in the Pannonian woodlands during the war, and even in the woods surrounding the imperial villa at Tibur. A poison when drunk, for sure. Could it be as damaging just to the skin?

Whatever the case, Rufinus was now sure that the scroll case itself was somehow poison, from which Crispinus had protected himself. Rufinus felt the stirrings of panic. The prefect was offering the scroll, and Severus had no reason to suspect foul play. He was preparing to reach for it. Rufinus could not warn him without giving the game away to his two wicked companions. For a moment he dithered, considering ending his entire investigation now and having the two of them killed.

In the end, his gaze fell upon Mercator, who was watching him intently. Aware that both Crispinus and Florianus were intent on Severus, he risked it. A small shake of the head was all, but his eyes darted to the scroll that was close to changing hands.

Come on, Merc...

Severus reached down, hand open.

'Wait,' called Mercator from the rear of the room, stepping forwards, and Rufinus tried not to let the sigh of relief he heaved show too openly.

Severus stopped, his hand curling into a claw upon empty air.

'What is it, soldier?'

'Domine, why does he wear but one glove?'

Severus frowned, peering intently at Crispinus even as he leaned back away from the scroll. 'Indeed. Is the feeble emperor of Rome so panicked at his diminishing position that he now stoops to poison? I had heard that the Guard had sunk to new depths, but I had no idea how low they were.'

Crispinus let out an angry growl and stepped back. 'Your accusations are awry and foolish, Governor.'

'Then swap hands with your burden.'

Crispinus stood, vibrating with fury as his impossible position declared his guilt to the world.

'I am insulted,' he snapped.

'Escort Prefect Locusta here to the walls and see him on his way,' Severus said in a slow drawl, referencing the infamous woman poisoner of Rome a century ago.

The prefect reached down to his side, his hand going to the hilt of his sword.

'Just how foolish are you feeling?' Severus asked menacingly.

The sword jerked from the mouth of the scabbard just a fraction, and Rufinus made sure to keep his own hand far from touching his hilt. On the far side, Florianus was exhibiting less caution. Encouraged by the prefect's rash boldness, Florianus held nothing back and pulled his blade from the scabbard, gripping it almost as tightly as his teeth were clenched.

Severus raised an eyebrow. 'I would urge you to caution,' Severus said, that same threat hanging in the tone. In response, though it irked him to be so powerless, Crispinus slammed his blade back into the sheath. Florianus, lip twitching, continued to brandish his.

The man on the high seat lifted an arm, and there was a dull thud. Florianus made a surprised sound and his eyes rolled down to the flights of the arrow jutting from his throat. He gurgled as blood gushed around the shaft and reached up with his free hand to touch it, before folding up and collapsing in a twitching, bubbling heap.

Crispinus had gone extremely pale. He turned and looked down at his expiring deputy, and then back at Severus, his face filled with hate. 'The next time we meet it will be in combat, and I will give no quarter.'

'As it should be,' nodded Severus.

The prefect cast a last look down at his man and turned on his heel, marching away from the very basic and makeshift throne. Rufinus hovered for a moment. He'd said he'd stay the course and finish his task, rooting out the corruption in the Guard, but once more he wavered, considering the possibility that the Guard was beyond saving. Perhaps it might be best to end it here and simply kill Crispinus, staying on and marching along with his friends in Severus' army.

His head turned and he looked at the retreating figure of Crispinus, and when he turned back, Severus had him fixed with a look. The usurper emperor gave Rufinus a small shake of the head and then motioned for him to follow the prefect. Still, Rufinus dithered, but finally gave the tiniest nod and turned, marching away after Crispinus.

They stepped out into the sunlight, Rufinus having caught up with his commander at the door. Their reins were proffered to them, and the commander of the nearest cavalry turma frowned. 'The tribune, sir?'

Crispinus shook his head as he mounted. 'Now we ride back for Rome.'

Rufinus pulled himself up into his saddle and turned his mare as the column began to move. They rode in silence through the streets of Ravenna, a menacing atmosphere to the entire city, and it was only when they were out of the gate and clear of the Severan army that the prefect spoke once more.

'Our one chance at ending this without a fight died with that scroll. We could have cut the head from the snake. Without Severus, they might well have been susceptible to bribery or coercion. Now, they will march on Rome and they will come to put him on the throne. Damn that sharp-eyed soldier who ruined it all.'

Rufinus felt a small thrill of victory. Not only had he saved Severus' life, but as an unexpected bonus, Florianus had managed to get himself killed. This really had actually turned out to be quite a successful day. He pasted an accordingly grim expression across his face and turned to the prefect.

'We can't win a war against that army.'

Crispinus nodded angrily. 'No. And we cannot stop them coming. Our only hope now is to somehow make the possibility of fighting their way into the city unacceptable. I cannot quite see how, but perhaps it can still be done.'

'And if not?' Rufinus urged.

'If not, then I believe it will be time to cut the strings on our puppet and let him fall.'

'Abandon the emperor?'

Crispinus nodded. 'We made him, perhaps it is appropriate that we break him. If we cannot avert what is coming, then it will be time to separate ourselves from the doomed Julianus. The Guard is still the strongest and most respected military force in the empire. If we cut Julianus free, Severus can be persuaded to negotiate with us.'

Rufinus frowned. 'You really think Severus will bargain with the Guard?'

'Of course. He must. No emperor can stand without the Guard. Even Trajan and Aurelius gave healthy donatives to the Praetorians on their accession. Even the strongest of emperors knows they must win over the Guard if they are to rule in stability.'

Rufinus nodded, though inside he screamed his denial. Somehow, he could not see the day Severus would negotiate with the Guard, let alone with Crispinus himself. Whatever was coming, there would be an end somewhere.

Why had Severus sent him back, though? He must have known that this was going to end in conflict now. Musing, Rufinus remembered the look on the African's face as he closed his hand on the empty air and leaned away from the murderous prefect.

I saved his life. If I hadn't been with Crispinus, Severus would be dead now. I am his agent among the enemy, and why would he want it any other way?

Somehow that didn't sound promising. Still, the fact remained that he was going back. He would have to see this through to the bitter end.

The bitter, bitter end.

XXVII – ROME IN PERIL

The emperor of Rome, Marcus Didius Julianus, was sweating, his face waxy and pale. Rufinus had, in his long life of imperial service, stood close to Marcus Aurelius and beside both Commodus and Pertinax and, good or bad, those emperors had been confident and strong. Each of them had even in the worst of peril walked proud to their fates. It made Rufinus twitch all the more to be in service to this man whose gleaming eyes darted back and forth from citizen to citizen in the crowd, as though each and every one might suddenly lift a bow and nock an arrow to end his reign.

The worst thing was that his fear was well-founded. Emperor of Rome he might be, but his rule was maintained now through a thin, frayed thread of control, and mostly through a fear created by the Praetorians. The people of Rome glowered at their ruler, the mood of the crowd made clear by the lack of cheering at the sight of Julianus. Instead there was but a low murmur of dissatisfaction.

The Praetorians were his only real support, and Rufinus' task was becoming a little easier, for even the Guard was beginning to polarise around their support of the emperor. The majority still marched with impassive faces, the emperor's coin good enough to secure their loyalty, but Rufinus could see in the faces of men their unhappiness with their lot, and those men perhaps were less subject to the rot within the corps.

The Urban Cohort were no more enamoured of their emperor than the man in the street, as was clear from the expressions of the soldiers who stood in lines keeping the crowd in place while the emperor's entourage passed. They had never liked the Praetorians, and had only a couple of months ago fielded their own commander as a potential emperor only to watch him cast aside by the Guard in favour of this man. They were hardly likely to feel any great loyalty to him.

Rufinus' eyes lifted from the lictors, who stomped along in front, to their destination. The curia sat like a fortress of republicanism ahead, a redoubt of Romanitas. The senate lurked within that fortress, armed only with barbed words and sharp wit, and they, of all the Romans who faced the emperor today, probably hated him most of all.

It was said that Commodus' fall had more to do with his disastrous relations with the senate than any personal grudge or dissatisfaction with his rule, yet while Commodus might have disenfranchised them and taunted them with a statue outside the curia door pointing a bow at them, he had never directly threatened them as a body. They must be ruing the day Didius Julianus first came among them.

The emperor had brought his Praetorians that day and surrounded the senate, demanding they hail him as emperor, and only once since then had he deigned to consult that august body, whereupon he had once more surrounded them with his Praetorians and demanded they name his opponents enemies of Rome. Such seemed to now be the role of the senate: a body of minor administrators there to announce the emperor's whim at the point of a Praetorian blade. Rufinus could feel the anger rising once more at the thought.

And now here they were again. For a third time Didius Julianus needed the senate, so for a third time he would threaten them with the Guard to be sure that they would agree.

Disgusting.

The doors of the senate house were closed and as the column approached the emperor's lictors were sent out ahead. The Praetorians came to a halt in the heart of the forum, still flanking Didius Julianus and his small entourage of toga-clad supporters as one of the lictors stepped out and hammered on the great bronze door with his bundle of rods.

There was a long and heavy silence, and Rufinus wondered how far the emperor was willing to go. Would he react badly? Would the Praetorians be ordered to force the curia doors? To besiege the senate? Did he need official ratification that much, given how far he had already devalued the senate's approval?

Fortunately, his questions remained unanswered for with a deep metallic clonk the doors were drawn open and the senate house awaited like the maw of a beast. Rufinus took a last deep breath of warm Junius air, for it would be stuffy and unpleasant inside.

As Crispinus' most senior man now, Rufinus was given the nod and led his century into the dark doorway, ahead of the column. In their pre-planned strategy, he immediately dispersed his men as they emerged into the great hall of Roman government. A contubernium at a time, they moved into position, securing the speaker's floor. Once his men were in place, another century entered and began to filter around the room into position.

The curia was designed to hold a maximum of six hundred bodies, the full number of senators of Rome, though it had probably never seen a full assembly in all the years of its existence. The most anyone would ever expect to see was half that number, and most senate meetings were held by less than two hundred men. In the height of summer when Rome's elite generally retired to the country or the seaside, that number could easily drop to less than a hundred.

Rufinus estimated sixty bodies constituted the assembly today. The soldiers brought to threaten them numbered more than twice that. Once the room was filled with angry, impotent senators and menacing guardsmen, finally the lictors entered and then the emperor. The doors were closed behind them, limiting the light in the room to that beaming in through the high windows. It would not do, after all, for the common man in the forum to hear his emperor threatening the senate. Fictions had to be maintained.

An uneasy silence descended upon the crowd within.

'Noble conscript fathers of Rome,' the emperor announced in a clear, flat tone, 'I greet you.'

The senate sat and glowered in response, and Julianus cleared his throat in the tense silence.

'Enemies close on Rome for the first time in generations. A usurper. An African. A soldier with a soldier's temperament and no legitimate claim, who you yourself have branded an enemy of Rome. The usurper Severus approaches, his legions traversing the mountain roads even now, passing Spoletium and only three days march from this very city.'

More silence greeted this. It was old news. All of Rome knew that Severus' army was coming. All of Rome could see the twelve thousand or so men gathered in the city, drawn from the Guard, the Cohort, the vigiles and the fleet, and knew them to number less than a quarter of Severus' army. Moreover, they were a motley bunch, poorly prepared and largely poorly equipped, while the approaching legions had spent their entire career on the very border of the empire, armed and trained for war.

No one was under any illusion as to what would happen when the two forces clashed. All that mattered to the city's population was that their emperor bravely decide to march his mismatched army out of the city and meet Severus in the field, so that Rome and its populace survived unharmed. Rufinus knew Didius Julianus well enough now to know how unlikely that was to happen. And he had suspicions as to how Julianus' army would feel too. He could not see the Urban Cohort taking the field for their emperor. The vigiles were no fighting force anyway and would break in an instant. Only the Praetorians and the fleet would remain to face the veteran legions of Severus, and they would number no more than eight or nine thousand at the most.

'Rome should not be threatened by such conflict, as I am sure you agree,' the emperor said, and though that was undoubtedly a fact, still the toga-clad assembly remained silent. Julianus was starting to get irritated. The sweating had stopped, to be replaced by a rising colour in his cheeks. 'There can be no doubt that military victory is uncertain at this moment,' he admitted. 'But conflict should not be encouraged anyway. Roman fighting Roman is an abhorrent notion. As such I intend to do all I can to avoid war with the usurper.'

That, and because you know you'll lose, Rufinus thought to himself.

'How do you intend to avoid war?' called a voice from the gathering, bravely addressing the emperor without a single form of respectful address.

Julianus' angry face snapped around, but the speaker was unidentifiable within the toga-clad crowd. 'I seek the senate's approval to mint a new coin. A gold coin with an original image on the reverse – an image showing Concordia with the emperor at one hand and the legions at the other. A symbol of loyalty and peace. An image that will strike deep into the heart of every man who views it.'

Rufinus could hardly hold in the sneer. Every man who viewed such a coin would only be doing so because the emperor had bought his loyalty with it. It was Julianus' way. Ever since those days in Carthage the man had believed that money could buy him anything he wanted, and sadly his belief had thus far been borne out. He had bought the Guard, and then bought the throne. And when the Guard had realised they had been cheated with valueless coin, and were close to throwing out their support for him, Julianus had bought them afresh with real coins drawn from the imperial treasury.

Now, with Severus' veteran legions closing on the city, he intended to do the same thing again. He would have the city's mint working day and night to produce his new coins, and the moment the Pannonian and Moesian legions hoved into view across the Tiber, he would throw money at them and promise them the world in return for their support.

There was a worrying possibility that he might succeed. The legions had proclaimed Severus emperor, and they felt a great deal of loyalty to their commander, as Rufinus had noted in Ravenna, but how far would that loyalty stretch in the face of gold? The common soldier was a simple creature. The legions had honour, but the men who comprised them still, when you got right down to it, fought for their wage. Money could buy a lot of loyalty these days. Rufinus would not be willing to put a wager on those legions standing by their commander in the face of gold.

The only real question was whether there would be time to mint and distribute sufficient coin to buy the enemy out.

There was a strange silence in the room now. The senate might not like their emperor, and in ordinary circumstances, the majority of them would throw petals in the path of Severus and turn their back on Julianus, but the stark truth was that no Roman wanted civil war in the streets of the city, and the senators were close to being swayed even without the threat of the Guard. Voting Julianus further power and legitimacy and whatever gold he needed would leave a sour taste in the mouth, but it would almost be worth it to avoid the coming cataclysm.

Rufinus found himself willing the venerable conscript fathers of Rome to refuse their emperor. Cestius had been convinced that when faced with Severus and an approaching force the senate would turn on their emperor and condemn him, but it seemed he was wrong. Perhaps Cestius had underestimated the power of Praetorian threats upon that august gathering.

'Where will the funds be drawn from?' demanded a voice. A different voice to the last, but equally unidentifiable within the crowd. Again, Julianus' flushed face snapped this way and that trying to spot the speaker, and then gave up in irritation.

'The finances will be drawn from the imperial treasury. A tax will then be levied on exports in all provincial ports to refill the vaults, so the senate need not worry about the emptying of the treasury.'

Rufinus felt his lip curl again. Such a tax would have long-term ill effects in those port cities, but that mattered not to the majority of the men in here. As far as they were concerned the city would be saved from war and the treasury kept healthy. Small matters of provincial finance could be dealt with by procurators in due course. It was a seductive notion, and Rufinus could sense the senate tipping to voluntary support. He felt the disgust rising.

'On that basis, your request has merit,' someone announced, and Julianus did not bother to try and identify the source of this voice, for support was acceptable wherever it came from.

Satisfied that he had them on side, Julianus straightened. The senate had procedures to follow, regardless of how valueless and influenced they might be. 'Inasmuch as it may be good and fortunate for the Roman people of the Quirites, we bring before you, conscript fathers, a request for the minting of five hundred thousand gold aurei for the continued security and peace of the empire. What does it please you should be done about this matter?'

There was a moment's pause, and then the senate began to voice its support, according to tradition, the most senior first, running down the strict order of position for those present, ending with the most junior of senators. Once again, it seemed Julianus had got away with it, his reign secured by a combination of threat and bribery.

'Let your will be known,' Julianus declared, gesturing with both hands. 'Those in favour to the left, those against to the right. Divide.'

It came as no surprise to Rufinus to see the entire gathering shuffle off to the left, accompanied by a low murmur of conversation. Julianus beamed a sickening grin of victory.

'You have your money, Majesty,' someone announced. 'The instructions will be delivered to the mint this morning.'

Julianus bowed his head in a futile gesture of respect, and turned, motioning to his lictors. At the entrance, Crispinus threw open the doors, allowing the sunlight to fill the room with dazzling brightness.

It was eerie emerging from that place to the forum, for the great heart of Rome was never silent, even in the depths of night, yet this morning the only sounds to greet them were the caw and cry of birds and the very distant hum of the city. The crowds in the forum stood silent, watching the curia. Rufinus wondered how long two centuries of Praetorians might last if the Roman mob decided to take action. Not long, he decided with a shiver.

Entirely surrounded by Praetorians and preceded by his lictors, the triumphant emperor stepped into the light and began to make his way back east along the Via Sacra. Rufinus marched along on the left flank, and his unease grew as they passed along the silent crowd-lined street. Something was wrong. Something had changed. He could feel the danger. His face turned to the watching mob as they marched, and his eyes played along the lines of people, held back by a thin cordon of men from the Urban Cohort.

His heart jumped as a single figure in the mass, just at the shoulder of one of the soldiers, pulled back the hood of a drab brown cloak. Icarion watched him from the crowd and Rufinus' eyes widened as he realised that the cloaked figure beside the man had to be Mercator.

What in Jove's name were they doing in Rome? Severus' army was supposedly still at Spoletium, several days' journey away. As he marched, he suddenly realised that his two friends were not alone.

His gaze swept forwards along the crowd they were passing, and back over those figures they had already passed. Cloaked figures were everywhere, yet there was no need to wear a cloak on such a sunny Junius morning...

Hundreds of them, hidden among the crowds. He boggled. Julianus had men of the fleet, or of the Guard, or the Cohort or even the vigiles at every road into the city. No force could have passed by unreported, so either someone had let the entire group into the city knowingly, or Severus had been sending men ahead in dribs and drabs well in advance of his army's march.

There was only one reason they could be gathered here, and now. Rufinus tensed. Trouble was about to start, and his duty was to warn the emperor.

His lips stayed shut. That surprised him more than anything.

'Tenth Gemina, ad signum!' came a voice from the crowd, its tone martial, strong. A centurion's voice. The entire column halted for just a moment in shock as the voice echoed in the odd silence, and then with a roar, soldiers all along the street-side crowd threw off their cloaks. Mailed beneath and armed for war in contravention of Rome's most ancient laws, the men of Rufinus' old legion suddenly surged forwards through the press.

Crispinus turned and bellowed to the Praetorians around him. 'Protect the emperor. Make for the palace.' And then with a gesture to the men of the Urban Cohort lining the Via Sacra and holding the crowd at bay: 'Seize those men!'

Rufinus was not remotely surprised at the lack of movement from the soldiers of the Urban Cohort. Even as the imperial column began to move, the soldiers of the Tenth Gemina were bursting from the lines of the crowd, the members of the Urban Cohort doing nothing to stop them. Rufinus found himself wondering whether perhaps even the Cohort were in on the entire thing. Had they conspired to let a cohort of the Tenth Legion into the city under cover of darkness?

Crispinus was bellowing now at the column, urging them to move faster. The emperor, who had arrived on foot, wanting to put forth to the people of Rome the impression that he was one of them rather than some aloof aristocrat, was probably now wishing he'd come on a horse or in a carriage as he ran along, rather undignified, alongside his men. The entire column was moving slower than it should, due to the encumbrance of togas, which were far from the easiest garment to run in, and it was but moments before Crispinus gave them the order to abandon the traditional garments. It was the most humiliating imperial procession in living memory as the entire entourage, soldiers, lictors, and even the emperor, let their togas fall and ran on in tunics alone, trampling the expensive garments into the ground beneath their boots.

Rufinus ran, undecided as to what he should do. Genialis would be in the office on the Palatine which had, over the last month and more, been turned into a veritable fortress, and there would be two centuries on duty there with him. All in all, that would put the military at around three hundred men when this column reached the place. There were almost certainly twice as many legionaries now forming in the forum behind them, untouched by the men of the Urban Cohort, but if the emperor was allowed to reach the palace it would take a veritable army to dig him out. Even as Rufinus turned to look back at the legionaries, a man in a senior officer's uniform detached from the soldiers of the Tenth and marched towards the senate house.

Rufinus felt his heart beating faster. Things were happening. What would the senate do? The Praetorians were powerless to threaten them right now, and faced with Severus' soldiers it seemed unlikely that their support for the troubled emperor would continue. He had to get out of this column... had to speak to Severus' men. But would he be of more use in the Palatine with the enemy? A thought struck him, and he gestured to the prefect, and to Gamburio, his faithful optio.

'Get to the Palatine, sir, and secure it.'

'Where are you going?' demanded Crispinus.

'To the Castra Praetoria,' Rufinus lied glibly. 'Reinforcements.'

'Very good. Good luck, Rufinus. The gods watch over you.'

Rufinus saluted and, as they continued to run on towards the Palatine, Rufinus veered off and ran at the crowd of people along the street side. As he closed on them, two of the Urban Cohort made to stop him, the people behind jeering angrily. Rufinus let them grab at him for the look of it until he was sure that Crispinus and the imperial fugitive were paying him no attention and far ahead.

'Take me to the Tenth,' Rufinus said in an authoritative tone.

The men of the Cohort frowned at him but glanced at the centurion's vine stick under his arm, and finally nodded. There was something in the Roman military character that demanded respect for a centurion no matter who he was. Still, Rufinus was left under no illusion – he was being escorted as a prisoner, as they marched him back along the Via Sacra towards the formed cohort of legionaries. As he neared them, he saw Icarion and Mercator both carrying their own vine sticks, gathered with a knot of other centurions. The two soldiers escorting Rufinus marched him up to them.

'This Praetorian demanded to see you,' one announced.

The centurions turned as a group. One of them, who looked vaguely familiar to him, blinked and threw out a finger. 'Rufinus?'

Icarion and Mercator grinned, the latter gesturing to the two guards. 'Leave him with us. Thank you.'

As the two men from the Cohort marched back to their place, other centurions in the group started throwing around questions. 'He's alright,' Icarion told them. 'He's a good one. Used to be one of us.'

Another of the centurions snorted. 'Like *you* used to be one of *them.*'

The familiar face, who Rufinus vaguely remembered as serving in his century back in the day even if he couldn't put a name to the face, waved his hands to calm the argument. 'We're all on the same side. Act like centurions, for Jove's sake.'

This cut through them, and the arguing stopped. 'What's happening?' Mercator asked him.

'They're retreating to the Palatine. The palace has been turned into a fortress recently. You'll have a lot of trouble taking it until the rest of the legions get here.'

'The legions aren't coming here,' Icarion told him.

'What?'

'Severus has no intention of fighting a war in the streets, and he knows Julianus won't come out to face him. He's marched with his legions to show his strength, to panic his enemy, but we're the force he's sent to end it.'

'You'll not take the Palatine,' Rufinus said. 'It's sealed tighter than a duck's arse and defended by three hundred Praetorians.'

'But we have a secret weapon,' Mercator grinned.

'What?'

'You.'

Rufinus rolled his eyes. 'Who's the officer with you?'

'Gaius Fulvius Plautianus. Severus' top general.'

'I need to speak to him.'

The two old friends of his nodded and escorted him away from the ranks of the Tenth towards the curia. Just as they approached, the officer emerged with half a dozen senators in tow, including the outspoken Falco. The officer stopped before Rufinus, eyebrow raised.

'Who is this Praetorian?'

'A friend, sir,' Icarion said.

'Praetorians are to be arrested and disarmed on sight,' Plautianus said flatly.

'Not this one, sir. He's a friend of the emperor.'

'I don't care who he...'

'Not Julianus, sir. *Our* emperor.'

Plautianus' frown deepened. 'I remember you. You were the one at Ravenna.'

'The one who tipped me the warning, sir,' Mercator added.

'Was he indeed. Rufus, wasn't it?'

'Rufinus, sir.'

'What are you doing here?'

'I split off from the column, sir, to warn you. The Palatine is fortified and garrisoned with three hundred men. It's going to be near impossible for you to take it.'

'I have no intention of storming the Palatine,' the officer replied in patient tones. 'We shall seal it up with men and demand that any loyal subject of Rome inside execute the pretender Didius Julianus. Someone in there will do it. And once Julianus is dead, there will be no value to the palace.'

Rufinus shook his head. 'There are a few good and loyal men in there, sir, but the majority of the Praetorians inside are the men who put Julianus on the throne. They know damn well that their chances of survival are small if they surrender to Severus, and they won't let anyone get to Julianus.'

The officer straightened. 'An offer of amnesty will be made. The senate have just voted to a man to condemn Didius Julianus as an enemy of Rome. He has already been sentenced to death, and any man who carries out that sentence or even assists in any way will receive commendations. It is all we can do.'

Rufinus chewed his lip, glancing up and across at Mercator and Icarion. 'There is another way.'

'Yes?' Plautianus enquired.

'I left the column on the grounds I was heading for the Castra Praetoria to secure reinforcements. If I turn up with a column of Praetorians, they'll let us in.'

The officer shook his head. 'We cannot trust the Guard,' he reminded Rufinus. 'And the emperor has given orders for their arrest en masse.'

Rufinus shivered. He remembered Severus' opinion. That the entire Guard should be dismissed and re-formed from new men, that this was the only way to clear the rot. Rufinus had been drawn gradually to the same conclusion. It seemed that this was to happen at last.

'You don't need Praetorians, sir.' He gestured to his friends. 'These two served in the Guard, and they look just like the rest of your men. All you need is white tunics and togas. A century of men from the Tenth in white will look just like any other Praetorian unit.'

'You think you can get them in? Get to Julianus?'

'I guarantee it,' Rufinus answered with a feral grin.

Plautianus nodded slowly and turned to Mercator and Icarion. 'Deploy the cohort. I want two centuries of men at the Palatine, blocking every entrance between them. Three centuries are to be dispatched to the Castra Praetoria to demand their surrender, and the remaining century are to secure white tunics and togas.' He turned back to Rufinus. 'We'll try it your way. Be warned that I will reward any treachery with the harshest of punishments.'

Rufinus straightened. 'I vow to remove the enemy from power, sir.'

For the first time in years, he felt confident that he was doing the right thing.

XXVIII – ENEMY OF ROME

Rufinus eyed the men of the Tenth Gemina, standing in straight lines in gleaming white togas in the warm summer sunlight. They would pass at a glance, for certain. There were a number of differences between they and the real Praetorians, though, for anyone checking close enough.

Men who had been serving for years in the Guard knew instinctively how to hang a toga, for a start. They could dress one another in the weighty and unwieldy garment swiftly and look like a statue of Augustus it was so neat. Many of these provincial border soldiers had never worn a toga. Dressing them had taken longer than he'd expected and teaching them how to simply walk without it all unravelling and falling to the ground was even more difficult. They only needed the white woollen wrap until they were in the palace, of course, but they needed to look the part until then.

Then there was the state of them. These men had marched from Pannonia to Ravenna, and then moved at breakneck pace to Rome, entering the city cloaked and under cover of darkness from all directions. They had not been to the baths since Ravenna, and they smelled like beasts of burden and sported a thick layer of travel dirt. There was no time for a proper bath, and each man had taken turns dipping in a fountain basin near the forum, scrubbing as best they could. The more pungent had been given a scent of rose and pine oil, which helped.

But the real giveaway was their very form. These men were hardened provincial veterans. Men more like Rufinus than Crispinus. Though there had been no official war throughout the reigns of Commodus and Pertinax, it does not require a war to find trouble on a border, and these men had been fighting on and off their entire career. Consequently, many were scarred and marked, even facially. This was unusual in the Praetorians, who had been on tedious guard duty in the city for that entire time.

Rufinus had spent the last quarter of the hour rearranging his century so that the prettiest and cleanest were more visible at the front and on the near flanks, while the most aromatic and disfigured were nicely hidden at the back. Even as he nodded his satisfaction someone's toga unravelled in the middle of the crowd, accompanied by a bark of 'Minerva's tits this thing is heavy.' He tapped his foot impatiently as the man's two closest companions helped him back into it.

'Are you ready?' murmured a centurion nearby, who looked extremely unconvinced.

'Just about. Can't go more than an hour. Crispinus might buy that it took me an hour to get to the Castra Praetoria, persuade them what was happening, arm up a century and get back to the Palatine. That's feasible. Any longer and he'll start to get suspicious.'

'Won't he be expecting a full cohort?'

'There will be plenty of men in the fortress unwilling to commit now, and he'll know that. He'll just be grateful for any reinforcements, I think. You've briefed your men?'

The centurion nodded. 'They'll be ready for you. Make it look good.'

'We will. Right; no time like the present.'

He was about to give the order when General Plautianus emerged from a nearby doorway with a grim expression. This entire area had been cleared of civilians by the Urban Cohort, who had declared their unanimous support for Severus and who now kept a wide perimeter of empty streets and buildings. All it would take was word of this little subterfuge leaking back to the Palatine and it would be entirely in vain.

'Problem sir?' Rufinus asked as the senior officer came to a halt next to him.

'Not really. I may have inadvertently started another war.'

'Sir?'

Plautianus huffed. 'The Praetorians have produced all the men they say killed Pertinax and sealed them up in the Athenaeum, offering them to the emperor. I suspect they thought that would buy them his favour. In response I had the men who'd rounded them up arrested and thrown in there with them.'

'Why, sir?'

'Because the emperor's order is explicit. All Praetorians are to be arrested. What will happen to them in due course I don't yet know, but they should all submit to arrest. When I had the Urban Cohorts take that lot in, a couple escaped. Now the Guard is sealed up in its fortress like a besieged city. I can't see them bending their knee to the emperor any time soon.'

Rufinus sighed. 'By rights you should be arresting me too. They can't stay in the fortress forever, though. Severus will have to arrange some kind or compromise'

'He's not known for his compromising.'

Rufinus gave a snort of agreement. 'Well, taking Didius Julianus out of the equation can only help.'

'Agreed. You're ready?'

'We were about to depart, sir.'

'Good luck, Rufinus.'

The centurion saluted and, adjusting his toga slightly, waved his vine stick. A moment later eighty white figures marched away, clacking on the flagstones of the street. They rounded the horrea piperatica with its heady aroma of spices and pepper, recently reconstructed following that fire Rufinus had fought through which had burned it almost to the ground. Between there and the sanctuary of the Penates, the Urban Cohorts kept their perimeter, and the men stepped aside to allow the small 'praetorian' column to pass.

Rufinus glanced to his right. The muster position and their route had been carefully chosen to keep tall buildings between them and the Palatine, to reduce any risk of the men up there spotting the white clad column. Only narrow cracks between buildings allowed such a view and a man would have to be fortunate indeed to be looking at such a narrow space at the right time. Besides, the men defending the Palatine had other things on their plate right now.

They disappeared behind the Temple of Venus and Rome and emerged into the wide square surrounding the great Flavian amphitheatre. There they moved on around the northern arc of that immense building until they came to the southern side, beneath the great terrace of Claudius' temple, where they marched off to the south, heading for the Palatine's less grand approach.

While the main public approach faced the forum, there were numerous other entrances and exits to the imperial palace, the rest largely ancillary portals and posterns, only used by guards and slaves. One such door, used on occasion by Rufinus when on duty, stood close to the aqueduct that marched across the valley, bringing water from the Caelian Hill.

Rufinus cast a professional eye over the exterior of the palace as they approached. As part of Julianus' futile preparations over the past month, iron lattice grilles had been put in place over every window. The door atop this approach, at the end of an ornate flight of stairs, had been strengthened with iron bands and studs to prevent easy destruction. Likely it was braced inside too. Above, an arcade ran along the wall just beneath the red tiled roof, and Rufinus could see two figures within the shadows of that columned portico.

As they climbed the street in silence, Rufinus could see figures lurking in the arches of the aqueduct. The men of the Tenth sent to make sure the Palatine was sealed in. The men who had hopefully been adequately briefed.

Closing on the position, Rufinus could see that there had already been one casualty here. A soldier in madder-dyed red lay face down on the steps ten feet from the door, his blood pooled around him and pouring from step to step. His head was a mess and half a dozen broken tiles around him filled in the blanks. That was what the two men in the arcade were doing, and that was why the men of the Tenth lurked in the shelter of the aqueduct.

At the sight of Rufinus and his century approaching, there were cries of angry alarm from those hiding men, who suddenly emerged from the arches, swords bared as they ran to intercept the approaching Praetorians. There were seven of them. Realistically it would be a brave tent party of legionaries who attacked a full century of Praetorians, but then they were trapped between Rufinus' men and the door with its rain of heavy tiles.

The leader of the men bellowed his anger as he ran directly at the column. Rufinus allowed his toga to fall from his arm, ripping his sword free, and yelling to his men to arm. The man barged into him and the entire column staggered and faltered.

Rufinus was impressed. The man really did look like he was trying to kill them. Rufinus dodged and parried a couple of blows and then managed to get the man into a position where he could strike the fake blow. His sword tore through the tunic next to the man's ribs and emerged at the back. From the angle of the arcade it should look like a good killing blow.

The man gave Rufinus an irritating wink and cried out, folding up and dropping to the ground.

By the time Rufinus had fought off another man the entire tent party of legionaries was engaged. He was impressed at the realism of it all, and two of the Tenth made it past them, running as though for dear life and shouting about reinforcements. Rufinus turned to look at his men. Two of them lay on the ground, 'killed' by the legionaries. With luck, at such a distance the men above the gate would not notice the lack of blood, especially conspicuous around the white, toga-clad bodies.

Urging his men on, they ran now, togas unravelling, heading for the gate, shouting for the defenders to open up. The show had been adequate. The men in the arcade above gave the order and behind the portal there were scrapes and thumps as blockages were removed. Finally, with a clunk the heavy door was unlocked, and drawn open.

333

Rufinus and his men rushed inside. As he passed from the daylight into the gloom of the corridor beyond, Rufinus spotted two men who had been keeping the door barred. As he approached one, he was pleased to note Mercator and Icarion hurrying forwards at his shoulders. The man on guard looked relieved.

'Thank fuck you got h…'

His voice tailed off as Rufinus brought the pommel of his sword down on the man's head, driving out his wits in an instant and rendering him unconscious. Icarion mirrored the attack with the other man and, in an instant, they were alone in the corridor. It had been an agreed upon tactic that they would attempt to subdue rather than kill any man they found. Right now, they might be considered the enemy, but there would be Praetorians here who did not deserve a grisly death for having been caught up in this disaster. The fate of the Guard would be decided by Severus when it was all over.

The subterfuge had now been seen through, as the men in the arcade above the door bellowed an alarm. The last few of Rufinus' men ran for the door. The two who had been lying on the stairs feigning death along with the legionaries leapt to their feet alongside their friends, allowing the togas to unravel and fall away, and hurtled for the door.

Rufinus winced as the barrage of tiles began once more, and one of his fake Praetorians failed to make it to the door, along with one of the legionaries who had been watching the entrance, both struck down with heavy tiles.

'Where do we go?' Mercator breathed as they began to move hurriedly along the corridor.

'Julianus will be in the imperial apartments. It's furthest from the front door, and the most luxurious place. He has to be our prime target.'

'Tell me you're comfortable with this?' Merc pressed as they hurried along past the doorway to the great stadium garden.

'What?'

'Killing an emperor. Like him or not, and labelled enemy or not, you took an oath to him.'

'Severus is the emperor now.'

'I know, but *I'm* still not really comfortable with the idea, and I know you suffer stronger morals than me.'

Rufinus bit down on the thought. He'd been trying not to consider it, keeping himself focused on what they were doing, and assuming he'd be able to do the right thing at the end. Damn Mercator for bringing it up.

'I'll do what I have to.' *He hoped.*

'Good.'

They reached the door to the porticoed fresco room where Commodus had liked to relax after exertions in the stadium garden beyond, and Rufinus paused, listening at the wood. He could hear nothing and nodded at the others before pulling it open.

A slave who was busy rubbing the frescoes with a rag gave a startled cry of alarm, and Rufinus put a finger to his lips as he hurried between the columns, glancing out into the water garden. White clad Praetorians were visible out there, and at the slave's shout, they were now mobilising. This entire thing could close in very fast, and Rufinus might have a century of men with him, but there would be four times as many Praetorians spread throughout the palace awaiting him.

Ignoring the danger on the far side of the ornamental pond, Rufinus waved his men on, running between the next set of columns and through the open door. Bursting into the smaller decorative room beyond, Rufinus ran across and ripped open the next door. His heart leapt as he saw white figures ahead falling into a line. Six or seven men, but they would present a dangerous delay, for they blocked the corridor. Swords were drawn with a metallic rasp, and Rufinus chewed his lip. He turned.

'Back?'

Icarion shook his head. 'They're coming from the water garden.'

Damn it but this had started to fall apart far too quickly. He'd been hoping that the element of surprise would buy them adequate time to get somewhere useful. Well, with a strong force gathering behind them, six or seven heads would have to do.

Rufinus fixed the men ahead with a fierce visage and roared a battle cry. 'For the emperor!'

There would be no quarter given here. No pommels in evidence, for this was a time for lethal blows. Rufinus felt his spirits sink as another group of white clad men emerged behind the ones they faced. Double the numbers made it less likely they could break through at speed and every delay allowed more and more of the enemy to find them and block them in.

He could hear those other men coming up now from behind, ready to trap them here. This was going wrong far too fast.

'Rufinus!'

He frowned at the shout, which came from ahead, and a moment later that fresh arrival of men suddenly launched into an attack on those Praetorians lining the corridor against them. Rufinus stared as the men who'd faced them were swiftly overcome with blows to the head and the odd lethal swipe of jab of a gladius.

Optio Gamburio stepped over the bodies, blood spattered across his white tunic.

'Gods, Gamburio, but that was good timing.'

'We heard the alarm. It had to be you.'

'We need to get to the emperor. He's in the imperial apartments?'

The optio nodded. 'He is.'

With the blessed support of his friend, Rufinus led his men on. A small group of his unit took up a rear-guard position in the next doorway, ready to face the growing number of pursuers who were now racing along the corridor in their wake. They would not be able to hold them long. Hopefully it would be long enough.

Through corridors and doorways, they ran. Every now and then a shout would greet them as defending Praetorians emerged from side passages and ran at them. At each such encounter, men broke off from Rufinus' force to hold back the attackers, and twice men turned and halted at the rear, forming a fresh barrier against pursuers.

They rounded a corner into a vestibule and Rufinus drew them to a halt. Two men stood guard on a door that led to the private apartments. There were three exits from here out into the main areas of the palace, and Rufinus jabbed at them with a finger. In response, Gamburio dispersed their men as they arrived, one by one, securing each doorway against anyone who might come for them, settling the last few men at the entrance through which they had come. Rufinus winced. Their entire force now numbered perhaps twenty men, the rest left to fend for themselves throughout the palace as they held off the enemy.

Three men suddenly limped into view, catching up, but it was still a pitifully small army now. He would have to hope they could manage now. The pair of men on the door held their swords ready, defending their position, though their eyes were wild, and the sweat poured down them.

'Stand down and no one else needs to get hurt,' Rufinus snapped at them.

The two men shared a look and, in a heartbeat, threw down their swords, holding up their hands.

'Wise choice.'

He gestured to Gamburio, who had two men gather up the swords and begin to bind the men's hands with strips of linen torn from their tunic hems. They could spare no men to advance now, every available body blocking those three doorways. Even as the two captives were secured, there were cries of fury and crashes of weapons as men bore down on the interlopers from all around the palace. His soldiers braced themselves in each of those three entrances, watching tensely, waiting for the attack that was coming.

Mercator and Icarion were with him now. He turned. Gamburio was directing the defence of the three doorways, and the optio waved him away. 'Go. We'll hold here.'

Rufinus nodded and stepped forwards, pushing the door inwards.

The room beyond, Rufinus had seen on occasion when he'd been on duty in the palace. One of the more sumptuous chambers in the place, its walls were a riot of red and gold, painted to resemble marble on the lower half. A couch of Serican fabric in silver and red sat against one wall, and a statue of Venus occupied the corner, red drapes all around and a carpet of Persian origin showed designs of winged beasts. The single doorway at the far side led deeper into the emperor's private rooms.

Three men stood waiting for them.

Prefect Crispinus was dressed in just tunic and boots, sword in hand and expression sour. To each side he had a Praetorian in similar state, each armed and prepared. They were strong looking men, almost certainly drawn from Florianus' villains in the Fifth.

Merc and Icarion moved out to each side, both facing the enemy. Rufinus stood silent and motionless, facing Crispinus.

'You were a traitor all along,' the prefect said, his tone flat.

'I was a loyal soldier of Rome all along,' Rufinus corrected.

'Frumentarii.'

'Yes. And Praetorian. And loyal to Commodus and Pertinax from beginning to end. I have watched you and your cronies since the time of Cleander, spreading rot and wickedness among a unit that should be proud and honourable.'

'Wake up, Rufinus. The Guard has never been what you seem to think. You think I'm rotten? Check your histories. What of Sejanus? Macro? Paternus?'

'What do you hope to achieve now, Crispinus? Your emperor is no more. He's an enemy of Rome with a sentence of death hanging over him. Severus has ordered the arrest of the entire Guard. You can't win any more.'

'I have survived worse disasters. The Guard will find a way to bargain with Severus. It's what we do. But I cannot have you muddying the waters.'

With that the prefect suddenly lunged, his sword lancing out. Rufinus threw himself backwards, taken by surprise. The tip of the blade nicked his left forearm and he hissed as he countered, sword swiping out. He was vaguely aware of Icarion and Mercator engaging the other two men to each side but focused his attention on his opponent.

Crispinus parried his blow and slashed out. Rufinus sidestepped and tried to strike low, but the man was no novice and his own sword caught the attack once more, turning it aside. Rufinus roared and charged in, sword slicing from the prefect's right shoulder to left hip. Crispinus leapt back, and the two met once more, swords clanging together as they backed into the doorway beyond.

Rufinus was vaguely aware not only of the twin struggles going on in the room behind him, but of the sounds of furious combat further back, where Gamburio held their rear against all comers from the palace defenders. Then suddenly his entire world was the narrow doorway and Prefect Crispinus.

The prefect's sword came lancing out once more, constricted by the lack of space, and Rufinus saw an opening. His blade cut down, aiming to sever the hand and the sword it held. Crispinus somehow saw the attack coming and managed to move his arm just enough to avoid a disaster for him. Still, Rufinus' sword connected, though too close to the hilt to do much more than draw a narrow line of red across the arm. The strength of his blow, though, was sufficient that it numbed Crispinus' arm, and at a shocked gasp from the prefect, the sword fell from his grip.

Rufinus gave him no time to recover, pulling back his sword and lunging.

Crispinus was ready, though. As Rufinus made to impale him, the prefect leapt to the side, flattening himself against the wall, and Rufinus staggered past him, carried by momentum. He took a heavy blow to the back as he passed and felt himself falling forwards. Keeping a grip on his sword, he landed heavily, the breath temporarily knocked from him, and suddenly Crispinus was there again. The prefect gave his wrist a heavy kick and Rufinus bellowed in pain as his hand spasmed and the sword fell from his grip.

He rose with a roar, turning as he did so, but Crispinus had the upper hand now. As Rufinus turned, the prefect's arms were suddenly around him, folding around his throat and tightening, trying to choke him.

Rufinus staggered backwards at the unexpectedness and ferocity of the attack, as well as the sheer weight of the man now on his back. As he gagged, gasping for air, his eyes narrowed. Now the bastard was fighting in Rufinus' territory. He'd been in this position before in the boxing arena, and this time he had the added bonus of there being not just a boundary rope, but walls.

Turning with an asphyxiating grunt, he braced himself, straightening, and then threw himself backwards. He heard a grunt and a crack as he slammed the man on his back into the wall. It was to Crispinus' credit that he managed to maintain his grip throughout.

Rufinus could feel his lungs burning now and his head filling with pressure at the lack of air. Grunting, he slowly stepped forwards and then threw himself backwards again. Another bang and another grunt, yet still Crispinus clung on. A third time, gasping, stars dancing in Rufinus' vision, he slammed himself backwards and suddenly the arms were gone from around his neck.

He lurched away, heaving in air, recovering as fast as he could, aware that Crispinus would be doing the same. As he straightened, heaving breaths in and out, he spotted the prefect, left arm clutched to his painful side where the wall had probably broken ribs, staggering towards the pair of fallen swords in the doorway.

Rufinus ran at him, hitting him full in the side with a shoulder barge, and the two men thudded against the wall where Crispinus cried out now as his damaged ribs suffered a fresh blow. As he straightened, Rufinus let go all the fury that had been building in his months of investigation. This man had been at the heart of it all.

His left fist met with Crispinus' cheek with an audible crack, and the prefect fell back again, blood spraying from his mouth as he staggered. Rufinus' right hand slammed into the man's gut and this time both of them cried out, for Rufinus' wrist had clearly been damaged when the prefect had kicked it. Still, he didn't stop, fighting through the pain. Using only his left, he slammed it into Crispinus' face again and again, predictable moves by rote that would be anticipated in a boxing match and easily avoided, but the prefect was no boxer and had no way to expect what was coming. Again and again, Rufinus hammered his powerful fist into the man's face.

When he finally let up the flurry of blows, still roaring his fury, Crispinus was unrecognisable. His face was little more than a pulp of red and pink, with white bone showing in places. The flesh of Rufinus' hand was torn and battered, but it would recover. The prefect, though, was done for.

The moaning form of Crispinus was still somehow upright, staggering this way and that and emitting a pathetic keening noise. Rufinus felt his lip twist with hatred. He was half tempted to deliver this mess to Severus alive and whimpering, but the memory of all he and his friends had suffered over the months hardened him, and stepping forwards, ignoring the pain in his wrist, he wrapped his hands around Crispinus' head, tightened his grip, and wrenched them around in a clockwise motion.

There were a crunch and a number of smaller snapping sounds, and the head lolled at an unnatural angle as Crispinus' shuddering, dying form staggered one more step and then fell.

Rufinus heaved in a breath and stepped back into the room. For a long moment, he couldn't quite make out what he was seeing, and then the weight of the scene crashed in on him.

Icarion was holding Mercator up. Both men were cut and bruised, but Mercator's tunic was soaked with crimson and wet through, and Rufinus could see the blood, fresh and flowing, sheeting down from beneath it. A vicious belly wound. He'd seen the like before in battle. Men who were stretchered back with that sort of wound were dead men already. They would either perish on the way to the medicus, or while he examined them. If they were *really* unlucky, they lasted until they were wrapped in linen and shuffled into a corner where they could leak until they passed away or acquire an infection that ate away at their insides.

Whatever the case, no one walked away from that sort of wound.

Rufinus felt his stomach lurch at the sight, his eyes brimming with tears.

'Gods...'

Icarion simply nodded, his expression grave.

'The emperor,' Mercator grunted, wincing. 'Make sure you finish it.'

Rufinus' old friend suddenly collapsed, knees buckling beneath him, and Icarion caught him, lowering him gently into the growing lake of dark blood beneath him. Merc had already gone deathly pale.

Rufinus took a deep breath, nodded, and turned, unable to watch his friend. He thought he'd got past this. A lifetime ago he'd watched his eldest brother die, watched the spirit leave his eyes, and for years afterwards, even in battle and even against a bloodthirsty savage, he could never bring himself to watch that moment when life departed. It had been the death of the traitor Paternus that had changed things, and he'd thought he was over it now, yet somehow it was back. Mercator was in many ways as close as a brother.

He couldn't watch.

Wiping the tears from his eyes, Rufinus walked to the doorway, crouched and collected his sword, and then strode on into the next room. As he entered, the door opposite opened with a click. Rufinus tensed, bringing his sword up.

Prefect Genialis stepped from the gloom beyond, gladius held down by his side, blood dripping from the tip of the blade. Rufinus narrowed his eyes. He never had known where Genialis stood, other than wherever suited him best at the time. Just in case, he did not lower his own sword.

'The criminal Didius Julianus is dead,' Genialis said in a weary tone.

'You killed him?'

'I think I prefer the term executed,' the prefect said, face grave.

'So once more you make yourself useful to Severus? Once more you walk into something a criminal and emerge a hero?'

'I'm too tired to argue with you, Rufinus. Think of me what you will, but I just saved you from having to kill an emperor.'

And that was true.

'And... the empress?'

Genialis shook his head. 'The empress lives. And the children. I'll have no part in that. If Severus wants their heads, he can do it himself.'

Rufinus nodded. Perhaps the man did have a moral or two in there somewhere after all.

The sounds of combat still rang out from the lobby, and Rufinus blinked. 'If you want to make yourself really useful, go and tell the rest of them to stand down.'

Genialis stepped past him, sword point still lowered and dripping, and Rufinus walked on through that far door. He didn't really want to see it, but his trust in Genialis was shaky at best, and he had to be sure.

Marcus Didius Julianus, brief and unfortunate emperor of Rome, lay on the floor in a large pool of his own blood. His throat had been cut from ear to ear. There could be no doubt that he had been killed, but Genialis had made it quick, at least. The sound of weeping from the next room made the family's location clear. Rufinus had no desire to see them and have to explain anything. Wearily he turned his back on the scene and walked out.

There would be much to do before the new emperor arrived in Rome.

EPILOGUE

It was surprising, and more than a little saddening, to see the sum of a man's life spread out on his cloak. Fortunately, Mercator had taken his personal effects with him when he and Icarion had left for Pannonia, and so they hadn't needed to gather anything from the Castra Praetoria. Fortunate indeed, since that great fortress remained sealed tight.

Rufinus glanced across at the charred remnants of the funeral pyre, standing a little back from the Via Nomentana, and the sad little urn on the stone block awaiting their attention. With the Praetorian Guard sealed in their fortress there had been no chance to request a withdrawal from their old funeral club, and it seemed wrong somehow to prevail upon the Pannonian legion with which Merc had served so briefly. Fortunately, Icarion knew more about their friend than most people. He knew, for instance, that among the properties the man had been acquiring over the past few years was a nice domus on the Esquiline, where he kept a sizeable vault of money. Securing the service of builders to put together a tomb at the third mile marker and paying a mason for an elaborate tombstone was no real difficulty.

They had held the funeral this afternoon and now the small gathering who could attend followed tradition as they each selected a keepsake from Merc's possessions. There were few of Merc's original compatriots here, for those men of the Guard who had known him well held out in the fortress, defying the new emperor. Only a few Praetorians were here; Gamburio and his men who had proved their value to Severus in the battle for the Palatine. The others were legionaries from the Second Adiutrix with whom Mercator had served since going over to Severus. Indeed, this small gathering of Praetorians represented the entire membership of the Guard that had not been condemned by the emperor.

Rufinus watched the men taking the last few things: a bronze strigil with a wolf's head embossed at the end, the set of ivory dice Merc had always said brought him luck, a phalera showing the head of Minerva. Rufinus was not looking forward to choosing. He didn't want anything. It would feel wrong to carry something from that remaining collection of trinkets, yet it was tradition. It was what was done.

When it came round to him, he reached down, still undecided upon which to choose, but Icarion's hand came down and gripped his wrist.

'None of them.'

Rufinus turned a sad frown on his friend. 'What?'

'Merc knew the risks when we marched on Rome. He knew what might happen, and we both made our own arrangements. Merc had already selected what he wanted you and I to have.' He patted the leather satchel over his shoulder. 'Documents for me, granting ownership of a latifundium near Capua. I now own a sizeable vineyard. I think he was determined to keep me in Italia instead of heading back to the family. And he had something for you.'

He fished in the satchel and hooked out a scroll case. It was not sealed, and Rufinus took it when offered, still frowning. 'I haven't got time to run an estate.'

'Open it.'

He did so, pulling out the papers held inside. Unfurling them, his brow furrowed further as he read down the deed of sale. He blinked in surprise.

'Is this real?'

Icarion nodded. 'Don't you recognise the name at the bottom?'

And he did. They'd not seen eye to eye for a very long time, but Rufinus knew his own father's name, and recognised his writing. The deed of sale of a coastal villa and associated estate and winery east of Tarraco in Hispania.

'How did he get this?'

Icarion laughed. 'Your father tried to sell that place to every senator he could find, but none of them wanted it, even when he kept dropping the price. I think it was because of the connection to you. Merc bought it for an absolute song in the end. I don't think he ever intended to keep it. He was going to let you buy it back from him at cost, but you've been a bit wrapped up in things these last couple of years. The time was never right, but he wanted you to have it back.'

'Won't his family want it? He's got brothers, I think. They'll leap on what he left in his will.'

'He didn't put these two in his will. Merc's been buying land and property for years. His family will be ecstatic with what he left them without these two places.'

Rufinus stared at the document, a tear welling up in the corner of his eye. He thought they had lost the family's estate forever, and with it his brother's burial place. *Mercator, you sly old bastard.*

Everyone having taken something, one of the legionaries lifted the cloak, gathering the last few items in the folds. Reverently, he finished folding and then proffered the bundle to Icarion, Merc's oldest friend. Icarion took it and turned, gesturing to the small gathering of slaves nearby.

'Take this and the urn back to the domus and wait there for us.'

The slaves bowed their heads and collected the cinerary urn, carrying both it and the bundle with great care. Rufinus had no idea what they were going to do about the domus until Mercator's family came to take possession, but for now it was the best place to keep the urn until the tomb and marker were complete.

Gamburio waited until the arrangements had been made and then gestured to Rufinus. 'They're still waiting for us. We'd best go and join the emperor.'

Rufinus nodded, and the gathering straightened themselves out and smoothed down their uniforms. The time had come.

Lucius Septimius Severus, emperor of Rome by popular and senatorial assent, sat astride his horse dressed in the garb of a general. His small group of officers were similarly mounted close by as they all waited close to the Porta Decumana of the Praetorian fortress, outside the sprawl of the city.

There was a dangerous tension in the air.

It had been two days since the morning of Julianus' death and the confirmation of Severus as emperor. Following what had happened on the Palatine, and knowing that although they outnumbered Severus' forces in the city, the new emperor closed on them with a massive army, the Praetorians as a unit had retreated to their fortress and shut the gates. Rufinus had finally given up any hope of salvation for the Guard then, when it became clear that not a man among them was willing to admit to their wrongdoing and throw themselves upon Severus' mercy. In their arrogance they simply believed they could hold out and persuade the emperor to strike a deal.

There would be no deal, or not one for which they might hope. The emperor had reached the city a little after noon, while Rufinus and his companion stood around the blazing pyre of their friend, and had immediately launched into action. His legions would not enter the city itself but would camp outside, close to the fortress, and the Guard could hardly have felt more threatened. General Plautianus and his men, including the Urban Cohort, had the Praetorians pinned down from the city side, and now a huge army sat outside to the east.

Rufinus winced as he fell into position close to the emperor with the other officers. He could almost hear the screams from the Athenaeum, though he knew it to be only his imagination. The moment he had arrived, Severus had pronounced the death sentence on all those guardsmen who had taken part in the murder of Pertinax. Rufinus had not been there, but it was said that the scenes of butchery at that makeshift prison had been unlike anything seen since the days of Sejanus.

Similar might just happen here shortly, unless the rest of the Guard came to their senses.

As the last few officers and men fell into line, the standards gleaming and the pennants hanging limp in the still summer air, Severus walked his horse just a few paces forward towards the gate. White-clad figures lined the parapet above, some with blue crests, some in senior officer's uniforms.

Rufinus tensed. Surely they could not resist now? They had to know how outnumbered they were, but then they would have heard what had happened to their compatriots at the Athenaeum, too.

'Men of the Praetorian Guard,' Severus called out in a strong voice, 'you are done. We outclass you and we outnumber you and now you are commanded to submit yourselves to imperial judgement. The Praetorian Guard were created to be the bodyguard of emperors, and in less than half a year you have murdered two such rulers, abandoning your sacred oaths and the honour of your unit. Corruption and crimes, cowardice and disgrace have become your watchwords.'

He paused, yet the gate remained shut and no answer came.

'I have deliberated on what punishment is fitting for your crimes and have come to the conclusion that there is no suitable penalty. The men directly responsible for Pertinax's death have paid their price, and the killers of Commodus have all been executed before I arrived. The rest of you...'

He paused again.

'No, I am feeling merciful. You *deserve* little more than death, but I give you this offer, and it shall be given only once. Every man within those walls is hereby cashiered and removed from service. Your pensions are forfeit. You will be stripped of arms, armour, uniform and all insignia. In just your tunics and boots, you will leave this place and find somewhere distant to live out the rest of your miserable lives, but at least you will live. Should any of you refuse to depart, or henceforth be found within a hundred miles of Rome, your heads will be forfeit.'

Another pause to let the deal sink in. The Guard had expected to strike a deal with their new emperor, but this could hardly have been what they had in mind. Severus lifted a hand and then dropped it. With a menacing low rumble, siege engines were brought forth through the lines of legionaries, facing the fortress wall. Ballistae and onagers, alternating all along the Castra Praetoria's eastern rampart. Rufinus could imagine the panic inside now, at the sight of an intended siege. The fortress was strong enough, but it had been designed to house a force, not to withstand a proper assault. Any attack would be over within the hour.

'You have until the last rock is loaded to make your choice. If the gates open I will stand down the artillery. If not, I will give the signal. Time to decide.'

At another gesture, baskets of rocks were heaved forward by teams of men, who began to wind and load, preparing the weapons. The hum of desperate argument issued from within the camp.

Rufinus turned to Plautianus, who stood close by.

'What of Gamburio and his men?'

'Amnesty,' the general replied. 'The emperor will reconstitute the Praetorians from chosen men of the legions, but this small group will be commissioned back into the new Guard. You too, assuming you wish it? We shall need good and loyal officers.'

Rufinus nodded. It was something he'd been pondering. It had made him feel uneasy serving in the Guard as he watched it slide into criminality. Perhaps it would be good to serve once again if the Guard could regain its honour and its values. He had a feeling that Cestius might want him for further work yet too, but the twin appointments might not be mutually exclusive. And the tantalising word 'officer' hung before him.

'What of Prefect Genialis?'

The man who had executed Didius Julianus had been allowed so far to maintain his rank, but his future remained undecided. Certainly he would not be retained in the new Guard, and his murky history put his loyalty into serious question, but he had also done a service for the new emperor and had in truth done nothing directly that Rufinus could really pin on him.

Plautianus shrugged. 'A provincial command, I think. Maintaining his rank and his pay, but with minimal authority and a long, long way from the emperor.'

Rufinus nodded. Probably for the best.

The activity all along the artillery lines was slowing now, as each machine was made ready. Severus lifted a hand, but before he could drop it in signal, there was a thud and the fortress gate swung open. Men began to issue from it, unarmed and in simple white tunics and boots, maintaining only their military belts. As they began to gather in a large crowd before the new emperor, it was impossible to tell who was who, though here and there a striped tunic marked an officer.

'A wise choice,' Severus called to them. He waited until the entire force was gathered before the fortress walls, facing the army, and then turned to Plautianus. 'Have these men escorted along any road they choose to the eighth mile marker and then set them loose and return.'

He spun back to the gathered former praetorians.

'You are free to go, but heed my threat. Rome and Latium are forbidden to you on pain of death. Now leave.'

The silent mob stood still for a moment until three of Severus' centurions began to bellow at them, at which they jumped and began to move, leaving the city, penniless and homeless, never to return. Taking a slow, calming breath, Severus turned to the small knot of officers, which included not only Plautianus, but also Rufinus and the few surviving praetorians. '*Tribune* Gamburio,' he said, which made the former optio blink in shock.

'Imperator?'

'Have your squad take control of the Castrum. In due course your ranks will be swelled with new officers and men, but until that time you are in effective command of the fortress. The Tenth Gemina will need to be barracked there for the time being, while the rest of the legions are encamped nearby. See to the arrangements. You may appoint such clerks and purchase whatever slaves you need to put the fortress in order.'

Gamburio saluted, beaming like a fool.

'Plautianus, the Tenth will remain at Rome for now. Have the other legions move some distance from the city and set up a temporary camp. We will be in Rome for a month and no more, unless Pescennius Niger decides to submit to me. Otherwise we must move east and deal with him.'

Plautianus inclined his head and the emperor turned finally to Rufinus.

'I feel it is safe to say that any debt you owed me is counted as paid. Should you wish to remain part of my imperial familia, that would be pleasing, though. As to your rank and position, Plautianus sees you as tribune potential in the new Guard, though I recognise that you may want no further association with your former unit.'

Rufinus bowed. 'With respect, Domine, might I be permitted time to consider?'

Severus nodded. 'One month, and then I must deal with Niger. If you are to join me I would know by then.'

Wearily nodding his thanks, Rufinus fell silent, watching the broken Praetorians departing.

It was over.

An hour later, sagging under the twin burdens of exhaustion and grief, Rufinus rapped on his domus door. When it opened, he strode in thanking the doorman, bowed his head to the household gods and paced through the atrium out into the peristyle garden past the image of Brigantia who seemed to observe him disapprovingly. Senova sat on the curved marble bench beside the pool, alongside Publius. It came as little surprise to see Vibius Cestius leaning against an arbour pillar opposite them.

'It is done,' Rufinus announced. 'My job's over. The Guard have been cashiered and exiled. A caretaker force looks after the fortress until the emperor rebuilds the Guard from his loyal legions.'

Cestius nodded. 'A satisfactory conclusion to events, I would say.'

'I guess so.' Rufinus walked round to join the three of them. 'I have been given a month to ponder on my future. Plautianus wants me in the new Guard. I suspect you would like me to continue working for you?' he added, looking across at Cestius.

'Probably. On an ad hoc basis if nothing else. I don't like to lose touch with my resources.'

Rufinus rolled his eyes at being so described. Disturbed from his rest in the sun, Acheron stirred only enough to look up at his master, drool a little, and then settle back into a happy snooze.

'For us, though,' he said, 'I feel the need to do what all noble Romans do in the summer, and get away from the city for a few weeks.'

'A country estate?' Publius murmured.

'Something like that,' smiled Rufinus, producing the scroll case and tossing it to his brother. As Publius opened it and read down the document with wide eyes, Rufinus stepped over to Senova. 'Frankly I don't care anymore about proprieties. We'll go to Hispania for the month, all three of us, and while we're there, why don't we get married? Properly, I mean. Officially.'

'We aren't allowed,' Senova reminded him.

'That's if I'm a serving soldier. Right now I'm not. The Guard is currently no more. It's a small loophole, I grant you, but a valid one. And if I decide to go back to the Guard as a married man, it would be as a senior officer. Severus is known to allow such things, and senior officers can get away with a lot.'

Senova smiled warmly. 'And *will* you go back?'

Rufinus sighed. 'Probably. I don't know much other than soldiering. And Pescennius Niger is still claiming the purple in the east. Severus plans to deal with him soon.'

'But for now, we go to Hispania?'

Rufinus smiled. 'I think so. Time for a well deserved holiday.'

THE END

HISTORICAL NOTE

Firstly, after the complexity of pulling together the threads of Lions of Rome, I felt a great deal of relief in being able to move onto a new book where I was not quite so constrained by the need to tie it to another work. This would be a new story, a separate story, and a very Rufinus one.

His arc as a character has been largely planned since the second volume of this series, such that by the time I'd finished that book, I knew he would next spend time in Dacia, then in book 4 come back to Rome in various guises to deal with Cleander. As such I had always planned book 5 to be the surgical cleansing of the rot in the praetorian guard. I also know what books 6 and 7 revolve around, though I'll keep that quiet as yet.

When it actually came to the more detailed planning, though, I discovered that my story had to conform to more than just that one simple idea. I wanted to tell the story of Rufinus' cleansing of the guard, yes, but to do so I really needed to deal with several major issues. I needed to show the guard at its very worst, and I needed to have a solid conclusion to the arc. Fortunately both of those things were metaphorically painted purple and jumping up and down and waving at me.

The worst moment in Praetorian history has to be their recognised nadir: the sale of the throne to the highest bidder in 193. This provided me with plenty of ammunition and readily suggested Didius Julianus as a potential villain. And the conclusion simply had to be Severus' complete disbanding and recreating of the Guard – especially since Severus and Rufinus were already closely linked.

This, of course, meant that I had to deal with the fall of Commodus, the uncomfortable and short reign of Pertinax, the disaster that followed, and the rise of Septimius Severus. All of this I was planning on covering anyway, but since the day I first thought of this story arc I have also written 'Commodus', the second book of the Damned Emperors. Needless to say, in that book I dealt with the fall of Commodus. There is never a need for an author to hash out the same events twice, and so I decided to largely gloss over the end of Commodus' reign here and go straight for the aftermath, hence Rufinus' year-long secondment to Africa where he would see nothing of the end of the reign. If you wish to read about how the emperor fell, I would point you to the aforementioned book on Commodus. Plus, of course, it's a great read!

Thus I had the bones of my story.

The angle was good, too. The frumentarii are an interesting, enigmatic and very hazy group. They often appear as bad guys in fiction, but here they are the pinnacle of honesty (here, if you have not read them, I must also point you at Nick Brown's 'Agent of Rome' books centred on a frumentarius). They *have* to be honest and loyal here, because the Praetorian Guard are already the very opposite. I had Rufinus back in the Guard, but also as a grain man. This is not impossible, especially when you consider Rufinus' true history. On the tombstone from which I took the character he had the most impressive career, and in the series he has already been a centurion in the Praetorians, a centurion in the Urban Cohorts and a prefect of the Fleet, all things mentioned among a plethora of impressive roles on his tombstone. Frumentarius is hardly stretching it much further than the historical record.

The use of the Speculatores is perhaps somewhat fanciful, but it fitted my need to have the remnants of Cleander's rotten web hidden among the Guard. The speculatores were used for nefarious tasks at least from the reign of Claudius to that of Trajan, likely including executions and intelligence gathering. They were to some extent the forerunners of the frumentarii, and their subtle nature is evidenced by the fact that Suetonius has them wearing a special boot called the 'caliga speculatoria'. This was likely a light, more subtle boot used for hunting and sneaking. Trajan is believed to have disbanded the speculatores and dispersed them among the Praetorian cohorts. When Hadrian founds the frumentarii in the early 2nd century, the need for the speculatores diminishes, as the new unit takes on much of that role, and Trajan's Singulares Augusti the rest.

However, it is enticing to wonder whether in fact the speculatores were truly disbanded or merely dispersed and hidden. This is the interesting premise I have worked with. If the speculatores were the emperor's torturers and executioners among the Guard, which seems to have been the case, the frumentarii did not take on these tasks, for there is no record of that, and we know that the praetorians continued to execute and probably torture on the emperor's orders, then it seems quite reasonable that the speculatores continued within the Guard in some form or other. I had my network of villains.

On to the characters, then. Severus, Pertinax and Pompeianus have all appeared throughout this series and are already known historical personages. Laetus is new to the series, though is dealt with in detail in Commodus. He is the last Praetorian Prefect under Commodus and one of those conspirators who bring about the emperor's death. In the sources, Laetus is not the most heroic of characters. Cassius Dio and the Historia Augusta both have him not only implicit in Commodus' death but disloyal to Pertinax and leading the plot against him. In this book I have toned down Laetus' culpability somewhat and made him more or less a tool of his own tribune.

Aper is a fictional character representing the worst the guard had to offer, though he takes his name from the tribune Aper who in one of the sources brings Didius Julianus to the Praetorian camp. His boss is a different matter. When I was first trying to settle upon who would be the linchpin of the villainous agents in book 5, I found him in the form of Tullius Crispinus. All we know of Crispinus comes from but five mentions in the notoriously unreliable Historia Augusta. The first we hear of him is when Didius Julianus is made emperor, and the new ruler immediately makes Crispinus prefect of the Praetorian Guard. This seemed to me suggestive of a favour owed, and with no previous mention in history, Crispinus became mine to play with. As such, I made him the Praetorian officer at the root of it all. In the HA, Crispinus dies when he meets with the vanguard of Severus' force, but I felt he needed a more personal end.

Didius Julianus, of course, is a solid historical character, albeit a short-lived one. He was governor of Africa at the time of Commodus' death, and does not truly enter the political stage until the end of the reign of Pertinax. Since he was a sidekick villain already in my tale, having Rufinus assigned to him in Africa solved the problem of keeping our hero out of the way of Commodus' fall.

A short word on locations. Clearly most of the action in this book was going to take place in Rome, either in the Praetorian camp or on the Palatine. And with Africa now occupying a quarter of the book, I had a nice distant place to throw in too. I needed locations for several of my scenes, and I always like to use places I've experienced if I can, especially if they are impressive and memorable.

I needed an opening location for the book, somewhere complex and interesting for a manhunt. Just a couple of months earlier I'd had the fortune to visit the immense imperial bath complexes at Baia, and the place seemed a natural fit. What I have used as location in the book is but a tiny part of what remains one of the most impressive and enigmatic Roman ruins on the planet.

The Lucus Furrina and the Janiculum mills that appear early on cannot, sadly, be visited now. One can stand atop the Janiculum hill at the Terrazza del Gianicolo and experience some of the best views in Rome, covering the whole of the ancient city, but even the precise location of the Lucus Furrina is unknown. As is its precise form. And the deity to whom it was dedicated. It does seem to have fallen out of favour by the imperial period and have been at least partially abandoned. The Janiculum mills must have been an impressive structure, and their location has been confirmed with excavation, though there is nothing now to be seen of them. Something of their impressive nature might be discerned from examining the similar mill system at Barbegal in southern France, whose remains *have* survived well. The precise line of the Aqua Traiana is lost too, since much of it was incorporated into a later aqueduct. It is said to have delivered much needed water to Rome, so as well as feeding the mills and probably the naumachia on this side of the river, it seems likely it crossed the Tiber on a bridge and from there was distributed among the city like the rest of the aqueducts

The Urban Cohorts had been based in the Castra Praetoria since the early days and it is commonly accepted that they only received their own barracks under Aurelian. A statue base dedicated by a soldier of the urban cohorts dated 182 AD discovered in the Via del Corso area, however, lends credence to their camp being a Commodian creation.

Carthage is well enough preserved to be able to build a good idea of the locations, especially the ancient port, which still retains its shape and is visible from the city's high places. Carthage is known to have had a mint, though the mint only had its own marks from sometime in the 3rd century. Where the building was and what form it took is entirely unknown. My descriptions of the governor's palace, forum and outlying villas are drawn from a mix of the existing ruins and some impressive reconstructive images that have been put together over the years.

I mentioned Pupput (modern Hammamet), though we never saw it. Hammamet has a few small remains to view, including an impressive collection of mosaics. The great aqueduct of Carthage, though, still stands in many places and is an impressive sight, especially near the Roman city of Oudna, and the water temple of Zica is faithfully illustrated here as it still stands, now called the Temple des Eaux at Zaghouan. On a side note, not connected with locations, but pertinent to Africa, the existence of extensions of the

Urban Cohorts in certain important provincial cities took me by surprise when I first heard about it. It is, however, fact.

In writing historical fiction there is always a balance to be sought between the two words. Without sufficient history, it weakens the premise and redefines the genre. With too much rigid adherence to historical fact, it risks being uninteresting and more resembling a textbook than a novel.

In "The Cleansing Fire", I have taken a number of historical events and real characters and woven them into a story. That there was by this time a great deal of corruption in the Guard is clear from their activities. While the rot had probably always been there at some level (power corrupts etc...) and certainly with characters around like Sejanus, it seems that the corruption had blossomed into something frightening at the time of the dreadful Cleander. The Guard had been used as a tool of police-state violence against the public now. It would not be the last time, sadly, and I have recently written about a similar event under Maxentius a century later, but it shows a marked change in the attitude and form of the Guard. That it culminated in the infamous 'auction of the empire' says it all.

Severus brings a new period of stability after this, though the fundamental nature of imperial rule changes forever now as we enter the era of the 'soldier emperors', as Cassius Dio says: "history now descends from a kingdom of gold to one of iron and rust." But one thing Severus is noted as doing is disbanding the Guard and dispersing them to lesser units, while reforming it from his trusted Danubian legions. It is possible to see this as simply removing a potential enemy and replacing them with one's supporters but, given all that had happened, it seems almost inconceivable that removing the rot that had become endemic was not at least part of his motive.

With the actual auction, Dio, Herodian and the Historia Augusta do not entirely agree, though they all recall the same basic event. Herodian has Julianus rushing to the camp and shouting up offers, then Sulpicianus arriving to counter-bid, the Praetorians only denying the latter because of his connection to Pertinax and the danger of repercussions. Dio has Sulpicianus already in the camp, sent there by Pertinax before his death, ready to be made emperor when Julianus arrives at the walls and persuades the Guard to accept him partially through that same fear, but largely from an insane sum offered (25,000 sesterces per man!) The Historia Augusta also has Sulpicianus already in the camp and ready, and has Julianus head to the senate to have himself proclaimed, where he finds the senate house closed up. Aper and Florianus then appear and lead him to the camp, where Julianus warns the Guard not to accept a man who might turn on them for their murder of his son-in-law. Interestingly, the HA does not make any mention of the auction, though it does agree that Julianus had promised 25,000 to them. I merged these versions into my own, and given that Julianus is called a 'wanton spendthrift' by Dio, I manufactured a reason for him to have sufficient money to easily outbid a man who might well have had more money than him.

With the closing events of the book, I have somewhat conflated the historical record from Ravenna onwards, given the varying accounts of the three main sources and the need to tie everything together into this pot. In our sources:

Cassius Dio has Julianus performing a very unlikely human sacrifice, sending men to assassinate Severus more than once, with them not only failing but joining Severus before he secures Ravenna. He then has the praetorians becoming unhappy, Julianus persuading the senate that he could share power with Severus. The praetorians arrest the killers of Pertinax and offer them up to the senate, who then pronounce Julianus to be an enemy of Rome, legitimise Severus, and Julianus is killed in bed in the palace with a last plaintive and pathetic plea.

Herodian has Severus marching on Rome and cities throwing open their gates. Julianus then throws money at the praetorians, who take it but are not bought over. Julianus ignores advice to block the mountains, gathers his army at Rome, including elephants. Severus slips most of his army into the city in small bands unnoticed. Julianus in a panic offers Severus a share of the power, and the senate initially support him, but quickly side with Severus, who is now in Rome with his men. The praetorians abandon Julianus, who shuts himself in the palace, begging to be allowed to resign in favour of Severus. The senate legitimise Severus, and a tribune is sent to kill Julianus in the palace.

The Historia Augusta has Julianus sending Crispinus first to stop Severus at Ravenna and secure the fleet, but failing. He then comes up with several mad plans, using his praetorians to threaten the senate, until eventually settling on offering Severus a share of power. Crispinus is then sent again to Severus with the offer, but in the belief that he was actually sent to assassinate him, Severus has Crispinus executed. Julianus then attempts his ridiculous child sacrifice. Julianus, now desperate, has the gladiators at Capua armed and offers a share of power to old Pompeianus while the whole empire starts to give itself over to Severus. Severus then demands the arrest of the praetorians who killed Pertinax. In the HA, Julianus ends up abandoned, shut in the Palatine with Prefect Genialis and the senate condemning him and legitimising Severus. A common soldier slays Julianus in the palace.

As you can see, events become a little muddled when one tries to fit a timeline to all three sources, and so I've tried to put forth a sequence of events that takes in the best of all three sources while also fitting my own plot. The bones of the plot are the same, after all, even if the face changes.

Thus has Didius Julianus fallen and Severus risen to the throne.

Where will Rufinus go next?

Well, I am working through the era chronologically, and there are two threads that still dangle, waiting to be dealt with, and have been doing so now for 2 books. One of those threads now controls Asia and the other Britannia. Severus may be on the throne, but his accession is far from settled. Pescennius Niger and Clodius Albinus begin to stir, and Rufinus's mission to cleanse the guard is complete. Time now to turn his attention to new battlegrounds…

Simon Turney. October 2019

If you enjoyed Praetorian why not also try:

The Damned Emperors Series

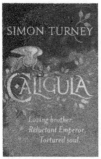

Caligula by Simon Turney

The six children of Germanicus are cursed from birth. Father: believed poisoned by the Emperor Tiberius over the imperial succession. Mother and two brothers arrested and starved to death by Tiberius. One sister married off to an abusive husband. Only three are left: Caligula, in line for the imperial throne, and his two sisters, Drusilla and Livilla, who tells us this story.

The ascent of their family into the imperial dynasty forces Caligula to change from the fun-loving boy Livilla knew into a shrewd, wary and calculating young man. Tiberius's sudden death allows Caligula to manhandle his way to power. With the bloodthirsty tyrant dead, it should be a golden age in Rome and, for a while, it is. But Caligula suffers emotional blow after emotional blow as political allies, friends, and finally family betray him and attempt to overthrow him, by poison, by the knife, by any means possible.

Little by little, Caligula becomes a bitter, resentful and vengeful Emperor, every shred of the boy he used to be eroded. As Caligula loses touch with reality, there is only one thing to be done before Rome is changed irrevocably.

The Marius' Mules Series

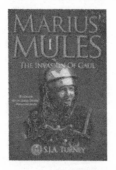

Marius' Mules I: The Invasion of Gaul

It is 58 BC and the mighty Tenth Legion, camped in Northern Italy, prepare for the arrival of the most notorious general in Roman history: Julius Caesar.

Marcus Falerius Fronto, commander of the Tenth is a career soldier and long-time companion of Caesar's. Despite his desire for the simplicity of the military life, he cannot help but be drawn into intrigue and politics as Caesar engineers a motive to invade the lands of Gaul.

Fronto is about to discover that politics can be as dangerous as battle, that old enemies can be trusted more than new friends, and that standing close to such a shining figure as Caesar, even the most ethical of men risk being burned.

The Templar Series

Daughter of War by S.J.A. Turney

An extraordinary story of the Knights Templar, seen from the bloody inside.
Europe is aflame. On the Iberian Peninsula the wars of the Reconquista rage across Aragon and Castile. Once again, the Moors are gaining the upper hand. Christendom is divided.

Amidst the chaos comes a young knight: Arnau of Valbona. After his Lord is killed in an act of treachery, Arnau pledges to look after his daughter, whose life is now at risk. But in protecting her Arnau will face terrible challenges, and enter a world of Templars, steely knights and visceral combat he could never have imagined.

She in turn will find a new destiny with the Knights as a daughter of war... Can she survive? And can Arnau find his destiny?

Made in United States
North Haven, CT
01 June 2023

37230569R00221